# Tex and the God Squad

## by

## Stuart R. West

*Tex, the Witch Boy, Volume #3*

**Tex and the God Squad**

Cover Art by *Lea Schizas*

The Wild Rose Press, Inc.
PO Box 708
Adams Basin, NY 14410-0708
Visit us at www.thewildrosepress.com

Publishing History
First Edition, 2023
Trade Paperback ISBN978-1-5092-4781-3
Digital ISBN978-1-5092-4782-0

*Tex, the Witch Boy, Volume #3*
Published in the United States of America

No one understood why the cheerleader killed herself. Her death had the entire student body of Clearwell High, even those who didn't know her, dazed. Everyone was baffled. Scared, almost.

It especially seemed frightening for those of us not blessed to be in the popular cliques. Popular and pretty, Brittany Gerlach had a bright future ahead of her. If she couldn't make it through the hell of high school, what chance did those of us who struggle every day have? Brittany's suicide made us feel even more vulnerable, more susceptible to the whims of the fragile mind and the pressures of high school life. An unspoken fear that any one of us could fall prey to whatever compelled Brittany to take her life loomed like a shadow over us.

It happened during our senior year at Clearwell High, with only one month remaining and springtime in full bloom. But the shocking news dampened our excitement that we'd almost fulfilled our tour of duty in war-torn Clearwell. I couldn't help but wonder how miserable Brittany must've been if she couldn't hold on for one more month. Things *have* to get better once we leave these hallways of horror forever.

## Dedication

I'd like to dedicate Tex And The God Squad to my parents. Like Tex, my dad lived in a wheelchair with Multiple Sclerosis for many years. Sadly, he's no longer with us, but I'd like to think his memory lives on in the Tex trilogy. And unlike Tex's mother, my mom very recently passed, a two-time cancer survivor and warrior. This one goes out to you, Mom and Dad. Love and miss you.

Chapter One

No one understood why the cheerleader killed herself. Her death had the entire student body of Clearwell High, even those who didn't know her, dazed. Everyone was baffled. Scared, almost.

It especially seemed frightening for those of us not blessed to be in the popular cliques. Popular and pretty, Brittany Gerlach had a bright future ahead of her. If she couldn't make it through the hell of high school, what chance did those of us who struggle every day have? Brittany's suicide made us feel even more vulnerable, more susceptible to the whims of the fragile mind and the pressures of high school life. An unspoken fear that any one of us could fall prey to whatever compelled Brittany to take her life loomed like a shadow over us.

It happened during our senior year at Clearwell High, with only one month remaining and springtime in full bloom. But the shocking news dampened our excitement that we'd almost fulfilled our tour of duty in war-torn Clearwell. I couldn't help but wonder how miserable Brittany must've been if she couldn't hold on for one more month. Things *have* to get better once we leave these hallways of horror forever.

I didn't really know Brittany Gerlach. We didn't run in the same social circles. But we'd shared several classes over the years, and she'd offered me warm smiles when I passed her in the hallway. Maybe not the brightest student at Clearwell, but she didn't appear to make anyone's life miserable either. To me, that goes a long way.

I should've taken it for the portentous omen it presented. Just as Brittany's vacant, pretty smile covered up a soul in agony, something dark was once again coming to the town of Clearwell, hiding behind the façade of goodness and righteousness, a fierce wolf in sheep's clothing preparing to devour everyone in its path.

**\*\*\*\***

The time had come to fulfill my mandatory meeting with the guidance counselor. After four years of having never met her, it seemed kinda odd to put my future into the hands of a stranger. I'm sure the various popular kids had been guided like the wind, but I seemed to have slipped under Mrs. Bennesh's radar. With one month to go, she'd need to guide me at hyper-speed.

A couple knocks on the door, and Mrs. Bennesh called out, "Come in!" As I sat across from her, she held a tissue to her face and honked loudly into it.

"Sorry, sorry," she said. "Damn allergies get me every time this year." Her eyes widened behind wire-rimmed glasses. "Excuse my 'French.'"

"No problem, Mrs. Bennesh. I suffer from allergies, too."

She pulled the tissue away so I could finally see what a guidance counselor looks like. Gray spots dotted her wiry black hair, a scouring pad riddled with flecks of soap. She set her mouth in a grim line and squinted at me suspiciously. Either that or her allergies were really getting to her. Staring down at a folder on her desk, she groped for a coffee cup proclaiming *World's Greatest Counselor*.

"A shame about Brittany. A real shame." She shook her speckled head. "Did you know Brittany?"

"Um, not very well. I knew who she was. She seemed nice."

"She was very nice, Robert." She leaned back in her chair, capturing me with her prison matron's steely gaze.

"Ahhh…it's Richard, actually."

"How's that?"

"It's Richard. Richard McKenna. You, ah, called me 'Robert.'"

One side of her mouth curled up. "I *really* don't think so, Richard."

I had to wonder if it's time for Mrs. Bennesh to retire and hang up her guiding spurs. "Okay. Um, does anyone know why Brittany…took her life?" Sure it was a bold question, but everyone wanted to know.

She frowned, but since her smile perpetually turned upside-down, I didn't take it personally. "I couldn't tell you that kind of information even if I did know, Richard." She smiled bitterly, a step up from her previous grimace.

"Yeah, of course. I didn't mean anything by it. It's just that everyone's wondering why—"

"Yes, well." She went back to thumbing through my folder. "So, I see Mr. Hastings has red-flagged you several times in your personal record. What do you have to say about that?"

*It's a frame-up?* Vice Principal Arville Hastings is the imposing and terrifying zookeeper of Clearwell High, who's decided to make me his pet project. Not in the way he favors his football players, either. No, Hastings has become my own personal stalker. Every time I turn around, Hastings is ready to blame me for the usual high school shenanigans like, I don't know…murder, black magic, global warming. Over the past several years, he's come perilously close to finding out the truth about me. But, somehow, I've always escaped unscathed.

"Um, what exactly does it say, Mrs. Bennesh?"

"Mr. Hastings believes you're involved with black magic. And you were mixed up with…let's see here…*two* murderers?" I thought she might drop the coffee cup that had yet to reach her lips.

"Um, that's not *really* true. It was just a bunch of misunderstandings." I guess that's one way to describe it. I had been involved with two murderers through no choice of my own. Well, other than the fact they were both friends of mine. And I'm really getting sick of my friends ending up being murderers.

"I *see.* You're going to sit there and tell me being involved with two murderers is a mere…*misunderstanding?*"

I sighed, settled in, and told her—the edited versions, of course—of my last two years of high school. During my lengthy speech, I kept seeking solace in the poster on the wall behind Mrs. Bennesh. A kitten hung perilously for life onto a window ledge with the slogan emblazoned *Hang In There, Baby!* at the bottom. I kept telling myself I had to "hang in there" for just one more month.

"Huh," she said. "That's *quite* a story, Richard." She tilted her head, grimacing at me.

"I know it is. But it's true. The newspapers…and

4

Detective Cowlings of the Clearwell Police can verify it all." This isn't how I imagined my counseling session would go. I felt like I was on trial with Mrs. Bennesh acting as the "hanging judge." I also worried this information might be passed on to colleges I wanted to apply for. Especially with Hastings's unwarranted bias against me.

"I see. And what of this…black magic?"Her scary eyebrows raised in black-cat arches.

"That's not true!" Well, the *black* magic part, at least.

She finally took a loud sip out of her coffee and clunked the cup down. "Fine. Let's move on, shall we?" She drew in a deep breath and flipped a few more pages. "I see Mr. Jensen has put in a few good notes about you." She once again raised an inquisitive eyebrow, signifying the impetus lay on me to explain this apparently baffling phenomenon. Mr. Jensen's one of the good guys. He's the football coach, but I also had him as a sociology, psychology, and now, philosophy teacher. He helped me during sophomore year in taking down a murderer. But more importantly, I agreed with a lot of his viewpoints. He's a stand-up guy. For a football coach and teacher, that is.

Not knowing exactly how to reply to Mrs. Bennesh, I spread my hands and said, "Well, Mr. Jensen's a good teacher. I'm glad somebody's willing to vouch for me."

"Yes, well. We do think highly of Mr. Jensen around here." Yay for the cavalry. "Now, your grades are…actually very good." Disappointment lowered the stridency in her voice. "Although they fell off a little late last year."

5

"Yeah, um, I was going through some stuff."

"But you've pulled them up again this year. What is it you have planned for your future, Richard? What are your interests?"

Once again I turned to the endangered Zen-kitten on the poster for true guidance, as these are both very good questions. What exactly *are* my interests? I couldn't very well tell Mrs. Bennesh I'm a witch. Not that witchcraft is a true interest of mine. My witchcraft abilities are something I inherited from my late mother, also a witch. And I doubt any university will offer a scholarship in "witchcraft."

College is definitely the right path for me, as I don't relish the idea of a tough, manual labor job for the rest of my life. With only one school month remaining, I know I'm cutting it close with my waffling, but I've been wrestling with some issues. Earlier this year, I applied for an English scholarship to the University of Kansas. I enjoy writing. But other than teaching, I have no idea what I can do with such a degree, especially in today's overcrowded and economically sucky marketplace.

But an even larger concern could be blamed for my foot-dragging. If I went away to KU, who'd take care of my dad? Dad has had multiple sclerosis for nearly as long as I can remember, and recently, I've seen troubling signs of his health worsening. On several occasions, he's fallen out of his wheelchair. He's a big man. It took some work getting him up each time.

One evening, I came home to find him sitting on the bathroom floor. With his back against the toilet, he'd been stuck there for over three hours, unable to reach the telephone. I pleaded with him to get a cell phone, but he shook it off with the aggravating excuse, "You can't teach an old dog new tricks." But what if he falls when I go off to college?

I'm responsible for the house cleaning, yard work, and giving Dad rides to and from work. Sure, he has his girlfriend, Ruth, but she's not about to move in with him without a ring on her finger. Very nice and proper, Ruth would never consider "living in sin." I suspect Dad feels the same way. I also sense his hesitance in marrying Ruth, probably out of respect to my mom, who died in an automobile accident several years ago. He isn't quite ready to let go of her yet. His love for Ruth is genuine enough but seems different from the relationship he shared with my mom. Regardless, Ruth isn't going to be there full time, not any time soon.

Dad insists I not worry about him, nor let his welfare color my future decisions. In fact, he's adamant about my going to a good university. Once, he told me, "Worst case scenario, I'll hire live-in help." But I know he can't afford it. Being a bank employee, he doesn't make much, and his meager savings have been going into my college fund. Besides, after a few cryptic comments, I could tell the future of his employment status worried him. Rumors are his bank may not be long for this world. When money-making institutions can't make it in today's economy, you *know* something's wildly messed up.

Then there's Olivia. Olivia Furman, my girlfriend. We broke up briefly last year but managed to put it back together and grow even stronger as a couple. The idea of leaving her behind's not an easy notion to accept. Sure, a long-distance relationship is an option—and really, KU's only an hour away—but, from what I hear, the reality of college kids successfully maintaining a weekend relationship isn't very viable. She plans on going to the Clearwell Community College for a couple of years and then transferring elsewhere. The community college is reputed to be a good one. But what if Olivia tires of an absentee boyfriend? Worse, what if she meets some new guy? Olivia's damned determined to remain committed to us and laughed off my fears, but…I don't know.

As I said, I'm dealing with issues. All of them *scary*. Last year, Mr. Jensen told our sociology class, "Life will get easier once you leave high school." So far, it seems I'm just trading one set of fears for another.

"Richard?" Mrs. Bennesh slammed her cup onto her desktop. "What *are* your interests and plans?"

"Oh, um, I guess I kinda like writing." Again, I focused on the poster kitten, forever fated to live one step away from plummeting to certain death. I hope I won't sway in the wind without a safety net as long as he's destined to. It's no way to live life. *Hang In There, Baby!* You and me both, brother.

"Okay, writing." She scribbled hastily on what I presume is my permanent record, obviously ready to finish this "guidance session" and write me off as one more obligatory student she can send out into the world, having done her job. "You might consider a degree in English. What universities have you applied to?"

"I'm thinking about going to Clearwell Community College." Her face wrinkled. "Until I make up my mind, that is," I added quickly.

She slapped her pen down on the desk. "Richard, your grades are good enough to get into a *real* school.

You're not doing this for a girl, are you?"

"No! No, no, no. Nope, never, not at all. Nuh-uh, no way. It's not like that." But, yeah, maybe it is.

She lobbed another acidic smile my way, the judge back in full disbelieving, prosecuting mode. "How is your financial situation?"

"I guess probably not the best."

"I *see.*" She said this like she most definitely did *not* "see." "It's getting late in the school year. Have you considered applying for a scholarship?"

"No." I lied. I didn't want to feel strong-armed into making a hasty decision from a guidance counselor whom I've known for twenty minutes. But I need guidance. Guide, damn you, *guide!* Guide like the wind!

"Uh huh. Well, I guess I've done everything I can here." She extended her thin hand toward me, long fingernails poised to scrape.

Somewhat taken aback by her hasty dismissal of me, I jumped to my feet, feeling no more guided than a blind man in a blizzard. "Um, okay. Thanks?"

"Good luck, Rob…Richard."

"Yeah, okay." I inched my way toward the door, hoping for a last-minute reprieve saving me from terrifying indecision. She sipped out of her coffee cup and thwacked my file into the small shelving unit on her desk, forever closing my case. *Next!*

\*\*\*\*

We managed to retain "Our Table" in the cafeteria during our senior year, and for once, most of my friends shared the same lunch period.

"How'd it go with your guidance counselor, Tex?" asked Olivia. Taking a quick glance around, she darted toward my lips with a quick peck, practically daring any on-looking teacher to bust her for PDA—the forbidden "public displays of affection." Giggling at my embarrassment, she brushed back a stray magenta strand of hair.

"O', you're gonna get us in trouble."

"Yeah? Just wait until the last day of school. I'm gonna wipe everything off the table, throw you down, and we're gonna make out like 'Skinemax!'" She pumped a fist into the air, defying the world.

Ian rolled his eyes. "Gawd. Some of us are trying to eat here." Outside of Olivia, Ian Stapleton's my best friend, definitely the one I've had the longest. We've shared a long path of trial and tribulation through two schools full of bullies, abusive gym teachers, and an endless array of ludicrous classmates. Ian doesn't really live the goth lifestyle but chooses to look and dress that way to maintain his individuality. As much as I admire his decision, it also makes him an easy target for bullies. Every time I attempt to defend him, it makes me an additional mark for the fun-loving bully set.

Watching Ian eat, I winced when he couldn't wrestle three of his fingers around a fork. A bully who wanted to run me down with his car ruined Ian's hand permanently two years ago. I sorta blame myself for his injury.

"Oh, shut up, Ian," said Olivia.

"I think it's cute," said Lance, the newest recruit into our world of students no other clique wanted…

****

Five months ago, Olivia dragged Lance Nguyen over to our lunch table.

"Hey, guys," she said. "This is 'Adorably Gay

Lance!'" Somewhat taken aback by Olivia's labeling him in a seemingly demeaning manner, I waited for the other shoe to drop. But Lance appeared to be good-naturedly enjoying his introduction. "He's in my psych class. Isn't he the cutest thing ever?"

We laughed, some of us awkwardly so, but I took note of Lance's obviously—against all odds, particularly in Kansas—sunny disposition.

"Hi, everybody." New to Clearwell, Lance recently transferred from Ridge View during his junior year. With American-born Vietnamese parents, his great-grandparents had immigrated here years ago. By far the best-dressed kid in our group, his wardrobe looked like it cost a bundle. He wore his hair immaculately curled, gelled, and teased into a stylish cut, the kind you only see on pampered television actors. Extremely striking-looking, many students secretly coveted his clear, smooth skin, I'm pretty damn sure. Although slight of build, you could tell he was muscular, athletic, and when needed be, very fast. Turns out, he needed to be fast. A *lot*. Clearwell's bullies came out of the woodwork for him, yelling racial slurs including the completely ignorant, *"Go back to China!"* and the typical homophobic epithets. Openly gay and proud of it, he only acted like a flamboyantly gay stereotype when egged on by Olivia. She dragged him around like a purse puppy, showing him off, and more or less visually threatening students to deride him.

Everyone immediately liked Lance, impossible not to. Even while pursued by bullies, he found something to laugh about. Nothing rattled him.

At first, Ian felt a little bit uncomfortable with Lance. I told Lance Ian's not homophobic, just "edgy."

Lance grinned, said he'd take care of it. I found out about their confrontation later. Wish I coulda been there. Lance had said to Ian, "Just because I'm gay, doesn't mean I've got the hots for you, dude. You're not my type anyway." Knowing Ian, it probably pissed him off someone—*anyone*—didn't find him hot. After that, though, they became the best of buds, hanging out after school together.

I welcomed Lance's charm and wit, a much-needed emotional antidote to the last two morose years we experienced.

A few months later, Lance invited us to his home for an eye-opening family dinner. I couldn't believe the affluent neighborhood he lived in, or the most lavish, gorgeous house I'd seen since visiting Elizabeth Blackmer's mansion.

We drove up the winding driveway, and stopped by a large gate. I pressed the button on the attached box, announced who we were, and the gates automatically opened, giving us safe passage into unknown territory.

Once we exited the Bucket, we couldn't find the front door. Three stories' worth of long windows set into white stone foundation towered over us, teasing us, yet not a door to be found. Feeling hopelessly stupid, we at long last discovered a sidewalk, which dumped us into a strange garden. A long, rectangular, man-made pond—complete with odd vegetation and large Koi fish—sat in the middle of the yard. A ginormous vase barred our path. Edging around the vase, we discovered a shrine with an Asian-styled dome above it. A long trek down the open walkway led us to what *had* to be Lance's front door. *Finally*. Lance's home had nothing on a carnival funhouse.

Dressed in casual business attire, a pretty woman answered the door. After seeing the elegance Lance lived in, I didn't know if she was Lance's mother, a servant, or what.

"Hi, um, we're Lance's friends?" I said.

She smiled, a living photocopy of Lance's grin, and I had my answer. "Hello. I'm Mrs. Nguyen, Lance's mother." A frown dissolved her friendly demeanor as she stepped outside, pulling the door closed behind her. "It's so nice to meet you all, but I need a minute to talk to you before dinner."

"Okay," I said, fearing the worst, because these days, that's the way I roll.

"I assume you all know Lance is gay," she said.

Olivia's eyes widened while the rest of us stupidly nodded.

"Make no mistake, I'm happy he's comfortable being who he is," she continued. "But I would greatly appreciate it if you don't make it a topic at dinner. Lance's father doesn't know yet...and I'm concerned with how he might handle it."

"Oh, um, sure, no problem." I suddenly felt part of a familial conspiracy. Happens a lot.

Lance greeted us and showed us around his palatial estate, while his mother wandered off to parts unknown. Flooded with sunshine, the house had more windows than a greenhouse. The walls were constructed of what I later found out to be decorative mud-wall. Large, bright red tapestries hung like paintings, punctuated with giant Asian symbols in black. Tall, exotic plants climbed out of gorgeous vases, hindering one's pathway through the long halls. The floors were spotless, light wood, gloriously resplendent and shiny.

If Mrs. Nguyen didn't have a staff of servants, she had to be one very busy woman.

We sat down at an oddly out-of-place, modern décor, glass dining room table in front of a slatted, folding wall built of wood and paper. Blown away doesn't even begin to describe how we felt.

Lance laughed at our reactions. "You guys never saw an Asian home before?"

"Jeezus," said Ian. "I had no idea you were rich."

"I wouldn't say 'rich,' but my parents do okay, I guess."

"Yeah, I guess," said Olivia. Laughter replaced our initial shock. "A little notice next time, maybe."

"Hello, children," rang out a deep, resonant voice. Dressed in a tailored, crease-free suit, Mr. Nguyen's power tie seemed as fully knotted and tight as his demeanor. No doubt styled to intimidate, his perfectly coiffed haircut demanded your attention, *dammit*! Contemporary, narrow-rimmed glasses practically bragged of his being in tune with the times. His unwaveringly serious disposition combined with his soothing, monotonic voice told me everything I needed to know about him. A world-class corporate raider, no one dared to jack with him.

After some awkward introductions, Lance grew solemn. Mr. Nguyen sucked the fun out of the table like an industrial-strength vacuum.

Like a magic fairy, Mrs. Nguyen floated in, spreading good-nature dust about the dining room. Even Mr. Nguyen smiled as she entered.

The food tasted fantastic. I couldn't believe Mrs. Nguyen had time to cook it—homemade Sushi, nonetheless—because Lance told us she worked as well.

"What line of work are you in, Mrs. Nguyen?" I asked.

"I sell real estate."

"Oh, that's what my mother did."

"What a coincidence. Is she retired now? I know it's a tough market out there."

Olivia's loud exasperated sigh sort of embarrassed me, but that's my gal. "Uh, no, she passed away several years ago," I said.

"Oh. Oh, I'm sorry." She looked mortified while Mr. Nguyen still appeared...*immobile*.

"Way to go, Mom," said Lance quietly. His father shot him a killer corporate look.

"No, it's okay. I'm fine talking about it. She died in a highway wreck several years—"

"Wait, are you Elizabeth McKenna's son?" Her smile opened up again like a blossoming flower. Apparently she only had two expressions, but I much preferred this one. Her husband? I think he'd mastered sleeping with his eyes open.

"Yeah. Did you know her?" Generally, when I say I'm okay talking about my mom, people usually drop the topic. But now faced with someone who obviously wouldn't back down, it hit me hard. My throat dried up, and I gulped down half a glass of water.

"I did. She was a very nice woman and a great realtor. I'd met her on many occasions through work. She mentioned how proud she was of you and showed me your picture. I should've recognized you...even with the hair." She tugged at an imaginary long strand of hair.

"Um, yeah, I get that a lot...about my hair, I

mean." Silence fell across the table, expectant eyes upon me. "She was a great mother, too." Kinda a dumb thing to say, but I had nothing.

Lance shot up from the table, blessedly running interference. "Okay! Great dinner, Mom. I want to show my friends my room."

Mr. Nguyen banged a fist on the table and glared at his son. He pointed back toward Lance's seat. Sheepishly, Lance returned to his chair. Mr. Nguyen took a long look at us. For a really, *really* long time. At last, he said, "You are released." I couldn't wait to get the hell out of there. The four of us ran up the stairs like Satan himself prodded us with a pitchfork, Lance giggling and leading the Hell-escaping prisoners to freedom.

On the way home, we all agreed Lance's father seemed like a very scary guy.

While Mr. Nguyen wouldn't win any charm school awards, I found Mrs. Nguyen to be pretty awesome. Any friend of my mom's is a friend of mine. I thought I might even like to talk further with her about my mother.

Little did I know then that I'd soon get the chance…

****

So, that spring day, when Lance brought his usual vibrant optimism to the lunch table, I couldn't help but wonder when the topic of conversation would turn dark and back toward Brittany Gerlach's suicide.

"So, yeah, *anyway*," said Ian, "what did Mrs. Bennesh say, Tex? About your interests and all that crap?" Ian had a personal stake in my future. He desperately wanted me to go to KU because that's where Ian—or at least, his father—decided he'd be staked out in three months. The thought of his sharing a dorm room with a stranger scared the hell out of him.

"She didn't really, um, guide me very much. She didn't even know who I was."

"Yeah, me either," said Ian.

"What about you, Allie?" I asked. "What are you going to do this fall?"

Allison set her fork down and finished chewing a mouthful of food before speaking. "Well, I wanted to go to art school. In New York, maybe, but my grandma can't afford it. She wants me to go to a Christian college." Allison's shoulders sunk, her large frame appearing smaller.

"What about a scholarship?" asked Olivia. "You're definitely a kick-ass artist." We all agreed.

Allison turned a shade redder and managed a slight smile. "I don't know. You guys really think so?"

"Hellz yes," said Olivia.

"I just don't think my grandma will let me do it."

Allison Brubaker had come a long way since I met her a year ago. She used to be so painfully shy that she self-consciously covered her mouth every time she spoke. Partial to wearing clothing more suited to a farmer's wife, she'd now developed her own style with Olivia's sartorial guidance. She layered interesting combinations and made an art form out of accessorizing, scarves wrapped tightly and jewelry jangling while she walked. On the downside, she's now the huggingest person I know.

Last year, I thought Allie and Ian were heading toward happy couple-land. But after a few dates, it just fizzled out. I never did find out why. When I asked Ian, he just sort of shrugged and said it didn't work out. I didn't dare ask Allison about it. She's a very private person. I found that out last year when I questioned her about her parents. Still don't know the story.

"Allie, it's not your grandma's life." I felt like a hypocrite saying it since I'm considering my dad's needs in front of mine. "You can do whatever you set your mind to."

Allison beamed. "Come on. Not really." Her words spoke of denial, but her smile radiated unbridled enthusiasm.

"No, really." Lance leaned in and draped his arm around her shoulders. "Dream big, girl."

"You're a killer artist, Allie," said Ian. Somehow, Ian and Allie bucked the odds and were able to start over from scratch and develop a friendship again. I tried it with Olivia last year when we broke up and failed miserably.

"Hey, where's Dickers?" I asked. It looked like Allison needed a respite from attention.

Ian said, "I think he's with the counselor now."

"Well, let's hope he gets more guidance than we did." I looked down at my plate and wondered what hidden atrocity lay waiting underneath the gravy. "What *is* this stuff, anyway?"

Ian laughed. "It's chopped beef and gravy. Don't be a candy-ass. If you don't want it, I'll take it."

The gravy had congealed into a clotted substance. I think I might've seen a few bubbles bursting through the surface, a creature struggling to crawl out from the deep, dark depths of his brown lagoon. I pushed the plate toward Ian. "Have at it." Ever since I started eating school lunches, I'd lost weight. I couldn't really afford to, since I was pretty lanky to begin with, but I didn't want to risk food poisoning. Ian, on the other hand, had a rock-solid constitution; his super-power.

"Did you guys hear about Brittany Gerlach?" asked Allison. A knot formed in my stomach, possibly from hunger. Or, more than likely, a troubling fear bad things awaited me on the horizon. I've learned to put faith in these sensations, especially since they've been occurring more frequently. Maybe they're connected to my witchcraft powers. I need to ask Mickey about that. Either way, my neck hairs felt like they were thrashing about.

"Yeah, how could we not?" asked Lance. "It's all everyone's talking about. Has anyone heard why she did it?"

No one had an answer. "Um, did any of you guys know her? I mean...*really* know her?" I asked.

"She was always nice to me," said Allison quietly.

"Yeah, she wasn't a *total* bitch," said Ian. Olivia blasted him with an icy glare. "I mean, you know, for a cheerleader. 'At's all I'm sayin'."

Our lunch table memoriam for Brittany Gerlach felt sort of lackluster and sad. The only thing we *truly* knew about her was she seemed to be a rare, nice cheerleader who didn't go out of her way to cause others agony. I looked around the cafeteria. Across the room, a gaggle of cheerleaders, despite the passing of their comrade, smiled, giggled, and gossiped. Several jocks hovered over them, flirting, no cares. Yet aside from the raucous popular table, an unnerving quiet draped heavily over the cafeteria, broken only by the sounds of plates clanking and utensils clinking. A hushed melancholy, an uncertain fear, lingered over the "common" students as they contemplated why someone so well-liked would take her own life.

I wondered if anyone truly knew Brittany Gerlach. Or what private pain she had carried around inside her. Or if anyone cared.

## Chapter Two

"Hi, son. How was your day?" I helped Dad lift his feet and swing them into the Battle Bucket. Not so long ago, he used to handle that by himself.

"Not bad," I said. "How was yours? Did you foreclose on anyone today? Make anyone cry being the big, bad banker?"

He grinned. "No, not today." I knew that's not his style, but I felt it my responsibility to rib him for being a corporate, money-grubbing fiend whenever the opportunity arose. "Say, I heard about the cheerleader girl at school."

Of course he did. Dad had a pipeline into the goings-on at my school, especially those of a violent nature. The security guard at his bank, a particularly chatty retired cop, kept him in the loop. I knew Dad would find *some* reason to worry—his favorite pastime—so I figured let's just get it out of the way. "Yeah, it's pretty sad."

"Did you know her?"

"Sorta, I guess. She was in some of my classes. We didn't really talk."

"I'm sorry, son. Are you doing okay?"

"Dad, I didn't *really* know her. I mean, it's sad and everything, but no one knows why she did it. That's what's got everybody freaked out." I pulled onto the highway, getting in line with the stalled rush-hour traffic.

The lines on Dad's face had doubled over the span of a year. When he frowned, new creases and folds appeared like a shirt left too long in the dryer. "You know, suicide is never the answer. No matter how bad things look, things will always get better."

"Dad, I'm *not* stupid. I know suicide isn't the answer. Don't worry." I forced a chuckle to allay his fears.

"I know you make smart decisions. It's just I can't help but worry." I believe a lot of his worry stemmed from the sudden, unexpected death of my mother. Ever since then, we've shared an understanding of how truly tenuous human life is. The McKenna men are award-winning, card-carrying, gold member worrywarts.

"Speaking of being smart..." Oh boy, here we go. The *other* topic I didn't want to tackle. "...have you heard back from KU yet?" I hadn't told him I applied for a scholarship, but I let him know I applied. He'd been riding me so hard I thought it best to toss him a bone.

"Not yet. I still don't know that's what I want to do, even if they do accept me."

"Son, you need to do what's best for you." He licked his lips, a sure sign of impending lecture time. "I've told you before, don't base your decision around me. I'd hate to see you throw away a good thing. I'll be all right."

"Dad, you can't get to work by yourself. You won't even get a handicapped-accessible van." He constantly pooh-poohed the van idea, considered it an unnecessary bell and whistle. But the truth lay in our finances.

"I have Ruth and Bill at the office—"

"*Whatever.*" I didn't mean to be short with him, but we constantly performed this dance, both of us leading, ultimately going nowhere.

We sat in uncomfortable silence, the car inching home through the deadlocked traffic, the minutes slowly crawling by. To the right, a billboard with a large smiley face beamed down on us. Next to the grotesque, nose-free face, the slogan, *"Smile! Your Mother Decided To Have You!"* practically screamed at us. Ironically, some sociopathic joy-rider had riddled the face with a shotgun blast, blemishing the yellow mug with unsightly blackheads. Hoping to lighten the mood, I pointed it out to Dad.

He sighed. "Yeah, it says 'Presented by the Clarendon Baptist Church.'" He shook his head and muttered, "They're something else."

"How so?"

"You haven't heard of them?"

"Guess not. What's up with them?" It somewhat surprised me to hear Dad disparage a Baptist church. The three of us used to attend a Baptist church regularly. Neither one of us had been back since my mother died. Church sorta became a casualty of our despair.

"This Pastor Don…whatever. He started a church down in southern Texas, and now he's bringing it to Kansas City. The Clarendon Baptist Church. I don't mind telling you, son, they're a bunch of wackos." My dad usually never rants and rails against anyone, but when he calls someone a "wacko," look out!

"Why are they, um, wackos?"

"Well…" He shimmied on the bench seat to face

me. "...they believe most of the world is destined for Hell. They think divorce and remarriage are sins. And they think homosexuals are destroying the world."

"You're kidding me. How come I've never heard of them?"

"You don't watch or read much news." Oooh! Ten points to Dad. "Anyway, I don't understand all of it, but they picket funerals of people who died from AIDS—even children born with it—and for *whatever* reason..." He tossed his hands into the air. "...they protest dead war heroes' funerals."

"U.S. troops? *Our* troops?"

"'Fraid so. This so-called...*church* believes God's striking the soldiers down righteously, punishing them because the world's evil."

"That's, wow...that's unbelievable."

"I'm telling you, son, they're wacko. Unbelievable, as you said. They think most Christian churches are evil and anyone who preaches that God loves everyone and Jesus died for our sins is a liar. Just...wacko." Dad had rolled onto a real wacko-palooza.

"That is...wacko." Yeah, I said it. I think I now understand the *true* meaning of "wacko."

"Anyway..." Dad wound down, stepping off his platform. "...Tex, you *really* need to clean your car." He looked around in disgust at the fast-food wrappers and cola cans strewn about.

The rest of the drive home, I couldn't help but think about the Clarendon Baptist Church. I mean, what are they trying to accomplish with their doctrine of hatred, anyway? It certainly doesn't sound like love, acceptance, or tolerance, three of the most important teachings of traditional religious faiths. And they'd rather condemn souls than save them. So what are they truly about? Other than spreading hate?

I saw the billboard's gun-riddled smiley face as an apt metaphor for the Clarendon Baptist Church. Underneath that golden, happy countenance lurked an insidious cancer, now creeping to the surface, revealing its true sickness.

And little did I realize the Clarendon Church would soon tear holes through Clearwell and those closest to me.

**** 

Clark Dickers stood next to my locker, attempting but failing badly to appear casual. Restless, he constantly scratched himself like he had a poison ivy reaction. His unfortunate high-water jeans rode up on his long legs, making him an even larger spectacle.

"Hey, Dickers," I said. "What's up? Where were you at lunch yesterday?"

"Hey, McKenna." For some reason, Clark's the only one who insists on calling people by their last names. Actually, he probably took his cue from us as we all call him "Dickers" because, frankly, it's kind of a fun name for obvious reasons. "I was busy with the guidance counselor yesterday."

"Yeah? How'd that work out for you?"

"Not bad. I'm going to Parkway Christian College to become a priest." He looked at me as if anticipating mockery.

"Good for you. At least you know what you're going to do." I think Dickers is the only one of us who has a set plan. The rest of us are at the mercy of the winds of fate, stray leaves blowing randomly across the backyards of life.

\*\*\*\*

Olivia and I had known Clark Dickers for three years, but we never really talked to him beyond "Hey" and "How's it goin'?" Last fall, Olivia and I went to see the school production of *Guys and Dolls*, knowing Dickers had a large role in it. What we *didn't* know at the time was how horribly he sang. Dickers played the father of the lead girl. When he burst into his singing solo, a horrified hush interspersed with laughter flooded the audience. Totally off-key to the point it made my teeth fillings throb. I hung my head in embarrassment for him. Olivia fought to stifle her laughter. Tension finally released once he'd finished.

When the production ended, Olivia grabbed my hand and rushed the stage.

"What are we doing?" She dragged me behind her while plowing through the fleeing audience members.

"We're going to tell Dickers how good he was."

"Olivia, you're *not* going to make fun of him, are you?"

"No! He needs all the support he can get after that. We're gonna lie to him. Do our good deed."

"Um, okay." I didn't know if lying seemed like the best way to handle the situation, but it took real courage for Dickers to get up on that stage and sing. Even if he did manage to kill off a few cats doing so.

The rest of the cast members were enjoying their doting friends and reveling in their ten minutes of fame. Dickers looked lost. He stood alone, his thrift store costume too small, his white socks clearly visible by several inches. I could relate, being tall myself, but you'd think the props department would've at least found pants to fit him. Or maybe there's a sadist in the

26

costuming crew.

To my surprise, Olivia threw her arms around Dickers in a warm hug. He returned the affection, too enthusiastically in my opinion. His arms enveloped her, rubbing, patting, exploring her back, his hands quickly traveling south. Later, Olivia deemed Dickers "King of the Inappropriate Hug."

Olivia broke the embrace. "Yeah, um, hey, you were really good, Dickers."

His lips spread into an arrogant grin. "Whaddaya' know? I've got chick fans."

Olivia rolled her eyes.

"Well, you don't *really* have her," I muttered. "But, congratulations. We, um, thought you did a great job."

"Thanks, man. I thought I was pretty good, too." Olivia and I created a monster, his ego running amok. *Texenstein's Monster.*

The next day, Dickers showed up at our lunch table. "Hey, guys, can I sit here?"

We all sat silent for a moment before Ian said, "Yeah, I guess so."

Dickers slid into the chair next to Olivia, wanting to keep his fan club close, I suppose. "Hey." He ignored the rest of us, his lecherous gaze all over Olivia.

"Hey," she replied.

"So, you guys thought I was pretty good last night, huh?" he asked, obviously fishing for further validation from the rest of the table.

"That's not what I heard," mumbled Ian. I jabbed my elbow into his side.

For the rest of that lunch period, Dickers talked about his theatrical success and told us of his future plans for a stage and screen career. But somewhere along the way, Dickers ditched any interest in theatre, replacing it with a sudden zeal for the Bible and religion. He joined several Bible groups in and out of school and, on a rare occasion, asked us if we'd like to attend a meeting. Most of us responded with fake excuses, except for Ian who insisted on antagonizing Dickers about his beliefs. When Dickers stopped preaching to the non-believers—or quit inappropriately hugging females—he seemed like a good enough guy. You could always count on him to help you out. Easy-going, amiable enough. But for some reason whenever we asked him about his family, he turned somber and responded with, "I don't want to talk about it."

\*\*\*\*

Clearly, something bothered Dickers that morning.

"Hey, McKenna," he said. "Have you heard why Brittany Gerlach killed herself?" Antsier than an anthill, he rocked back and forth against the locker.

"No, I haven't. You knew her, right? Wasn't she in your Bible group?"

"Yeah. I just can't figure it out. She quit going to the group the last couple of months. I'm worried for her soul."

"Um…why?" I didn't really want to get into a religious debate, especially since he treaded on the precipice of good taste, but he obviously needed to talk about it.

"God despises sinners." He stared at me disbelievingly.

A divine interference, Ian bounded up with Brandon Townsend sauntering behind him.

"Hey, brahs," said Ian, a familiar spark of anarchy

in his eyes. "Dickers, get a haircut already. You look like a lesbian."

Dickers forced a chuckle. "Shut up, Stapleton. *You're* the one wearing eyeliner."

Ian punched Dickers in the shoulder and cackled.

Brandon watched quietly while taking bites from a cookie, crumbs dropping onto his T-shirt. Brandon Townsend isn't too bright but has one thing going for him. Every girl—and some guys, including Lance—find him irresistible. Blessed with the looks and body of a Greek golden-skinned god, he's either oblivious to the fact or just doesn't care. I used to be insanely envious of him but have since made my peace and now even consider him a friend. He's also bi-sexual, meaning he could literally have *anyone* in the school he desired.

"Man." This is the kind of scintillating commentary Brandon's known for.

"Morning, boys," said Olivia behind me. I turned to meet her as she threw her arms around my neck. Dickers angled up behind her, in preparation for his inevitable, mauling hug.

"Hey," I said. "What's up?"

She released me and twirled around. "The sun. The birds. All that crap."

Out of nowhere, a figure dressed in a long, black, flowing gown rushed by, his head obscured by a hood. He tapped a student on the shoulder and in an affected tone, drawled out *"deadddddad!"* The student said "Dammit" and begrudgingly followed the cloaked figure down the hall.

Olivia said, *"No!* Not *this* stupid crap again." Yep, it appears it's time for our yearly "DDAD." On "Drunk Driving Awareness Day," members of the student council dress up as Reapers and "kill" people throughout the school. Once tagged as dead, they lead students into a room where their faces are painted white, one solitary black tear punctuating their cheek. The newly "dead" is also required to remain silent for the rest of the day. While I agree with the importance of DDAD, I've never really understood the theatricality behind it all.

It also struck me that having this event the day after a student's suicide was in pretty poor taste, but nothing can stop the punishing, bureaucratic empire Arville Hastings built.

"Well, at least we'll get out of class for the rally," said Brandon, obviously having given this more thought than his future plans. I'm sure he had no plans, which gave me a little comfort. Solidarity in slackerdom. Brandon's immediate driving goal in life appears to be missing a class.

"It's so stupid, " said Olivia.

"What's stupid?" The fingernails-on-chalkboard voice belonged to Parker Pennett. An awful-looking smirk spanned most of his pale face.

"Hey, Parker," said Ian. "Oh, you know, DDAD and all the Reapers."

Parker shrugged, jerking his chin out. "There's a reason for it."

"Whatever," said Ian.

Although I was the only real witch in the hallway, Parker Pennett truly looks like your classic storybook witch. Long, straight blond hair framed his gaunt face. His small beady eyes orbited the planet of his hooked nose, his light eyebrows barely visible. When he frowns—which he often does—his eyes narrow and his square jaw sags, his disdain obvious. Yet he's inexplicably popular with girls in the school, particularly the lower classmen. They'll follow him, hang on his every word, laugh exaggeratedly at his jokes, hoping he'll notice them. Olivia says it's because he's such an incorrigible flirt. It's certainly not because of his looks, but, hey, I've been wrong before. I just don't get it.

Allison had brought him into our group, as she'd known him from her church. Even though he'd attended our school for four years, I'd never met him nor had him in any of my classes. Until this year. He sat next to me in Mr. Jensen's philosophy class.

Like Dickers, Parker's heavily involved in church, Bible studies, and groups. But unlike the kinder, quieter teachings of Dickers, Parker wears his religion on his sleeve, constantly turning his hawk's nose up at those he deems less worthy, ready to lambast anyone who doesn't share his views. He isn't a constant mainstay in our group. An anomaly, he bounces back and forth between cliques with ease, even hanging out with the cheerleaders and football players at times. Why he's considered "socially acceptable" while we're treated as pariahs is beyond me. But I'm okay he doesn't hang with us 24-7. He's arrogant, snide, and condescending. I try to keep an open mind and open door for everyone, but he makes it tough.

Possibly the oddest thing about Parker is his relationship with his girlfriend, Shannon Booth. Parker keeps her hidden away from us as if he's ashamed of her. Or us, more than likely. On the one occasion we met her, she rarely spoke and remained stand-offish, a surly frown cemented onto her face. But she's a completely different person around others, screaming and laughing animatedly, showing off her tongue stud to her *real* friends whenever the chance arises. Olivia nicknamed her "The Queen Of The Toads" due to her constantly flitting tongue. And because, you know, she doesn't like her.

We never saw any physical contact between Parker and Shannon. Most couples manage hugs, quick kisses, and handholding, even under the watchful vigil of Arville Hastings. With Parker and Shannon, their relationship is comprised of walking alongside each other, the tall and the short, scurrying to their next class. Olivia posited the theory he's gay and everyone knows it except for himself. My scientific theory remains he's a judgmental jackass.

"Anyway," said Parker, "I guess you guys heard about Brittany Gerlach."

"Yeah, sucks." Frankly, I wanted to put a stop to Brittany being put through the rumor mill. Let the poor cheerleader rest. But with Reapers running rampant through the halls, it's no wonder everyone's constantly reminded of their mortality.

Parker shrugged. "God has his reasons." His upper lip curled into a hint of a smile, maybe a sneer.

"Parker...man. You're *not* going to tell me this was, I don't know, 'ordained' by God or something." My temper-pot bubbled, ready to boil over.

Dickers nodded and hung his head, knowing better than to vocalize his beliefs.

Parker laughed. "No, *I* don't speak for God." He held his gaze on me, ready to spring into a debate.

"Okay, boys," said Olivia. "Time to put 'em away." She wisely stepped between us. "You can play cavemen some other time. Oh, wait, you *do* believe in cavemen, right, Parker?" Even though Olivia set out as an emissary of peace, her tart tongue pushed her behind enemy lines. Ian and Brandon laughed while Parker shot them an evil glare.

"Hey, Parker, maybe we can take it up in philosophy?" I said, hoping to diffuse time bomb Olivia.

"Yeah, maybe we can."

"All right," said Olivia. "Time to go to class. Try not to get dead today, y'all." Her smile faded quickly, replaced with instant regret, usually an alien concept to Olivia. "You know what I mean." She gestured down the hallway toward another Reaper, who just claimed an unhappy student.

Olivia spun on her black high-tops to face me. She tossed her arms around my neck and said, "And *you...*" She stretched up on her tiptoes and planted a long kiss on my lips.

Dickers said, "Gross. Get a room."

Ian's mock-gagging stopped with a hiccup-like sound, his voice diminishing into a whisper. "Guys. Hey, guys."

"*And* we have two detentions," caterwauled the dreadfully familiar voice. I turned around and looked into the madly grinning face of Arville Hastings, resident redneck tyrant in charge of reducing students into quivering piles of fear.

"I had something in my teeth," said Olivia. "Tex was trying to help me get it out, Mr. Hastings." Usually good at thinking on her feet, this had to be a new low for her.

"Yes, I can see that. Was he using his tongue to

help?" Hastings licked his lips, obviously savoring his big arrest.

Olivia huffed. I gave her arm a quick squeeze to keep her from saying something multiple-detention worthy. From the sidelines, Parker chuckled, enjoying the show. Brandon just stared, possibly contemplating a nap.

"Sorry, Mr. Hastings." I tried my best to work up false remorse. An actor, I'm not. "It won't happen again."

"We'll see about that," said Olivia quietly.

*"What* was that, Ms. Furman?" bellowed Hastings. "Would you like double detention?"

Olivia frowned, blinked, lost in thought. "I've considered your offer. But, no, I would not like to have double detention. Thanks, anyway."

Oh boy. Hastings's formidable eyebrows flew up like tossed caterpillars. "I've had about enough of your smart talk, little lady! I'm going to—" The bell for first class rang and just in time. "Detention. Tomorrow. Miss Swanson's room. And you'd best both be there," he shouted over the bell.

"It's a date," called out Olivia as she ran down the hall.

I chased after her. "Olivia, are you *trying* to get us expelled?"

She laughed. "We only have *one* month left. *Chill!* I think we're going to make it."

"Not like this we're not."

She peered down the hallway before latching onto me again. She kissed me, this time a short smack. "Olivia, come *on.*"

"I swear, Tex, on the last day of school, I *am* going

to throw you down onto the lunch table and make out kamikaze-style right under Hastings's hairy nose."

"Okay." I knew it wouldn't be the smartest thing to do, but I had to admit the possibilities of it sounded absolutely liberating. Amongst other sensations.

Olivia's words put a light bounce in my step. Not the ones about the ultimate Public Display of Affection, although that promised its own merits. She said we only had one month left, and for the first time, I felt like we might truly make it. After four years of living in Hell on earth—all the trauma, tragedy, and sadness we've endured—I finally allowed myself the luxury of believing we *are* going to survive.

But once again, the nefarious Fates were plotting a different ending than the one I naively hoped for, one that wouldn't leave us unscathed.

\*\*\*\*

As we piled into the gym, I scoured the bleachers for friend sightings. Ian sat slumped next to Allison, while Lance chatted up an indifferent Brandon. I scaled the crowded bleachers and made it to the back row, our preferred area for any event.

"Hey," I said. "Where's Olivia?"

As if on cue, I saw Dickers climbing the steps, Olivia's jean-jacketed arms swaying behind him. Dickers grinned as he stepped aside.

*Uh-oh.*

"Don't say a *damn* word," shouted Olivia over the laughter of the crowd. Even though Olivia's face had been painted white, she apparently made several cosmetic alterations. She expanded the single black tear into a star surrounding her eye, giving her the appearance of a glam-metal rocker.

"Those...*bastards.*" She plopped down next to me, Dickers flanking her other side.

"Hey, you're not supposed to say anything," said Ian.

Olivia reached across and punched him in the shoulder, those of us in the middle catching part of her "friendly fire."

"They killed you, huh?" I coughed to cover my involuntary—and ill-advised—laugh.

Lance said, "White becomes you, girl."

Allie's chin met her chest as she stared into her lap, her head bobbing up and down. Smarter than the rest of us, she'd mastered laughing while ducking and covering.

"And you think I'm *not* going to say anything? Well, just watch me." Olivia cupped her hands around her mouth and yelled, *"Jackasses.* It's all *so* stupid. "

"Who got you, O'?" Dickers excluded Olivia from his using last name only protocol.

"Beats the *hell* outta me. Can't tell who's who in those *stupid* cloaks and hoods and makeup. But if I find out—"

A brassy burst of instruments erupted from the band stashed away by the locker room doors. An ear-piercing whistle shrieked, followed by sirens. A dozen Reapers exploded out of the locker room doors, running helter-skelter across the floor, taunting the students in the stands. Our student council hard at work. A pumped-up power anthem blared over the speakers, a hissing defect making it much worse. Several Reapers broke into something resembling dance steps while others ran randomly amok. The Clearwell cheerleaders trotted out, performing high kicks on the sidelines.

Finally, a tall Reaper stepped onto a wooden platform, his arms held high. The students applauded. Olivia rolled her eyes and looked at me aghast. As if carsick, Ian doubled over, his face in his lap.

The Reaper slowly lowered his hands until the music came to a crashing halt. The other Reapers mercifully ceased their awkward gyrating and gathered around the platform. Cheers and catcalls filled the auditorium. The Reaper patted the air. Unbelievably, the students instantly quieted. The Reaper king slowly pulled back his black hood, exposing the well-coiffed head of Donovan Goode, student council president extraordinaire. The other Reapers yanked off their hoods as well. While the lowly Reaper minions' faces were painted white, Donovan Goode somehow escaped this indignity.

"Fellow students of Clearwell High," he yelled into the microphone. "We are gathered here today for our annual Drunk Driving Awareness *Dayyyyyyy.*" The audience roared with approval, hopefully for Donovan rather than drunk driving. "I'm your Student Council President, Donovan Goode.*"* More cheers as Donovan used the infamous political "power thumb" trick—his thumb pointed toward the sky, signifying optimism, while the fist below balled up, representing power, I suppose. But he made it look *good.*

Donovan Goode's a sure-fire politician in the making. Handsome, smart, well-liked by the faculty and students, he's even friendly to a degree, although he insists on sticking with "his own kind." And he has perfect hair. Even his name's a campaign manager's dream—Donovan *Goode* For You! He'd occasionally say hi to us in the hallway, although I suspect he has no idea who we are. Maybe he's just hitting the campaign trail extra early.

"Look around, fellow students," he continued, his hands resting firmly on the podium. "Go ahead. Look around you." Everyone followed his lead. "What do you see?"

*"Reapers,"* yelled out a voice from the bleachers.

"Well, yes, there are Reapers," said Donovan. "But...I see...dead students!" More inexplicable and inappropriate cheers. I imagine Donovan could gain votes by singing the praises of lima beans. He raised his arms again to quiet his captive audience. "We're here to make sure this doesn't become a reality. When you drive drunk, you're not only putting your own life at risk, but everyone else's as well." *And* more cheers. "So, remember...if you *must* drink...if you *absolutely* to drink..." The way he thrust around those power-thumbs, he came dangerously close to putting his eye out. "...have a designated driver. And *don't* drive drunk." The students went nuts, cheering, applauding, and stomping the bleachers with their feet, a tribal drumbeat from some uncivilized jungle. Donovan stared around at his constituents, nodding and smiling at each section. The band fired up a rallying song that I'm sure doubled for a victory anthem on the football field. Finally, Donovan raised his hands again, silencing the audience one more time.

"Before we get to our movie..." Olivia groaned while Brandon's eyes lit up. The films are amateurishly acted, clichéd, and full of mind-boggling gore, the better to instill the message into our heads. *Forever.*

"...I'd like to dedicate today's 'Drunk Driving Awareness Day' to the memory of Brittany Gerlach." I couldn't believe he went *there*. I met Olivia's gaze, also stunned by the announcement. For the first time, a hush fell over the stadium. "Let's close our eyes and have a moment of prayer for her."

I glanced at my friends. Dickers's hands folded into his lap, his head bowed while mouthing silent words. Allison, Lance, and to my shock, even Brandon, were also praying, leaving we three heretics—Olivia, Ian, and myself—out in the cold.

I have no problem with religion, but I couldn't believe that a day represented by grim Reapers and topped with a bloody film should be dedicated to Brittany Gerlach. In fact, the entire day felt like some sort of strange pagan celebration of death.

****

The movie ended. The lights came up, and many faces appeared nearly as white from nausea as Olivia's painted features. Students flooded the stadium floor, surrounding Donovan Goode, his adoring groupies. I spotted Parker patting Donovan on the back, congratulating him on a job well done. Typical Parker behavior, nothing new there.

But it jolted me to see Elizabeth Blackmer land a quick kiss on Donovan's cheek. Definitely a public display of affection, but one so chaste, I'm sure even Hastings would heartily approve. I guess I really shouldn't be so surprised. Who other than Elizabeth would make the perfect first lady for the future president of the United States, Donovan Goode?

My relationship with Elizabeth Blackmer is a complicated one. Very rich, stuck-up, and snooty, Elizabeth's downright mean. A junior this year, she's accomplished more in a short time than we have in four years. Her ultimate goal in life is to get into an Ivy League school and then, I suppose, take over the world. Frankly, if anyone can do it, she can. We have a very uneasy friendship, if you can even call it that. She'll greet me in the hallways at times, but if I attempt to communicate further, she brushes by me as if I'm not important enough for her social-climbing networking. Which, I have to say, is an improvement on how she treated me last year.

On the flip side—a *very* flip side—is Elspeth Chambers, the dead, yet undead, punk girl who Elizabeth used to channel. She's everything Elizabeth isn't. Friendly, clever, funny, mysterious, warm, open, badass, *sexy*. Last year, she helped me get rid of a particularly nasty spirit and uncover a murderer. Long story. Sadly, I haven't seen—nor heard—from her for a year. Her last words to me, like a goth "Terminator," were that she'd be back. I hope she'll return before the school year is out. Before I have to move on. I miss her.

But school waits for no one. My stomach finally having settled, I stood up and stretched.

"Dudes, that movie kicked ass," said Brandon.

\*\*\*\*

Keeping an eye out for Hastings, I held Olivia's hand while walking down the main corridor. While I headed to the basement for geometry, Olivia would splinter off upstairs to English.

"Tex," she said, "did you know Brittany Gerlach?"

"Sorta, I guess. She was in a lot of my classes over the years, but I never really knew her." I'd been using that excuse a lot lately. And I felt more than a little guilty about it. A couple of years ago, I made it my intent to get to know everyone I could. Even though

Brittany maintained a very visible profile, hot in the spotlight of popularity, somehow she'd escaped my attention.

"Well, she *was* a cheerleader. It wasn't like we hung out in the same circles."

"I know. I just can't help but think…what *if* I took the time to befriend her? Maybe…maybe she wouldn't have—"

"Oh, for… Tex, *not* your fault. Don't take the whole world onto your shoulders. You're only human." She reached up and hugged me.

"I guess you're right. I just hate that someone was walking around…in such obvious pain…and we were all blind to it—"

"She had her friends. She was, you know, popular."

"I know. I wish…" I let out a long sigh. "Anyway, are you off to English?"

"Yeah, but first, I'm gonna go wash this crap off my face."

"Olivia, you might get in trouble for that."

"What're they gonna do? Give me top-secret double detention?"

"Well, yeah, maybe. See you after school." I watched as she bolted for the girls' restroom.

I entered the empty stairwell. As I walked down the steps, the door behind me swung open. Another procrastinating student, no doubt. Light footsteps scurried to catch up with me. Turning, I glimpsed a Reaper's black robe. A gloved hand lashed out, shoved my chest, forcing me backward. I twisted, hoping to land on my hands and feet before I tumbled down the stairs. My hand wrenched on the steps, the momentum carrying me down to the landing. In shock, I looked at the top of the stairs, catching the tail end of a robe flowing back into the hallway. Attempting to climb to my feet, my throbbing knee forced me to give up. I sat in stunned silence.

What the hell was *that?* Whoever it was pushed me down the steps on purpose. I could've been seriously hurt. Maybe an over-zealous Reaper carried away by the rallying cries of Donovan Goode? Or could it be something else, something possibly much, much worse?

## Chapter Three

Mickey Goldfarb's my witch mentor. She supplied the same services to my mother in years past. When I first met Mickey, she seemed like a stereotypical, doddering, little old lady. But I've since realized she has one of the sharpest minds around (not to mention the fastest dope-slap) and is a walking dictionary of witchcraft knowledge. I suspect she enjoys giving people the wrong impression about herself. It might be one of the shrewdest weapons in her seemingly bottomless arsenal of tricks.

A couple of evenings ago, Mickey called and said to get ready for a field trip, which both intrigued and filled me with trepidation. During our three-year mentor/student relationship, we've never set foot out of the confines of her house.

Waiting for me on her front porch, Mickey appeared impatient and clearly excited about our outing. She'd gone nuts on the make-up, her cheeks burning fiery red, unnaturally blue eye shadow smudged on her eyelids. Wearing a dark floral-patterned dress and a large matching purse slung over her shoulder, she could've been a grandmother anxious to get to Sunday church.

"Hey, Mickey."

"Howdy," she said. "About time. Let's go."

"Are you driving, or do you want me to?"

She narrowed her eyes. "Oh, you're going to have to drive. My eyes ain't what they used to be." She bounced down the porch stairs. "You're sure you can drive?"

"Well, yeah. I, um, drove over here."

"I mean without killing us. I know how you kids are today with your hotrods and reckless driving."

"I'm a good driver," I said, with a gesture toward the Bucket. "And that doesn't actually qualify as a hotrod." I opened the passenger door for her, and she slid in. "Seatbelt, Mickey." She fumbled at the belt for a seeming eternity, dropping a few choice words until she finally strapped herself in. "Where we going?" I fired up my trusty steed and slowly pulled into the street.

"Go to 'Hippieville.' We're gonna go shopping first."

"'Hippieville'? Where…*what* is that?"

She whipped her head at me as if I'd offended her. "You've never heard of 'Hippieville'? Just drive over to downtown Trellington Park."

"Ah." I knew about Trellington Park but had never heard it referred to as 'Hippieville.' Smack in the middle of suburban Kansas, Trellington Park's shops are specialized niche stores catering to new-agers with endless trinkets, candles, and whatsits. "So, Mickey, I've heard of hippies before, but I've never really seen one. What are they?" Maybe a tad risky pulling her leg like that, but I thought it'd be fun to hear her definition of a hippy.

"You've never seen a hippy before? I *swan.* If you weren't driving, I'd smack you upside your head." She studied her hand as if disappointed she couldn't use it.

"Hippies were all the rage in the '60s. They had sex, did drugs, didn't work, and protested everything you could think of. Why, once my daughter…" Her words fell away as she stared out the passenger window.

Last year, when the topic of her daughter came up, Mickey turned hostile. I let it drop. "Ah, okay. But what are we going to do in 'Hippieville'?"

"I *told* you already. We're shopping.*"*

We finished the rest of the drive in uneasy silence. I turned the radio on, and she immediately changed it to an oldies station, humming along hoarsely and off-key. I hoped we wouldn't have to do too much more driving today.

Upon Mickey's barked directions, I found a parking spot on a store-lined, cobbled-brick street. Several bearded men in porkpie hats watched us from the patio of a bistro as we crossed the street. Subversive hippies, no doubt.

We stopped in front of a store, the window cluttered with candles, votives, and robes. Homemade fliers hung on the inside of the window, alerting us about upcoming book signings and a string quartet performance. Scrawled in yellowish-green paint across the window were the words "Moonlight Dawn," which didn't make a lot of sense to me…but whatever.

A chime jangled as we entered. The scent of incredibly strong incense filled my nose. My allergies kicked into high gear while my eyes watered. I've never understood the pleasures of incense; to me, it always smells like burning perfume.

Seemingly from nowhere, a deep, resonant voice with a hint of an unrecognizable accent said, "Hello, Mickey, how are things?" A very short man hopped onto what I presumed to be a stool, behind a glass case full of ceremonial knives. Beneath his dark brown and wavy hair, his face appeared handsome and stoic. "Is this your new 'boy toy'?" He inclined his head toward me.

"Ah, heh, well..." I laughed awkwardly, attempting to give the impression I can take a joke. Of course, I failed.

The man pursed his lips, stared at me, and shook his head.

Mickey howled. "Oh, Max, you just *slay* me." Her shrill laughter rose above the low, repetitive chanting emanating from a speaker behind the man.

Finally, he broke his stolid glare and managed a wry smile.

"Tex, don't just stand there looking like a deer caught in the headlights," said Mickey. "Come over here. Meet Max LaCastre, the proprietor of this store, and the King of Clearwell, Kansas."

Max stared at me indifferently as I approached him. He grabbed my offered hand and squeezed with an iron grip, belying his diminutive status. I yelped girlishly and pulled it back as if a mousetrap snapped at me.

"Um, hi, Mr. LaCastre. I'm Tex McKenna—"

"Wait." His eyes widened, his laconic expression slipping away. "*You're* Elizabeth McKenna's boy?" He stood up on his stool, placed his hands on the glass case, and leaned over to get a closer look. I felt on display, along with a sudden empathy for zoo animals.

"Yes, I am," I said quietly.

He studied me further. "Max. Call me Max."

"Okay, Max."

"I've heard a *lot* about you, Tex. Your mother was a very special lady."

"Thanks. I thought she was, too." Apparently, my mother's reach sprawled farther than I'd ever imagined.

"'Twas a pity what became of her." He shook his head.

The door chimed again as a thin, tired-looking woman walked in. Mickey motioned for me to follow her as she grabbed various herbs off the well-stocked shelves. Presumably funny bumper stickers and T-shirts filled a barrel, but I didn't understand them. Witch humor, I guess. Throughout the store, practically every religion was represented by statues, icons, and other artifacts—except for traditional Judeo-Christian beliefs.

I eavesdropped on the customer speaking with Max. She asked about "ear candles," and Max took great pains to explain to her the proper methodology to use them in his low, pleasing monotone. From what I gathered, ear candles are used to cleanse the spirit and are actually placed and lit in one's ears. Max warned the timid woman not to attempt to do it alone, or she might end up on fire. He roared with laughter while the woman promptly paid and left.

"Got everything you need, Mickey?" Max began to ring up Mickey's handful of items.

"I think so."

Unexpectedly, Max dropped a bottle of herbs on the glass countertop. He stepped off the stool and stood paralyzed, his eyes rolling up as if having a seizure.

"Mickey, is he all *right*?" I leaned over the counter, preparing to vault it. I wouldn't know what to do once I got there, but that's all I had.

Mickey placed her finger to her lips to shush me.

"Just watch. And listen," she whispered.

Max trembled, his eyelids fluttering. His knees shook, the resultant ripples rising through his body like waves. The speed of his convulsions increased. Locks of hair flapped about his face. He moaned, his voice steadily rising.

*"Something bad is coming,"* he said. *"Something bad. Only you can stop them, Tex McKenna. Soon you will be tested. Beware. Danger will come from more than one."*

Max's tremors slowed. Sweat built on his forehead. His shoulders drooped as if he'd been literally let off a hook. Eyes rolled back into view, narrowed, then opened wide. He stepped up on the stool again, business as usual.

"Sorry about that," he said. "That was a bad one. Where was I, Mickey?"

"What just *happened*?"

"Oh, simmer down, Tex," snapped Mickey. "Max is one of the finest clairvoyants in the country—"

"The world, Mickey. The *world*," he said.

Mickey laughed. "When Max goes into one of his visions, it's best just to listen and hear him out. He's got at least an eighty-five percent accuracy ratio—"

Max tilted his head and frowned. "I think it's more like ninety-five percent."

"Okay. Okay. I *understand* you're great, but you're not really helping me out here." While Mickey and Max discussed percentages, I kinda wanted to…you know, find out about the newest threat to my life.

"Excitable one, isn't he?" Max wiggled his eyebrows several times, a mini Groucho Marx.

"Well, it *was* a little disturbing, Max," said

Mickey, finally—*finally*—acknowledging the mega-disturbingness of it all.

"Why? What'd I say?"

"You said something bad is coming, and Tex is the only one who can stop it. I think you said… 'there is trouble from more than one.'" Mickey looked toward me for corroboration, and I nodded frantically. "You said the kid would be tested."

"Huh."

"*'Huh'?* That's all you *got?* You practically scream that I'm in real danger, and all you can say is *'huh'?*" I realized I sounded a little rude, but manners shouldn't count when your life's in danger.

Max shrugged. "I think it's…quite fortuitous…you happened to be here when I delivered the message. That rarely happens. People usually write down what I say. I can't remember it. And I don't have any more knowledge about it than *you* do."

Mickey dragged her fingernails across her chin, scratching madly away. "This is kinda…concerning, Max. Tex has been a supernatural trouble magnet since I first met him—"

"I see."

Mickey glimpsed at her watch. "Well, crap, look at the time. Gotta get to the meeting. Max, do me a favor and keep your ears open?"

"You know I will, Mick," replied Max. "Say hi to the girls."

Mickey snatched my arm, still in a state of shock as she dragged me behind her. "Bye, Max," she called out. "And thanks again."

*Yeah, thanks a whole lot.*

\*\*\*\*

My hands shook over the steering wheel. I felt my life spinning out of control again, impending danger my constant unwanted sidekick. Yet I had no idea what to expect.

"Mickey, what am I *supposed* to do?"

Mickey twisted in the car seat and glared at me. "Quit being such a cry-baby. Just relax—"

"Max's five percent margin for error *isn't* very comforting."

"Yes, well, I don't suppose it is." She set her mouth tight. "I'll be here to help you. But right now, we don't know anything. Once the big picture becomes clearer, we'll take some action."

I felt slightly better knowing I had Mickey in my corner. Maybe it meant the chances of doom not coming for me rose to six percent. "Why does this always happen to me? I know I'm a witch, but if this is what it means to be a witch—constantly dodging death and danger and evil or *whatever*—how do I go about...rescinding my witch powers?"

"Now you're just talking dumb, kid. You've been given a gift. And even if you *could* throw it away, do you know how stupid that would be? The 'powers that be' already know you're a witch and seem to have hand-picked you as their tool—"

"Yeah, I sure feel like a tool, lately," I said, under my breath.

"What was that?" Mickey furrowed her brow.

"Never mind."

"Well, anyway, even if you could lose your powers, that don't mean the bad side of things will stop targeting you. They'd keep on coming for you, and without your powers, you'd be helpless against them.

What would you do then, kid?"

"I don't know. I never *asked* for this. I never wanted this!"

Mickey sighed. "I know, kid. Just deal with it, okay? Look at all the good you've done in the last couple of years."

I thought about all the murders and the loss of Josh and Danny. Kinda tough spotting the silver lining around the coffins of so many people caught up in the supernatural games in which I'd become a pawn. "What about the bad, Mickey? What about all the...*misery* my powers cause?"

Her head shot up straight, displaying more of a neck than I thought she had. "You're talking stupid again. You helped put away two—no, three—murderers. Sure, there were some casualties, but...without you, more people would've died."

I suppose I knew this to be true, but a little reinforcement's always a helpful boost. "Maybe you're right, but—"

"Of course I am." Her smile stretched face-wide, temporarily wiping out many wrinkles. "Now quit talking stupid and let's go." She pointed her bony index finger ahead of us. "Go down the street and take a left till I say don't go no more."

I eased into the traffic, following her directions. "I'm just scared. Every time things seem to be going right for me, *bam!* I get the rug pulled out from beneath me. I'm *this* close to graduating." Having said it, I realized more than Max's ominous warning frightened me. I wondered if I *would* graduate. Even more frightening than that, what would I do afterward? My entire life felt stuck in flux—in free-fall—and here I am, still holding onto the cat's ledge, trying not to be dumped unceremoniously into the void of nothingness. Or a career in the fast food industry.

Mickey patted my shoulder. "Don't worry, kid. You made it through everything else. You'll get through this, too. Whatever it is. You know, the fact you have survived some bad situations, I think—I *feel*—the good side is watching out for you, too."

"Huh. You mean...I have an angel on my shoulder? Or something?" In spite of my fears, I managed a grin.

"Something like that, yes." I hadn't really considered this before, but I'd gladly take any comfort doled out.

"So what's the deal with him? Max, I mean."

"Max? He's one of a kind—"

"Yeah, I kinda gathered that. But what's his story?"

"No one really knows. There're rumors he's from France. Others say he's from the Bayou. He's never been forthcoming about his background, and I think he enjoys the mystery. Actually, he lives for it. I know the FBI has gone to him several times for help to find missing people. Usually he finds 'em. It's not an exact science, though, you know. He can't turn it on and off like a water fountain. I don't think even *he* knows where his information comes from. Or if he does, he's never told anyone."

"Yeah. Keep going straight, Mickey?" For several miles, we traveled on the same street, the similar-looking boxy houses blurring by in a suburban parade of blandness.

"I told you so, didn't I?" She shook her head

exasperatedly. "Anyway, Max is a great example of a clairvoyant who could've used his powers to get ahead. To make his fortune. Maybe even for black magic. But, thankfully, he's chosen the side of good. Now he bides his time running his little store. And those *prices.* Land's sakes! He's charging five bucks for a piece of hematite I can get at a Stuckey's for fifty cents." She chortled. "That scoundrel." Her laughter quickly transformed into her standard coughing fit. Although it horrified me the first time I witnessed this happen to Mickey, I learned to just ride it out. It sounded like music to my ears compared to the oldies station she insisted on torturing me with. "Anyway, Max is admirable in that he chose the high road. You get my meaning?" She glowered at me to make sure today's lesson penetrated my thick skull.

"Yes, I do, Mickey. White magic, good. Black magic, *evil.*"

Mickey hooted again, and now I wished I hadn't triggered it. "So, where *are* we going?"

"We're going to a witches' meeting," she said. "Mind if I smoke?" She already popped a cigarette into her mouth.

"Well, yes, I would appreciate it if—"

"Thanks, kid." She lit the cigarette and sent a huge cloud of smoke billowing off the dashboard and window.

I groaned and rolled down my window. Coughing into my hand a few times, I tried to get the message across in a less than subtle manner. She continued to "chimney" me mercilessly. "Mickey, would you at *least* please roll down your window?"

Her mouth fell open, as if I had asked her to jump

out of the car. Finally, she reluctantly complied.

"So. A 'witches' meeting?'"

"Yep. I think it's time to start socializing you, kid. You know, what do they call it nowadays? 'Networking.'"

*This should be interesting. A witch's world apparently isn't so small after all.*

"Okay, pull in behind those cars." The house looked like any other house on the street—a modest ranch, with a well-trimmed yard and of course, an immaculately kept garden. *I've found that a healthy garden is a sure telltale sign of a witch. I wondered if the neighbors knew that beneath this seemingly bland, gray aluminum siding façade, lurked a witches' coven. I imagined witches dressed in black robes, performing outlandish ceremonies, and hoped sacrifices and nudity wouldn't be mandatory.*

Mickey rang the doorbell and told me to relax. Seconds later, a plump elderly woman opened the door. She wore a blue jacket draped over her gray dress, with a white belt cinching it around her waist. *"Mickey,"* she screamed, leaning in for a hug.

"Hello, Esther." *They could've been two dotty aunts at a picnic rather than two witches gathering for a meeting.*

"And *you* must be Tex. Elizabeth's boy."

Following Mickey's lead, I offered the woman a hug, thinking this to be a traditional witch's welcome. As I felt her shrink uncomfortably away from my embrace, I knew my first witches' meeting had kicked off with a rip-snorting start.

"Um, yes. Hello to you, too, Tex." Mickey, of course, enjoyed my graceless moment, cackling away like a more traditional witch. "You can call me Miss Philpot."

"Ah, hi, Miss Philpot."

"Well, don't just stand there, you two," she said, flapping her hand as if trying to put out a fire. "Come on, before you let all the cats in." The two women tittered. More witch humor, I presumed.

We stepped into the front hallway, and Miss Philpot directed us around the corner. "The others are in the living and dining rooms. Please make yourselves at home, and, Tex, do get to know everyone." We entered an adjoining room, awash with a sea of blue-and-gray-haired women swirling about like dancers on a wobbly cruise ship deck. Their high-pitched laughter, occasionally pierced by one woman's particularly horrific scream of mirth, jangled my nerves. Every few seconds or so, like a crazed coo-coo clock, a woman would drop another searing laugh-bomb.

The rooms themselves appeared similar to Mickey's house, cluttered, but arranged neatly and precisely. A cracked, leather sofa sat against one wall, where three women nested, busily clucking away at one another. Photographs of children and grandchildren, trinkets interspersed between them, lined the mantle over the fireplace. A large burgundy Persian rug covered the worn tan shag carpet. The only sign that I'd stumbled into a witches' meeting, rather than a family reunion, were the abundance of candles—different colors, shapes, and lengths—illuminating the rooms with minimal lighting. Shadows stretched and bobbed along the walls as if the restless spirits of the women's deceased husbands had found them, asking for one final dance at life.

Feeling incredibly uncomfortable and extraneous, I sought a face younger than sixty-five for solace. Bingo! A child, no more than nine years old, sat in a corner of the dining room. Her legs kicked back and forth underneath her chair, sweeping the floor for dust bunnies out of idle boredom.

"Hey," I said. "Um, not too many young people here, are there?"

She blew a gum bubble before popping it loudly.

"Uh, I'm Tex." I offered my hand to her.

She folded her arms, legs still swinging rhythmically beneath her.

"Hey, um, are you, you know…a witch?" I sat down in the chair next to her.

*"Nooo,"* she said, utilizing three harmonic syllables. With a loud sigh, she finally acknowledged me. "Grams makes me come to these stupid things. She hopes I'll be a witch someday. I'd rather be home." Her eyes rolled several impressive orbits.

"Yeah, I kinda get that."

"I'm Darleen." Even though I thought I'd finally broken through her icy demeanor, having found common ground in our outsider status, she still kept her arms guardedly folded. "This is *sooo* way boring." Darleen's constant gum popping sounded like someone taking pot-shots at me, the lone male intruder.

*"Snicker-doodle?"* Startled by the booming voice, I looked up at the woman holding a tray of cookies. Extremely large, she wore a yellow sundress, circa 1976, adorned with psychedelic blotches of green, orange, and aqua, giving her the unfortunate appearance of an old hippy bus.

"Don't mind if I do." I stood and snatched a cookie

off her tray. Not the sort of hors d'oeuvre I would expect from a witches' gathering, but if I have to seek comfort in food, so be it. "Thank you."

"I see you've met my granddaughter, Darleen." Her plump cheeks shoved her eyes into slits. "Isn't she as cute as a bug's ear?" She leaned down and pinched Darleen's cheek.

*"Grammms,"* whined Darleen. I tossed her a glance and nod to suggest I empathetically know what it's like to be in her shoes. Embarrassment and I are old acquaintances.

"I'm Wilma Garrington," she said, turning her attention back toward me. "And who might you be, young man?"

"I'm, um, a friend of Mickey's. Tex McKenna." This time I followed proper witch protocol and extended my hand, withholding an undesirable hug.

*"Oh!"* She took my hand, squeezed it hard, pumping wildly away. "You're Elizabeth's boy. I've heard a lot about you." The other women within earshot stopped what they were doing to stare at the long-haired, skinny elephant in the room.

"Yeah, I've been getting that a lot lately."

"Well, isn't that something?" She continued working my hand like a crank.

"I guess it's something, all right." Finally, she released her grip.

"I hope you enjoy your first meeting, Tex. Be sure and say hi to all the sisters. I *must* be making my rounds. *Ta.*" She floated off humming, touching everyone's shoulder as she passed.

I returned to my seat, trying to blend in with the chair's woodwork. "Well, she seems nice."

Darleen rolled her eyes and snapped her gum. "What*ever*. Why are *you* here?"

"Well, I guess 'cause I'm a witch."

For the first time, something close to interest passed over Darleen's face as her jaw dropped, the pink wad of gum hanging perilously close to her bottom lip. "Don't be silly. *Boys* can't be witches." She rocked back and forth on her seat, my having entertained her so thoroughly.

"Yeah, I'm beginning to wish that was the case."

A dinging sound filled the room. Miss Philpot stood in front of the fireplace, tapping a wine glass with a small fork. "Ladies! Sisters! May I have your attention, please? Everyone take a seat, and we'll begin our monthly meeting of the Clearwell Sisterhood of Witches." I wonder if they were unionized.

As the women scrambled for their seats like a game of musical chairs in a seniors' home, the raucous laughter died down. Many women still stood while the victors relished their comfortable squatters' rights. I considered giving up my seat, but that would entail crossing the large room and making another spectacle of myself. Better to forgo courtesy and remain unnoticed in the corner. I tried to spot Mickey, but with the candlelight darting around, I only saw dark blotches where eyes belonged and an occasional highlighted outthrust jaw.

"Welcome, sisters," began Miss Philpot. "Oh, and young man, of course." She inclined her head toward me. The women laughed, straining to get a good look at the oddity in the dining room. "The Clearwell Sisterhood of Witches welcomes you all. I know most of you, and there are a few new faces here tonight, as well. I certainly hope when I've wrapped up tonight, you'll take a few moments to greet our new sisters...and *brother*, of course." More sniggering, just *killing* it tonight.

Miss Philpot dropped her smile and scanned the audience like a well-rehearsed politician. "Now, I'm quite aware we have witches of all different types and sorts amongst us tonight. We're not here to start arguments over which type of witchcraft is best, or whose goddess is the *right* goddess. We accept each other unequivocally. We're here to form a bond—our sisterhood—over the wonders of witchcraft of all types. If this should prompt healthy discussions later, so be it." A smattering of applause. "But we keep things civil and, above all, open-minded. We don't judge, and we accept everyone. Okay, that's the end of my disclaimer for the evening." I joined in the laughter (even though nothing struck me as particularly funny) while Darleen rolled her eyes again. I seriously considered telling Darleen her eyes would get stuck that way if she kept it up, but I didn't feel quite ready to join the "older generation" yet.

"Let us start by a simple invocation to the Great Goddess of Night," continued Miss Philpot. In the dark room, I made out bowed heads, the candlelight fleetingly touching upon their graying heads. I bowed my head as well. "Oh, Great Goddess of Night, overseer of the four forces of nature—life, fertility, death, and rebirth—we have gathered here tonight to give thanks to thee. And to offer our debt of gratitude to you for allowing us to utilize your four natural elements—fire, water, earth, and wind—for the betterment of womankind...and mankind. We seek enlightenment with the goal being to bring ourselves into balance with the universe, thus exploring ourselves fully. We promise to honor and worship all living things in nature and our agreed upon creed to never harm any living thing…" Miss Philpot fell silent, the only sound the faint clicking of a few of the more testy candlewicks.

Tonight held many surprises, perhaps the biggest one being that this coven of witches truly preached tolerance and acceptance, something that seemed to have been vanishing lately from some of the more traditional Judeo-Christian churches. Particularly, the new heinous-sounding Clarendon Baptist Church. I toyed with the notion of telling Dickers and Parker they could learn a thing or two from witches, but I'm sure they'd consider it blasphemy. And, of course, there is the whole issue of my being a witch, one not open to sharing. Nope, I'm filing the idea into my brain's "dead files."

"Okay, let's get started, sisters." Mercifully, she omitted my intruding gender this time. "Now. First up, where will the next meeting be held? More importantly…whose turn is it to bring treats?"

The doorbell rang. A hush fell over the gathered women. Muffled voices floated in from the entryway, followed by the closing of the front door. Whispers volleyed back and forth as a large figure filled the living room door.

Another teenage boy, possibly my age, stepped into the candlelit room. Overweight by thirty pounds, his Nehru jacket wrapped around him tightly like an over-achieving python. A wild purple and black paisley pattern swirled about the material, nearly psychedelic in its outdated outlandishness. Extra skin squeezed out over the buttons snapped up to his neck, making me worry about his circulation. A mop of his black, greasy hair brushed carefully down over one eyebrow, the newest in "Cyclops Chic." With a dramatic flourish worthy of an arrogant stage magician, hand raised, he swept his gaze across the room.

"Good evening, ladies," he said, attempting to affect a suave air, and bowed. Instead, he came across as completely silly. To my surprise, however, he succeeded in holding sway over the Clearwell witches as they responded with a sort of hushed reverence. He stepped forward into the middle of the room, taking his sweet time, just a casual stroll through the garden of witches.

"Who's *this* guy?" I whispered to Darleen.

This time Darleen's eye-roll seemed to be more than warranted. "That's Spencer. The only *real* boy witch. But he's *such* a tool."

Choking back my laughter, I nodded in agreement.

Amazingly, one of the women sitting on the sofa jumped to her feet with lightning quick speed. "Here, Spencer. I'd be greatly honored if you take my seat."

Spencer hefted one unnatural looking black eyebrow—a move I'm sure he perfected in front of a mirror—and sashayed toward the now vacated seat.

Before I could instruct my inner censor to leave things be, I bolted from my chair. "No, no." My voice broke from nervousness, not unlike when my voice finally changed last year. "Why don't you take my chair, so she can stay seated?" Blood rushed to my cheeks as gasps made the rounds. "Um, I don't mind. Really." I tried to chuckle casually, but it sounded more like a feeble cough.

Spencer whipped his head toward me, sneered, then looked back at the standing woman, who continued to beckon him toward her sofa seat. Weighing his options, I guess. Finally, he inhaled deeply. "Okay. *Fine.*" Like a shamed puppy, the woman nervously hunkered back to her shelter. Spencer sniffed as he walked toward me. Within inches from my face, he spat, "I'd be *delighted* to take your seat.*"* Nostrils flared, and his dark eyes didn't waver. With a loud, breezy *flumph,* he fell into the chair. He stuck his black-jeaned legs out and crossed them. The only way for me to stand somewhere unobtrusively would be to vault over his legs; clearly, he wouldn't budge.

"Excuse me." With the grace of a drunken hippo, I high-stepped over his legs.

Finally, Miss Philpot broke the tension and brought the attention back toward herself. "Well, sisters, it truly is a special night as we have with us Spencer, whom we haven't seen in some time..." She smiled warmly at him. The women applauded reverently as if amongst true royalty. To me, it looked like Miss Philpot's smile had been glued on, betraying her true feelings regarding Spencer. Or it could have been a trick of the candlelight.

I had a hard time focusing on the rest of the meeting. I kept wondering if I'd broken some sort of unspoken witch protocol about seating and some sort of pecking order. Just when I thought I found a bully-free zone, a place where all are accepted openly, here comes Spencer, my first "witch-bully."

I probably would have zoned out for the rest of the meeting, anyway. From what little tidbits I picked up here and there, the main topics included planning future social events, recipes, and an occasional anecdote remotely related to witchcraft. I nervously stole glances at Spencer, who likewise—unrelentingly, doggedly—glared back at me. Does this kid not blink?

The meeting finally came to an end. Candles blew out as the overhead lights flipped on. Readjusting my eyes to the new brightness, I gave a quick wave to Darlene and scrambled to find Mickey. I saw her by the front entryway speaking with another woman whose stance seemed oddly familiar.

"Hey, Mickey."

The woman spun around. "Hello, Tex." Mrs. Nguyen, Lance's mother. "It's so nice to see you here." She placed a hand on my arm, and I practically needed her support to keep from falling over in shock.

"Mrs. Nguyen. You're a...*witch!*" I knew it sounded like an overly-ripe line from some crappy television show, but this unexpected revelation floored me. My once insular world of witchcraft was rapidly expanding to include more people. Three years ago, I didn't even know witches existed—and now I had to wonder who else might be one. How about Mrs. Carbody, Arville Hasting's right-hand goon? Or maybe the abominable lunch-lady, lurking in the kitchen, doling out potions in the pseudo sloppy joe mix?

Mrs. Nguyen placed her fingertips to her lips and suppressed a laugh, her eyes alight with amusement. "Well, let's just say...I'm a witch-in-practice."

Mickey chortled away. "I see you already know Christine, Tex. Small world, ain't it?"

"Uh, yeah, you could say that. Does...Lance know about your witchcraft?"

"Yes, he thinks it's 'cool.'" She giggled like a shy schoolgirl.

"You, um, won't tell Lance about me, will you? I mean, about being a witch and everything?" My excitement crammed my words together like a multi-car pile-up. It seemed I might've found a new ally, or at least someone else whom I could talk to about everything witch-related.

"Don't worry. Unless you specifically say it's okay to tell him, I'll keep your secret for you."

"Um, maybe it's none of my business, but, ah, does your husband know?"

Her mouth drooped down at the corners. "No, I'm afraid I haven't told Mr. Nguyen. He thinks I go to monthly book clubs." She shifted nervously as if I'd stepped on her toe. This is a family who're keeping a *lot* of secrets. And from past experience, I know how secrets have a way of germinating to the point where they grow wild, eroding a relationship with weeds of distrust.

"Oh." Great comeback, as always. "Anyway, wow. Is Lance a witch?" The thought of having a friend as a witch seemed too super-cool.

"No, no. As I said, Tex, I'm a practicing witch. I'm not a witch born with power. That kind of witchcraft isn't hereditary."

"Oh...yeah. Of course. I knew that." Attempting to not sound like an idiot, I think my results spoke for themselves.

"Come on, kid," said Mickey, grabbing my arm. "Let Christine be. She's got a family to tend to."

"Tex, if you ever need to talk to someone, or have questions, give me a call." She held her hand to her head, feigning a mock phone; apparently, she thought I needed the extra clue in all of my denseness.

"Thanks, Mrs. Nguyen, I just might do that."

Mickey tugged forcefully at my arm. "Now. Let's go. It's getting late, and I have some 'stories' to catch up on yet before the night's done."

I unlocked Mickey's door to the Bucket, and she clambered in. As I opened my door, a hand whipped out and slammed it shut. I turned around and looked once again into the eyes of Spencer, a very angry boy witch.

"Why'd you do it?" He huffed loudly, either from rage or being winded.

"Um, do what?"

He tilted his head slowly, which I assumed was for maximum dramatic effect. "Were you trying to make me look *foolish* in there?" Viewing him up close, under more adequate lighting, I noticed he doctored his eyebrows with black dye. A disastrous run of blemishes blasted his face, a light-colored facial product failing miserably in providing sufficient coverage.

"No. Spencer, isn't it? No...I didn't think you needed any help looking foolish." I knew my smart-ass mouth should've taken the night off, but I honestly didn't consider this kid as a threat. Never saw him coming.

He smacked his palm against my car window. "You'd better be careful whom you talk to that way," he whispered through clenched teeth. I noticed Mickey squirming in her seat, attempting to open her car door. One of these days, I really should get that door fixed.

I sighed and attempted to retract any damage done. "Look, sorry if we got off on the wrong foot. I'm Tex McKenna." I held my hand out to him.

He ignored it. "I know who you are. The reason I came to this...*amateur* hour was because I heard you'd be in attendance. I wanted to see what all the talk was about." He slowly swept his gaze up and down my body. "You're not all *that.*"

"Well, damn, Spence, that really hurts. Because I think you're a teenage dream." Okay, "smart-ass sensors" set to *stun.*

Spencer said nothing, but smacked the poor Bucket again, while Mickey still struggled with her unmovable door. She began to shimmy toward the driver's side, a slow process.

"All I did was offer an old lady my chair." I took a cue from Darlene's playbook and obnoxiously rolled my eyes. "I didn't *think* I was...hurting anybody's feelings. If it makes you happy, at the next meeting, I'll pull the chair out from under her." I smiled, hoping the effect would prove contagious. It didn't.

"There *will* be another meeting between us, McKenna. Only you won't have the protection of the 'old lady squad' to back you up next time." He glanced at Mickey who had scuttled approximately halfway across the car's front seat. He snorted, snapping his head back, his hair remaining plastered to his skull. "Nobody...*no one*...humiliates 'The Spencer.'"

"I really, really, *really* don't know what I did to humiliate you, '*The* Spencer,' but it looks like '*The* Tex' did somehow, doesn't it?"

Spencer suddenly swept his hand up, prompting me to flinch. Grabbing a handful of my hair, he yanked hard.

"*Ow!* What the *hell,* Spencer?" I wobbled back in shock and rubbed the area where he'd pulled. Slowly lifting his hands, he balled them into shaking fists and pounded them on his chest like a gorilla. Looks like "The Spencer" isn't fully wrapped. Time for me and Mickey to go. "Well, this has been fun, 'The Spencer', but I really *must* be going. I think I have some other people to humiliate. Ta." As he stood quivering freakishly in the street, I yanked my car door open.

"Move over, Mickey," I whispered. "This guy's *nuts.*"

With Mickey scrunched next to me, I realized it'd take a while for her to repeat her crabwalk back across the car seat. Out of options, I sat there and uncomfortably listened to Spencer's threats through the rolled-up window.

"This isn't *over,* McKenna." He accented his newest rant with another impotent hand slap on the Bucket. "Not in any *way.* You just made a *dangerous* enemy. You better *watch your back.*"

I stared straight out the window as nonchalantly as I possibly could, while a few of the straggler witches watched the eruption. Spencer's tirade continued unabated with every threat he ever heard in a movie.

"Hurry up, Mickey," I said under my breath, my lips unmoving, so as not to show Spencer how much he unsettled me. Because ventriloquism is brave, I guess.

I finally heard the reassuring *clack* of Mickey's seat belt as she said, "Let's roll." Being the obedient Clyde to her cigarette-toting Bonnie, I slowly pulled out, hoping not to leave Spencer dead on the road. I glanced back in the rear-view mirror, only to see Spencer pirouetting in the street, hands raised to the heavens, shrieking a litany of evil down upon me. Several of the Sisterhood witches cautiously approached him, trying to tame him like a wild, enraged lion in the circus. Good luck, ladies, remember Siegfried and Roy.

To my amazement, Mickey cackled—all just fun and games. "Kid, what in the world did you do to get little Spencer so beside himself?" The inevitable coughing ensued. "Good on you, kid, good on you."

"Mickey, what's *up* with him?"

"Who? Spencer Pritchett? Oh. Excuse me. I should say *'The* Spencer.' He's trying to drop his last name and wants to just be called 'The Spencer.'" She took her glasses off, wiping tears of hilarity away. "You know…like that rock star you kids love nowadays?"

I looked at her, no clue.

"Oh, you know. Charo. *No. Cher*! That's it. Cher.*"

"Um…" I'll just let that one slide, even though she's about five decades too late.

"Anyway." She placed her glasses back on the tip of her nose. "Spencer Pritchett is just a snotty little punk kid. Too big for his britches, if you ask me."

"But…I mean, what is he? Why do the, um, 'sisters' treat him with such respect?" I hadn't realized until now my hands were shaking. Apparently, Spencer had rattled me more than I realized.

"Well, he's a witch. I think he's over-rated, personally, but some of the sisters think he 'walks on water.'" She shook her head. "There've been rumors that he's levitated…and that he's even done a 'Cloud Eye Rite.'"

"What's a 'Cloud Eye Rite'?"

"We haven't got to that yet in our studies, kid. But it's where a powerful witch performs a spell that transfers her consciousness into a cloud. I've *never* heard of anyone doing such a spell, and frankly, I think it might be a bunch of hooey, but I'm damn sure Spencer Pritchett hasn't done any such spell."

"Um, why would anyone *want* to transfer their mind into a cloud?" I couldn't see the obvious benefit.

*"Heh,"* she chortled. "Tex, you're something else."

"Thanks?"

"It's like science, kid. It doesn't become science until someone *makes* it science. Maybe they'll discover a useful application for it someday. Maybe these witches will be the weathermen of our future—they sure can't be any worse than what's on the TV now." She shrugged. "Or maybe not, but you get my point. Right?"

"Oh, sure." *Absolutely not.*

"I'm still not convinced it's even a 'doable' spell. But if it is, I'm willin' to wager that it's just a bunch of show-off witches who do it for the fun of it. And that ain't right."

"No, guess not." I cleared my throat. "So, you don't think Spencer has any powers?"

"Oh, I wouldn't say that." She scratched her chin, a match failing to strike the first five times. "I just think a lot of what the girls say about him is fabricated crap started from his own big mouth. He started his own hype, believes in his own hype, and now has a lot of the sisters believing it, too."

"Has anyone you know ever seen him do anything? I mean, anything big?"

Mickey watched the passing convoy of suburban houses. "Not sure," she said, nearly inaudibly. "Some of my friends swear to it. But for every witness, a naysayer will gainsay it. I personally think you're ten times the witch he'll *ever* be." She smiled at me warmly. If I weren't driving, I would've hugged her for the vote of confidence. Self-confidence is in short supply for me these days.

"Thanks, Mickey. What else do you know about him? I mean, is he a real threat, one I have to worry about?"

"I don't think so. There…are a few strange similarities between you two boys, though." She winced as if in pain. "His mother was also a very powerful witch…and she also died unexpectedly."

My knuckles over the steering wheel looked like white bones, and I'm sure my face matched. "How did she die?" I didn't know if I really wanted to hear the truth.

"It was a car accident, Tex. Like your poor mother. Another senseless, unavoidable, tragic, stupid car wreck."

I said nothing. Every time I think I've come to peace with Mom's untimely departure, some outside force reawakens my sorrow. It's as if the cruel Fates think that Tex, their favorite whipping boy, should never have any downtime from grief. And I'd inevitably feel deep sadness again for my mother, whom the bastard Fates robbed of another glorious fifty years of life. If I could pour my tears down on the Fates, causing them unworldly pneumonia, I surely would. It'd be small retribution for what they cause throughout the sad lifetime of earth's inhabitants.

Now I'm told I share an almost brother-like bond of grief with Spencer Pritchett. I wish I hadn't been so flippant with him. Yes, his behavior was horrible, but I can almost understand where the false bluster comes from now.

Before I dropped Mickey off, she said, "Don't fret too much about what Max said We'll deal with that when—*if*—it happens. And for Heaven's sakes, don't worry about Spencer. He has no powers to speak of. He's *not* a threat."

Unfortunately—and for one rare time—Mickey's parting words would prove to be wrong.

## Chapter Four

Olivia shot out of her house like a bat out of hell. She galloped toward the Bucket, the band buttons pinned across her jean jacket jangling like so many cymbals. She yanked open the car door, jumped in, and planted a kiss on me.

"Whoa! Good morning to you, too," I managed after I came up for air.

"Spring is in the air," she sang. "And school's gonna be just some soon-forgotten nightmare. What else could you want, Tex?"

"Well, I hate to tell you this but—"

*"Wait! Hold* on. You're *not* gonna harsh my buzz." She pulled the purple-died strand of hair back from her face to glare at me better.

"Yeah, guess I am." I recounted my strange encounters of the day before, first with the Reaper, and then Max and Spencer. I also told her about Lance's mother, as I'd learned keeping secrets from Olivia is toxic.

She collapsed back against the car seat. "Oh, boy, here we go again."

"Yeah, that's kinda my thought."

"What do you think it means? I mean, what this Max guy told you?"

"I don't know. It doesn't sound good, that's for sure. But Mickey says not to worry about it. *Yet.*" I am *so* not ready to face the forces of evil again. Not when I have my own life—my future—to straighten out.

"And what's the deal with this Spencer guy?" She burst out laughing. "He sounds like a real...what'd you call him? 'Teenage dream.'"

I grimaced at how harsh I'd been toward him. "Yeah. I don't know. He was kinda a jackass, but after Mickey told me about his mother..."

"It's okay." She placed a reassuring hand on my shoulder. "Whatever's going to happen, you won't go it alone." The corners of her mouth turned up, immediately brightening my sulky disposition. "That's pretty wild about Lance's mother. And Lance knows?"

"That's my understanding."

"*Cool!* Maybe we should, you know, tell him about you."

"I don't know, O'. I think it's better if our friends don't know. It seems like when they do find out, they get a bull's-eye on their back."

"Yeah, maybe you're right." Although unspoken, I knew we were both thinking about our friends lost over the last two years. "Hey, so all those old ladies at your 'meeting' last night? They were all witches? Like, 'Tex-Style Witches' with superpowers and stuff?"

"No. Mickey said most of them are 'witches-in-practice.' They study and follow the beliefs but don't have any, um, 'superpowers'...so to speak. Like Mrs. Nguyen."

Olivia nodded as if this made perfect sense. "Cool, cool." It struck me as odd we were discussing such things so matter-of-factly. Yet that's the way my world rolls these days. "Hey, you think I can go to the next meeting?"

I grinned. "As long as you promise to be cool, I think we can probably arrange that."

"Yes!" She jerked her arm up in a victory gesture, only to have it rebuffed by the Bucket's disapproving roof. "*Ow!* Dammit."

Walking through the crowded parking lot that morning, I noticed the students stepping more lively, laughing louder; enjoying their final days of school before summer rolled in and pushed them on to other pursuits. The dark storm of Brittany Gerlach's suicide apparently had been whisked away by a cleansing breeze, leaving nothing but an occasional gust, a fleeting cloud of memory. Already going up in smoke like a cigarette butt discarded onto the highway. But for some reason, I couldn't put it behind me. Not completely.

The gang crowded around my locker, their energy level high.

"Hey, what up, McKenna?" Dickers propped a leg up behind him onto the locker.

"Dickers," said Olivia, "what did I *tell* you about tryin' to be cool and talkin' 'homie'?"

Dickers, looking appropriately chastised, mumbled something and dropped his foot to the floor. Olivia snickered and gave him a make-good hug. Dickers took advantage of the situation, hands roaming up and down her back.

"Ah, yeah, break it up, you two," I said.

Ian burst out laughing. "Jeezus, Dickers."

Dickers dropped his octopus-like hands and burned crimson, wearing his well-earned scarlet letter of shame.

"Hey," said Brandon, "Ian, Lance, and me are

74

goin' to the skate park after school. Wanna hang?"

"Wish I could, but Olivia and I have a very important date with detention after school."

"That sucks, dude," said Ian. "We'll be thinkin' about you when we're hookin' up at the park with the chicks." Lance giggled at the inherent absurdity of Ian's boast, while Allison squirmed uncomfortably. Maybe some unresolved feelings going on there.

"Yeah, like I'll be hookin' up with all sorts of chicks, Ian," said Lance. "Dumb-ass!"

"Whatever." Ian shrugged. "Well, Bran and I will take up the slack." Olivia shook her head disapprovingly. "Right, Brandon?" When Ian entered testosterone overdrive, it changed him completely, and not in a good way.

Brandon simply shrugged. Sometimes I wish I had Brandon's brain—no worries, no problems, no work whatsoever.

"Lissen' up," said Lance. "I'll bet I can score more phone digits at the park than the both of you combined."

"Dude! It is *so* on," exclaimed Ian.

"Okay, I'm in. I've gotta see this," said Dickers.

Disappointment undercut me as I wouldn't be able to witness the grudge match. Between Lance's seemingly endless charm and Brandon's godlike appearance, it'd be a tight race. Then again, a betting man'd say Ian would handicap Brandon's team.

Allison forced a pained smile, obviously not enjoying Ian's display of machismo. I sidled up next to her. "Hey."

"Hi, Tex." The others ignored us, braying and bleating like billy goats, while Olivia took them all down a notch.

"You okay?"

"Yeah. I guess I'm just not feeling well, that's all." She gave me a liquid smile, her lips visibly trembling.

"Come on, Allie." Usually she offered the first hug, but I felt she needed it more. "Hugs make everything better."

Burying her face into my shoulder, she laughed. "Yeah, you're right." She held on tight, clinging to my life raft, while she struggled to keep her head above turbulent waters.

"Hey, how about we talk later? Cool?"

"I'd…like that." I thought it best to not push any further. Knowing how it sucks to cry in public, I released her.

The guys were still trading jokes and threats when Parker sauntered up. Buzz-kill. "Hey, girls." He exposed a shark-like grin.

"Parker! Hey, Parker… *YAC Power*." Ian shot his arm up in front of him, palm open.

*"And* here we go," I whispered, nudging Olivia.

Surprisingly, Parker laughed. "Brah, you really should come to a meeting sometime. It'd probably do your way-damaged soul some good." His nasty grin dissolved into a warm smile, and for a brief moment, I could almost—*almost*—see what girls found attractive about him.

"Allie," I asked, "what's 'YAC'?"

"The Young American Christians," she said before quickly moving toward Parker, the recipient of another long hug.

Did she want to make Ian jealous? Or did she truly like this worm? I knew they went to the same church, but I sincerely hope that's all there is to it.

"No *way* in hell am I going to your 'YAC' meeting!" Ian bounced up and down on the balls of his feet like an adrenaline-fueled basketball player.

"Whatever. Hell may be where you'll end up if you don't go." Parker punctuated his message with a slam to Ian's shoulder. I noticed Lance scooting down the row of lockers, like an escaped convict trying to avoid the searchlights.

"Guys, Parker's a little over-the-top, but really...you're *all* invited to a YAC meeting," said Dickers. For all of Parker's holier-than-thou attitude, Dickers seemed more than earnest. Maybe even a little excited about winning over new prospects.

"All right," I said, "So what's YAC all about?"

"We're just a cool group who meet and discuss our Lord and Savior, Jesus Christ, and His teachings. Even if you guys aren't super-religious...it's helped me figure out some things in my life. Really, come to a meeting." He nearly hyperventilated in his over-zealous proselytism. While I didn't feel ready to board the YAC train, I had to admit a part of me felt envious Dickers believed in something so strongly. Obviously, YAC impacted his life. I wondered if it'd helped form his future vocational choice of becoming a priest.

"Hold up, hold up," said Olivia. Everyone quieted. Although short, Olivia projects a much larger persona, impossible to ignore. She strutted in front of Dickers and Parker, arms akimbo, ensuring she held everyone's attention. "I already see a problem here, boys. It's called the Young *American* Christians. What about those who *aren't* American? Or *Christian,* for that matter? Can they not join your little club?"

Parker let loose an indignant chuckle. Olivia challenged him with a formidable glower. "Olivia, we live in America! *Duh!* And if you're not Christian, then you wouldn't be going to the meeting. And frankly...there's not much hope for you, anyway." He smiled, feeling he'd won this one. I nearly felt sorry for him.

Olivia dropped her arms and pulled a fist back. I stood ready to intervene, hoping things didn't turn physical. She exasperated loudly, blowing the purple strand of hair away from her eye, and crossed her arms. Physical crisis averted. For now, at least. "That's...some of the *stupidest,* backward, non-Christian *crap* I've heard in a long time, Pennett!*"* Annnd, we're off! Passing students stopped to watch the poor soul unfortunate enough to evoke the wrath of Olivia Furman.

"What happened to Jesus' teachings about tolerance and *loving* everyone? Huh, Parker? What about it? You think *He* turned people away because of differences in *color, race, or beliefs?* What kind of red-neck, cracker, ignorant...inbred...crap are you *YACCERS* all about, anyway?*"* Parker squirmed, giving passers-by an acknowledging smirk, faking complete control while being accosted by this insane she-demon. And, of course, that stoked Olivia's fires further.

"It's not like that, Olivia," said Allison. "We believe in the same Jesus you do."

"Oh, no! *Tell* me you're not a YACCER, Allie! Tell me you don't buy into all this...anti-Christian *crap* posing as...*crap*." When Olivia's on a tear, her vocabulary sometimes comes up short, but the intent is never anything but crystal clear. I felt bad for Allie and wanted to stop Olivia, but knew from experience you can't pull a hungry dog away from his meal.

Allison stared at the ground, her head nodding. "I'm in YAC...but you're not getting what we're all about."

"*Dickers*!" Olivia's favorite whipping boy's turn. "Dickers, are you going to just *stand* there and say nothing? Do you believe Jesus doesn't accept people of other beliefs and colors?"

He pursed his lips, clearly searching for the safest vocal exit. "You're misinterpreting Parker's words. Of course, we believe in a just and loving Jesus. Come to a meeting, so you'll understand better..." As soon as the words left his mouth, Dickers flinched a bit, fearful of Olivia's retaliation.

Olivia shook her hands and let loose a cathartic shriek. We stood around her in a circle, waiting to call in the bomb squad if necessary. She stamped her feet and barreled through us, running down the hall. I gave pursuit, bumping into students in the crowded hallway, uttering apologies.

Parker called out to us, "Looks like *somebody* needs Jesus more than we thought!"

"O', wait up!" Once I caught up, I grabbed her shoulder. Abruptly, she stopped. I collided into her, and we tumbled to the floor. Olivia hit the floor face down, while I stared at the gathered students gazing down at the freak show.

Beneath me, Olivia shook. She lifted her head and let out a magnificent bray of laughter. I sat up, puzzled, then soon realized how ridiculous we looked and joined her in her mortified amusement. The crowd grew bored and split up, seeking more interesting trauma elsewhere.

"Dammit, Tex, did you have to tackle me?" She wiped away tears of laughter.

"Well, I didn't *really* tackle you." I stood and pulled her to her feet. "Hurricane Olivia sort of wiped us both out."

She snorted and clapped her hands. "That was fun."

"Olivia...really? What happened? Why'd you freak? I mean...what Parker said was stupid, but—"

"I don't know. It's just one thing that gets me— *really* gets me—is hypocrites. Especially when they hide behind God and Jesus. They're friggin' predators. They *suck.*"

"I totally agree. It's just you seemed to take it...personally."

Olivia snagged my hand and pulled me through the students and into the cafeteria. She scanned the area and found an empty table near the back wall. Without saying a word, she guided me to a chair and pushed me into it, sitting down across from me.

She gave me a sad half-smile. "Here we go..." I had no idea where we were going. "Tex...when I was a little girl, life was...*wonderful*. My mom, my dad, and me. We went to a Catholic church. I went to catechism classes. And you know what?"

I shook my head, deciding to withhold my tongue until Olivia finished her tale. It's super rare for her to talk about her past.

"I *liked* it." She nodded, signifying I could do likewise. "I lived for it. I believed every word, every story, every...lesson that was taught to me. I even kicked it up to the next level. I pretty much taught myself to read by reading the Bible. Every night, I'd kiss my parents good night, run to bed, grab the Bible and a flashlight and stay up late, trying to unlock the mysteries and the...*wonder* of the Bible." She chuckled. "Can you believe how lame I was? I must've been the only kid in the world who was supposed to be sleeping but rebelled by reading the Bible at night."

"I don't think it's lame. I think it's kinda...sweet."

"I can't believe my boyfriend's such a dork. *Anyway*, I began to think that God was even talking to me in a way. That He had a special plan for me. Maybe when I'm older or something, I dunno, but maybe, like Jesus, I was...destined to help people. I began to take my questions—and I had a *lot* of them—to Father O'Flanaghan. He was your typical Irish-Catholic priest—fat, graying, hammered, smelled funny—but he always had time to talk to his 'little Olivia.' That's what he called me...his 'little Olivia.' Like I was nothing but a stupid, inconsequential, little wind-up toy he could claim ownership over, or something..." Her good humor darkened, a drawn nightshade shutting out her sunshine. "But Father O'Flanaghan *always* made time to help me understand Jesus. Unlike my parents, who'd grown more and more distant. Not only weren't they talking to each other, but they ignored me, too. I didn't know it at the time, but that's when their marriage began to break up."

"I'm sorry, O'. It must've been rough not understanding at a young age—"

"Just *whose* story is this, anyway, Tex? Damn! Yeah, I didn't get it at the time, but I always had Jesus, the Church, Father O'Flanaghan...and for a while, they got me through those tough times. I even tried talking to Father O'Flanaghan about my parents, and he'd patiently tell me that sometimes adults don't get along. It didn't help much, but it was all I had."

"Wow."

"Nice comment, Tex! So, one Sunday, I was all dolled up in my Sunday's finest and ready for church— you should've seen me—I mean, I was *goddamn adorable."* I strapped in next to Olivia on her emotional rollercoaster, with ups and downs and all-arounds. "And my mom, looking more tired than I'd ever seen her before, told me we weren't going. I asked why not. She said 'because some bad things happened, and we won't be going back'. My whole world fell apart. The last thing I counted on had been taken away from me. I felt like I had nothing."

"That's…horrible."

"Soon after that, my father left. Just up and left. Didn't even say goodbye…" Olivia wiped back a tear with her palm. "Once again, I didn't get a good answer as to why he did that. I kept pestering my mom to go back to church, and she kept saying '*No.*' I asked why. She ignored my questions. She told me we'd soon find a new church to go to. We never did. Finally—I guess because she was sick of my constant badgering—she sat me down and told me what happened. She said Father O'Flanaghan had been caught doing something bad—something terrible that went against Jesus' teachings. Something so bad, she couldn't speak of it. She looked at me and asked me if he'd ever done anything 'naughty'…to me." Olivia raised her moist eyes to stare into mine.

"Olivia…he didn't—"

"No…no, no, *no!* He was never…*that* way with

me." She stared off into the distance at nothing in particular. "So…get it? The one last thing that I had in my life was Jesus, the church. Father O'Flanaghan. And I found out it was all…a lie. A big, fat hypocritical lie. This man who taught me about the Bible…couldn't even live by the oath he swore to. Everything I believed in…wanted *desperately* to believe in…were just lies."

"That totally sucks." At the risk of getting punched, I dared to add, "But you know not *all* religion is hypocritical." I intended to help Olivia rather than cause more damage. Apparently, it's a trait shared by males across the world. While it's one thing to understand females don't want males to fix problems— just to understand and listen—it's another task entirely trying to adhere to this commandment. Mansplaining's been around since the cavemen.

"I know that *now*," she said. "But when I was a little girl…." She drifted off again. "Anyway…I absolutely hate religious hypocrites. They take something that's supposed to be good, something that people turn to in times of need…and twist it to suit their own selfish, icky needs. Damned *predators*!"After whipping her head about, she regained her poise. "And if I can do anything—*anything*—to help tear them down, well, dammit, I'm gonna *grab* the hypocrites by the short and curlies and do just that. Maybe *that's* my purpose in life, Tex. You have yours. And maybe…just maybe, that's mine."

At least someone proclaimed to know my life's purpose. If only she'd clue me in. "I…feel the same way you do, Olivia. If you ever need my help in fighting the hypothetical, hypocritical windmills…well, you know."

"I know." She fired a staccato burst of laughter. "Now you know why I totally lost my crap when Parker started spewing his poison back there." She raised her arms straight into the air as if refereeing a football game.

"Yeah, you totally did. But…your story, well, it sucked for you, but I hope you don't rule out religion, like, forever, if it means that much to you."

"I'm still working that out." She smiled, a small, sad, beaten smile. "But *that's* between me and my God."

"Yeah, I get that. But, you know, I don't think Allie and Dickers are as bad as you sorta made them out to be."

She hung her head in her hands. "Oh, God… Poor Allie. I probably owe her a big, freakin' apology."

"Maybe. Yeah, probably. But don't *even* apologize to Parker."

"No way."

"Hey…do you like Parker? I mean, do you think he's an okay guy?"

"*Hellz* to the no. He gives me 'douche-bumps.'"

I laughed at her gross, yet undeniably funny, ailment. "Kinda funny…but after knowing you for three years, this is the first time we've ever really…I mean, *really*…talked about religion."

"Well, yeah, it's not something I like talking about." She leaned toward me. "Tex?"

"Yeah?"

"Do *you* believe in God?"

Good question. I closed my eyes, buying time, a tactic I'd picked up from Dad. Delaying the inevitable. Waffling. Waffling's what I do best. I'm a world-class waffler. Waffle, waffle, waffle. Let's pour some syrup on that baby and let it soak in for a while. Finally, I answered. "You know, I've always wondered…what kind of God would take my mother away at such an early age…in a pointless accident that could've easily been avoided? What sort of *just* God is He? How do you explain all the war, the famine…the homeless, the sad, the lonely, the sickness? The damn tragedy. Simple: He just doesn't exist." Students were leaving their tables, preparing to head off to class, but I needed to finish what I started. "Then again, we've had personal experience with the dark side."

"So, it's a 'yes?'"

I felt I might be letting her down, especially after she just spilled her guts out to me, but I had to speak the truth. Even if it's a sad truth. "No."

"What? 'No?'"

"No."

"You just said you believe in the 'dark side.'"

"Yeah, well…I've *experienced* the dark side. But, I haven't heard any celestial trumpets, seen any miracles, you know? Decent humanity…witchcraft, those are the things I—"

"Oh, whatever, Tex. Grow a pair and face facts."

"But they're not facts! I can't explain them. Frankly, after everything you've been through, I'm sorta surprised that you—"

"Whoa, whoa, hold up, son. Just 'cause I had one bad experience, doesn't mean I quit believing in God. Organized religion and all the crap that goes along with it? Yeah, it sucks. But I never said I'm a non-believer."

"Huh." Surprised is putting it mildly. Olivia's faith had been truly tested. Yet she still carried on. Her unflagging faith made me a little envious, and I wanted to tell her so, but mostly, I wanted to smirk. Neither option seemed the smartest choice. Smart man's move? End the conversation. "You know what? This is way too early in the morning for this kinda talk. We probably better get to class."

"Way to avoid."

"Yeah, that's me."

She did give me a lot to think about, though. I'll put it on my increasingly growing list of "Things I Need To Deal With."

I really wouldn't mind believing in God. Might smooth some issues over. Have a few questions to ask the big fella.

But as such is the case with my life, I would soon meet the Devil instead.

\*\*\*\*

I don't understand detention. I mean, I can see why there's a need for punishment—to deter wrongdoers from repeating past trespasses—but Clearwell High's version of detention is a particularly nasty circle of Hell. Rather than allotting time for studies or something productive, Arville Hastings and his minions of evil have concocted a torturous method to while away the extra-special hour spent at school. We're given a piece of graph paper with literally thousands of minute squares on either side. The detention Hell-master chooses an arbitrary number—today's winning number was 2,978—and it's our lot in life to fill in those boxes, counting down until we reach zero. As I said, I just don't get it. All it did was promote hand cramps and ill will.

I entered Mrs. Swanson's classroom, checking out

the rest of my fellow inmates. No surprise, the perpetually-stoned Paul Jacobsen slumped deep into his chair, more holes in his jeans than a piece of Swiss cheese. He acknowledged me with a slacker's chin-bob. I wonder if he's set a course for his post high school endeavors. No doubt it involves video games and ganja. Who am I kidding? He probably *does* have a plan. I felt like the last student standing with no idea where my life should head.

After tossing my backpack to the floor, I slid behind a desk. The other six students either had their heads down, catching a quick nap before the fun began, or were dreamily staring out at the nice weather, wishing to be anywhere but here. Olivia barreled in, struggling with her over-sized backpack, and sat down next to me.

"Hey," she said. "Thought I was gonna be late."

"No, the games haven't begun yet." I reached across the aisle to hold her hand.

Mrs. Swanson cleared her throat and inclined her head toward our knotted hands. "Oh, sorry," I muttered as we broke contact.

Filling in the endless, tiny boxes, my eyes began to strain, and my mind wandered. What a truly *weird* week. For whatever reason—karma, the Fates, bad luck, whatever—religion seemed to be on everyone's mind. I'd become embroiled in more religious debates this week than I had over the last three years. I couldn't help but wonder if the sad suicide of Brittany Gerlach had something to do with peoples' mindsets—maybe it forced everyone to confront their own immortality, and everyone desperately scrambled to choose a side before their number came up. Or maybe the sudden intrusion of the Clarendon Baptist Church cretins and their non-stop advertising campaign had worked its subliminal magic on us all. But I've learned to start watching 'patterns' in life. They're usually trying to tell me something.

Olivia grinned at me, cracked her knuckles, and went back to her diligent box filling. It had taken a great deal of courage for her to tell me what she did earlier. And it explained a lot about who she is today. She went from being 'God's little soldier' to 'Olivia's fiercely independent soldier,' a necessary defense mechanism to make sense of her unbalanced world and her war within. What a huge burden for a young girl with an AWOL father to take on.

My eyelids grew heavy, the boxes blurred, and my head dropped. I caught myself, and jolted upright. Olivia comically frowned at me and proceeded to go back to box filling. Those *damn* boxes…

I felt a slight tingle. It began in my cheeks and rose to my brain. The sensation traveled down my arms to my over-worked fingertips and rebounded back to my spine where it hitched a quick ride to my toes. Uh-oh. Heart attack? Or something else? Something unpleasant. It finally struck me it felt similar to when I confronted Bob Bellman's spirit last year. Yet much different this time. Last year, Bellman's appearances prompted a bowel-shaking, disturbingly nasty, electric sting. This felt more like soaking in a hot tub, my body pummeled by hot plumes of water, the cumulative effect ultimately relaxing.

I glanced over at Olivia. Her head slumped, her chin resting upon her chest, eyes shut. I looked around at the other torture victims. They, too, appeared to be asleep. Completely stretched out, Paul Jacobsen had his head and one arm draped over the back of the chair, snoring at the ceiling. Mrs. Swanson did a face-plant on her desk, pen still in hand. The clock on the wall had stopped dead at three thirty-five.

"Olivia?" No response. I looked around to see if anyone else had stirred. Quieter than an urgent care ward. "*Olivia!*" Still nothing.

In a dream-like state, I stood up slowly, my cheeks numb, but my brain sizzling like melting butter. I shook Olivia by the shoulder. Slowly, she toppled forward, and I reached out to guide her toward a safe landing onto her desktop. The lights flickered, hissed, and popped on and off, finally staying off. A light agreeable shade of blue fell across the room like a slowly drifting cloud bringing respite from the sun.

Out of the corner of my eye, I saw—more like, sensed—movement. I swiveled toward the door. The small glass window set in the door was now empty, but I knew I saw something there. Creeping slowly into view, three thin, white fingers slithered across the pane, like snakes on a parade.

I shuddered, yet still felt compelled to go toward the door. Hand on the knob, I pulled the door open and stepped out into the hallway. The neon lights above were all out, the hallway barren of students or teachers. A deeper shade of blue originated at the far end of the hallway and floated toward me. When it ensconced me, I felt an inner warmth fill my belly.

"Texxx," whispered a voice from behind me.

I turned, my legs uneasy, threatening to give out. Brittany Gerlach stood two feet in front of me, awash with blue, except for the dark shadows rippling over her face like a spilled oil slick in an ocean. Dressed in her cheerleader outfit, her arms hung limply at her sides. Her blonde—blue?—hair appeared immaculately combed, the long tresses flowing down her chest.

"Um, Brittany?"

"Tex...don't let him do it again," she said, evenly, slowly, as she took a step toward me.

"Brittany...what are you talking about? Don't let *whom* do *what*?"

Shadows skittered away from her eyes, leaving two pale rings, one inside the other. "You've got to stop him. Before he hurts someone else. You've got to stop them. Don't let what happened to me...happen to someone else."

"Brittany! *Please*...help me understand!"

She looked right through me, rather than at me. "Find out about me. Search...talk...read."

As if someone had yanked her back by her long hair, she swiftly receded down the hallway until she silently imploded into a round, swirling ball of blue radiance. In front of the window, it spun, sending off blue sparks until it collapsed upon itself into nothingness.

*Clack! Clack!* The lights overhead snapped on, startling me, filling the hallway with a harsh, artificial yellow tint. Quite a sensory shock after the relaxing blue luminosity.

*"Crap."* As if startled awake by a dream, I realized the reality of my AWOL status from detention. I turned and made a beeline back to the classroom. After yanking the door open, the previously slumbering students sat up, looking groggy and puzzled (nothing new in Paul Jacobsen's case). Curiosity filled Olivia's

eyes. Mrs. Swanson sat at her desk, yawned, and stared at me.

"Mr. McKenna," she drawled. "And *just* where have you been?"

"Um, the bathroom?"

"I don't recall giving you permission." She tented her ancient hands.

"Oh, well, um, I tried to ask you permission, Mrs. Swanson, but you...I guess you were asleep." The classroom broke out in laughter.

Mrs. Swanson's eyes grew in horror at her own negligence. "Well, have a seat, Mr. McKenna." She waved her hand toward my desk, appearing totally humiliated. "Class, get back to your squares."

As I sat, Olivia mouthed, "What the *hell?*"

I whispered, "Later."

I could feel Olivia watching me, hoping for a quick, satisfactory answer.

Yet I had no answers. The only thing I knew for sure? I'm all in. To what, I had no idea. But I now knew there appeared to be more to Brittany Gerlach's suicide than any of us could possibly imagine.

Chapter Five

"So, green light's bad and blue light's good?"
Olivia drove the Bucket as Brittany's visitation still
shook me.

"Yeah, I guess so."

"What do you think it means? What does Brittany
want you to do?"

"Beats me. But it seems there's more to Brittany's
suicide than we know. She said to stop *them*. That's the
same thing Max said. It can't be a coincidence."

"Oh, for God's sake... Where are we supposed to
start?" With Olivia gaping at me, the Bucket bounced
up and off a curb.

"I really don't have a clue. She told me to search,
talk, and read. And I have no idea what that means. I
guess I could start by talking to Dwight Louden."
Dwight Louden had been Brittany Gerlach's boyfriend
over the last several years. He's a thuggish, hulking
football player, and trying to get information out of him
didn't sound like much fun.

"Yeah, good luck with that! Tex, you think
Brittany was murdered?"

"I really don't think so. From what I've heard, her
parents found her in her bedroom. She took a bunch of
pills from their medicine cabinet."

"Then I don't get what she wants us to do."

"Yeah, me neither. Hey, so, did you not feel

anything? Did you just fall asleep?"

"Didn't feel a thing. I mean, I was getting sleepy from filling in all those stupid boxes. The next thing I know, you walked into the classroom. Weird."

"Yeah. A 'weird' I wish I didn't have to deal with. I've got a bad feeling coming on."

Driving by the Clearwell cemetery, we saw several policemen standing by their parked cars, watching a gathering of people across the street.

"Oh, *hell* no!" Olivia wrenched the steering wheel abruptly and popped the car onto the curb, this time intentionally.

"Olivia? What's going on?" By the time I asked, Olivia already bolted from the car, running at full speed, her jean jacket flapping against her back. By the time I caught up, the policemen had stopped her.

"Hold on, girl," said one of the cops. "Where are you going in such a hurry?"

Olivia pointed at the crowd across the street. "If those…*bastards* get to have their say, then so do I!" Protesters carried signs and marched in a small circle, bobbing along as if on a merry-go-round. One sign read GOD DESPISES SUICIDES. Another said SUICIDES GO TO HELL! I'd forgotten Brittany's funeral was this evening.

The two policemen exchanged a knowing glance and waved her on. "Okay, then. Just keep it non-violent." The policeman lowered his voice and added, "Give 'em hell, girl."

This was *not* going to be pretty. I followed Olivia toward the protesters.

"What in the *hell* do you think you're doing?" she snarled. The picketers dropped their fake smiles, held tight to their signs, and glared at Olivia.

"Well, it should be obvious," an overweight woman huffed. The flab of her bingo arms jiggled as she lowered her sign. "We're protesting sinners. And suicide is a sin."

"Don't you people have any *respect*? There're *people* in there who've lost someone they love!" Olivia hitched a thumb toward the cemetery. "And you...*jackasses* are making their trauma even *worse*!" She stood, fists coiled, ready to leap into action.

A shrill laugh disrupted the inevitable showdown. "Well, well, well, you *are* a firecracker, aren't you, little lady?" A short, rotund man in a light gray suit stepped forward. A wealth of gray wavy hair curled out from his cowboy hat and a bolo tie wrapped tightly around his neck. His bushy white eyebrows raised, highlighting his ruddy, sunburned red face.

"Don't call me '*little lady.*'"

"Now, let's not get all in an uproar, young lady," said the man in an exaggerated Southern accent. If not for the inherent evil in their message, he'd seem like a kindly, drunken uncle. "We're just having a little peaceful get-together here." He waved his hand at the protesters. "We're within our legal rights to do as such. We're three hundred feet from the cemetery...and the funeral of the sinner doesn't start for another hour."

"Well, then, *I'm* within my legal right to let you all *know* that you're *disgusting, filthy, hypocritical...jerks*!" As soon as I grabbed Olivia's hand to calm her, she shook me off.

The man chuckled. "There's no need for such harsh words, child." He placed his stubby hot-dog fingers together under his double-chin. "I'm Pastor Don

Danvers of the Clarendon Baptist Church. And you are…?"

"*Pissed off*!"

So this is what the face of evil looks like. Don Danvers, the head of the Clarendon Baptist Church, was hardly what I expected. I suppose I thought he'd be a gaunt, menacing supervillain, not the jovial, unassuming man we faced. Yet, underneath his friendly veneer lurked the mind that gave birth to a vile ideology based upon hatred, ignorance, and self-righteousness.

"If you'd just settle down a bit, girl, I'd *love* to have a little chat with you about our message," he said. "Maybe it's not too late to save you."

Uh-oh. "Oh, *no*, you don't! *You* don't get to judge *me*. *You* don't know me. And even if you did, I wouldn't spend any more time with you than I have to. You're *nothing* but a bunch of small-minded *hypocrites*. What gives you the right to judge people? How come *you* get the say in who goes to Hell and who doesn't?"

"I, um, agree," I mumbled. Olivia shot me a quick, sour glance. I'd probably catch all kinds of hell later for my insubstantial backup.

"Why, we're just preaching the words of our Lord from the Bible itself." Danvers splayed his fingers in a well-practiced form.

"That's *crap*! You *distort* the Bible to fit your own…stupid…*evil* beliefs."

For the first time, Danvers frowned, the smile falling from his face like the obvious mask he wore. His eyes narrowed, his cold gray pupils seeking to sear a hole through Olivia's soul. "Girl…you had best mind your manners and your elders," he said in a low growl.

He cleared his throat, smiled at his gatherers, and pulled himself together. "Any time you'd like to go over the Bible with me, I'd be glad to point out our righteous beliefs. I can tell you where it says God hates suicides—"

"And I suppose you can show me the passage that says God hates homosexuals, too."

Danvers laughed, stomping his booted foot onto the ground. "I certainly can do that, young lady. I certainly can." His followers joined him in his glee, pissing off Olivia even more.

"That's nothing but...*bullshit!*" She kicked at the ground like an enraged baseball manager.

As the crowd continued to laugh, I took my cue to get Olivia out of there. I snatched her around the waist and pulled her back. Olivia swung her fists, cutting a swath of rage through the air.

"*Jackasses,*" she shouted in parting.

"I'll pray for your sinner's soul, child," called back Danvers.

I finally wrestled Olivia to the Bucket and pushed her inside.

"*Dammit.* I wish I knew more about the Bible to *throw* in their ugly faces!"

"Yeah."

"And *thanks* for your *support* back there, Tex!"

"Olivia, you *can't* argue with that kind of people. They're completely narrow-minded, with blinders on. They won't hear you. It's pointless. Besides, as you said, they'd just take their so-called knowledge of the Bible and turn it sideways. You just can't win an argument with them."

"*Gawd.* They just suck so bad."

"Yeah, they do." I watched the crowd across the street continue their fools' parade. Danvers stood off to the side, admiring his flock like a shepherd. Next to him was a tall, handsome, smartly-dressed, silver-haired woman. Her arms folded across her chest, eyes hidden behind large tinted lenses, she appeared as serious as Danvers was cheerful. And she had her gaze locked directly on us.

Feeling a shiver ski down my spine, I shook it off. "We'd better hurry up, Olivia."

"Why? What are you talking about?"

"Well—like it or not—I guess we've got to go to a funeral."

****

At the funeral, Brittany's parents sat in front of the gathered mourners, sunglasses covering their no doubt tear-filled eyes. Throughout the service, moans and sobs overpowered the quiet droning of the pastor. Brittany's contingent of cheerleader friends held onto one another for support.

Both Parker and Dickers showed up. By the gravesite, they approached us.

"Hey, guys," said Dickers. "What're you doing here?"

"What do you think, Dickers?" snapped Olivia. "Paying our respects."

"I see someone's still having her time of the month," said Parker.

Olivia got right up in his face. "Yeah, I guess *you* are, Parker. Or do you just suck *all* of the time?"

Before things spiraled out of control, I stepped in. "Guys, come on. This is a funeral."

Olivia huffed and reluctantly folded. "What are *you*

doing here? I didn't even think you *knew* Brittany."

Dickers shrugged. "Yeah, we knew her. She was in YAC with us until she quit going the last couple of months." Olivia bristled at the mention of the dreaded YAC, a cord in her neck tightening.

"Yeah, she was cool," added Parker.

"Huh," I said. I knew Brittany had been in one of Dicker's Christian groups but didn't realize it was YAC.

"Are you guys going to Brittany's house?" asked Dickers. "They're having a get-together for friends and family."

I raised my eyebrows expectantly toward Olivia. She nodded. I might be able to do some digging there and talk to some people. "Yeah, I think we'll go."

\*\*\*\*

Brittany Gerlach's house looked pretty much like what I imagined it'd be. Upper middle class suburban two-story house, complete with the obligatory white picket fence and two yapping, twin poodles kicked into the backyard so as not to disturb the proceedings.

Brittany's parents parked themselves on a sofa in the living room, their spirits and bodies sunken deeply into the cushions. Their demeanor was one that I, unfortunately, knew too well—dazed, confused, puzzled, lost, and ultimately, angry. Feeling like an intruder—even though I felt Brittany probably wanted me there—I exchanged brief salutations and shared sorrows. I remember at my mother's funeral wanting the well-wishers to simply shut up and go away.

Dwight Louden lumbered about in a suit too small for his build. He appeared agitated and carried around a Big Swallow cup that was more than likely spiked with booze. It wouldn't be easy pinning him down. I had a little bit of history with Dwight. A very vocal bully, he never threatened any real physical harm. But his favorite pastime appeared to be calling me and my friends, "fags." When he stepped outside, I took my chance.

He stood on the front porch, staring out into the yard. "Um, hey, Dwight. I'm really sorry about Brittany."

He snapped around, his eyes rimmed with red. "Did you even *know* her?"

"Oh, yeah, sure. I knew Brittany."

He approached me, menace etched on his square face. "That's funny. She never mentioned *you*. Faggot!" Even his girlfriend's funeral couldn't dampen his fun.

"I, um, didn't know her very well, but I always liked her. She was nice. I'm sorry, Dwight." Now standing in my personal space, a whiff of his breath corroborated what I suspected earlier. "Um...do you know why she...killed herself?" Talk about "all in." Surely, Dwight wouldn't beat on me here? I also still believe in Santa Claus, I guess.

Dwight slammed his cup down onto the porch railing. "What the *hell* are you asking me that for? On the day of her *funeral*? You come into her home *asking* me something like *that*?" Ready to burst out of his suit, his face blew up with purple anger.

"I didn't mean anything by it. I'm just trying to...make sense of this tragedy." I backed up, pinned against the house.

He grabbed my collar and yanked me toward him. "*Why?* So you can post...your shit all over the Internet?"

"No, *no!* Dwight, I *wouldn't* do that. As I said, I just want to try and understand."

"Understand *this,* faggot!" He pulled his log-like arm back and formed a fist.

"What's happening?" asked a soft-spoken voice. Jasper Stafford stepped out of the front door. "Why don't you let him go, Dwight? It's Brittany's funeral."

Dwight shook me like a ragdoll and then released me. "Faggot," he muttered as he stumbled back into the house.

"Um, thanks for the save, Jasper." I attempted to straighten my suit collar while stilling my nerves.

Although a football player, Jasper Stafford could be considered somewhat of an abnormality. Laid-back, smart, and never a bully, he treated me and my friends with a level of cool the other players lacked. He also didn't run with the rest of the football players, pretty much a lone wolf. His height prevented him from pursuing college football, yet he was cut like a diamond. So soft-spoken you had to strain to hear him speak, you could tell a fierce intelligence hid behind his heavy-lidded blue eyes.

"What was that about?" Typically uncombed, his shaggy blond hair hung over his brow.

"I, ah, just wanted to know if Dwight knew why Brittany...did what she did."

He stared at me quietly before chuckling. "That's really not too cool, Tex. You're lucky Dwight didn't pound you. I think I might've if I was in his shoes."

Realizing my own stupidity, I could do nothing but nod in agreement.

"Why do you want to know anyway?" He folded his arms as he crossed the porch.

"I don't know. It's just got everyone bummed out…and wondering, I guess."

He tapped his barely visible soul-patch. "Yeah, it's kind of a drag."

"Did Dwight say anything to you about why she did it? Or have you heard anything?"

"No, not really. But over the last month or so, Dwight was complaining…"

"Complaining? About what?"

"I don't know if I should be telling you this or not."

"Don't worry, Jasper. I'm *not* going to go viral on you or anything."

"Dwight wasn't happy with Brittany. During the last two months, he was bitchin' and moanin' she wouldn't put out anymore. He said she acted like she wanted to break up with him. Became quiet, distant. Wouldn't even make out with him. He said he hardly ever saw her anymore. She was too busy with some Christian group—"

"YAC." It sounded like I tried to bring up a hairball or something.

"What?" he asked then shrugged it off. "Anyway, that's what Dwight said…over and over again."

"Huh." I wondered if YAC had something to do with her sudden change. Or maybe she suffered from depression. Dwight Louden's hardly anyone's idea of a dream. "Well, thanks. I mean, for saving my ass back there."

He hitched up his broad shoulders. "Whatever."

"Hey, Jasper, if you hear anything else about Brittany, would you let me know?"

He eyed me suspiciously. "Really? What's going

on? I've heard about you, you know. You always seem to be getting involved in…stuff."

Uh-oh. I guess my reputation for being a trouble-magnet made the rounds. "No, really, I'm just trying to understand. There's no 'stuff.'"

"Whatever." He casually sauntered back into the house, and I followed, not too far behind.

Olivia stood beside Dickers and Parker, looking uncomfortable. She didn't wear skirts often and kept picking and brushing it like she'd fallen into a thatch of poison ivy.

"What's up, guys?" I whispered. "Hey, did you notice anything funny about Brittany over the last two months?"

Dickers shrugged. "I didn't really see her much. She just quit coming to the YAC meetings."

Parker nodded in agreement. "I think something was going on with her."

"What do you mean?"

Parker looked at me as if I'd been smacked with the idiot stick. "Well, she quit coming to the meetings. Duh."

Olivia rolled her eyes. "Oh, whatever, Parker. Maybe she wised up."

I tuned my friends out, only to hear Brittany's cryptic words rummaging around in my head. She said to talk, listen, and *read*. I needed to look in her bedroom. If she had a diary or something, maybe that's what her ghost had meant.

"Uh, guys, I'm not feeling well," I said, my hand positioned over my stomach. "I need to find the bathroom." Olivia let slip a hint of a smile. Feeling sick to my stomach is my "go-to" move for covert operations. I used it quite a bit over the last several years. I hope I'm not gaining a reputation for it. In my yearbook photo, it'll probably say, "Tex McKenna...Most Likely To Become Incontinent."

Olivia occupied Parker and Dickers while I scooched my way upstairs. After reaching the landing, I pushed open the closest door and entered a room crawling in pink.

Pink curtains framed the window, a large pink rug lying underneath the immaculately-made bed. Posters of bands and actors flanked the large vanity in the center of the room. I looked underneath Brittany's bed and found nothing, not even dust bunnies. An ornate jewelry box sat on top of the dresser next to the bed. Inside nestled rings, earrings, necklaces, bracelets, and a temporary tooth brace. Underneath the box, I found a stack of papers and some concert ticket stubs. The papers consisted mainly of school assignments, tests, and notes to friends. Quickly skimming the notes, I found nothing more interesting than the fact she thought Dwight couldn't kiss worth a damn. *Shocker.*

Hidden at the bottom of the pile were three folded pieces of yellow stationery. The first one—written in a hastily scrawled, barely legible script—read *I KNOW WHAT YOU ARE.* The second one said *GOD DESPISES YOUR TYPE.* The third one had been wadded up many times by the looks of it. *GOD HATES HOMOSEXUALS.*

Placing the letters into my jacket pocket, I wondered about the ramifications of their contents. Had Brittany been gay? I never had a clue. For as long as I'd been at Clearwell High, Brittany supported Dwight Louden as his arm candy. Yet, why would someone send these to her? Or did Brittany write them?

Disappointed I couldn't find a diary I spotted her computer on a desk. I powered it on, to be met with the password prompt. I typed *Dwight* and got knocked out. Next, I tried *Pink* to no avail. Looking around the room for clues, I unsuccessfully attempted several more passwords. Finally, out of desperation, I typed in *Brittany*. The reassuring musical cues brought the computer to life. *Really*, Brittany?

In the corner of the screen, a folder sat with the designation *Brittany's journal! Keep out!* Feeling somewhat like a ghoul preying upon the memories of the dead, I mentally apologized to Brittany and lamely reassured myself she'd want me to read it.

I began with an entry from two months previously. Brittany's writing consisted of happy, inconsequential malarkey, expounding upon her jealousy over another girl's hair or how nice a smile a boy had. Although dating Dwight at the time, she pulled no punches in announcing his many faults, including stupidity, halitosis, and gross masculine hygiene. She wrote at great length about how being in YAC filled her with hope—a new purpose almost—a zest for life amongst her Christian friends.

Then something odd happened. Her entries became shorter, more urgent. The everyday vanity that filled prior entries had gone the way of the dinosaurs, replaced by a more introspective tone, very self-reflective. And seemingly self-loathing.

Brittany Gerlach developed feelings for a fellow cheerleader. A female cheerleader. At first, she wrote of her extreme confusion. She didn't understand these feelings, didn't *want* these feelings. They frightened her. Soon, she grew to despise herself. She wrote how her new feelings weren't natural—several of her later entries appeared to be addressed to God himself as she asked Him why he'd made her this way, since He hated homosexuals. She felt abandoned, rejected, and let down by God. And I felt awful for Brittany. How terrible it must've been to go through this by herself, not letting anyone share her secret. And to have found such joy in the YAC group, only to have it snatched away from her...because she felt unworthy of God's love.

My heart pounded as I read her final entries.

*I never should have told him,* she wrote. *He was the only one I trusted with my secret, and now I KNOW it's him sending me the hateful letters, making the late night calls—threatening to tell the entire school about my secret. He can disguise his voice all he wants, but I know it's him. And he keeps telling me the same awful thing! GOD HATES PEOPLE LIKE ME!*

The day Brittany killed herself, she wrote, *I can't do it anymore. All because of something I can't help. God doesn't love me anymore. There's nothing to live for.* And that awful, pain-filled sentence was the last thing Brittany Gerlach would ever write.

My stomach churned with misery. Poor Brittany. Pissed off didn't even begin to describe how I felt. I had to find out who sent her those letters. I'd do it for her.

The door slammed open. Dwight Louden bellowed, "Oh, you've got to be *kidding* me!" He galloped across the room, grabbed the back of my jacket, and slung me to the floor. *"You're gonna pay for this."*

"Dwight, it isn't what it looks like!"

He pulled me up by my jacket, his mouth gaping

open. "What are you, faggot? Some kind of sick...*pervo?*" Slapping my face, he threw me onto the bed. I scrambled back, performing a clumsy somersault to the floor. As I attempted to get to my feet, he tackled me, bringing us both down with a dull thud. "I can't *believe* the balls on you!"

I tussled with him, somehow managing to gain leverage and pushed him off. As I raced for the door, I nearly knocked Jasper over as he entered.

"Tex, you just can't stay out of trouble, can you?" Jasper looked behind me at Dwight, who now standing, prepared to lunge at me again. "Just go! *Now*," Jasper ordered. "I'll take care of Dwight."

"I'm gonna *kill* him," roared Dwight, rattling the windowpanes of Brittany's room.

I fled as I heard Jasper mumbling platitudes, trying to soothe the beast. Nearly tumbling down the stairs in my haste, the crowd looked on at my antics.

"Come on," I said to Olivia. "Let's go before they throw me out." Parker and Dickers appeared puzzled.

"Okay. Later, boys." Olivia slung her purse over her shoulder and pulled me behind her.

Once we got outside, she said, "Way to go, Tex. I've never been kicked out of a wake before."

\*\*\*\*

"So...*wait*," she said. "Brittany Gerlach was...*gay?*" Her eyes popped open nearly as big as her gaping mouth.

"No, I didn't *say* that. All I know is she was, maybe...bi-curious, bi-sexual. Maybe she was gay and just found out. Either way, someone in her YAC group found out and was harassing her about it."

"Bastards!" Olivia planted a punch to the much-

106

abused Bucket's glovebox. "And no one knew about Brittany? Not even her Cro-Magnon boyfriend?"

"No, in fact, I'm absolutely positive he didn't know, especially since he's so fond of tossing around hurtful homosexual epithets. I think if he found out, it would damage his...sense of masculinity."

"Good! I hope he *does* find out."

"Yeah, maybe it'd teach him a thing or two."

"And Brittany didn't write who it was who sent her the letters?"

"No. I just know it was a guy." With the sun falling fast, I turned on the Bucket's headlights. "And I'm going to find out who it was and make him answer for it."

"How?"

"I don't know. I guess maybe...I may have to join YAC."

"*Really*?" She chortled, failing miserably in hiding her amusement.

"Yeah, I can't think of anything else. Are you in?"

She stared at me in silence before answering. "Oh, man. I *guess* so. I wouldn't mind taking these guys down, too. But joining YAC?" She wrinkled her nose as if she'd tasted Ruth's cooking. *"Not* what I consider fun."

"Tell me about it. But, Olivia, somebody more or less *pushed* Brittany to suicide! I *have* to do this."

"You think this is what Max and Brittany warned you about? I mean it's not like...something dangerous or anything. Is it?"

"Hope not. But I think this guy—whoever he is—might try something like this again. Then there's the Reaper who pushed me down the stairs...and the threats

I got from The Spencer and—"

"You think it all might be connected?"

"I'd be dumb not to read *something* into all this. There's something bad going on, and we're stuck in the middle of it."

"Okay," she said. "Bring it. *Hoo-yah!*" Olivia pumped her fist in the air. "I'm ready to take on the hypocrites of the world."

I wish I could share in Olivia's giddy excitement, but I had a nagging feeling—a creeping dread—there's something rotten lurking about the quiet, placid corners of suburban Clearwell. And soon I would be plunged right down the crapper into it.

## Chapter Six

I shooed the cats away from the front stoop, entered my house, and heard voices in the kitchen.

"Hi, son," called out Dad. "Have you had dinner?"

"Hey, Dad. Hi, Ruth." They sat at the kitchen table, polishing off their supper.

"Hi, Tex," said Ruth. "We have some leftover Coconutty soup for you." I suppressed a laugh when Dad shook his head briefly and mouthed, *no*. These days, Ruth took sadistic pleasure in experimenting on the McKenna males with her horrific food recipes, some much more appalling than others. Coconutty soup definitely sounded like it belonged in the latter category.

"Um, no thanks, Ruth. I ate something at the, ah, wake."

Dad raised his eyebrows. "Oh, you went to the Gerlach girl's wake?"

I nodded. Ruth placed her fingertips over her lips, batted her eyelids, and said, "Oh, my."

"How are her parents doing?"

"As well as can be expected, I guess. They looked…out of it."

Dad grimaced. He'd been there. "Say, Mickey called and wants you to call her back."

It baffles me why Mickey refuses to call me on my cell phone. It's not like I haven't given her the number many times. I suspect it has to do with her unwillingness to embrace modern technology. She still watches "her stories" on a VCR, for crying out loud.

For once, Mickey picked up on the second ring. Something must definitely be wrong.

"Hi Mickey," I said. "It's Tex."

She took a moment of silence before she responded. "It's Mickey, kiddo."

"Yeah, ah, I know. Um…you called?"

"Tex, the more I think about it, the more worried I am." It sounded like she carefully weighed every word before she spoke. *Totally* unlike her. Anxiety kicked in.

"What are you worried about?"

"I'm not real sure, kid. Just gotta bad feeling. Maybe it's about Spencer, maybe it's about what Max foresaw. I don't know. But something ain't right." She expelled a long breath. "I'm not sure what's going on exactly, but I can feel *something* in my bones." I've learned to count on the scientific accuracy of Mickey's bones, more reliable than a weather forecaster or political polls. "Has anything else happened to you lately?"

"Well, yeah, as a matter of fact…" I related the incidents of the past few days.

"I think you may need some protection."

"Okay."

"We need to prepare you for magical or spiritual attacks."

"'Kay."

"Tex, do you have a ring? Something special? Something that's important to you?"

I wiggled my naked fingers. "No. No rings. *Wait!* My mom had a ring. I found it in her witchcraft stuff."

"Perfect." I heard Mickey puff out a bloom of cigarette smoke. "Bring that to me in the next day or so. The sooner the better."

"All right. But…what good will a ring do?"

"I'll show you how to charge the ring. We'll invoke the Spell of the Witch's Ring. It *should* provide you protection from any black magic spells, provided you wear it."

"Okay, but why now? I mean you didn't seem to think Spencer was a threat the other day."

"I can't really say why, kid. Told ya it's just a feeling I have." Yeah, the *bones*. "And with everything that's been happening to you lately—especially with the warning from the dead cheerleader—it seems supernatural energies are converging around you again. That's usually an omen black magic's getting ready to move."

The old song "Black Magic" played through my mind. Obviously, the singer didn't know anything about black magic, because he sounded so happy. My experience with black magic could be defined as *anything* but "happy." I told Mickey I'd see her soon and hung up.

Warnings. Sooooo way sick of warnings. That made, what, the fourth one in the last couple of days? It'd be different if spirits, mediums, threatening boy witches—*whatever*—might, you know, give me actual concrete information. But, no, apparently being cryptic is cool. And wouldn't it kick ass if someone, like, I don't know, warned me I'd win the lottery or something?

I sighed and remembered another call I'd promised to make.

"Hey, Allie."

"Oh, hi, Tex." She sounded distracted, with little time for me.

"Just wanted to see how you're doing. I know Olivia was a little rough on you today."

"That's okay. I'm used to having to defend my religious beliefs. I think that's just part of being a good Christian. I know Olivia didn't mean anything by it."

"Well, I think she's going to apologize anyway. Hey, if you don't mind my asking, whatever happened between you and Ian? I mean, I thought things were going great between you two...and then..." So way pushing it. Allie didn't like to discuss things of a personal nature. But I could tell unfinished business between the two of them needed to be resolved. I waited for the fall-out.

"Tex, I don't know *what* happened, really. It just sort of...went away. I mean, we were never officially boyfriend and girlfriend, but Ian just sort of pulled away."

"Sorry. Um, if you'd like...I can talk to Ian—"

"*No*! Please, just let it be." I understood her hesitation. I wouldn't want anyone interfering in my love life either, but since Ian opens up to me more than anyone else, I thought I might have a shot at talking sense into him. *Matchmaker Tex.*

"Okay, I won't say anything. But, Allie?"

"Yes?"

"You don't...*like* Parker, do you? I mean, *like-like?* Or were you just trying to make Ian jealous?"

Long pause, uncomfortably so. "I've known Parker for a long time. We practically grew up in church together. Maybe I think he's cute, or *maybe* I was trying to make Ian a little jealous. Honestly, it's none of your business."

"Gotcha." I forced an awkward laugh. I'd brought out the tiger in Allie and didn't want to get clawed up. "Yeah, I know it's none of my business. I'll back off. I just want you to be careful, okay?"

"*Still* none of your business."

I thought it best to change the subject. "Hey, I'm curious about the Young American Christians group. Do you think I could talk to you about them sometime? Maybe even go to a meeting?"

Her voice brightened. "I'd love it if you came to a meeting. That'd be *awesome*."

I thanked her for the offer and said goodbye. Obviously very open to talking about God, the YACCERS, and anything religious, but Allie drew the line on her personal life. I wondered if I'd ever find out what happened to her parents. Or just what the deal is with her creepy, feral little brother. If she told me a pack of wild wolves raised him, I'd believe her. I still shudder at how he cowered along the stairwell at Allie's birthday party last year, throwing things, tittering, and just…*watching*.

I switched on my computer, checked social media, email—the usual hangouts. Nothing but typical name-calling, idle gossip, preposterously cheesy fiction about fellow students, and spam for sexual enhancement.

Suddenly a window popped open. Dressed in a dark robe, Spencer Pritchett sat at a desk, candlelight spiking shadows across his face. Heavy metal music droned in the background. Hard to tell through the video's fuzziness, but it appeared he sat in front of a black sheet pinned to the wall, a large white pentagram painted over it.

He checked his wristwatch and glared into the camera. For minutes. A very uncomfortable cybernetic staring contest. Finally, he realized he'd made contact. "McKenna," he hissed. "I told you we'd meet again and this was *far* from over." His voice broke a few times, puberty reminding him where he stood. "What you did to me was *unforgivable*. I'm coming for you. When you least expect me, I'm coming for you." He glowered into the webcam with well-rehearsed drama. Interrupted by something, he looked off camera. "Just a minute," he shouted to an unseen intruder. When he reached to turn off the webcam, he muttered "Jesus" under his breath before the screen went black.

*Great!* Not only is he a black magic-practicing vengeful witch with a huge grudge-on against me, but he also appears to be an expert computer hack. The thought he'd somehow invaded my computer felt unsettling enough, but I wondered what he could do if his witch powers are as potent as the rumors have them be.

At close to midnight, I crawled into bed. While nearing the early stages of sleep, the guttural meowing of two cats, obviously in the throes of sex, awakened me. I wondered how something supposed to be so wonderful could possibly sound so...*horrible*. I drifted off to sleep thinking what an appropriate metaphor that is for my life lately. On the surface, everything seems tranquil, happy—*normal*—but just like one of Ruth's foul concoctions that sat in the refrigerator for too long, once opened, its rank odor permeates the air. It might have smelled good at one time, but the expiration date has long passed.

\*\*\*\*

"Hi, Olivia," said Allie. "We missed you at lunch yesterday."

Olivia dropped her tray onto the lunch table and threw her arms around Allie's neck. "I know, I just didn't feel like seeing people after…yesterday morning. I'm sorry for my, um, outburst."

Allison smiled as she tapped Olivia's arms. "It's okay. Everyone has a bad day once in a while."

Olivia turned her attention toward Dickers. "You, too, Dickers. Sorry."

Dickers wiped his mouth with a napkin and stood, arms reaching toward Olivia like a hungry toddler.

"No hugs for you, Dickers!"

Dickers, looking mortified, slumped back into his chair.

"It's called hugging, not groping, Dickers," said Ian. Lance tried to stifle his laughter, failed, and let out a loud hoot.

"Okay, now that we have *that* out of the way," I said, "I've been dying to find out the results of yesterday's skate park challenge." Ian averted his eyes, a sure sign of his ego-crushing loss. "Dickers? You were the judge. What was the outcome?"

"Well," he began, "Lance got two phone numbers—one from a girl and one from a guy. Ian doesn't think the guy's number should count—"

"Yeah," said Ian, "it was supposed to be about getting chick's numbers."

"And Brandon thinks Ian's failure to get *any* numbers should give him additional points," said Dickers.

Brandon shrugged. "I got two numbers."

"If that's the case," said Lance, "I should *clearly* be the winner since there was only one person on my team. *Not* the other way around." Olivia leaned into Lance, tapping their shoulders together. "And I'm going to totally call the guy."

"What about you, Brandon?" Olivia asked.

"Haven't given it much thought." *Of course you haven't, Brandon.* Brandon didn't give much thought to anything. He didn't need arbitrarily grasped phone numbers from a bet, anyway.

Ian shoved his tray away. "What*ever*."Again, Allison looked on edge, busy twirling spaghetti around her fork.

"Sounds to me like we need to have a rematch." I couldn't help but stoke the fires.

"I'm game," said Brandon.

"I'm in, too," said Lance.

"*Fine.*" Ian tried to dismiss the topic with a wave of his hand and a harrumph.

"Come on, Ian." Olivia stood and poked his arm. "We can't *all* be winners."

I spotted Elizabeth Blackmer sitting at a nearby table, holding court over a slew of other preppie girls. Time to have a chat with her. I wanted to know if Elspeth had made another appearance recently. Why not? Everything else supernatural had poured down from the skies. "I'll be back, guys." I felt Olivia's gaze burning a hole into my back as I made my way toward Elizabeth's table.

Braving myself, I stood in front of the girls for a seeming eternity before Elizabeth finally acknowledged my existence. "Yes?" Her chilly, blue eyes sent an avalanche of ice tumbling down my back.

"Um, what's up, Elizabeth? Can I talk to you? Alone?"

Elizabeth licked her lips and held one regal, expertly manicured hand into the air. "Girls, if you would excuse me, I have to talk to Tex about a school assignment."

I thought I'd depart *with* Elizabeth, but the other girls at the table suddenly and obediently took their leave. Apparently, Elizabeth had climbed to the head of her pack over the past year, lording it over them with an iron fist.

"I just wanted to ask you if you've had any, ah, visitations from Elspeth lately?" I took a seat across from her.

"No. She hasn't come back since last year." Planting her head sideways, she jutted out her jaw suspiciously. "*Why* do you ask?"

"No reason, really. I've just been thinking about her lately. Her last words to me were she'd return when I needed help. I think that time might be now."

Elizabeth rolled her eyes. "Oh, no, not *this* again."

"I know, right? It just seems like something…bad's coming. And I could use some help."

"Hey, Elizabeth," said a beautifully toned voice. Donovan Goode stood behind Elizabeth. "Where're the girls?"

Elizabeth smiled affectionately—something *totally* unaccustomed—and rushed to stand up. She placed a short, demure kiss on his cheek. "I sent them away. I had to discuss a homework assignment with—"

"Oh, sure," he interrupted, holding his hand out to me. "I know who Tex McKenna is."

I accepted his firm handshake, twice up and down

and released, like that of a practiced politician. Just like Elizabeth's cement-solid mane, Donovan's product-covered hair remained stolidly in place. I self-consciously patted at my out-of-control waves of hair. No way I could compete—let alone be in the same room—with the Hairstyles of the Gods.

"Yeah, hey, Donovan," I squeaked. "It's a pleasure to meet you…finally."

"Even though we've never actually met, Tex," he said, smiling, "I know a *lot* about you." He had me at "I know who Tex McKenna is." "You helped put Red away a couple of years ago, and I understand you were instrumental in putting a stop to the gang problem last year."

"Yeah, well…" I looked away, uncomfortable with my own notoriety.

"It's a shame one of your friends was implicated." Obviously, Donovan Goode made it his business to know everything about the school he reigned over. He has my future vote. He's simply…*wonderful*.

"Yeah, a shame," I echoed. Quickly changing the uncomfortable topic, I added, "So, you guys are dating?"

Donovan, in a very sweeping fashion, sat down next to Elizabeth, grabbed her hands, and stared into her eyes. "Yes, we are." They *radiated* at one another like two beautiful angels. If they weren't such a perfect, gorgeous couple, I would've gagged. But they *mesmerized* me, something out of a fairy tale. "We've been going together for the better part of a year. We met at a Young American Christians' gathering."

I felt the blood rush out of my face. Was *everyone* a member of YAC?

Donovan's friendly expression gave way to a look of genuine concern. "Is something wrong, Tex? You don't look so well."

"Ah, no, it just seems like I've been hearing a lot lately about YAC." My voice drifted away like dandelion seeds floating on the wind.

"Well, we could *always* use someone like you in our group, Tex. To help spread the Word. And to discuss God, of course."

"Of course."

"So," he said, slapping his legs. "How do *you* two know each other?"

I started to say we're friends before Elizabeth answered for me. "We've shared some classes. I had to help Tex out with some assignments." Same ol' Elizabeth. Apparently, she still didn't consider me worthy enough to be a "friend." And to add insult to injury, I'm now just a "dumb" fellow classmate.

I managed, "Yeah, that's right." I looked at Elizabeth, hoping she'd see how she pissed me off. But she only had eyes—and a generously, toothy smile—for Donovan. Not that I could blame her. I nearly felt blessed to be in his presence. He was the cream of the crop of future young presidents, the savior of modern society, possessor of perfect hair and a dazzling smile. *Jerk.*

"Well," he said, jumping to his feet, while simultaneously straightening his khaki pant legs, a master of multitasking. He clapped his hands once as if summoning celestial trumpets from above and again held his hand out to me. He clamped down on my hand with both of his—nice, warm and snug, just like a cozy sweater. "It was a real pleasure to finally meet you,

Tex." He smiled as if he meant it. I'll just bet he has a perfect singing voice as well. Two hand-pumps and gone, golden glitter left in his wake. After having thoroughly bathed in his warm persona, I wanted him to tuck me in at night.

Shaking off my ridiculous—yet *totally* heterosexual—man-crush, I plummeted back into the chair across from Elizabeth. I said nothing for a while, cleared my throat, and uttered a very quiet, "wow."

To my shock, Elizabeth giggled. "Yes, he *does* have that effect on people. Listen, Tex, if I should 'hear' from Elspeth, I'll let you know, okay?"

I nodded, still in a state of stunned silence.

"Goodbye." She abruptly left me sitting by myself.

I took a cleansing breath and stumbled back to my friends, legs wobbly from being in the presence of Royalty.

Olivia shook her head in disgust. "So, you're now hanging out with 'The Young Republicans of Clearwell?'"

Lance and Ian burst out laughing as I thought to myself, "*I wish.*"

\*\*\*\*

I watched the newly blossomed tree limbs whip back and forth outside the classroom window. The wind wheezed asthmatically against the panes, and debris flew in every direction. The change in weather—and, yeah, the weirdness of my life—made it next to impossible to pay attention to anything being taught today.

Parker brushed up next to me, tore off his backpack, and fell into his seat. "Hey, McKenna. How do you think you did on the test yesterday?"

*Not very good.* "Pretty good, I think. How about you?"

"Aced it." He grinned triumphantly at me. "Easy as pie."

"I never really thought of 'pie' as being easy, Parker."

"Whatever."

Mr. Jensen surveyed his philosophy students from the doorway. After walking into the room, he stood with his knuckles burrowing into his sides, his short sleeves straining at his arms. His purple and black necktie—much too short for his long torso—provided me a focal point because I couldn't hold his nerve-wracking stare-down for long. Mr. Jensen is a master of intimidation, but unlike, say, someone like Arville Hastings, he generally uses his dominating powers for good. Something was on his mind, never a good sign.

"Okay, guys." He continually batted a fist into an open palm, warming up for the mound. "Who here's heard of the Clarendon Baptist Church?"

Of *course* it had to be about them. Most of the students raised their hands.

"I'd like to hear some of your thoughts about them," he said. "Go!"Everyone appeared to be too frightened to answer. "Tex?"

"Um, well, I don't *really* know a lot about them, Mr. Jensen. Ah…I don't like what I've heard…or seen."

Mr. Jensen raised his eyebrows expectantly. "Go on."

"Well, they protested Brittany Gerlach's funeral yesterday. I don't think that's right…or even Christian, for that matter." A hush fell over the previously buzzing classroom. Obviously, I'd stepped into a huge, stinking pile of controversy.

"Why do you say that, Tex?"

"Um, they believe that suicides go to hell, that God hates them. How is that Christian? I mean, who are they to judge, to define God's meaning? It's like they take one or two random passages from the Bible and twist it to their own agenda." A few of my classmates nodded in agreement. Good. Maybe I won't get slaughtered.

"Oh, I don't know, Mr. Jensen," interjected Parker. "It *clearly* states in the Old Testament that suicide is a sin. And for a mortal sin like that, Hell's the obvious journey's-end—"

"Parker, I don't *know* the Bible as well as you do, but I'd be willing to bet—"

"That's right, you don't! And for someone like *you* to be casting judgment on true believers, well..." He shook his head, his long blond hair slapping his face like punishing whips.

"Let me ask you this, Parker," said Mr. Jensen. He finally relaxed his prison guard patrol and sat behind his desk. "Do you believe in what the Clarendon church teaches?"

"I don't know if I believe in everything they espouse, but there *is* some merit to some of the things they have to say." Parker sat back, smug in his self-perceived superiority.

"Like *what*?" I jumped to my feet, feeling terrifyingly out-of-control. "That suicides go to Hell? And that it's cool to protest their funerals?"

"Well, yeah. As I said, the Bible clearly states it." Paul Jacobsen groaned from the back of the room. "Look," Parker continued, turning to face the students one by one, "I know it has to be tough for Brittany's parents hearing their daughter's going to Hell. But I'm not gonna say God's words—the Bible's words—are lies. I'll leave that to McKenna."

"I never said that. You're putting words in my mouth!"

"Kind of like what you're trying to do with the Clarendon Baptist Church."

"I'm just saying *they're* the ones twisting the words of the Bible around—"

"You show me *where* in the Bible *anything* contradicts what they're saying!"

I faltered, coming up empty.

"*That's* what I'm talkin' about. You can't back up your own words."

My throat swelled up, on the verge of tears; not a sign of weakness in the face of adversity but rather an unfortunate side effect I suffer when I become angry. And I hate making a spectacle of myself. *Too late*. "Yeah, Parker. I *don't* know the Bible as well as you do…but there's such a thing as common, human decency! And that's what I think being a Christian should be. Seems to me these Clarendon people are *definitely* not practicing that,"

Parker bolted out from behind his desk. "You're not even a *Christian*, are you?"

"Well…um, not practicing."

"Do you even *believe* in God?" We faced off, our noses inches from colliding.

"I don't know…"

Parker held his hand out toward the students as if presenting incontrovertible evidence. "Well, there you have it."

"And what about Clarendon's stance on homosexuality, Parker?" A desperate trump card at best, but the only one I could think to play. Being on the losing side of our impromptu debate called for desperate ploys.

"What about it?"

"Do *you* believe homosexuality is a sin?"

"It *clearly* states in the Bible—"

"Here we go again!" The class stared at me, eyes wide, mouths slack-jawed.

"It *says* that 'Man shall not lie down with another man,'" said Parker.

"What about the stories of Jesus having welcomed homosexuals? Huh? What about *that*?"

*"Where* does it say that?"

I fell silent for a moment. "Um, historians…" I offered as a last resort. I *thought* I remembered reading something about that…*somewhere*. Maybe not.

Parker trumpeted his lips. "'Historians.' What do *they* know? The Bible is *God's* word."

I felt my fists clench into weapons. "So says who? The Clarendon Baptist Church? If their word is the *absolute* word…then their small congregation will be the only ones *in* Heaven! It's gonna be mighty sparse up there, Parker." To this, a few students laughed.

"They're *right* about a lot of things, McKenna!" Spittle flew from his mouth.

"What about where the Bible says 'Beware of false prophets'?"

"*Exactly*, McKenna."

*"What?* Gah!"

Parker's upper lip curled, his teeth grinding. "I'll *pray* for your soul."

I so wanted to swing my fist at his snarky, sharky face. Thankfully Mr. Jensen interrupted, saving me from a lifetime of detention. "Okay, guys, okay." He walked out from behind his desk. "Have a seat."

I sat down, my hands shaking uncontrollably. Parker's eyes smoldered, a fireplace of hatred.

"We've had a, ah, lively discussion about religion," said Mr. Jensen. The classroom let out a barrage of relieved laughter. He swayed his hands to calm everyone down. "Now, this *is* philosophy, not theology. And while I appreciate your comments and your views, Tex, Parker, I think we better leave the heavier themes of religion to the churches. Before I get into trouble." More nervous laughter. "I just wanted to make everyone aware of what's going on in Kansas now with the Clarendon Baptist Church. And I think both sides have been clearly represented. Just be *careful*, people. As I always ask you to do, *think*. Gather all the facts first. Don't run into anything blindly." He tapped the side of his head. "Use your brains, people. Contrary to the popular belief of a lot of teachers around here, I know you have them. The brains God gave you." He chuckled, and the students followed his lead.

Throughout the rest of class, I sat fuming, unable to even look at Parker. But I felt him *shimmering* with victory next to me.

\*\*\*\*

Humbled and embarrassed, I walked toward my locker, keeping my head down.

"Dude," said Brandon, slouched against the lockers. "Heard you threw down with Parker in class today." He stared at me, unblinking, awaiting a play-by-play.

"What'd you hear exactly?"

"I heard you guys got into a fight. Don't see any battle wounds, though."

"It *wasn't* like that. It was more of a, I don't know…heated argument."

"Well, everyone's talking about it." By the way he shifted his attention to passing students, he had already lost interest in the topic, and I couldn't be happier.

Olivia bounded up, dragging Ian behind her by his shirtsleeve. "Tex," she shouted. "Are you okay?"

"Gah! Yes, I'm okay, no, I didn't hit Parker, and as far as I know, I'm not suspended, expelled, or banished into super-secret double-detention. Yes, most of the school thinks I'm a psychotic anti-Christian, and no, I haven't been struck dead by God's vengeful lightning bolt." I managed a smile when Olivia's concern became obvious. "That should cover it."

Olivia placed her hands on her hips and glared at me, an all too familiar glare. "And you're okay?"

"Yes, I'm okay, no, I didn't hit—"

"Okay, already! Let's *not* go over your life story again."

"Sorry, O'. It's just…damn Parker gets to me."

"Jesus, Tex," said Ian. "Are you *trying* to get expelled before graduation? Just simmah' down."

"Oh," said Olivia. "Speaking of Parker, guess what happened to me after lunch today?"

"Are you gonna tell us or what?" asked Ian.

A testicle-shrinking scowl from Olivia rewarded his effrontery. "Okay, I was going to the bathroom—"

"Sounds like a killer story so far," said Ian.

"*Anyway*," she continued, "in the stall next to me, I heard crying. I asked if everything was okay, if she needed me to grab the nurse. If I could help her with anything. You know, feminine stuff." Ian frowned while Brandon looked puzzled. "She didn't answer me, so I kept up. I knocked on the stall door, and she just kept crying and *finally* stopped. I waited a few minutes longer until she came out. It was Shannon Booth."

Brandon furrowed his brow. "Parker's girlfriend," I whispered. He snapped to, once recognition kicked him in the head like a mule.

"Okay, you guys *know* I can't stand her." She stuck her tongue out in disgust.

We all nodded in obvious agreement.

"But, I *hate* to see anyone hurting. And even though she's treated me like *crap*—the snotty lil' bee-*yotch* that she is—I still thought I'd try and help her out. At first, she kept on being all, *get away from me, ho*! And I was like, come on, Shannon, obviously, there's something wrong. Just talk to me. *Finally*, she said she and Parker broke up." Olivia took a breath, waiting for our astonishment.

Not too surprised, I managed an, "Oh, really?"

She nodded animatedly. "So, I asked her why. Told her they made a great couple." Olivia took time out from her story to poke the tip of her finger into her mouth. "She finally—*finally*—said it was because of YAC!"

Suddenly, Olivia's bathroom saga became more interesting. "Huh," I said.

"*Yeah*! She said Parker came back from a YAC meeting, and the instructors, I guess, or whatever, told him he *had* to break up with her…because they went to third base!"

"*What*?" shouted Ian. "That's crazy."

"You guys, shhhh." I didn't see the need for Shannon's sex life to become hallway talk fodder.

"So, they told Parker he had to purge everything bad from his life. Leave it all behind him. And *that* included his ho' of a girlfriend who let him go to third base," she said.

"Wait, so it was all Shannon's fault?" I asked. "Parker's not held...accountable for any of this?"

"*That's* what I asked her. So, she looked at me and said it was all her fault. Parker blamed her...and never wanted to see her again. Can you *believe* that *crap*?"

"Wow," I said, "just...*man.*"

The Young American Christians were beginning to have an impact on the everyday goings-on at school. Not only did they affect people's personalities—mostly, for the worst, from what I could see—but like an unseen virus, they spread their toxins into the student body, infecting even those who weren't members. And it fell upon me to find out who the "carrier" was.

Chapter Seven

"Richard? Excuse me, Richard?"

I turned around to see Alf Lampbert, Clearwell High's security guard, pop his gray-haired head out from his cubbyhole office. Much to Alf's dismay, he'd been taken off foot patrol and relegated to computer screen watching. A retired cop, rumors circulated that he'd shot himself accidentally in his foot. *Twice.* I didn't buy it for a minute. Peel away his mask of dottiness and you'll find a pretty shrewd mind.

"Oh, hey, Alf." I tossed him a wave. "What's up?"

"Um, if I could have a few minutes with you? Alone?"

Olivia took the hint. "All right," she whispered into my ear. "You go play with your friend, and I'll wait for you at the Bucket." She planted a quick peck on my lips.

Alf appeared embarrassed, his small ears glowing tomato red. "Aw, is that the little gal you were so broken up over last year?" He ushered me into his office.

"Yeah, as a matter of fact, it is." Last year, Alf became somewhat of my romantic guru, dispelling wisdom and common sense when it came to the opposite sex. "How are things going with you and your, ah…"

"Don't have to call her my 'ex-wife' anymore." He

129

turned a picture frame on his desk toward me. In the photo, Alf had an arm draped around a plump, amused-looking woman, the joy on their faces infectious. "We got remarried."

"That's great. Belated congrats and all that."

He studied the photo for another moment before setting it carefully back into place. "I gotta say your choice of gals this time is a little better than the one you brought to the dance last year." Referring to Elizabeth, he showed good taste. "Anyway, here, let me pull something up." He jabbed some keys on the keyboard and toyed around with a few knobs. "Dag-nab computer. Here. I want you to take a gander at this." Discovering the short length of cable wouldn't allow him to turn the monitor toward me, Alf waved me to join him on his side of the desk.

I stared at an image of me standing in the darkened hallway outside of Mrs. Swanson's classroom. "Hmm. Not a very good picture of me, is it?" I tried to affect a look of casual nonchalance, but Donovan Goode I'm not.

"That's the odd thing. It's not just a picture. That's a moving image of you during detention yesterday."

"Whoa. That's kinda weird." I sat across from him. "I *do* remember feeling kind of sick, so I asked Mrs. Swanson if I could go to the bathroom. She sorta fell asleep."

"You're kidding me." Alf had a way of keeping me off-guard by switching between his good ol' boy persona to inquisitive overseer of the odd and unjust.

"No, really. But don't tell anyone." I gave him an awkward wink. Winking doesn't come naturally to me. I feel like I'm attempting to dislodge a foreign particle from my eye.

"Your secret's safe with me, Richard. Old Mrs. Swanson's getting up there in years." She *can't* be any older than Alf, but it's a point best not brought up. "But, it looks to me…like you're speaking with someone. And I don't see anyone else in the hallway. I've looked at it from different angles, on several different cameras. You're alone, but you're clearly talking." He raised his bushy eyebrows. "C'mere, take a look."

I waved him off. "I believe that's what it looks like, Alf, but as I said, I guess I wasn't feeling well. Maybe running a fever or something. I really, *really* don't remember much 'cause I was feeling so bad." Once again, I placed my hand over my stomach and made a sour face. Stomach, don't fail me now.

"That *is* strange." I had the feeling he didn't believe me for a moment. "Even stranger, the cameras shut down for a few minutes right after those hallway lights went off." He leaned across his desk. "You wouldn't know anything about that, now, would you, Richard?"

I made a big to-do in searching my mind for any light-altering incidents I'd forgotten, complete with eye squints and furrowed brow. "No. No, can't say as I do."

"Well, I rushed on up there. Two flights! By the time I got there, the lights came back on. And I looked through Mrs. Swanson's window and saw you back in your seat. Tell me… did you ever make it to the bathroom?"

"Um, no, guess I didn't."

"Curious." He leaned back, rocking in his chair, scrutinizing me. The clock above Alf ticked out eternal seconds, cutting through the silence like pounding drums. Suddenly, he tilted forward, squinting closely at one of the screens. "What the *hell*?" He leaped up from his desk, bumping into his wedding photo. "I've got to go, Richard."

"Alf? What's wrong?"

"Oh, looks like some damn hi-jinx. I thought we were finished with those silly Reapers a coupla' days ago."

The memory of my own personal Reaper attack brought my heart knocking at my chest. "You saw a Reaper?"

"Yep." He hitched his pants up, ready to spring into action. "Saw him run into the boys' bathroom up there on the third floor."

It might be nothing, but the fact a Reaper still lurked in the hallways two days after DDAD seemed too strange to ignore. And I had a niggling notion it could be the same Reaper who pushed me down the stairs. I set out after Alf.

Alf moved faster than I thought possible, vanishing up the stairwell. I bounded up the steps after him, two at a time. Practically skidding to a halt in front of the third-floor bathroom, I pushed the door open.

Water from a sink gushed full blast, hissing out cloudy steam of vapor. Kneeling, Alf's hands hovered over someone lying on the floor. A pool of dark blood inched across the floor.

"*Richard*," he screamed, his face white as chalk. "Call 9-1-1…*now*!"

I fumbled my phone out of my pocket and dialed. "Um, there's someone in the bathroom at Clearwell High, third floor, lots of blood, hurry…" My words jumbled out, nothing making sense. The woman on the phone may as well have been speaking in a foreign language. I rushed toward Alf.

I immediately recognized Calvin Sturgess. Not unfriendly, but he always stuck to himself and remained quiet in classes, either extraordinarily shy or so self-confident, he felt no need to burden himself with friends. Rumors also persisted about his homosexuality.

"What can I do, Alf?"

"I don't know! He's losing a lot of blood." Alf had stripped off his tie and now held it to Calvin's head. A dripping mess, the tie had been stained dark red. Blood continued to creep across the floor like a fire-angry sunset. "Hold on, young man," Alf repeated over and over like a prayer. "Help is coming, hold on, young man…"

From off in the distance, I heard an ambulance or police siren. The door slammed open behind me, and a loud voice screamed out, "*You!*" Arville Hastings chugged toward me, a two-legged weapon of destruction, his extended finger guiding him like a heat-seeking missile.

His eyes grew large when he saw Calvin. "Alf, *what's* going on here?"

"I don't know, Mr. Hastings. I ran up here after seeing footage of one of those Reapers enter the bathroom…and found the boy on the floor. He's lost a lot of blood!"

I couldn't see Calvin's chest rising, just so much blood. I ran to the nearest toilet stall to empty my stomach.

"And what's he doing here, Alf?" said Hastings. "What's he got to do with…*this?*"

"Nothing. He was with me when this happened…"

I exited the stall, wiping my mouth on my sleeve. The three of us looked at one another, each one unsure of his next move.

Hastings finally said, *"Richard, my office…now!* And stay there."

I nodded and left, my legs unsteady, bumping into the paramedics as they entered the bathroom.

\*\*\*\*

Over the past three years, I've seen my share of physical violence and even a dead body, but I've never seen that amount of blood before. I felt queasy, sick to my stomach, moving in a half-daze.

Olivia pounced on me when I entered the main hallway.

"Tex, what's going on?" She could tell something had happened and cradled me in her arms.

"It's…Calvin Sturgess. He…was in the bathroom…bleeding…so much *blood...*"

"Oh my *God!* Poor Calvin. Is he…all right?"

"I don't know. Hastings told me to wait down here for him."

"Oh, he doesn't think that you—"

"Of *course* he does. Anytime he can pin something on me…he does it." I shut my eyes, attempting to block the lasting imagery from the bathroom.

"Did Calvin fall? Or did somebody—"

"I don't know. Alf saw a Reaper go into the bathroom before he found Calvin lying up there…covered in…"

"Do you think this Reaper was the same one who attacked you?" She pushed me toward the hall lockers, steadying me against them.

"I'd bet money on it." I don't know why I felt so certain, but I've learned when there are weird, violent things happening that make no sense in the rational world, they're usually tied into *my* world. With a less than happy resolution.

"Who'd want to do that to Calvin?" Olivia's gaze vacantly wandered the hall as if searching for enlightenment.

The hallway door cracked open, and Hastings led a parade of two policemen behind him. He mumbled something to one of the cops, and the officer went into Alf's office. Hastings jabbed his finger at me and said, "I thought I told you to wait in my office." He then switched his menacing digit toward Olivia. "And *you,* Ms. Furman. Do you have any business being here?"

I saw defiance rise in her eyes. "Yeah! If my boyfriend's in trouble, it sure as hell *is* my business." She placed a hand on my chest as if protecting me from an attacking bear.

"Leave the premises *now,* Ms. Furman. This does not concern you."

Olivia ignored his command and looked into my eyes. I whispered, "It's okay."

On tiptoes, she gave me a caring, life-affirming kiss, the consequences be damned. Hastings huffed but obviously had more pressing matters to attend to. "I'll wait for you in your car. Give me your keys."

I fished them out of my pocket, the keys jangling in my quivering hands like a tambourine, before following Hastings and the officer into his office.

"Now. This is Officer Barrows. Officer, this is Richard McKenna," said Hastings.

Officer Barrows's facial hair so prominently

overwhelmed his face that he looked like a giant, walking mustache. I sought distraction—a day at the zoo—in his walrus-like appearance.

"Richard, why don't you tell me what happened?" asked Barrows, all business. Forget about the zoo.

"I was sitting in Alf Lampbert's office, just talking to him. Suddenly, he saw something on one of his computer screens—"

"What'd he see?" asked Barrows.

"He said it was one of those Reapers going into the third-floor boys' restroom."

Barrows squinted at Hastings for clarification. "Reapers are something we use every year as a dramatic device to illustrate the dangers of drinking and driving. Our Drunk Driving Awareness Day was held three days ago. On Tuesday."

Barrows nodded as if he understood, but the way his animate mustache danced and twitched told a different tale. "Okay, go on."

"That's really about it. I followed Alf up there and saw Calvin lying on the floor, his blood everywhere…" The image struck me again, blinding me with the indelible memory.

Hastings leaned forward, his hands clasped together. "And…*why* did you think it necessary to follow Alf, Richard?" His inquisitorial eyebrow flew up.

"Because after Tuesday's pep rally, someone in a Reaper's costume pushed me down the stairwell!"

Hastings and the cop exchanged impossible-to-read glances. "If this is true, why didn't you report it?" asked Hastings.

"I don't know. I guess I thought it might have been

an accident. Maybe, someone just goofing around and—"

"That seems *highly* unlikely," said Hastings.

"Well, *who* would I report it to, Mr. Hastings?" Uh-oh. Somewhere the Fates punched my "Pissed Off Button." "If I took it to you, then you'd turn it around on *me*, make it my fault or something. And I couldn't report it to *your* Hastings's Hallway Heroes. They're as bad as the rest of the bullies."

"'Hastings's Hallway Heroes?'" asked Barrows.

Hastings beamed like a proud father. "Yep, that's my baby. To stop bullying from going on at Clearwell, I put together a group of kids to patrol the hallways. Keep things on the up and up."

And that's the problem with Hastings's special elite task force. Hand-picked by Hastings himself, the "Hallway Heroes" are comprised mostly of football players, themselves some of the worst bullies at Clearwell. Several top honors students earned spots in the "Heroes," but they tend to turn a blind eye out of self-preservation. Generally, if the "Heroes" aren't bullying, they're messing around, flirting with cheerleaders, *anything* but doing the job they're supposed to be doing.

Barrows shook his head as if to clear it of unimportant details. "Okay, what can you tell me about this, ah, Reaper?"

"Nothing really," I said, trying to reclaim my dignity. I wouldn't give Hastings the pleasure of losing my cool again. "I mean, he didn't say anything, just shoved me. I didn't even get a good look at him."

"'Him'?"

"What?"

"Richard, you said 'him.' Are you certain it was a male?"

"I guess I just kind of assumed it was a guy and—"

"Richard, you know what happens when you 'assume,'" interjected Hastings, desperately trying to be a part of the interrogation. I sometimes wonder if he suffers failed dreams of being a cop. Or an evil dictator.

Barrows immediately blew Hastings off. "Anyway, you're pretty sure it was a male?"

I nodded. "Look, how is Calvin? Is he okay? How's Alf doing?"

Barrows and Hastings traded looks again. "I haven't heard yet," said Barrows. "I know it doesn't look good."

"Oh."

"Richard, were you a part of this?" Hastings lowered his voice—"bad cop" to Barrow's "good cop." "Did your little friends have anything to do with this? Maybe a little bit of horseplay, things got carried away. Now's the time for you to come clean, son."

The hair on the back of my neck prickled when he called me "son." Not once in my four-year term of incarceration has he treated me remotely like anything but a hardened criminal not good enough to walk the halls of Clearwell High. I boiled over with anger, ready to pop at any given second. I bit the inside of my lip and exhaled deeply. "I had absolutely *nothing* to do with what happened to Calvin, and neither did my friends." I turned my attention toward Barrows. "Maybe you should quit wasting your time with me, Officer Barrows, and hunt down this Reaper."

"Okay, we may need to talk to you again later." Barrows smiled and jerked his chin toward the door. I glanced once at Hastings, who looked perturbed he wouldn't get to wrangle a confession out of me.

Walking out of the Office of Doom, I almost collided with a dreadfully familiar figure.

"Hello, Tex," said Detective Cowlings. "I'm sorry to say, it now looks like we have a murder on our hands."

I like Detective Cowlings, but unfortunately, every time I see him, he brings a load of trouble for me, and usually, bodies trailing in his wake. Not that it's his fault. But we seem to be locked into a recurring dance of bumbling into and solving murder cases. Extremely smart, he's also highly suspicious of my "trouble-magnet" ways. I often wonder if it wouldn't be easier to just level with him and tell him I'm a witch. But I'm sure that'd ruin our dance partner status.

"What?"

"The boy, Calvin Sturgess..." He consulted his faithful companion, the ever-present notebook. "...he died at the hospital, not too long ago. Someone cracked his skull, and he lost too much blood in too short a time. There're obvious signs a struggle took place in the bathroom."

"Oh, no...no..." I felt my legs giving out.

Cowlings grabbed me, holding me up by my arms. "Let's go sit down, Tex, and have a little chat." He spotted the open doors to the cafeteria and guided me in there. The room sat empty except for the creepy lunch lady, who took time off from cleaning dishes to watch us from her hole in the wall.

"What? No hair nets anymore?" asked Cowlings, once he spotted our observer. He deposited me in a chair and sat next to me.

I had to chuckle, appreciating the relief it supplied. "You'd be surprised at what goes on in that kitchen."

"No doubt."

"Anyway...hey. It's nice to see you again. I guess."

"Yes. So, Tex, tell me, what's your involvement in this?" He stared at me, unblinking. "And, why is it I'm not exactly surprised to see you're—"

"Whoa, hold up! I'm not involved...at least not directly."

Cowlings sighed and reached for his notebook, flipping it open. "Fine. How are you *indirectly* involved?"

I told him how a Reaper had attacked me and how I followed Alf to today's scene of the crime. He bobbed his head, grunting now and then, scribbling away, inducing fear that all signs point toward me as a suspect. Even though I'm never—well, usually—guilty of any wrongdoings, it's my natural reaction toward cops.

"And you think this, ah, Reaper is the same one who attacked the Sturgess boy?"

I shrugged. "I mean, it sorta makes sense, doesn't it? Two violent Reapers are harder to credit than one."

"Let me be the one to determine what the facts are."

"Okay. More than happy to."

"Who would want to attack the Sturgess boy and why? Tell me about him."

"I didn't really know Calvin very well. He was a private person, and didn't seem to have any friends. But I don't think he had any enemies, either." Cowlings continued writing, the cafeteria light gleaming off his bald scalp. "And there's the rumor he was gay…" Once the words left my mouth, I wished I could've taken them back.

Cowlings eyes narrowed into hardened slits. "What makes you say that?" *Crap.* I forgot Cowlings was gay.

"Okay, I know, I know. They're just rumors. And usually, I don't pay any attention to rumors, but everyone said Calvin was gay—" Cowlings glowered at me. "Not that I have a problem with that or anything. One of my best friends is gay. And another friend is bi and—" I could see my embarrassing mouth diarrhea had no effect on the detective. Cowlings obviously has a big, gay chip on his shoulder. But having witnessed the persecution homosexuals go through at Clearwell, I kinda get his chip-wearing crusade.

"Settle down, Tex," he said. "Why were there rumors? Did he date boys? Did he have a boyfriend?"

"Well, I guess mainly it was the way he talked and walked—" And double-crap! I just made things *way* worse.

Cowlings yanked his glasses off. I hope he's not ready to teach me a lesson with rubber hoses. "Tex, if I didn't *know* better, that sounds an awful lot like stereotyping."

My shoulders collapsed. I'm not homophobic, but everything I say is coming out damning. "I know it does and I apologize. I'm really just repeating what everyone else said and thought. He was awfully…flamboyant."

"Not all gay men are flamboyant or effeminate. That's an unfortunate stereotype perpetuated by years of ignorant people—"

"Oh, I get it, Detective. I mean I would never have

thought you're…um…"

Cowlings raised his eyebrows to heights heretofore unseen, almost daring me to finish my statement. Time to just shut up now. Finally, he let me off the hook. "I don't have time to debate this with you now."

"I wasn't trying to debate—"

"Why are you making such a deal about whether the Sturgess boy was gay or not?"

"You asked me what I knew about Calvin. I knew he was gay."

"No, you conjectured he was gay by listening to rumors." He slipped his glasses back on. "Tex, you have good…let's call them 'instincts.' Do you think this kid may've been targeted because he was gay?" He leaned in closer, carefully scrutinizing my reaction.

"I don't know. Maybe?" A distinct possibility, especially factoring in how Brittany'd been bullied and harassed into taking her own life. Yet I had no proof—and I didn't feel right in outing Brittany since she took her secret to the grave with her. But now? Who knows what the truth really is?

"If that's the case, why would this Reaper target you?"

Therein lay the million-dollar question. To which I don't even have a five-cent answer. "I can't figure that out."

"Maybe they're unrelated," he said thoughtfully. "It just seems to me you're always around when corpses pile up at your high school. And you've been around a *lot* of corpses in the last three years. Why is that, Tex?"

I squirmed in my seat. "Just unlucky, I guess?" I flashed a wan smile only to have it rebuffed by

Cowling's frown. "Detective, there *is* something…"

"Yes?" He flipped his notepad open again, preparing to spring into scrawling action.

"There's this group, a church group. They're called the Young American Christians, and I think they take a pretty anti-gay stance."

"Go on."

"Now, I just suspect this. But I know of one member who is *definitely* anti-gay. He thinks God has predestined homosexuals to Hell." I thought about naming Parker but decided against it. I had no proof of any foul play. And he is, I guess, if not exactly a friend, a part-time casual acquaintance. But he's also a world-class jerk. Ah, the hell with it. "You might want to look into Parker Pennett."

"Friend of yours?" Great, now he thinks I'm a homophobe who runs with other homophobes.

"Let's just call him more of a guy whom I have to deal with."

"Okay, fine." He snapped his book shut. "Is there anything else you're not telling me? It's not that I don't trust you, but you've withheld information from me before." He smiled. "Okay, so I *don't* trust you."

"Uh, no, nothing at all." Well, yes, actually there is.

"Uh-huh." I couldn't tell whether it was a declaration of belief or massive distrust. I leaned toward the latter.

"But…there's also the Clarendon Baptist Church," I said as an afterthought.

His lips tightened. "Yeah, I'm familiar with them. They've been nothing but a pain in my ass since they arrived in Kansas City. What about 'em?"

"Well, they're definitely anti-gay. Maybe they sent one of their congregation members to Clearwell to hassle gay kids or something."

"Tex, nothing would make me happier than to get something on this so-called church. But so far, they've abided by the laws. Such as they are. I find it highly unlikely they're involved in the Sturgess boy's death. Sadly so." He stood up and I followed his cue.

"Detective, I know it goes against the rules and everything, but if you find anything…weird in Calvin's belongings, would you let me know?" I thought of Brittany's mysterious, threatening letters.

He stopped and turned back. "'Weird,' Tex? Define 'weird.'"

"I don't know. I'm just spit-ballin' here. But maybe, with my knowledge of the…crap that goes on at Clearwell, I can help you make sense of it. Um, if anything weird turns up, that is."

"I'll take that into consideration. By the way, how are you and Olivia doing?"

"How'd you know we were a couple again?"

Cowlings jammed his hands into his pockets and hitched his shoulders up, holding them there for emphasis. "Oh, I don't know, Tex. I like to keep tabs on people who interest me."

"Well, I guess I'm glad somebody thinks I'm interesting."

"I didn't say I found you 'interesting,'" said Cowlings, master of the proper usage of the English language. "I said you *interest* me."

"Oh. Um, yeah. Anyway…we're doing great." I grinned, even though my mouth muscles wanted to go in the opposite direction.

"And I see you're still friends with that old woman…Mickey, is it?"

"Um, yeah, I help her around the house and the yard with stuff." Sweat drenched my back and not from the heat.

"Huh. Now *that* I find 'interesting.'" He let his ominous comment ferment my mind and uncomfortably soak into my paranoia. After enjoying my discomfort for a moment, he suddenly switched courses. "Okay, time to go talk to your friend, Mr. Hastings."

"Yeah, have fun with that."

"Then I need to look in on your security guard. See if he scoped anything else out on camera. I'll be in touch. And you call me…" He tapped my chest three times. "This time, you *call* me if you find out anything else."

"Okay. Still have your card in my wallet." I tapped my bottom for an unnecessary and ultimately embarrassing visual cue. "Bye, Detective." I called out after him, hoping to leave on a less adversarial note.

He stuck his hand in the air once, his gaze glued to the ground, deep in thought.

I checked on Alf before I finally left the murderous halls of Clearwell High. Shaken, but not stirred, Alf's the James Bond of the high school security set. I left him diligently scanning computer monitors, his determined security face back in place.

It'd been nearly an hour-and-a-half since I told Olivia to wait for me, and she would undoubtedly be freaking out. I found her lying on top of the Bucket's hood, her back propped up against the windshield.

"Tex, where you been?" she yelled, whipping off her sunglasses.

I crawled onto the Bucket's hood next to her. "Another year at Clearwell High, another murderer roaming the hallways." I smiled but felt no mirth.

"Good Gawd! What in *hell* is going on this time?"

"I wish I knew, O'. The only thing I know for sure is…well, nothing. I asked Alf if the security cameras picked up the Reaper after he left the bathroom."

"What'd he say?"

"Nothing helpful. The killer ran out the gym door and into the field. No cameras outside. But I bet the killer's the same person who drove Brittany to suicide."

Olivia sat up straight and faced me. "Why do you think that?"

"No proof. It just fits with the warnings I got from Brittany and Max. Brittany told me to stop him before he did it again. I think he just did do it again. And the one thing Brittany and Calvin had in common? They were both gay. Or maybe just confused or curious, in Brittany's case."

"What are you…*we* going to do, Tex?"

"Well, O', if you're game, I think it's time we found religion."

## Chapter Eight

As I waited for Mickey to unlock her door—she can whip up a spell at the drop of a hat but still can't master the locks on her door—I admired her thriving garden. Three strange plants I hadn't noticed before stood straight and tall, reaching for the sky. With their bulbous leafy heads, long thin necks, and arm-like stalks, they resembled a family of Dr. Seuss creatures. I had no idea what they were, but with Mickey's green thumb—and I suspect a little bit of witchcraft aid—surely the neighborhood envied her garden.

Finally, with some choice expletives, Mickey managed to unlatch her door. "Don't just stand there like a Bible salesman, kid. Get in here."

"Um, okay." It wasn't like I was dawdling on her front porch but whatever.

"Did you bring your mother's ring?"

I fished it out of my pocket and handed it to her. "Yep, here it is."

"Good. Good." She rolled it between two fingers, held it up toward the kitchen light, and licked her lips like she did over fried chicken. "And you're sure it fits?"

"Yeah. It's tight, but I can wear it."

"And it's amber. Good gemstone, kid." She pointed toward the table, indicating I should sit. "Taken from the blood of life itself."

And here I thought it was just a woman's ring. "Mickey, why the urgency for protection? Is it Spencer? Or Max's warning? Or is there something else going on?"

"It's like I told you…" She hopped onto her kick-stool, reaching for a cabinet. "I just got a feeling."

"Spencer threatened me the other day."

Mickey clanged some bowls onto the countertop and spun on her heels. "Did you see him? Did he visit you?"

"Well, sorta." I told her how he'd hacked into my computer and what he'd said. Mickey seemed alternately baffled by the existence of a webcam and horrified at Spencer's promised retaliation.

"I see." Looking out the kitchen window, she drew her fingers across her chin. "Well, I think we better set you up with a few more spells as well. Just in case."

"Just in case. So, you think Spencer's threats are serious?" Mickey poured salt into a cereal bowl and filled another with water. She placed these in front of me and brought over two more empty bowls.

"I still have my doubts as to his abilities. But if what the girls say is true about him, you can't be too careful." Mickey set a red votive candle in one of the bowls, incense in the fourth bowl, and lit them.

"Yeah, I guess not."

She pushed an aged piece of parchment paper across the table and sat down. "Read this and touch the ring to each of the bowls."

"I consecrate thee by earth, air, fire, and water," I read, while chinking the ring against each bowl.

Mickey bounced up and returned with a larger bowl. "You got any cologne, kid?"

"Ah, no."

She tut-tutted me and grabbed a bottle from the countertop. "Guess we'll have to use my going-out stuff, then." She poured the perfume into the bowl and set fire to it. Between the overwhelming smell of incense and burning perfume, my eyes watered. "Now, turn the ring slowly over the flame and read this…" She tapped the paper.

"I dedicate and consecrate this ring to be a ring of Witchery unto me with the powers of the Goddesses three, the Lady of all Witchery, as my word so mote it be." As the flame licked at my fingertips, I let out a yip.

"Okay, now pass the ring over each of the other bowls three times," she ordered. When I finished, she snatched the ring out of my hand and wrapped it in red tissue. "Now for the most important part, be sure to place the ring outside somewhere where the moonlight will shine on it tonight. Don't forget that part."

"Moonlight, got it. So…this will protect me from spells?"

"Well, you've gotta wear it." *Great.* I wonder how much grief I'll get at school for wearing a woman's ring. "It won't work for *all* spells. If you're close to a powerful witch who's put a spell on you, the power of the ring's diminished. But it's a start. Now, let's teach you some proactive spells."

Several hours later, I felt adequately prepared to confront Spencer on "witch-grounds" if necessary. But I wanted to try a different approach with Spencer first. "Um, Mickey? Do you know where Spencer lives?"

Mickey drew back her hand, and I knew what came next. *Thump!*

"Ow! What was *that* for?" I need to start wearing a

ball cap when at Mickey's. Any extra padding could only help my poor dope-slapped head.

"If I was you, I wouldn't provoke Spencer. Why would you want to go looking for trouble? It's not like you don't have enough following you around as it is."

"It's not… I guess I thought…if I could just talk to him, maybe we could start over. Come to an understanding…or whatever…"

Mickey roared with laughter, finishing with a loud, phlegmy cough. "That's really something, kid. You think you're gonna go over there and make friends? You *really* think ol' Spencer is just going to let you in and you kids can play your damn video games or something?"

"Well, yeah…kinda." I massaged the back of my head, thinking it wasn't too bad of a plan.

"Well, think again. It's a bad idea, and I'm not tellin' you his address."

"Okay, fine, whatever." I sighed. "It was just a thought."

"A really *dumb* thought. Now get it out of your head."

"Okay." But you know me.

****

On top of our roof, I worked at cleaning out the gutters. Instead of climbing up and down and moving the cumbersome ladder, I sat on the roof plucking out handfuls of leaves. It's probably not the safest method, but experience taught me it's the quickest option.

Earlier, I had tracked down Spencer Pritchett's address. It hadn't been hard. First I found him online, where he had a ridiculously gothed-up site, complete with a looming photo of him in black garb and makeup.

A self-proclaimed "Witch Extraordinaire," he offered his services to people for a price. From there, I found out he lived in Overland Park—just ten minutes or so from Clearwell—and cross-referenced that with the Pritchett addresses I found online. As soon as the dreaded gutter cleaning chore finished, I'd pay him a visit.

It might be nice to talk to a fellow "guy witch" and commiserate over the losses of our mothers. We could probably help each other. As long as he wanted to bury the hatchet. Um, not literally, I hope.

I sat, dangling my feet over the edge of the roof. Lying back, I closed my eyes, the sun's warmth caressing my face.

Darkness blotted out the brightness like a sudden solar eclipse. From above me, a voice said, "Hey, Tex. The bitch is *back!*"

Freaking out, I jumped to my knees and twisted around, my momentum carrying me back. First one foot, then the other slipped over the edge. As I fell, Elspeth Chambers grinned at me, decked out in full black leather regalia. "*Gah!*" My fingers scrabbled at the edge of the roof, desperately attempting to latch onto something, anything. Elspeth grabbed my wrist and tugged, falling backward onto her bottom, enough to slow down my descent. I managed to hook one leg up over the gutter. Elspeth continued to pull as I clawed my way to safety. I lay down on the roof, shaking and winded. You know, for a teenager, I sure do marvel a *lot* over how wonderful it is to be alive.

Giggling, Elspeth sat next to me. "You should be more careful."

I sat up and glared at her. "Really, Elspeth? *Really?*

And maybe *you* should learn how to—oh, I don't know—ring a doorbell or something!"

"Where's the excitement in that?" she said, a twinkle in her eye. "Besides, I saw your ladder, and it looked fun—"

"Oh, yeah. That was really '*fun.*' Anyway, except for your love of terrifying entrances, it's really good to see you again. I was worried about you."

Elspeth's tall, black faux-Mohawk stood solid in the breeze. To passersby, she probably resembled a very strange, punked-out weathervane. "That's sweet." She reached over, grabbed my ears, and pulled my face toward hers. She kissed me, her lips playfully exploring mine. I gently pushed her away. Just maybe not as soon as I should have.

"Um, I can't do this, Elspeth." The blood rushed to my cheeks out of embarrassment, shame, and more than a little excitement.

"Oh, lighten up. I know you're with Olivia again. The kiss is just a hello from an old friend."

It certainly didn't feel like a "friendship" kiss. "Well, still…"

She leaned back, crossed her ankles, and stretched out on the roof. "Besides, I've gotta get my kicks where I can. It's not easy being dead and all. Anyway, it's better than kissing Donovan Goode."

"You don't like Donovan?" It totally mystified me how anyone could *not* like Donovan.

"*Hell,* no." Her pale blue eyes widened. "It's like kissing cold salmon…wrapped in plastic."

I tried to imagine that particular sensation. "I dunno. He seems like a pretty good guy—"

"Oh, I know, everyone *loves* Donovan Goode. Not

me. He's just so…sanitized and boring."

"Um, can you feel what Elizabeth experiences?" I always wondered about that but never got around to asking Elspeth or Elizabeth. Well, I never would ask Elizabeth something like that.

"Sometimes." She wiggled her entwined feet. "But after Elizabeth's first kiss with him, I had to check out. Ew."

"Huh. Does, um, Elizabeth…can *she* feel what you do?"

"No. I don't allow that."

"Imagine that. Anyway…where've you been? I mean, what have you been doing?"

One corner of her mouth curled up. "You know I can't tell you that."

"Is there *anything* you can tell me?"

"Let's just say…I've been away on 'vacation.'"

"And now you're back." She nodded. "Which probably means trouble's on the horizon." I fell back on my elbows, anchoring in, waiting for the latest cloudburst of bad news.

"You know the drill, Tex. But you're hip-deep in trouble already anyway."

"Yeah, I guess I am. Do you know about any of this…stuff that's been happening lately?"

"I don't know any more than you do right now. But I've been sent back to help you…I think. There's a retreat coming up for the Young American Christians. I think you're supposed to go."

"A 'retreat'?"

"It's some sort of stupid camping weekend. The members are supposed to build, I dunno, bonds and beliefs and junk."

"Yeah, sounds like fun."

Elspeth laughed. "No one ever said this was going to be fun." She turned serious, at least as serious as I've ever seen her. "I can't believe Elizabeth is caught up in this YAC nonsense."

The irony of her statement gob-smacked me like one of Mickey's head slaps. It seemed odd Elspeth belittled spiritual beliefs when she obviously has first-hand experience with...*something.* "Elspeth..." She raised her black-painted eyebrows. "...do *you* believe in God?"

She cocked her head, batted her eyes, and grinned. "My lips are sealed. What I can tell you is there's something not quite right about these guys." When she waved her hand, her bracelets clanked together. "It looks to me like they're somehow involved with the death of two of your peers. From what little I've seen— from what little I could *stomach*—they almost seem to be brainwashing some of these kids. So far, Elizabeth seems to be immune to it. I think she just sees it as a strategic group to add to her résumé." She shook her head in disgust. "Anyway, what happened to that cheerleader chick really pisses me off. I want to help you take these bastards down."

"Yeah, I know what you mean. But do you have proof they're involved in the deaths?"

"No, not really. But it sure as hell seems that way."

"But...if there's just one kid responsible for the deaths of Brittany and Calvin, I don't really think we can put it all at the feet of YAC."

"Maybe, maybe not. But how do you think this 'kid' got that way in the first place? I wish I had the answers, but—let's call them 'The Powers That Be'—

154

they play fast and loose with the information they give me."

"Yeah. I kinda get that a lot, too."

"You get used to it," she replied. "Anyway, be careful, Tex."

"Richard?" called out a voice from below. I peered over the roof to see Mr. Cavanaugh, the resident nosy neighbor, with one hand on the side of our house. "Does your father know you and your 'little friend' are playing on the roof?" He smiled like he'd caught me red-handed at deviltry.

"Yes, Mr. Cavanaugh. I'm cleaning out the gutters."

"Well, it certainly doesn't look that way to me."

Elspeth leaned over and shot him an extraordinarily sexy grin, her eyes alit with mischief. "Would you like to come up and play with me?"

Mr. Cavanaugh sputtered. "Why, I *never*—" He stumbled back through the yard toward his front porch, mumbling to himself.

"Great, Elspeth."

"Oh, he's just an in-your-face busybody. *All* adults are just alike—"

"Yeah, well, like it or not, I have to deal with him. You don't."

"Tex, you're almost like an adult before your time. *Stop* it!" She leaned over and kissed me on the cheek, then smudged her black lipstick off with the palm of her hand. "Can't have Olivia seeing that, now can we?"

I ignored her loaded question. "Are you going to be staying for a while?"

She stood up and smacked the back of her leather skirt. "I'll be around. I'll help you when I can. Now?

Gotta bounce. Later." With a modicum of ease and a slew of recklessness, she literally bounced over the roof like a gymnast on the mats. She spun through the air, dropped onto the ladder, and vanished. Her head popped back into view, prompting a high-pitched yelp from me. "Don't forget to wear your ring," she said and disappeared again.

Okay, well, that's exciting…and scary. Having lost all interest in cleaning the gutters, I carefully made my way toward the ladder, wondering what Elspeth's appearance truly foretold.

\*\*\*\*

A ramshackle, one-story, yellow domicile located in the oldest section of Overland Park, Kansas, Spencer Pritchett's house needed some TLC. The blue shutters buckled at the hinges, in dire need of repair. Paint peeled off the sides of the house, the gutters hanging loose like faulty fake eyelashes. For all of Spencer's ballyhooed witchcraft powers, he obviously didn't apply the "craft" to his lawn. While surrounding neighbors yards appeared spring-green and blossoming, Spencer's lawn looked winter-ravaged. Barren for the most part, the yard looked more like a field of dirt sprinkled with patches of brown and yellow grass. Crumbling bricks encircled what might have once been a garden around the house but had now lapsed into a sad repository for fallen dead leaves.

I walked past a rusty pickup truck in the driveway and braved myself for my impending encounter. When I knocked on the door, a far-away dog responded with a mournful howl.

"Yes?" The man wore a stained wife-beater T-shirt and shorts. Long gray socks were pulled up nearly to his knees, his slippers falling apart. He weathered a beyond haggard face, ruddy in the nose, with wrinkles framing his eyes. Spencer had inherited his father's frown. "What do you want?"

"Uh, hi, Mr. Pritchett?"

"That's right." He remained disinterested and immobile, a battered statue.

"Hi, my name is Richard McKenna." He stepped back, studied my proffered hand and ignored it.

"So, what do you want?"

"Um, is your son...Spencer home?"

Without saying a word, he pushed the door open wider and jerked his chin. He mumbled "down the hallway" and slouched away. Personality obviously runs abundant in the Pritchett family.

Walking down the hallway, I glanced at the portraits hanging on the wall. Covered in dust, most of the photos were of Spencer. He looked much younger, less angry, like any typical suburban child. The last photo must have been of Spencer's mother, several sad finger trails drawn through the dust.

Loud music thrummed and shimmied through my body. The noise grew louder as I approached the last door in the hallway. My heels practically throbbed through my sneakers.

Yellowing, hand-drawn signs reading, KEEP OUT, THIS MEANS YOU! and SPENCER'S LAIR adorned the door. Spencer obviously hadn't upgraded his signs in a while, and they hardly provided a warm welcome mat. Low, monotonous vocals, accompanied by a sitar, sounded from within the room. I rapped on the door and took in a deep breath.

"I'm busy."

Fighting the urge to run, I poked my head inside. "Hey, Spencer."

Wearing a black robe, Spencer sat in front of the pentagram sheet I saw on his video message to me. Papers, books, and half-melted candles spilled over the top of his messy desk. Numerous wires poured out of his computer and onto the floor. Electronic components covered every inch of floor space within his immediate proximity. Handmade shelves lined the wall, threatening to buckle under the weight of witchcraft and magic books. Music pumped out of a small portable stereo behind him. Moth-eaten shades were drawn tight, the only light in the room emanating from his computer screen.

He jumped up, sending his chair into the wall. "What are *you* doing here?" His face tightened in anger, his teeth clenched.

I raised my hands as a sign of peace. "Ah, hi, sorry to bother you. I just thought we could talk. I wanted to apologize—"

"Too *late* for apologies. If you know what's good for you, you'll leave right *now*."

"Spencer, look, we got off on the wrong foot. I really am sorry about that."

He made a futile effort to rush out from behind his desk but his barrage of electronics waylaid him. After shifting things, he finally unburied himself to stand in front of me. "I have absolutely *nothing* to say to you."

"I know about your mother."

A hiccup erupted from his mouth. "What…do you know about my mother?"

"I know she, ah, died in a car accident." His hands rose in the air as if summoning something dark. I

158

quickly added, "My mother died in a car accident, too."

"What are you talking about?"

"We have a lot in common." I flashed a sympathetic smile. "Both of our mothers died...tragically, unfairly, in car accidents in the last couple of years. I know what you're going through."

For a moment, it seemed like I'd reached him. His lips quivered, and his eyes brimmed with tears. Sensations I'm too damned familiar with. He turned away, dabbing at his eyes with his sleeves. When he faced me again, he'd corralled in his emotions. No more Mr. Sensitive. "You don't get to talk about my mother," he said calmly. He pointed toward the door. "Get out...*now*."

A pounding at his door ripped through the room. "Spencer, what the *hell* is going on in there?"

"Dad, this kid's saying bad things about *Mom*."

"No! That's not true—"

The door burst open. Spencer's father grabbed the back of my neck, his strong fingers pressing into my flesh. "I *knew* you were trouble. You're leaving *now*!" He shook me with the ease of a can of shaving cream.

Spencer smirked. "Get him out of here, Dad! You'll be...*feeling* me shortly, 'Tex.'"

His father shoved me into the door, the impact breaking his grasp. I reached for the doorknob as his iron claw grabbed my neck again.

"Okay, okay!" I waved my hands in defeat. "I'm leaving."

Mr. Pritchett continued to prod me down the hallway, snapping at me with indecipherable grunts and curses. Wrenching the front door open, he pushed me into the yard. I stumbled, tripped, and fell into the dead garden. Mr. Pritchett rushed toward me. I clambered to my feet and ran toward the Bucket, car keys poised and ready to get the hell outta there.

"And *don't come back*!" Spencer stood behind his father, grinning, his pale face practically glowing from within the shadows of the house.

Well, *that* could've gone better. I really need to give up my goodwill missions.

Spencer's final words bothered me. What did he mean I would "*feel*" him soon? I had no idea, but I didn't like the sound of it.

Chapter Nine

"Tex."

I gripped my cell phone tight when I heard Detective Cowling's voice. "Hey, Detective. What can I do for you?" Staring out of my bedroom window into the encroaching dusk, I felt vulnerable. Jumpy, too. I thought I saw a small figure darting around where I'd placed my mother's ring in the backyard. Just a cat. They do take a keen interest in me, after all.

"The other day," Cowlings said, "you wanted to know if I found anything weird regarding the Sturgess boy's death—"

"Oh, um, yeah. Did you find anything...weird?"

An insufferably long silence. "I don't know if this constitutes 'weird'...but, we cleaned out the boy's locker today. I found a note..."

"A note..."

"That's right." His words were terse, impatient. Possibly expectant? "Do you happen to know anything about this note?"

I looked at the three notes on my desk I'd appropriated from Brittany's belongings. Should I tell Cowlings? "Um, were they handwritten? On yellow stationery?"

Another nerve-wracking blast of quiet. "I'm coming right over, Tex. We need to talk." He hung up without so much as a goodbye.

I barreled downstairs into the kitchen where Dad and Ruth busied themselves at the stovetop.

"Hey, um, what smells so good?" It did *not* smell good. A horribly offensive odor drifted out of the pot Dad stirred, bubbles belching up from the paste-like mix.

Humming merrily, Ruth rolled out dough with a pin on the countertop. "Potato and liver pie." Once Ruth turned back to torturing the dough, Dad shook his head and grimaced. The things we do for love. "It should be ready in about thirty minutes, Tex. Hope you're hungry."

"Oh, wow, sounds great. But, someone's coming over soon. Won't have time, I guess." I turned to leave, a hasty exit the best course for several reasons.

"Who's coming over?" asked Dad.

"Um, Detective Cowlings." I waited for the inevitable Twenty Questions game.

Dad gripped his chair's wheels and rolled toward me. "What's this all about? Are you in trouble?" His new mantra. Not that it's totally unwarranted, I suppose. A visit from a homicide detective doesn't sound like a slumber party.

"No, no, Dad, I'm not in trouble. It's just...well, you know that kid who was found bleeding in the bathroom yesterday?"

He took his glasses off, and wiped them. "Uh-huh. The Sturgess boy, I believe it was. What does it have to do with you?" He replaced his glasses, the better to glare at me with.

As I walked away, Dad rolled fast to keep up with me. "Nothing, really."

"Tex, you and I both know Detective Cowlings

162

isn't coming out here for nothing."

"Okay, fine." I took in a deep breath and dropped onto the sofa. "I guess Detective Cowlings found a note Calvin had." The map-like stress lines on his forehead deepened. "I think I know about some similar notes…sent to Brittany Gerlach."

"I don't understand—"

"Neither do I."

"What do the notes say? What's the connection to the Sturgess boy?"

"Dad! Gah! I don't *know!* Maybe Detective Cowlings can figure it out."

"Yes, well, *maybe* I'd better sit in on this 'meeting'—"

"That's not necessary—"

"Son, if this excuse is good enough for you to get out of eating potato and liver pie, then maybe it'll be good enough for me." He crossed his fingers, and we shared a laugh. "Honestly, do you smell that?" He hitched a thumb back toward the kitchen where Ruth warbled like a canary.

"Dad…how much longer is Ruth going to experiment on us?" I lowered my voice. "I miss our meals. We were getting pretty good there for a while."

He patted my shoulder. "Yeah, I miss them, too. I'm sure she'll run out of recipes soon." He widened his eyes as if suddenly frightened. "She *has* to."

"I know, right?"

"Say, have you heard back from any of the colleges?" Time for levity's over!

"No, I haven't."

"Have you given any more thought to your post high school plans? Time's getting short now. School will be out soon."

"I know. The more I think about it…maybe a year…or two at Clearwell JuCo until I make up my mind."

"Tex, you know I just want the best for you. If you're staying around because of me…or Olivia—"

"*Dad!* I know, I know. It's just…I've got a lot on my mind right now—"

"Like this business with Detective Cowlings?" he sighed and slumped back in his wheelchair. "Look, I'm *really* trying to be patient here—"

"I know, I appreciate it."

A hush fell over the room until Dad finally broke the tension. "Tex, how do you know about these notes? Of Brittany Gerlach's?"

A knock at the door saved me from answering.

As soon as I opened the door, Detective Cowlings strode in without waiting for an invite. "Can we talk in here?" He inclined his head toward the living room. "Hello, Mr. McKenna. It's nice to see you again."

Dad joined us. "Detective, if it's all the same to you, I'd like to be present during your chat with my son."

Cowlings frowned, rubbed his neck, but said nothing.

"Okay, well, I demand to sit in," said Dad. "He's still a minor. And he's my son."

"Tex, will your father's presence keep you from answering me honestly?"

"Uh, no, I don't think so."

"You don't *think* so?"

"No. I'll answer honestly."

"Fine." Cowlings sat on the edge of a chair.

Looked like it'd been a long day for him. His usually impeccable suit appeared wrinkled, and his eyes betrayed sleeplessness. "Tell me about these notes."

I handed them to him. He looked the sheets over, touching only the edges, and placed them delicately onto the table next to him. I sat down on the sofa across from him, Dad hovering next to me.

"*Where* did you get these?" Cowlings flipped open his notebook.

"Um, they were in Brittany Gerlach's bedroom. In her stuff." Dad leaned forward, hanging on every word. "I, ah, might've taken 'em…at her wake."

Cowlings said, "You *took* them?"

Dad cast me a disappointed look.

"Yes."

"Why?"

I scratched my head, buying time to work out a decent reply. "I don't know. I just sort of found them, I guess. You gotta understand, everyone—*everyone*'s— freaked out about Brittany's suicide. I'm just trying to make sense of it. To *understand* it. I don't know…"

Cowlings uttered a short guffaw. Dad reloaded his formidable eye-rockets and aimed them at Cowlings. "Okay, where did you find them? Exactly?"

"In her nightstand…next to her bed." Hoping to throw the spotlight off my questionable behavior, I asked, "Detective, did you find a similar note? To Calvin?"

"This goes without saying… Anything I tell you within these walls *stays* here. Is that understood?" We both dutifully nodded. "We cleaned out the Sturgess boy's locker today, and yes, there was a note…on the same yellow stationery, from the looks of it. It said, '*I know what you are. God despises homosexuals.'* The same content as your letters, Tex." He tapped the table next to him.

"They're not *my* letters."

Cowlings ignored the clarification. "What else can you tell me? About the letters?"

"Nothing. Wait! There's a diary you might want to look at—"

"Tex?" Cowlings nearly sang my name as if trying to connect with a small child. "Did you happen to 'take' that as well?"

"No! No, um, it's Brittany's diary. On her computer. She wrote someone was harassing her…" I cleared my throat. "…about confused…sexual feelings she was having for another girl—"

"Brittany Gerlach? The *cheerleader*?" I thought Dad might just pass out, so thoroughly had I just rocked his world.

"Yes, well…" said Cowlings. I hope Dad's not about to be lambasted about the dangers of stereotyping homosexuals. "How was she being harassed?"

"She wrote there was someone she met in the Young American Christians and she'd been talking to him about her feelings." Cowlings' eyebrows rose as he scribbled an entry in his book. "She didn't mention him by name…but it was definitely a guy. She also said she'd been getting phone calls and notes…and she just *knew* it was him. Whoever that might be—"

"Definitely a male," repeated Cowlings. "And you're sure she said he was a member of the Young American Christians?"

"Yeah. But I'm not sure if it's the same guy who sent the notes…or killed Calvin."

"Yes, Tex, I'm quite aware of what the difference is between suppositions and facts." He sighed and slapped his notebook several times against his thigh. "*Dammit.*"

"What's the matter, Detective?" asked Dad.

"It looks like I might have a hate crime on my hands. I *loathe* hate crimes." I wondered if that meant there are certain crimes he *did* like.

For once it thrilled me to see Ruth flit into the room, our disrupting angel from the Kitchens of Hell. "Oh, hello there, Detective Cowlings," she said as if welcoming an old friend. "You're just in time for dinner. Would you like me to prepare you a dish?"

He blinked his eyes rapidly as if weighing the secretly toxic offer. Dad and I tried to discreetly attract his attention without Ruth noticing. Too late. The newbie fish got hooked. "Why, I just realized I haven't eaten since this morning. Thank you very much, Miss Crandall. It's very kind of you." Ruth, appearing very excited to have another victim, leaped away like an evil palate-destroying fairy. Cowlings, smiling for the first time since his arrival, turned toward us and noticed our horrified expressions. "What's the matter?"

I snuck a fleeting glimpse at Dad, barely able to hold it together. "Um, never mind." I said.

Cowlings dismissed us with an exasperated sigh. "Tex, what else can you tell me?"

"Nothing. *Really.*"

"And what about this, ah, Reaper who attacked you?"

Dad gave me a double-take. "Hold on... What's this all about?"

I quickly filled Dad in on what had happened,

downplaying how serious it could've been. Cowlings watched with an amused expression. Oh, you're going to get yours soon, detective.

"Mercy," exclaimed Dad, wagging his head back and forth. His eyes were clamped shut as if trying to ward off pain. "Tex, why do these things happen to you?"

Cowlings nibbled on the end of his pen, working his big smile around it. "I've often wondered that myself, Mr. McKenna. Tex, what do you have in common with the Gerlach girl and the Sturgess boy?"

"Not much, really, as far as I can tell." Dad's audible intake of breath couldn't be missed. I think he halfway anticipated *my* confession about confused sexuality.

"Uh-huh," said Cowlings.

Ruth returned, carrying a steaming plate of grotesqueries. Cowlings politely accepted the vile offering. "Thank you, very much, Miss Crandall. This looks wonderful."

Ruth smiled and sang, "I'm sure you'll *love* it*."* She triumphantly paraded out of the room, head held high.

Cowlings pushed at the food with a fork, staring at it quizzically. "Hope you don't mind, gentlemen." He dug into Ruth's undead creation.

"No, we don't mind." Dad nudged me when he caught me smiling.

"So, Tex, if there's no connection between you and the two dead students...do you think your attacker is the same person...who...um..." Cowlings slowly chewed his first bite, working it around his cheek, unsure where to put it, no doubt. His eyes widened as perspiration broke out across his scalp. "The same person…who…um…sent the notes? And for the love of *God,* what *is* this?" He winced as the lump slowly crawled down his throat. Dropping the plate on the table, his usually unflappable demeanor set into a near panic. *"Seriously,"* he lowered his voice, "what *is* that?"

With a straight face, Dad managed. "Detective, *that* is potato and liver pie."

I felt like adding, *welcome to my nightmare.*

*"Why?"* Cowlings wiped his mouth with his napkin. He shuddered at the memory of the culinary abomination. "Anyway, if it's the same perpetrator, there has to be a connection between the three of you. I really need your help in finding out what that is." He aimed a glance at his dinner plate as if afraid it may come crawling back in retribution for his having abandoned it.

"Have you spoken to Parker Pennett?" I asked.

Dad interjected. "Your *friend?"*

I shrugged. "More like 'pseudo-friend.'"

"Yes, I spoke to him and his parents," said Cowlings. "The Sturgess boy's attacker couldn't have been him. His parents supplied him with an alibi, said he was home five minutes after school and studying." He pitched his shoulders up and dropped them. "They're parents, though. I've known them to lie for their kids before." He shifted his eyes between us. "It's not what you'd call ironclad, but right now, I have no reason to believe otherwise."

Oddly, I felt mild disappointment. For once, I thought I knew who the killer is. And for once, I wouldn't feel sucker-punched by that resolution. Better than the killer being someone who I actually like. "Well, I bet the YAC's a good place to start looking. Um, maybe?"

"Tex, *I'll* figure out where to take the investigation next." He slapped his legs and abruptly stood up. "Okay. I've taken enough of your time tonight. You call me if you, ah, *hear* anything," he said while sliding the notes into his jacket pocket.

"I will. Promise." I held two fingers up.

"Yes, well…" He took one last forlorn look at the plate on the desk. "Mr. McKenna, would you please tell Miss Crandall…tell her…." He waved his hand, sweeping the room. "Hell, I don't know, make something up."

Dad smiled at him. Both now members of the Brotherhood of Ruth Crandall Concoction Survivors. From the fires of Hell such strong bonds are made.

Before I closed the door on Cowlings, he said, "Tex, you do know if you ever want to talk to me— about *anything* else…you can trust me? Right?" I nodded. "Right?" he repeated, waiting for a verbal confirmation.

"Yep, thanks."

"Be careful," he called back from the sidewalk. "It's a dangerous world out there."

Don't I know it? In fact, there are several dangerous worlds out there.

****

I awoke in the middle of the night with twenty cats on my chest. At least that's what it felt like. I sprang up, struggling to take in a deep breath. My chest and throat clamped up, only able to take in small breaths at a time. I couldn't exhale. I moaned and tried to groan. Nothing but the sound of my lips smacking together. I flailed about, pounding at my chest, attempting to dislodge whatever jammed my windpipe. Yet I knew there was nothing there. I just *knew* it.

The full moon's beam flowed in through the venetian blinds like a lighthouse beckoning me to safety. That's when I remembered my mother's ring. I put it in the backyard for the moon's rays to empower it. And I remembered Elspeth's warning to wear the ring.

Chest on fire, I rolled out of bed, still unable to exhale. Sweat drenched my T-shirt, the fabric sticking to my back. Barefoot, I stumbled down the stairwell, deliberately using as little energy as possible, hoping to spin out my limited oxygen. *The backyard! I have to reach the ring*!

As if I had suddenly grown taller, I watched my feet flop about on the kitchen floor, a million miles below. I felt detached from my body, my brain having flown the coop. My vision dimmed, and stars and a dazzling light show became my new reality. Shag carpeting covered my head. Not too uncomfortable, sorta inviting, really. My mind wandered, running—no, strolling in slow motion—away with thoughts having nothing to do with survival. My chest expanded with each new gulp of air. *What happens when a balloon gets too full without any release? It pops*!

Staring down at the doorknob, I thought bed sounded like a better option. I felt tired and sleepy. *Wouldn't it be nice to go back to bed*? I lassoed my runaway brain, finding the idea funny. Shaking my head, I forced my eyes open, a myriad of psychedelic patterns melding together before me. To wake myself up, I jammed my hand hard against the door. The pain sent a jolt up to my brain. I wanted to cry out but couldn't.

The cool night air slapped me in the face, forcing the last breath I could inhale. I fell down the three stairs into the grass. Rolling over, I stared up into the round attentive visage of the moon. *How pretty the moon looks tonight.* Tinted blue with clouds flitting in front of it, the moon wanted to lull me asleep, a celestial babysitter humming a lullaby. *I once had a moon in my bedroom. Part of my solar system mobile. I wonder where it is now? Did Dad throw it away? Or is it in storage? Wonder what else is in storage? A long time ago, I put away my teddy bear, but I'd really like to hold his furry body for comfort. Especially now. What was his name? Rufus? Doofus? Mr. Spoofus? Mr. Spoon? Mr. Moon? The moon. The moonlight. The ring!*

I flipped myself onto my stomach with my last bit of energy. My jaw flapped open and shut, straining for air like a fish out of water. Clawing my way through the grass, my legs lost all feeling. My head pounded. Yet the night sky remained quiet. *So very quiet. Just let me get comfy on my back.*

Random images that might be real—or *not*—played out in front of me. Mr. Spoon, my bear, waved to me from the moon. *What a goon.* I need to close my eyes…*just for a second…just five more minutes, Dad…I promise I'll get up…so tired…*

A warm sensation tickled my face. I opened my eyes. Two cats, their eyes glowing, lapped at my face with their small, sandpaper-like tongues. I squinted at them. Their faces took on human-like expressions. *How funny!* They appeared concerned, but they both agreed that my skin tasted nice. My eyes watered. I felt like sneezing, but couldn't, the agonizing pressure on my chest increasing.

My hand fell on the red tissue-covered ring in the middle of the yard. My fingers, tingling, caressed the paper, attempting to open the package. *So damn tired!* My hands gave out from underneath me as I fell face forward onto the ground. The unexpected blow jerked me awake. I pulled the tissue off and with trembling fingers, slipped the ring onto my pinky.

I rolled onto my back and waited, hoping this would rectify my trauma. *Nothing.* My eyes felt ready to pop out of my head. Like being underwater, I held my breath, too far from the surface to refill my lungs with air. *Game over.* I need to accept it, inhale the water, and give in. I closed my eyes again, ready for sleep—or the water—to sweep me away.

Above me, I heard what sounded like a light ocean tide washing onto a shore. I forced my eyes open and saw a small blue wisp of smoke swirling over me, zigging and zagging. It slowly, yet unwaveringly, filtered into my mouth and nose. I pulled one last Hail Mary and took in a deep breath. Then let it out.

Never before had oxygen felt so sweet. It flooded over me, through me, filling me with sweet, life-sustaining air. I lay in the grass, inhaling and exhaling, assuring myself this wasn't a temporary fluke. My vision cleared; my thoughts became more lucid. I smelled things in the air that I never had before. I even welcomed a series of sneezes, caused by the cats. *The cats! They saved me!*

Testing my voice in the dark of the night, I croaked, "Here…cats…" I released a small hysterical laugh, surprised at hearing my own voice, which mere seconds ago seemed impossible.

"*Cats!*" I repeated, louder. The cats leaped on top of me, and I greeted them with glee, allergies or not. My allergic reactions reinforced I did indeed live again! Life—warts, allergies and all—is *wonderful*. For several long minutes, I continued scratching the cats' heads, stroking their backs, sneezing into the night, giggling like a madman. Once my head finally cleared, I noticed tears streaming down my face. I felt the moisture with my fingertips, marveled at its intricate beauty, tasted the salt.

I quietly set out a saucer of milk for my feline saviors and on weak legs, made my way back to my bedroom. I flipped on the lamp, sat on my bed, and pulled my knees up to my chest. What happened to me? Did I just experience the world's worst asthma attack, compounded by a chunk of steak lodged in my esophagus? But it hadn't been either of those things. I had been attacked, *wit*chcraft-style. And thanks to the intervention of several cats, the warning from Elspeth, and the witch's ring spell, I would live to see another day. *Barely.*

I ran various scenarios through my head, round and round, going nowhere. Sleep remained far at bay. I caressed my mother's ring, almost subconsciously. Then I heard a strange whirring sound.

Looking around the room, I spotted a red light on my computer. My webcam had been activated. Someone was watching me, and I now knew the identity of my attacker.

"I'm still here, Spencer," I said into the light. "Now I guess we *are* at war."

I slammed the computer shut and unplugged it just to be certain. Crawling back into bed, shivering, I waited for the comfort of morning.

Chapter Ten

"Kiddo, someone put a spell on you. A damn strong one, too," said Mickey.

When I woke in the morning, my bedroom mirror reflected someone I didn't recognize. My eyes were bloodshot, dark circles surrounding them. "Yeah, I kinda figured that. But *what* kind of spell was it?"

"Sounds to me like it was a breath-stealing spell." She smacked her lips with certainty. "That blue cloud you saw...that would've been your breath. Some witches think it's your life essence, it being blue and all."

*Wow*. Just *wow*. The fact Spencer can pull off this spell from a distance just made my world ten times scarier. "How'd he do it, Mickey? I mean, I kinda thought you had to be sorta close to the person you put a spell on."

"Tex, you know better than that. We've done spells before where the intended party isn't close. Are you not listening to me, kid?"

"No, I hear you loud and clear."

"He'd need something from you, though. Something of a personal nature or—"

Then I remembered. My altercation with Spencer at the witches' meeting. "He pulled my hair that night! At the meeting, out in the street."

"That'd do it, all right. You're sure it was

Spencer?"

"I'd stake my life on it." Which I guess I pretty much did already. "He hacked into my webcam, and I think I *really* set him off when I—" I stopped before I made a confession best not told.

"When you what?" Thank God, we were on the phone; otherwise, my head would've been ravaged by her stupidity-seeking hand projectile.

"Okay... I know it was dumb, but I went to see Spencer. Tried to talk to him—"

"*Dammit,* Tex!" I had to hold the phone away to tolerate her shrieking. "What did I *tell* you?"

"I know, Mickey, I know! Sorry."

"You just can't help yourself, can you?"

"Guess not."

"So, what came of your little meeting?"

"Nothing good. He wasn't open to talking or even hearing anything I had to say. He had his dad throw me out."

Mickey chuckled. "I could've told you that. That Spencer kid is just an uppity too-big-for-his britches brat, if you ask me."

"Yeah. What can we do?"

Mickey made a ticking sound like a tightly wound Grandfather clock. "Well, obviously you can't talk to him again. And we can't bring in the police. *That* wouldn't go over too well. I can try and talk to some of the girls. See if they can't intervene. But—" She paused.

"But what?"

"I just don't think any of the girls hold any sway over Spencer. Most of 'em think he's the greatest thing since beans and white rice."

I ignored my dislike for beans and white rice—something better left to Ruth's kitchen of iniquity. A chill crawled down my back. "Mickey, if Spencer is such a powerful witch…what *else* is he capable of?" Knowing there's a formidable sociopathic witch gunning for me scared me.

"Who knows? I suppose I underestimated Spencer."

"Ya' *think*?"

"Yes, I do," she replied, my sarcasm totally lost on her.

"Can't you—I don't know—talk to the witches and get his membership revoked or something? You know, for using magic for bad, personal reasons?"

"It's not like we're a fancy club, with rules everyone abides by. I'll see what I can do. Maybe Miss Philpot can talk to him." Mickey sounded less than optimistic, but it was a little bit of hope to cling to.

"Okay, thanks."

"In the meantime, keep wearing the ring. I can't believe you went to bed without it!"

"Mickey, I did what you told me. I put it where the moonlight could reach it."

"Not all night, kid." Well, *that* little tidbit would've been nice to know. "Just be careful. And let me know if anything else happens. And for God's sake, stay away from Spencer."

"Got it." I had no desire to see him ever again. Although that seemed highly unlikely. "Bye, Mickey."

Even though I dreaded it, I couldn't keep postponing what I needed to do next. I called Dickers.

"Hey, Dickers. What's up?"

"Hey, McKenna. What's going on?" He actually

sounded pleased to hear from me, a rarity in my world.

"Not much. A couple of days ago, you said I should come to a Young American Christians' meeting. Is the offer still good?"

The phone clumped and clattered as if he'd dropped it. "Yeah, awesome. We meet every Sunday at three at the Clearwell Rec Center. Room 312."

"Yeah, I know where that is. But, why there?" I guess I imagined them hunkering down in the basement of some church, plotting to save souls.

"Well, we're a non-denominational group," he answered. "We've got Baptists, Methodists...everyone." Everyone as long as you're a Christian. "We can't meet in a church. It might rile up some of the other members if it's not their chosen religion."

"Huh."

"Um, McKenna?"

"Yeah?"

"*Why* do you want to go? I mean, don't get me wrong. I'm cool with your going and everything...but I kind of thought you weren't into it."

"Well, let's just say I'm interested." That's an understatement. "I've sorta come around to not ruling out anything until I have all the facts. I guess. I just want to understand. I mean, a ton of my friends are in YAC, so—"

"Okay, cool. I mean, that's really what we're all about. Just hangin' and talking about God and His word."

"All right. Hey, is it cool if I bring Olivia? If she's available?"

Dickers' enthusiasm screeched to a halt. "Um,

yeah, I guess it'd be okay. It's just…well, she's not going to start yelling and raving at us, right?"

"Dickers, if she can't promise to bite her tongue, then I won't bring her. But, after a, um, chat I had with her last week, I actually think she's going to keep an open mind, too."

"Cool, sounds good. But—"

"What?"

He hesitated before finishing his thought. "I, uh, think it's probably best if…you don't bring Lance or Brandon."

His words bit like a snake in hiding. I'm sure he alluded to Lance and Brandon's alternative lifestyles, and it pissed me off. I expect better from Dickers. But going off on him won't help me infiltrate the YAC. "Why?"

"Don't take this the wrong way or anything…" Like there's a *right* way. "…but their chosen way of life doesn't really fit in with YAC beliefs. You know what I mean." Unfortunately, I did. "Now I don't have a problem with them, and I *personally* think God is more understanding, but, still—"

"Dickers, if you don't agree with the YAC stance on alternative lifestyles, why are you even a member of YAC?"

"Dude, they *totally* changed my life! I mean, really, without them, I probably wouldn't want to become a priest. And I think it's okay sometimes…to disagree." He sounded unsure of himself, almost guilty of defending YAC. Or his own beliefs.

\*\*\*\*

"So. I thought I was the only one who could take your breath away." Olivia grinned at her lame joke.

"Not funny, O'. Definitely *not* cool." I was surprised at her lighthearted take on my ordeal. "I mean, really, I almost died."

The wind blew through the Bucket's window, whipping her hair about as she struggled to tame it. "I know, whatever. Sorry. It just sounds so…freaky!"

"Yeah, I know, right? It was super bizarre and scary as hell."

"So, Mickey's going to help, right? This Spencer kid sounds like a class-A douche." I nodded at her douchiness assessment. "And there's nothing the police can do?"

"Really, O'? I'll just call up Cowlings and report a bad witch putting a breath stealing spell on me? I can see it now…" I lowered my voice, approximating a lofty adult's tone. "…'Okay, Tex, I'll issue a warrant for his arrest. Illegal witch spell.'"

Olivia sputtered before ripping out a loud guffaw. "Really crappy imitation of Cowlings. But just wear your damn witch protection ring. Even if it does look girly." She bit down on her lower lip as she stared at the large gem protruding from my pinky finger.

"Believe me, I'm going to. Never catch me without it." I brandished my hand through the air.

"Are you going to try and do anything to this Spencer guy?" Olivia played with the buttons on her blouse and fidgeted with her skirt. I told her to wear something not too "radical." For her, the nice outfit probably felt like wearing someone else's skin.

"I don't know what I'm going to do. I suppose I could take the fight to him, but I'm not really prepared for that. I'm still new at all this. I just hope that since he knows I'm on to him, maybe he'll chill out—"

"Maybe." Olivia sighed and placed her hand under her chin, her index finger scratching her cheek. "I can't believe we're going to a YAC meeting," she mumbled like a sullen kid forced to go to church.

"Olivia, you said you wanted to help. And with your past regarding religion and everything—"

"Tex! You *don't* have to remind me of what I said and how I feel! I *know* what we're doing is good. I just hate dealing with these stupid, backward-thinking *hypocrites*."

I had doubts about whether I should even involve Olivia in my investigation. But as she's told me on more than one occasion, she's a big girl. Even with all her grousing, she wouldn't have it any other way. "Yeah, you know I'm not a big fan of hypocrites either. But, keep in mind that some of these hypocrites are our friends." She shook her head as if in denial. "You've got to be on your best behavior today. Even if it kills you."

"Humph."

We pulled into the parking lot of the Clearwell Recreation Center. Conceived a dozen years ago by our then mayor, the Center provided a place free of drugs and alcohol, for Clearwell kids to gather. Although the sentiment seemed admirable, the plan flopped miserably. Kids stayed away in droves, and not only because of the uncoolness factor. You couldn't really do anything at the Center. Most of the building consisted of oppressive rooms resembling the school classrooms we spent a seeming majority of our life in. Activities included an indoor tennis court and a walking track—middle-aged and retired businessmen's sports of choice. The Center now largely rented out for seminars and meetings. Most Clearwell adults still resented the Center, seeing it as nothing more than a tax strain on their wallets. The mayor had *not* been re-elected.

Sleep-inducing oldies tunes played out over a speaker as we rode the elevator to the third floor. You know, the kind of music kids like.

"Remember, this is a search-and-discover mission. We're *not* here to take down the religious hypocrites of the world."

"*Okay,* okay, Tex! I get it already." She leaned against the elevator wall and shook her head. "I'll be a good, little girl." I laughed and gave her hand a quick squeeze.

When we entered room 312, Donovan Goode met us immediately, his pearly white teeth exposed in a dazzling smile. Somewhere angels applauded.

"Tex," he said, grabbing my hand within both of his. Like an expert fisherman, he hooked me immediately with his baited charm. "Clark told me you were sitting in on a Young American Christians' meeting." Took me a second to register "Clark" as our "Dickers." "We couldn't be more thrilled to have you." He was so stately, *so* presidential. I'll bet he could create a *much* better recreational center.

"Oh, hi, Donovan." I pressed my lips together in a tight, contained smile, so as not to let my pleasure out. Plus no way could my flawed teeth compete with his expensive dental care. "This is—"

"Olivia Furman! Yes, I know who Olivia is." He grabbed Olivia's hand and shook it gently. Olivia stared at him, obviously torn between distrust and cautious veneration.

"Um, hi." Olivia's grin looked forced at first but

slowly blossomed, Donovan successfully melting even her cynical nature.

"Terrible thing. Just terrible." Concern spread across Donovan's face, his eyebrows arched sadly.

I had no idea what he referred to, but I wanted to hug him. A manly hug. Anytime. "Uh, what's that, Donovan?"

"I understand you're the one who found poor Calvin's body."

"Oh! Well, it wasn't really me. It was Alf Lampbert—"

"Just terrible!" He gripped my shoulder. Hot damn, here comes my hug! "Tex, do the police know who'd do such an awful thing yet? Or why?"

"Ah, not that I'm aware of."

Elizabeth strolled up, shoulders held back. She sized us up, lingering on Olivia's outfit, before finally breaking out a trace of a smile. "Hi, Tex. *Olivia*." She spoke Olivia's name with ice dripping off every syllable.

"Elizabeth," muttered Olivia. Handshakes were *not* exchanged.

"I'm surprised to see you here, Tex. I didn't think this was…your thing." She tossed back her hair to emphasize her point, whatever *that* might be.

"Ah, just here to learn."

"And isn't that what we're all trying to do?" asked Donovan. "Come on, Olivia. I'll show you where the punch and cookies are." He herded her in front of him, keeping up a constant stream of amiable conversation. As he took her to the punch trough, she looked forlornly back at me, like a farm animal being led to the slaughter.

When they were out of earshot, I spoke quietly to Elizabeth. "Elspeth's back."

Elizabeth raised her thin blonde eyebrows. "Duh! She started leaving me notes again."

"Yeah, she visited me, said I was going to need her help again."

"What is it *this* time?"

"I'm not sure. You know how she is. Has she said anything to you?"

She shook her head, her hair an unmoving blonde helmet. "No. She said I was supposed to go to next week's YAC retreat. Like I wasn't going already anyway! And she said to bring her clothes."

"Huh. She said I should go, too."

"Look, Tex, if you find out anything about this latest excursion...Let. Me. Know!" Catching herself with her hands on her hips, she quickly clasped her hands in front of her. Very unladylike, after all.

"I will. So, are you glad she's back?"

Elizabeth let her guard down for a second, an unusual sparkle in her cold, blue eyes. "In certain ways, I think I am. She's sort of like the sister I never had. Sometimes I love her, others...not so much."

"Yeah, I think I get that."

Olivia rushed back toward us, Donovan scurrying to keep up with her. She exhaled loudly and glared at me. I'd pay later for Donovan having led her away. "I've just met some of the most *interesting* people," she said.

I glanced about the room. Under the artificial yellow lighting, everyone appeared jaundiced. There were probably sixty kids milling about, their conversations low and reserved. When an occasional laugh broke through the otherwise somber gathering, those closest to the perpetrators shot them looks of disapproval. Some of the kids displayed glassy-eyed, vacant looks, their movements slow and mannered. Others looked happy, excited about what wonders the newest YAC meeting might hold for them. It didn't feel or sound anything like what you'd expect from a gathering of sixty teenagers. As the Clearwell Recreational Center had transformed into a haven for old people, the YACCERS likewise had transitioned into boring adults, any sense of fun and wild abandon having long left the building.

Allison, Dickers, and Parker walked into the room. Allison rushed over, hugs all around, and said, "I'm *so* glad you guys came." Of course they wanted to know about Calvin Sturgess. I gave them the simplest, shortest version possible.

"That sucks," said Dickers. "But it's really cool you're here." He leaned toward Olivia, arms outstretched in a hugging formation. Olivia silently barred him with an outstretched hand. Parker snickered.

"Can't believe you're here," said Parker, eyeing us skeptically.

"Oh, Parker, leave them alone," said Allison. "Remember, we're about being open to everyone."

Parker pinpointed Olivia with his narrow eyes. "Well, yeah, that's true. I just *hope* their intentions are good, otherwise…it's a waste of everyone's time."

Donovan placed an arm around Parker's shoulders. More than I got. Sigh. "Come on now, Park, you're not being very Christian." Even Parker's cold heart seemed to melt a little as he begrudgingly agreed with Donovan. "It's all about brotherhood."

"*Ahem!*" interjected Elizabeth.

"Oh, my apologies, ladies." Donovan bowed toward the girls with a royal gesture. "It's also about sisterhood." Olivia nodded once, surrendering easily to Donovan's effortless charm. I couldn't believe it. "We can't leave out the fairer sex, after all." Olivia snorted. And Donovan just lost a future voter.

"Ladies and gentlemen!" A strong voice cut through the crowd's conversation. "If you could grace me with a few moments of silence." At the far end of the room, I saw the speaker waving a hand. A tall, striking-looking, middle-aged woman with prematurely gray—nearly silver—hair stood, commanding everyone's attention. Dressed smartly in a woman's suit, her poise nearly as perfect as Elizabeth's, she seemed vaguely familiar. "I would like to welcome everyone to another meeting of the Young American Christians." Cheers erupted. "A lot of you know me. But for those who don't, I'm Sister Augustine. I see a lot of familiar faces." She took a moment to scan us, nodding occasional recognition. "And I couldn't be happier to see some new faces as well. Praise God!" She stretched her arms in the air, raising the roof. *Hollah.* "It's our mission, as you well know, to spread the word of God to those seeking something missing in their lives. If you're one of these poor souls, then you've come to the right place."

Dickers clapped my back like a proud father. Olivia groaned, provoking a few stares from those closest to us.

The woman held her hands up quieting the boisterous crowd. "It fills my heart with God's good grace to see newcomers. It tells me we're doing *something* right! Our membership is growing daily. More and more of you are spreading the word, letting those around you know they're living in a world rife with sin." A few amens were tossed, religious verbal grenades. "It's a wicked world, full of temptation and evil, and the only way for us to rise above it, to accept our rightful place in Heaven—to live an eternal life—is to follow God's words." Her face took on a grim demeanor. "And God's words are *not* hard to find, ladies and gentlemen." She brandished a Bible above her head. "They're all...right...*here!* For anyone to deny the literal *truth* of the Bible...well, I feel sorry for them." She lowered her head solemnly then raised it with a smile. She'd be a good vice president for Donovan in the future.

Yet, something felt a little off about Sister Augustine. She carries herself like an aristocrat, her speaking elegant, her entire manner and appearance refined. It seems like she'd be more at home hob-knobbing with Kings and Queens instead of preaching like a fire and brimstone huckster.

"Do you kids know what you're doing?" she continued. "Do you? You're *saving* souls." She shook her coiled fists high above her head, inciting the audience into a roaring fit. "With your help and the generous donations from you and your parents,"—okay, *that's* what this is about—"we've become a nationwide organization, our numbers *many.* And if we can't change the sinful physical world we live in, by calling out the sinners we all know, we're going to take as many others as we can with us to Heaven."

While the crowd shouted their zealous support, Olivia looked appalled, her mouth ajar. The rest of my friends clapped politely and smiled serenely, basking in the after-glow.

The woman's words came across as strong, and she definitely had a commanding demeanor. Yet the words also seemed to be verging on dangerous; a sense of intimidation hiding behind the face value and somewhat vague and open to interpretation. Almost a call to war. What if these words are misconstrued by someone not so tightly wrapped? A teenage boy, already confused about his place in life? Or did Sister Augustine actually issue orders, subtly, maybe even bordering on brainwashing? From my limited knowledge of cults—mostly gleaned in sociology class—YAC could very well be one.

"Okay, settle down, ladies and gentlemen," she continued, once again quieting the crowd by gesturing with her hands. "All right. Please, let's not forget the weekend retreat coming up next Saturday. If you haven't paid your fees yet, please see one of my aides afterward..." She tilted her head toward an overweight man in a too-tight, green polo shirt and a prim woman in a gray suit standing to her left. "It will be at the Oakdale Resort in Oakdale, Kansas. Carpooling is always a fine idea." Well, at least she wanted to keep it green. "And, people, get out there and recruit! Bring as many newcomers to the retreat as you possibly can. We accept *everyone*." So *not* true, but that didn't stop the kids from applauding again. "It's up to *you*—the future of not only this world, but our *spiritual, heavenly afterlife,* as well." Another volley of amens rose up throughout the congregation. "Now, the donation basket to help fund our important work will be with Mr. Green." I guess Mr. Green wore his green polo shirt to color-coordinate with his name. "Before we break off into our small discussion groups, let us all bow our heads in a moment of silent prayer…"

I bowed my head in compliance with the others. Catching Olivia's eye, I gave her a chin motion to at least pretend to pray. Reluctantly, she obliged.

After the prayer, Elizabeth and Donovan worked the crowd, shaking hands and wandering about, finding a group more worthy of their stature. The rest of us gathered around a table.

"So, who was that?" I asked. "I mean, I know her name's Sister Augustine, but *who* is she? Is she really a nun?"

Allison slapped me on the shoulder and tittered. "Oh, Tex, don't be silly."

"Um, didn't think I was."

"She's not a nun," said Dickers. "We keep personal denominations out of it. She's just going by Sister because we're all about the brotherhood." Seeing Olivia scowl, he quickly added, "And the sisterhood, of course."

"*Brotherhood*," Olivia snorted. "I can tell you of *another* brotherhood from history—"

I kicked at her shin under the table.

Parker rolled his eyes. "Olivia, I *hope* you didn't come here to totally freak out again and make a scene."

I held my breath for a positive outcome. "No, you're right," said Olivia. "I came here to learn about *YAC.*" She pronounced YAC as if she had a hairball lodged in her throat.

Parker, looking vindicated, continued. "Good. Anything you want to know, just ask me."

While Olivia didn't acknowledge Parker's

suggestion, she didn't say anything, probably the best I could hope for.

"So, how did you guys get involved in YAC?" I asked.

"Parker and I got involved through some other kids in our Sunday School class. They said it was really cool and that we should come. It was, and I'm glad I did."

Parker grinned and acknowledged Allie with a firm nod.

"I just sorta saw the flyer at school," said Dickers.

"There were flyers?" I asked.

Parker shook his head. "McKenna, where have you been? The flyers are *everywhere*."

"I was looking for something," continued Dickers. "Something was missing. I was just sorta empty inside, I guess. I went to my first YAC meeting, and a whole new world opened up. I'd always been sort of religious—altar boy and all that—but YAC led me to my future."

"Good for you." Allison placed her hand on top of his.

"Back to Sister Augustine...if she's not a nun, is she a preacher? Or what?"

"McKenna, why are you so concerned about Sister Augustine?" Back on the defensive, Parker glowered at me.

"No reason, really. As I said, I'm just curious."

"You know, we never really asked her, and she hasn't said anything about her background," offered Allison. "Other than she was once a sinner until she found God—"

"Yeah, since we don't put labels on people or their choice of churches," added Dickers, "it's kinda like the military's policy of 'don't ask, don't tell.'" Dickers looked down at the table as if embarrassed he brought a sore topic up.

Parker exasperated loudly. "Not this again. I don't wanna *hear* any more about gays."

I saw an opening in the conversation, so I stupidly plunged in. "So, do you guys think Calvin Sturgess deserved to die? Because he was gay?" An uncomfortable hush dropped over our table. Tex McKenna, unpopular no matter where I go.

To my surprise, Parker looked hurt by my question. "Whatever. The YACCERS are *not* happy about Calvin's death if *that's* what you're asking. Yes, YAC believes homosexuality is a sin, but Calvin didn't deserve to die…not like that."

"Tex, I *can't* believe you'd even ask that." I read betrayal and sadness in Allison's eyes. Even Olivia looked somewhat aghast.

"Sorry, guys," I mumbled. "It's just…been weighing on my mind. I saw him in the bathroom and everything—"

Dickers leaned across the table and said, "Dude, it's cool. Everyone freaks now and then. Don't worry about it."

"You know," said Parker, "possibly the saddest thing about Calvin's death is that it sped up his arrival in Hell."

Olivia threw her hands into the air and let them fall loudly into her lap. Yet she held her tongue.

But I could *see* it in Parker's eyes. He wasn't just being a jerk. He truly believes his own words. With *conviction.*

But I couldn't get anywhere in my research

mission. Other than managing to come across as a total jackass. "I'm sorry, guys. I didn't mean to hijack the meeting. But I do want to learn more. You think it'd be cool if I went to the retreat? Next weekend?"

Parker appeared deep in thought, considering my proposition. Finally, he nodded. "Yeah, sure, why not, McKenna? Maybe we'll make a YACCER out of you yet."

"Yeah, definitely," said Dickers.

"Um, what's the fee?"

"Four hundred fifty bucks."

*"What?"*

Olivia's hand flew to her mouth, suppressing a laugh at my response.

"Four hundred fifty *bucks*? Man…" How am I going to get that kind of cash? Fighting evil is costly.

"My, my, what an animated discussion you kids are having." Sister Augustine stood behind me, one hand cupped on her elbow, the other resting on the side of her classically lined jaw. "I could hear voices rising from across the room." Her smile stretched so tight I thought her cheekbones might puncture her skin.

"Oh, hi, Sister Augustine," said Dickers. "We, ah, were just explaining to our friends—"

"I see! So…who *are* your new friends?" Her gaze flitted back and forth between us.

"This is Olivia Furman," said Dickers. "And this is Tex McKenna."

Upon hearing my name, Sister Augustine's smile vanished. "'Tex'…what an interesting name. Is that your Christian name?"

"Um, no, ma'am, it's—"

"'Sister.'"

"Sorry?"

"You may address me as 'Sister Augustine.' We're all brothers and sisters in God's war. Besides, 'ma'am' makes me sound older than I am." I forced out a polite chuckle. Augustine put a halt to that with a glower that would intimidate Elizabeth. "So, tell me, Tex and Olivia, what did you think of your first YAC meeting?"

Olivia blinked and straightened up as if being caught napping. "Oh, um, it was really…something."

"Yeah," I squeaked, "I'd like to learn more. I'm really interested in coming to the retreat."

She tapped her hand alongside her jawline. "Is that right? Well, I think it would be wonderful to have you join us." Although her words spoke of encouragement, her tone smacked with suspicion. "Will you be joining us as well, Olivia?"

"I think so…if I can get the money."

Sister Augustine lifted her head to the ceiling and let out a braying laugh. "Oh, Sister Olivia! What *is* money but just a physical obstacle on our path to our rightful place in Heaven at God's side?" I wanted to ask if money's no big deal, could I forego the entry fee. "Four hundred fifty dollars is *nothing* when you think of the rewards awaiting you on your righteous path."

"Yeah, I guess, whatever," mumbled Olivia.

Sister Augustine snapped her head toward Olivia. "Yes. Well, I do *so* look forward to having you join us."

"Um, is it okay to bring the fee to the retreat?" I asked.

"That would be fine, Brother McKenna. We shall see you next Saturday." She hurried off to check in at other tables.

For the rest of the meeting, we talked about God

and how he impacts our lives, but it felt definitely strained. Even Parker and Dickers lost their zest. Totally my fault. I sullied their *hoorah* by bringing up fallen comrades and couldn't help but feel guilty over it.

We said our goodbyes, and before we left, I turned around one last time to appraise the room. Most of the kids were still huddled at their tables, embroiled in deep conversations. Then I spotted Sister Augustine. Standing in the center of the room, stiff and still as wood. Her gray-eyed gaze lanced me, a slight, but noticeable frown pressed onto her lips. I turned away, thinking surely she didn't just give me the evil eye. I dared one more look in her direction to find her still glaring at me, unblinking. I hurriedly ushered Olivia out the door.

"*Tex*," shouted Olivia as soon as we got into the Bucket. "That was a fun date! *Gah!*" She formed her hands into claws and scratched the air.

I laughed. "Yeah, it was."

"And Parker...what a dick! Tell me again *why* we hang out with him?" She threw several punches into the space between her and the windshield.

"I know, I know. I think he latched onto us, more than us reaching out to him. Doesn't matter, though, because—"

"Yeah, yeah, yeah. I know, we leave no man behind and all that crap. Maybe it's time for us to amend our charter."

"We only have to deal with Parker for another month at most. Then we can cut him loose if we choose to."

"I guess. Do you know how hard it was *not* to tell

those *idiots* they were full of crap?"

"I know. I tried my best, too." Honestly, maybe I could've tried a little harder.

"And that Sister Augustine! She's damn creepy!"

"Yeah, she really is." Something bothered me about her, something I couldn't quite grasp. "Olivia…did she look familiar to you?"

Olivia ran her finger over the Bucket's dashboard dust. "Oh my *God*!"Her sudden outburst caused me to swerve the car into the oncoming lane. "*She* was the woman at the Clarendon Baptist church protest. At Brittany's funeral!"

"Crap, you're right. I didn't recognize her because she had sunglasses on at the protest." Even though it was warm in the Bucket, I broke out in a cold sweat. Never a good sign. "Olivia, do you know what this means?"

"Yeah, I can guess."

"YAC is affiliated with the Clarendon Baptist Church." Olivia bobbed her head in agreement. "Maybe they're even the ones who created YAC—"

"Dammi*t*, Tex*!*" Olivia punched the dashboard. The Bucket lurched slightly, threatening to die as if in protest. "We should've known. Their…agendas are too damn similar."

"Maybe YAC's their young soldier branch, which they can mold into spreading their…word."

"Okay, now it's *really* personal. I'm going to this stupid retreat with you and you can't stop me."

"Where are you going to get the money, O'?"

She hung her head, staring into her lap. "From my dad," she said quietly.

"Your dad? Olivia…I didn't think you've even

*heard* from him since he left—"

"I haven't. But every birthday…he sends me a check for one hundred dollars." She held her hand up in the air, attempting to persuade her emotions to take a hike. "It's just his way of trying not to feel guilty. I never touched it. I have, like, nine hundred dollars saved up."

"Are you *sure* you want to use the money for this?"

"I'm not going to use it for anything else, Tex." She slowly simmered down and placed her hand over mine. "Maybe…his 'guilt money' will do something worthwhile." I nodded and said nothing. "Do you think the guys…Allie, Dickers, and Parker…know about YAC's connection with Clarendon?"

"I don't know. I hope not. I just can't see Allie or Dickers—even Elizabeth and Donovan—blindly going along with that. Parker? Maybe. But, even he seems pretty damn sincere in his beliefs—"

"They all seem sincere! Didn't you see them? Everyone in that room seemed like a zombie. It was like…'Night of the Living YAC.'"

I rubbed the weariness from my eyes, the intensity of the YAC meeting having tired me. "Yeah, they did seem sorta blindly following—"

"Tell me about it! You weren't the one who had to go meet all those…walking dead with Donovan."

I fought the temptation to laugh at Olivia's plight. "So…you're not a Donovan fan?"

"You've got to be kidding me. I know what he's all about. All phony friendliness and charisma, and he's way, *way* too slick. He's…*gag*!"

"I don't know. I kinda like him." Olivia punched me in the shoulder. "Ow! Dammit, O', not while I'm driving!"

"You *so* deserved that. You suck!"

"Whatever." I flinched when I thought she meant to repeat her attack. Now laughing, she settled down. "Olivia?"

"Yeah?"

"I think it's time we accepted what's going on in Clearwell."

"What?"

"Someone's targeting gay kids at Clearwell. And I'm pretty damn sure it's someone in YAC. It could even be one of our friends."

She shook her head, staring at nothing in particular. Finally, she said, "Crap. Here we go again."

## Chapter Eleven

As I stood outside the school doors waiting for the bus to arrive, Principal Puts-In-An-Appearance-Four-Times-A-Year stared at me, no doubt on red alert about my nefarious doings by Hastings. I tossed him a casual wave which prompted him to shift his attention elsewhere. Students filed past me, full of energy. Apparently, Calvin's death barely registered a blip on their grief radar.

The bus pulled to a stop, and the door opened with a *whoosh*. Near the end of the pack, Lance stepped off.

"Hey, Tex, what's up?" He leaned in and gave me a quick, one-second guy hug, totally cool as long as we didn't linger Dickers style.

"Not much. Hey, how about I give you a ride home today?" Since I needed to talk to Lance, Olivia had agreed to catch a ride with her mom since her car had blown a gasket or whatever.

"Yeah, dude, that'd be cool."

We walked up the stairs, past Principal Who-Are-You-Again? "Good morning, good morning," he murmured robotically.

Lance whispered, "That's our principal, right?" I laughed and nodded. Lance stopped in his tracks. "So…what's up with the ride offer? I mean, I appreciate it and everything, but, like, what's up?"

"I'll tell you after school."

"Uh-oh. This sounds important." He stared at me, hoping for immediate resolution. "Does this have anything to do with Calvin?"

"Um, sorta."

"Oh, you *girls* on a date?" Dwight Louden, in all his letter-jacketed glory, blocked our path. "Isn't that sweet? Coupla fags out for a morning stroll." His eyes narrowed above beefy cheeks.

"What, are you jealous, Dwight?" Lance shot me an amused look, seemingly carefree.

"Faggot! *What* did you just say to me?" Dwight poked his hot-dog finger into Lance's chest.

"I asked if you were jealous."

Dwight grabbed Lance by his shirt collar. "I should kill you right here." Students gathered, hoping for a nice hot cup of violence to kick-start their morning adrenaline rush.

When I stepped between them, Dwight shoved me into a locker. "Come on, Dwight," I said, after regaining my footing. "He didn't mean anything. Lance is just kidding around—"

"I don't joke around with fags! I don't have *nothin'* to do with 'em."

Lance, still in Dwight's grasp, said, "Then why do you have your hands all over me?"

Dwight slung Lance to the floor and pulled back his mallet of a fist.

A hand caught Dwight's arm in mid-swing. "Dwight, chill! You don't want to get kicked out of school." Jasper Stafford, his voice as cool as his blue eyes, emanated casual calm in the face of the beast. Dwight glowered at the shorter football player, finally relented, and lowered his fist. "Come on, man. Let's go walk it off." Jasper drove the grumbling Dwight through the crowd of students. I owed Jasper twice now. When it comes to Dwight Louden, Jasper Stafford's my guardian angel, always there when I need him.

I pulled Lance to his feet, unbelievably giggling like a maniac. "You believe that guy?"

"Lance, um, you know we just about got pummeled, right?"

"Ah, you worry too much. Everything's cool." I wonder if Mrs. Nguyen put some sort of protective spell on her son. He sure as hell needs it, although I admire his optimistic spirit in the face of adversity. And ass-kickings.

****

Ian greeted me with "Tex, what the *hell?* " I sat down next to him at the lunch table. "I tried to call you all weekend long. What's going on?"

"Sorry. Just really, *really* busy. Besides, you didn't leave any messages or anything." As one of my closest friends, and one of the few who knows I'm a witch, Ian probably has a right to know what's going on. But I wanted to keep him out of this and safe. I still had regrets over what happened to his hand two years ago.

"Who leaves messages anymore? What, are you stuck in 2010? I've been freakin' out! What the hell happened with you and Calvin Sturgess?" Even though Calvin's death happened last Friday, so much had occurred since then; I couldn't remember who knew what.

"Okay. So, I was talking to the security guard when he ran up to the bathroom. I followed him. Calvin was on the bathroom floor, his blood everywhere—"

201

"Wow. So…someone *killed* him?" Ian worked his fingers back and forth, three stubborn stragglers on his right hand remaining inert.

"Looks that way, yeah."

"Wow. Damn."

Brandon ambled up, apple in hand. At least his diet had improved over constant potato chips. "What's going on?"

"Tex discovered Calvin Sturgess' body in the bathroom Friday," said Ian.

"I think I might've heard about that." Of course you'd *think* Brandon might actually remember something like that, instead of recalling some vague notion. But, whatever.

"Well, technically, I didn't really discover his body." I hunkered down into my seat, hoping the unwanted attention would go away.

"Whoa, dude, that's sick," offered Brandon. "Did they catch the guy who did it?"

Before I could answer, Allison and Dickers joined us. "Hey guys," said Allie.

"Tex found Calvin Sturgess' body," said Ian.

"Yeah, we heard," said Dickers. Allie offered me a consoling look.

"Guys, no offense, but I really, *really* don't want to talk about it." I looked at the cafeteria clock. "Where's Olivia? And Lance?" Lately, anytime my friends were late became a cause for concern. If only I could steal a few pages out of Lance's easy-going playbook. Or Brandon's book of sleepy-time tales.

"Did somebody say my name?" Lance plopped into a chair, Olivia squeezing in next to him.

"Okay, okay," said Olivia. "So, now I'm Shannon

Booth's BBBF, I guess."

"Olivia," I said, "what's 'BBBF'?"

"'Best Bathroom Buddy Forever!'Duh!" Lance burst out laughing, lolling about in his chair. "So, there I was again, in the ladies' room—" She looked at Dickers, proactively awaiting a dumb, sexist comment. "*Don't* get excited, Dickers. Anyway, Shannon came in and just started bitchin' to me about Parker. And all guys in general. And she really, *really* let the Young American Christians have it." Dickers looked humiliated, while one couldn't possibly miss Allison's scowl, a totally new look on her. Olivia quickly realized her faux pas. "Sorry, guys, no offense. Anyway, I'm just sayin' what she was sayin'. First of all, the crazy chick never used to even talk to me. And now, she's all up in my face, repeating the same crap she did before. She so *totally* blames the YAC for Parker breaking up with her. You should've heard what she said."

"That's not true, Olivia," said Dickers quietly.

"I'm sure there's more to their break-up than YAC, Olivia," said Allison, surprisingly stern. "You don't know the entire story. I happen to *know* it's not Parker's fault. I think you should get the whole story before you… Oh, never mind!"

"Allie! I'm sorry," said Olivia. "I'm…just repeating what I heard. I'm not the one making accusations or anything…" She trailed off, looking beaten. Totally unsettling to see Olivia roll over like this, but I knew she did it out of respect for Allison and, to a lesser degree, Dickers.

Our old friend, awkward silence, joined the table. Allison, flaming red, finally spoke. "Okay, whatever. I accept your apology."

"We're all brothers and sisters," interjected Dickers, making an already uncomfortable situation way worse. "McKenna and Olivia should know that by now, right?"

Ian swiveled his head between us, confusion creasing his brow. "Okay. What's going on?"

"Oh, they didn't tell you?" said Dickers. "Tex and Olivia are coming to the YAC retreat this weekend."

"Wait! *What*? Wait!"

"Really?" asked Lance, obvious disappointment in his eyes.

I looked to Olivia for support. She spread her hands apologetically. "Um, yeah, we're just going to check it out...I guess."

"Am I the *last* sane person at this *table*?" yelled Ian. Brandon raised his hand, hoping to be counted amongst the sane. "What the *hell,* Tex?" He slammed his fork down on the table.

"Ian, I'll tell you about it later—"

"Jeezus, Tex, *whatever!*" Ian shook his head, seeking solace in his plastic-burger.

"Hey, guys." Jasper ambled up, holding a food-packed tray. "Mind if I hang?"

"Oh, hey," I said. "Yeah, no prob." Olivia appeared alternately enamored and horrified by the notion. She once told me she found Jasper cute, yet she couldn't stomach his football player status. Ian's eyes grew wide as if Jasper supplied the icing on his suddenly crazy world-cake.

"Thanks." Jasper fell into a chair, his tray landing with a *thwack*. "So...what's going on?"

"Jasper," said Olivia, "um, no offense, but...we're not exactly the most popular kids in school." She waved her hand around the cafeteria, a game show hostess presenting the popular kids on display. "And you're a football player."

Jasper sighed. "I just can't hang with the football players. Just can't deal with 'em."

We rallied behind him. Plus, he certainly couldn't hurt our hall cred, such as it is. Not to mention chances of survival. "That's cool," I said.

"Hey," said Lance, "thanks for helping me out earlier today."

Jasper stared at Lance blankly, nothing disturbing his karma of cool. "Yeah, no sweat. Dwight can be a real dick sometimes." He shrugged his shoulders. "Still...he is on my team. I've gotta show him a little respect. And, you know, he lost his girlfriend—"

"Wait, wait, wait!" said Olivia. "Back up! What happened with Dwight this morning?"

Lance glanced at me, then turned to Olivia. "Oh, nothing. Dwight tried to get tough with me, hassled me a little bit...but Jasper pulled him off. Right, Tex?"

"Um, yeah."

Olivia jerked her head toward me. "Tex! And you're *just* telling me this?"

"O', it's not like I've seen you until now or anything." I hoped she wouldn't consider this more secret-keeping. I've really worked hard to keep her in the loop on everything lately.

"Don't you *dare* boys-club me!"

"We wouldn't do that," said Lance. "Come on." He bumped shoulders with her, putting out her fire with a smile. I wish I had his powers to tame her.

"Anyway," said Jasper, "might be a good idea to steer clear of Dwight for a while. I can't watch him all the time."

I nodded. "Yeah, thanks." He shrugged, no big deal, and dug into his lunch—comprised entirely of meat. I think it was a first for all of us to be in such close proximity to a football player without having to worry about our safety. I noticed my friends stealing curious glances at him like a specimen under a microscope, a fascinating new species.

"So, Tex," said Dickers, "do you need a ride to the weekend retreat?"

"No, I'm gonna drive Olivia. Thanks anyway."

Ian harrumphed.

"What retreat?" Even though Jasper asked the question, he seemed only interested in his mountain of meat.

"Um, the Young American Christians' weekend retreat." It embarrassed me even saying it. Now that I had the potential to make a football player friend, I guess I didn't want to blow it.

"Huh." Although casual-sounding as usual, his sudden eyebrow leap betrayed his true feelings.

"Well," said Allie, "I'm going with Parker. Now, that Parker's broken up with Shannon, I don't see anything wrong with it." She looked around the table for validation, lingering on Ian's reaction in particular. Ian leaned back in his chair, his arms crossed over his chest, his hands tucked underneath his armpits, poster boy for pissed-off goth rebels.

"Hey, that sounds…yeah, okay…yeah." Well, I wouldn't win any eloquence awards, but since no one else commented on her bold proclamation, I thought *something* should be said. Even if it sucked.

Throughout our tension-filled lunch, Brandon took

in everything with lazy curiosity, his gaze flitting back and forth as if watching a tennis match. He finally broke his silence and without a hint of sarcasm asked, "Tex, are you going religious?" Dickers shot him a sour glance. Olivia sputtered, her hand flying to her mouth.

"*Thank* you," said Ian. "That's what *I've* been trying to find out!"

As fascinating as we found Jasper, he, too, studied us from his side of the microscope. He stared bemusedly at me, as if saying *interesting bunch you hang with, Tex.*

The ringing bell provided me with an escape strategy. I gave Olivia a quick kiss on the cheek, waved, and got the hell out of there.

Rushing toward my locker, I heard Jasper call out, "Tex, hold up."

Jasper's broad shoulders swam through the crowd, parting the flow of students without touching them. I suppose nobody wanted to take the chance of getting knocked over by him, yet he seemed careful to avoid bumping into anyone. Yet another anomaly. Why couldn't he have come around my first year of high school?

"Hey. Sorry about my friends. They're usually not that…weird or high-strung." *Yes, yes, they are.*

Jasper slashed his hand through the air. "Don't worry about it. It's cool. It was sorta cool after hangin' with the rest of the team all the time. I need to talk to you about something."

"Um, okay."

He nodded his chin toward the center stairwell, which appeared fairly abandoned. I followed him in there—the same landing where I'd been pushed by the

Reaper.

"You wanted me to let you know if I found out anything else about Brittany," he said. "I asked around a little bit, talked to Dwight after he'd been drinking. Seems Brittany was spending a lot of time with your boy, Parker."

"He's not really my 'boy.'"

Jasper shrugged. "Whatever. Just thought you might like to know. Dwight was super pissed about it. He thought Parker was moving in on her and brainwashing her or something. He also thought the Young American Christians was a bad deal for her."

"Really?"

"That's what he said. But I think he was just looking for a scapegoat because Brittany sorta quit paying attention to him. It was pretty obvious she wasn't into Dwight anymore."

"Huh. Jasper, why do you care about this?" Feeling like that came across as callous, I quickly altered my approach. "I mean, it's cool of you to tell me, but...why?" I had to tread cautiously. Even though Jasper seemed like the only decent football player in the world, he could still punch a hole right through me.

"You know...Brittany was all right in my book. She always treated me with respect. Not as an outsider, which is always how I feel. I mean, I want to play football, but not all the other crap that goes with it."

"Yeah, I'm intimately familiar with that feeling. Um, not playing football, I mean, not that there's anything wrong with that, but look at me, I'm way too skinny, and I don't want to play football...and, um..." *Quit staring at me, Jasper! Let me off the hook and shut me up, already*!

"Anyway, it sucked what happened to her and…" He paused while several students bounded by us, racing up the stairs.

"And what?"

"Something's not right about any of this. It doesn't make sense. It *feels*…wrong." I wish I could tell Jasper his intuition is anything but wrong.

Boldly, I placed my hand on his shoulder. He glanced at my hand, hefting an eyebrow. I quickly snagged it back. Our "friendship" hadn't reached that stage yet.

"Um…yeah, anyway, thanks for telling me about it."

"No sweat. What's it mean to you?"

"I'm not sure. But it's…interesting." And *now* I sound like Cowlings. I really need to quit letting adults rub off on me.

He had one hand placed on the door before he stopped. "If there's anyone responsible for pushing Brittany toward what she did…" He turned around, his eyes wide, his casual confidence lacking. "…get 'em."

"Um…"

He took a deep breath and tossed his shoulders back. As he pushed his way through the door, his stride filled with self-assurance again.

Okay! Everything's coming up Parker. His attitude and proximity fits in with what Brittany wrote, and now I have seeming corroboration from Jasper, a very unexpected ally. Yet Cowlings said Parker has an alibi for the time of Calvin's attack. His parents vouched for him, said he'd been home, studying. On the other hand, Cowlings did say parents lied for their children before. *Gah*!

I re-entered the hallway, still needing to hit my locker before class. Down the hall, I saw the unmistakable, bullish back of Arville Hastings, grilling some poor unseen kid. Grimacing for my kindred, beleaguered student, I couldn't help but watch. Hastings straightened, turned, and glanced at me. He swiveled back toward his prey and hitched a thumb my way as if I were the topic of conversation. Hastings left in a huff, exposing the student. Jasper caught my gaze and appeared shocked, nervous. Something not in his usual repertoire.

Something was up. Surely, Hastings hadn't sent Jasper to infiltrate our group to spy on us. It would explain Jasper's sudden interest in befriending us. Then again, he seemed genuine. And he told me about Parker's involvement with Brittany. Unless…he lied to me to put me off the trail of the real culprit. That's crazy thinking, though, right? *Right*?

\*\*\*\*

Lance stood next to the Bucket, idly swinging his backpack like a pendulum. "Hey, Tex." He looked energized, ready for whatever the fates threw in his path.

"Hey. Um, any more run-ins with Dwight?" I opened the car door for him.

"No. No more caveman sightings. I think he's afraid of me."

"Well, I don't know about that!" I fired up the Bucket and idled out of the parking lot, turning onto Johnson Drive.

"Thanks a lot for the ride home. I mean it."

I'm sure he did. I spent several of my early years trapped on the bus and knew it as a special circle of

Hell. Enclosed in a hot can on wheels, a loner surrounded by bullies with no exit or help available. The bus drivers usually either turned a blind eye or were embittered, aged bullies themselves. For the remainder of the school year, I intended to offer Lance rides even though he lived quite a distance from me. If I could make his life slightly more tolerable, I didn't mind adding some miles on the Bucket. I worried about Lance's future, though. For his senior year, he'd be on his own. Yet he's pretty fearless and able to take care of himself. Recklessly—even dangerously—so, Lance skates through life, feeling untouchable, not realizing just how truly vulnerable he is. It's an admirable, though maybe naïve, outlook on life. I felt bad about sticking a cynical, pointed pin into his optimistic balloon.

"Okay, let's talk, Tex." He swung his backpack to the floorboard. "I know something's up."

"Calvin Sturgess was gay."

He looked at me incredulously. "Ya' *think*? Is *this* what you wanted to talk to me about?"

At a stoplight, I turned to him. "I think Calvin was murdered because he was gay." The horrible words hung in the air, a menacing thundercloud ready to burst.

"What are you talking about?"

"I have reason to believe—*good* reason—Calvin was being harassed, given notes. Bullied. Then murdered…because of his, um, lifestyle."

"Notes?"

"Yeah. Notes on yellow stationery saying things like 'God despises homosexuals.' Hate crime crap."

Lance took a deep breath and leaned his head back against the car seat.

"Lance? You okay?"

"Oh…God." He reached for his backpack, unzipped the side pouch, and produced a piece of yellow paper. He unfolded it and waved it in front of my face. "Like this?"

Trying to drive and read the note proved troublesome, but it looked like the same cursive scrawling from the prior notes. *GO HOME! HOMOSEXUALS GO TO HELL!*

"Where did you get this?"

"Why? Is it the same letter?" Lance appeared as if his entire world just imploded. In keeping with his personality, he probably read the note, thought it a lark, didn't give it a second thought. Now his voice sounded uneven, the color draining from his face.

"Close enough."

"Whoa! This…is jacked up! You *really* think the person who wrote this letter…*killed* Calvin?"

"Yeah. I'm afraid so…I'm pretty damn sure about it. Where'd you get the letter?"

Lance crumpled the letter up and crammed it into his backpack. "I found it in my locker last week."

"That's where the cops found Calvin's letter. In his locker. There's more. You and Calvin weren't the only ones…"

"Who?"

I cleared my throat. "Brittany Gerlach received similar letters—"

"Brittany Gerlach was *gay*?" He scooted up in his seat as if to hear me better.

"I'm not sure what she was. I…don't think she even knew what she was. But, I know she was conflicted, having doubts about her own sexual preferences. I guess…she found herself liking another girl—"

"Oh, my God! This is just…goddamned crazy! *How* do you know this?"

"Well, I just thought something was weird. So I started nosing around. At Brittany's wake, I, um, found her diary…and the notes."

"Tex! You didn't! What are you? Some sorta Encyclopedia Brown or something?"

"Yeah, or something." I managed a pathetic smile. "Anyway, you need to know you might be in danger. You need to be careful. Any more notes—or if someone hassles you—or *anything* like that, let me know immediately, okay?"

"Yeah, sure, whatever…" His voice hollowed out, a shadow of his former vocal acrobatics. "Do the cops know about this?"

"Yep. When we get to your house, I'm going to give you the number of a detective—he's actually pretty cool—who's investigating this. I think you better call him and report the note."

He shook his head slowly at first before cranking it up into a violent back and forth motion. "I…can't."

"*What?* Why the hell not? I mean, your life may depend on it."

Tears fell down his cheeks. "If I call this cop, he'll come to my house…and my dad will find out—"

"Lance, it's probably best if your dad *does* find out your life's in danger—"

"You don't *get* it, Tex. That's *not* what I'm talking about." Then it dawned on me. His father doesn't know he's gay. "I can't tell my dad I'm gay! He'll be so…disappointed in me."

I pulled the Bucket over to a street curb and killed the motor. "Lance, come on. It'll be okay. Surely your dad will understand. He loves you."

"You just don't understand. He might love me now. But you don't know how he is. This will destroy him."

At a loss for words, I scooted across the seat and draped my arm around his shoulder. I awkwardly patted his back until he cried himself out. A neighborhood woman walked in front of the Bucket, taking a long look at us. Shaking her head in disgust, she stole backward glances while speeding toward her house. No doubt to call the police on the disgusting perverts parked in front of her home.

"I mean, your dad does seem kinda strict...but you're his son. If he only could see how brave and smart...and *awesome* you are at school. I mean, come on. What's not to love? Gay or not?"

Lance chuckled through his tears. "You really don't know anything about gay people, do you? Now get offa me." He straightened up and pushed me away.

"Well, I mean Brandon's bi—"

*"Get out!* I didn't know that. Hmmm."

"Yeah, well..." I wonder if I should have the same talk with Brandon. It probably isn't necessary. Outside of a select few, I'm fairly certain Brandon's preferences are the best-kept secret at Clearwell High. "Look, Lance, it's not that big a deal you're gay. I mean, not anymore. I think everyone...well, *most* everyone at school's okay with—"

"Oh, whatever. Maybe...*maybe*...kids are cool with it on the coasts and more liberal areas. But...I'm a gay Asian kid in a Kansas suburban school. That's three strikes right there. I mean, you saw how Dwight acts toward me. Besides, it's not the other kids I'm worried about. I've been thinking about this for a long time. About telling my dad I'm gay. I guess now I sorta have to move up the timetable. I just don't feel ready yet—"

"I don't know if you're ever going to 'feel' ready. Not completely."

"Yeah, easy for *you* to say. I'm scared. Would you come with me? When I come out to my dad?"

"Umm—"

"Please! If I have support, it'll be easier. Better."

"Ah…um…"

Lance punched me in the shoulder. "Tex! *Dude!* Just *do* it already."

"Crap." I fell silent, trying to think of a way out. But I didn't really have one. "Okay, whatever. Okay." I couldn't think of anything more terrifying to do, but Lance is my friend. And in trouble. "All right… Is your dad home now?"

"What? Are you kidding me? He works so much I really don't see him until the weekend."

"I don't know if you should put off calling the cops until the weekend—"

"I have to! A policeman's *not* telling my father I'm gay."

It flew against my better judgment, but I saw his point. "Okay. I'm worried about you waiting that long…but all right. We're going to have to do it Sunday evening, though. I've got to go to that stupid retreat this weekend."

Lance rolled his eyes. "Tex, why *are* you going to the YAC retreat, anyway? I mean, aren't they anti-gay?" A quick flash of anger darkened his features.

"I think, in some way, these guys are involved in Calvin and Brittany's deaths. I'm trying to find out what's going on."

"Okay, cool. It doesn't surprise me much they're involved."

"What do you mean?"

"Because they're anti-gay." He stared at me as if I'd been dipping into Brandon's dimwitted cereal stockpile. "The way Parker goes on sometimes—"

"Yeah, he's kinda a jackass."

*"Kinda?* Man, he broke the jackass mold!"

"I know, right? Hey, just promise me you'll be careful and watch your back, okay?"

"Always."

"Call me any time."

"Anytime. Got it. And Tex?"

"Yeah?"

He dabbed at his eyes one more time. "Thanks. I mean, thanks a *lot* for being there for me…when I talk to my dad."

"No problem. Friends help each other out. Now let's get out of here. Did you see the way that woman looked at us?"

"Yeah, I thought she was gonna stroke out." Lance's laughter sounded strained, over-compensating, trying desperately to keep his pain and fear at bay.

\*\*\*\*

No simple witchcraft spells or "apps" for it, I needed to ask Dad for four hundred fifty dollars. And I dreaded it like crazy. We're not exactly swimming in cash. But this is something that has to happen. Surely he'll understand.

"Hi, son." He rolled toward me across the marble

bank floor, a wide grin spread on his face. He wouldn't be smiling for long. Seems like today I'm the destroyer of delight.

"Hey, Dad, ready to go?"

I assisted him into the Bucket. "What's new at school?"

"Not a lot. Hey, um…I have a *huge* favor to ask you."

"Uh-oh." His grin turned down a notch.

I pulled the Bucket out into the rush hour traffic on Ward Parkway. "Okay, well, I know times are tough—"

He sighed. "Okay. How much do you need?"

To my left, a pickup truck seemed to be pacing my every move. The driver kept up with me whether I slowed or sped up. I glanced over. A white face bobbed up and down from within the dark cabin. The truck's passenger window rolled down. Spencer leered at me, wiggling his fingers in a childish wave. He swerved, cutting in front of me, barely missing the front of the Bucket. He burned rubber, his taillights vanishing down the road.

"Friend of yours, Tex?" Dad strained to see down the street, his forehead rippling with worry lines.

*This can't be good.* I tapped the brakes, felt nothing, and pressed the brake pedal to the floor. The brakes wouldn't engage.

"Uh…hold on tight, Dad!"

"What's wrong?" He grabbed the "Oh Hell" handle above him.

"The brakes! They're not working!" The Bucket picked up speed as we descended along the long stretch of road. Even with functioning brakes, the end of rush hour always slammed more traffic at me than I cared for. Today the roads seemed doubly jam-packed.

A car's back-end raced toward us as if it were at a standstill. Focusing straight ahead, I couldn't afford to take my gaze off the road for a second. I prayed silently—maybe not silently—that no one lurked in my blind spot and whipped the wheel to the right, inches before impact with the bumper ahead of me. A horn bleated behind us. Bright lights snapped on, flooding us, blinding me in the rearview mirror. Gripping the wheel tight, I continued pumping the brake. Nothing! As the decline grew steeper, the Bucket plunged faster.

"Try the emergency brake," yelled Dad. I yanked the handbrake and braced for a grinding, sudden halt. The handle swung back and forth with no results.

"Didn't work!" Hysteria mounted in my voice. Dad held on tight, falling against the door while I veered around another car. Having three lanes to maneuver, I kept to the far left lane. I repeatedly punched the horn as a warning to other drivers, my runaway car's staccato soundtrack.

A large fountain divided the road ahead. I tossed away the fleeting, crazy notion of driving into it. As we passed it, I instantly regretted the decision. I pulled to the right at the fork, the tires wailing, and headed down toward the Plaza.

*Hills*! *My kingdom for a hill*! I needed hills to slow my speed, and the area surrounding the Plaza has many. But traffic around the Plaza is a notorious cluster, day or night.

"Hang on, Dad!" A red stop light swam up to us where the road leveled out. My lane sat empty but we couldn't possibly stop. Even though my throat felt dry as sandpaper, I managed to screech, not proud of how I sounded. I laid on the horn, jackhammering the brake impotently. I held my breath, resisting the desire to close my eyes. We barreled through the intersection, barely missing a crossing car. Another car rocketed toward us, a hellish screeching of tires following its fishtailing. I wrenched the Bucket over to the far right lane. The two right tires popped onto the curb, the yards and intermittent driveways making for a bumpier but just as harrowing drive. Dad bashed his head but remained quiet. Maybe not. I couldn't hear anything over my banshee wailing.

I slammed the transmission handle into park. No response, almost as if it'd been completely stripped. Desperately, I turned the ignition off. The Bucket insanely ignored the laws of mechanics and continued chugging along on its manic flight.

Ahead on the right loomed a huge house—nearly a castle—a steep, ascending driveway leading up to it. I wrenched the car onto the driveway. The Bucket's bottom scraped the cement, a dinosaur's roar I felt all the way to my teeth. Our momentum slowed halfway up the drive, the Bucket winding down its joyride. We nearly crept to a stop, and I heaved out a sigh of relief. *Prematurely.* The Bucket sat still for one brief, almost pensive second, decided it had too much fun, and went for round two. Movement. Very little at first. I watched the trees slip past us as we rolled in reverse.

"*Here we go again, Dad!*" Our speed increased. Dad and I shared a crazed glance. Looking through the back windshield, I swiveled the steering wheel through the winding driveway, putting my best gaming skills to the test. Except that I had no joystick. I bounced in and out of the yard, striving to avoid threatening tree trunks.

Driving blind as a bat without radar.

The end of the driveway neared, ready to kick us out onto the busy four-lane road, a very ripe T-boning target. I turned on the hazard lights and bleated the horn. We continued gaining momentum like the worst possible sadistic rollercoaster. It would be only seconds until we entered the street. I awaited our inevitable splashdown. Dad, one arm hanging over the seat, looked back at the on-coming traffic. For once, luck joined our side. A traffic light down the road temporarily slowed the flow of cars. We hit the street, the Bucket's bottom grinding across the cement. More horns blasted while cars sped toward us. Our reverse journey slowed as we traveled across all four lanes. Car headlights gained on us like a swarm of vengeful fireflies. Finally, the back tire grudgingly lifted onto the large center island. The front tires followed. The Bucket groaned, rattled, and clicked. The engine died. Our wild ride ended with a light tap on the tree trunk behind us.

Neither one of us said a word. My shaking hands fell from the wheel as I collapsed into the seat, exhausted. Dad had his glasses off, wiping his eyes. Together we watched the traffic speed by us like we were drive-in movie viewers, stunned by the horror movie we just lived through.

But as they say in comedy, timing is everything.

"Dad, canIhavefourhundredfiftydollars?"

# Chapter Twelve

"Tex," said Olivia, "you know that's twice this Spencer ass-hat has gone after you."

"I know. Why do you think I'm not driving?" I had no more problems with the Bucket after our hellish ride but still felt kinda freaked out about driving. Dad insisted on having the Bucket checked out by a mechanic. Unsurprisingly, the mechanic said the brakes were tiptop. The brakes going out had nothing to do with faulty car parts. My gremlin went by the name of Spencer Pritchett.

"I did have Mickey put a protection spell on the Bucket." When I told Mickey about what happened that night, she hung up on me and twenty minutes later stood outside my front door, wielding a bottle. She called it a "witch's bottle" and instructed me to keep it in the Bucket's glove box, protecting the car from any further attacks. She swore she'd talk to "The Witches' Council" about Spencer. Of course I didn't even *know* a "Witches' Council" existed. Knowing little things like that might come in handy. "I'm just glad you got your car out of mechanic purgatory."

"Well, you can't stop driving forever." Maybe not, but I sure felt like hanging up my keys. I hadn't driven the rest of the week. Olivia took me to school while Ruth picked up the slack with Dad.

"Did you tell your dad about Spencer?"

"No. I didn't want to worry him. Any more than I already have."

"And *why*, again, is Spencer out to get you?"

"Beats me. I guess it's because he thinks I punked him."

"And that's it? Nothing else to it?"

"As far as I can tell, that's it."

"Huh. Anyway, your dad gave you the money?"

"Yeah. I don't think he's too thrilled about it, though." Dad had questioned why I wanted to go to a religious retreat. Long talks ensued. I told him everything. Well, no I didn't. But if he knew how much danger I've been in recently, he wouldn't have let me go. "I did tell him it was a loan. I really, *really* need to get a summer job."

"Yeah, me, too."

"There's something else we need to talk about." Last Thursday, I received a letter from The University of Kansas. They offered me a scholarship. Instead of celebrating and sharing the news with my friends and Dad, I kept quiet about it. I didn't know how to take it. Or how Olivia would take it.

Olivia took her sunglasses off and glared at me, paying very little attention to the highway. "What's wrong?"

"I, um, got a letter this week. From KU. They offered me a scholarship."

Olivia put her sunglasses back on and stared down the road. "Cool. I'm happy for you." She pushed a smile through her solemn demeanor. "You *are* going to take it, right?"

"I really don't know what I'm going to do, Olivia. I just wish…someone would tell me what to do."

Her hand lashed out and punched my leg. "Don't be an idiot! You have to at least seriously consider it."

"What do *you* want me to do?"

"It doesn't matter what I want. It's your life. Only you can make that decision."

"Tell me to stay, Olivia…"

"I can't do that."

"Well, you want me to stay, right? Tell me to stay…that you want me to stay."

"Gah!"She threw her hands up in the air before quickly reclaiming the steering wheel. "Of *course* I want you to stay, Tex! But I'm not going to be the one to tell you to. You'd end up…resenting me, maybe—"

"I'd never do that—"

"Oh, whatever. You can't say that."

"Besides, there're other things to consider." I folded my hands in my lap as I've seen Dad do so often. Maybe it'll open the gateway to the wisdom of adults. I'm still waiting.

"Like what?"

"Like my dad. He's getting weaker—"

"He has Ruth."

"But she's not around always. He's falling more."

"Oh." Olivia bit her lower lip. "Well…what does he want you to do?"

"He wants me to go. But I haven't even told him about the scholarship offer yet. I just need…I don't know…something. Gah!"

"Time's running out. You've got to decide what to do."

"Well, you know, if I went to JuCo for a couple of years, I could still go to KU later. Anyway…" We drove in silence for a very awkward fifteen minutes.

"So," she finally said, "what *are* we going to do at this stupid retreat anyway?"

"Dickers told me we're, ah, going to play paintball."

"*What?* I guess nothing promotes Christianity better than shooting others."

"It's supposed to help build a better brotherhood—"

"*Ahem!*"

"And sisterhood."

"Still sounds stupid to me." Olivia gestured toward the religious themed billboards lining the highway. "Looks like we're getting close."

Thirty minutes later, a weathered road sign announced the Oakdale Resort on the next right. Olivia turned her car into the nearly hidden entryway and gunned up the steep, one-lane dirt road. Heavy foliage blocked the sunlight, trees embracing one another overhead. After a mile, the road dumped us into a vast field, the sun brilliant after the darkness of the woods. Four large log cabins lined the perimeter of the field, trees guarding their backs. In the center of the cabins stood a large, stone-block two-level building, utilitarian in its bland design. Shutterless windows appeared unwelcoming. Like an afterthought, a chimney jutted out of the flat roof. If not for the sign merrily announcing the OAKDALE RESORT, it could've passed for a prison.

"Jeeze," said Olivia, wrinkling her nose, "you sure know how to show a girl a good time."

"I'm not exactly a world-class camper myself, O'. My idea of roughing it is no streaming TV."

In front of the cabins, a tetherball pole and a tall

white post with antiquated speakers attached to it rose out of the dirt. Further down the field, a joyless-looking game of volleyball was in progress. Hundreds of kids dawdled, some with a look of displacement, others smiling widely. Mr. Green, Sister Augustine's right-hand man, directed cars to park at the outer edges of the field. Still stuffed into a tight green polo shirt—not a good look for him—he gyrated and wiggled his hips, dancing to some sort of celestial disco soundtrack in his head. Using two flashlights, and enjoying his moment, he pointed us to a parking spot.

"All right," said Olivia. "Mr. Green's rocking it."

As soon as we got out of the car, Dickers pounced on us. "Hey, guys, it's cool you're here."

"And your outfit is *not* cool, Dickers," said Olivia. He wore a cheaply made T-shirt with the YAC logo emblazoned across the front, the transfer already peeling at the edges. His long white shorts gave him the appearance of a bottom-of-the-barrel cabana boy. "I am so not wearing that shirt."

"Um, everybody's supposed to. When you register and sign in..." He pointed toward the two-story building. "...they'll give you a T-shirt." Olivia snorted.

"Okay, so that's where we're supposed to go?" I asked.

"Come on. I'll take you." Numerous long wooden tables and benches filled the front colossal room. "Since there's no chapel here, this is where we hold our meetings. We eat here, too."

Dickers led us through the room to the central hallway, a stairwell in the middle with burgundy-colored carpeting treading the steps. "Up there's where the adults sleep." He jerked his chin toward the stairs.

"It's off limits to us."

"What, the adults are too good to camp?" asked Olivia.

Dickers smiled. "What*ever*. I hope you're not going to be a smart-ass the whole weekend."

"Oh, just…whatever."

"Okay, here's where you register." Dickers pointed toward a long line of kids in the hallway. "Tex, you're going to be in the cabin with Parker and me. Olivia, you're in Allison's group. Hey, I'm gonna bounce, but I'll catch up to you after you're done." Dickers waved as we joined the end of the line. A morose bunch, the kids looked like they were waiting their turn for mood-altering medications.

"This is already just too much fun," said Olivia.

"That's what's weird," I whispered. "Everyone's so quiet."

A boy in front of me distractedly rubbed his elbow up and down, a sure sign of a lice invasion. Or nerves. "First time here?" he asked.

"Um, yeah. You?"

"No, man. I've been to a retreat before." He tugged at his ear and scratched at his cheek. Just watching him made me itch. "They're great."

"Cool, cool," I said. "Um, what do we do here? For fun, I mean?"

He stared at me like I had a third eye. "It's *all* fun."

Upon entering a small office, two middle-aged men sat at a table, flipping through stacks of paper. One of them hoarded what appeared to be a moneybag, his hand constantly upon it.

"Name?" This had to be "Mr. Brown" because of the color of his polo shirt. "Mr. Blue" simultaneously took Olivia's vitals. I felt like we were being recruited into the army. *God's army*.

"Um, Richard McKenna." Mr. Brown stared blankly at me, his caterpillar-like mustache twitching. I *so* wanted to swat it.

"Ah, yes, Mr. McKenna. Entry fee?"

I handed Dad's check to him. He grabbed it and marked some papers. "Size?"

"Sorry?"

He glared up at me like he expected trouble. Adults' favorite way of looking at me. "The size of your shirt."

"Oh, uh, medium."

When he expelled a deep breath, I thought his lip caterpillar morphed into a butterfly, ready to take wing. "All out of medium. Here's a large." He tossed a bundled shirt at me. "Go get dressed. *Next*."

Olivia grimaced at her shirt. "Really, Tex? *Really*?"

"Olivia, if the worst we have to do this weekend is to wear this shirt...well..." I shrugged as she gave in grudgingly.

Leaving the building, we nearly ran over Parker and Allison. Parker stayed one step in front of Allie, as if embarrassed by her presence. "Hi, guys," said Allison, inching forward to stand at Parker's side.

"Hey," said Olivia. "Parker..."

"What up?" he said. "Have any problem finding the place?"

"Well, we almost missed the dirt road—"

"You guys better get your shirts on." He looked at his watch, no time for small talk. "We're meeting in the hall at...thirteen-hundred."

"Really, Parker?" asked Olivia. "Military time?"

"When at camp, do as the campers do. Come on, McKenna, I'll show you your cabin while the girls get prettied up." Allison smiled at the compliment, while Olivia's sneer suggested she wanted to punch out Parker.

I followed Parker to the farthest cabin, struggling to keep up with his long stride. The door opened with a creak as we entered. Nearly fifty small, lumpy-looking cots lined both sides of the log walls. In the back of the cabin sat the bathroom, several partition-free toilets sitting next to an open-spaced shower area. I guess it helped promote "brotherhood" or whatever.

A single overhead bulb, dangling from a wire, dimly lit the cabin. The walls were barren although some previous campers apparently tried to get their graffiti on, with mediocre results. Moth-eaten, lacy curtains adorned several windows, the sun bleeding in and illuminating a swirling smattering of dust.

"Pick a cot that doesn't have anything on it," said Parker. The floorboards creaked beneath me as I settled on a cot near the back. I tossed my backpack, containing one change of clothing, onto the thin mattress with a single green blanket resting on top of the sheet. I could only imagine Olivia's horror.

I changed into the T-shirt, my body swimming in it. Parker smirked at me. "Looking good, McKenna."

"Yeah, well, they didn't have my size—"

"Okay, it's about time to convene at the mess hall."

"You *really* need to quit the military talk, Parker."

The packed mess hall remained oddly quiet with only a few strained giggles slashing through the oppressive silence.

"What's going on now?" I asked.

"Don't know. I heard we're going to have a guest speaker."

Olivia, Allison, and Dickers joined us and scooted onto the bench. "*Don't* say a word," said Olivia. Her shirt looked too small, her chest straining against the yellow and green YAC letters.

"Oh, I think you look cute," said Allison. Dickers and Parker were obviously stealing not-so-casual glances at her chest.

"*Gah!* Whatever," she said.

Regal as ever, Elizabeth and Donovan floated in. Surveying the crowd, Donovan spotted us and mouthed, "*Ah!*"

"Hey, guys. May we join you?" They sat down before we could answer. I suppose being turned down's never happened to either of them.

Donovan curtly nodded his head at each of us, making sure to announce our names. Elizabeth dutifully dipped her head, a queen supportive of her king. It disappointed me I didn't get to shake Donovan's hand. His warm, double-handed greeting is *special*.

Behind me, a low, menacing growl grew. A black, green-eyed cat sat in the doorway. Its gaze locked on mine while its tail switched rapidly back and forth.

"That's Sister Augustine's cat ..Guinevere," said Dickers. Snarling, the cat circled behind me, darting closer a little bit at a time. "Don't tell me you're afraid of cats, McKenna." Dickers and Parker shared a laugh.

"Uh, no, not afraid. Just allergic." As if on cue, I sneezed and took special care to apologize to Donovan.

A back door opened, and Sister Augustine strolled in, her entourage of polo-shirt-wearing chubby henchmen close behind her. Wearing a navy blue business suit, she stepped onto a slightly elevated platform and crossed to a podium.

"Okay, ladies and gentlemen," she said. "Calm down." That demand felt unnecessary as everyone already sat adrift in a sea of tranquility. "It warms my heart to no end seeing so many of you at our newest Young American Christians' retreat. I'll have you know we've set a record for retreat attendance. There are nearly three hundred of you here today." Applause and cheers erupted. "And to honor this occasion, we have a special guest speaker with a *very* special message from God. And now, from the Clarendon Baptist Church, I present to you...*Pastor Don Danvers.*"

Olivia's eyes widened in horror. Elizabeth's eyebrows dipped slightly before regaining perfect formation. Parker grinned.

Danvers burst out of a back door, waving, running like a game show host. The crowd responded with a scattering of polite applause before several loud whistles and mass cheering broke out.

Danvers hopped onto the platform, swooping his cowboy hat at the crowd in a southern gentlemanly fashion. Olivia sat with her arms crossed while the rest of my friends mustered uncertain applause, the kinda "slow clap" you see in movies. Attired in a bolo tie and a light gray suit, Danvers worked the crowd, pointing out several kids and clasping his hands in the air triumphantly. Sister Augustine stood off to the side, enveloped in shadows.

When the hullaballoo died down, Danvers spoke. "Hello, youngsters, and hello to the Young American *Christians.*" The crowd went wild. Danvers waved one hand in the air to quiet them. "Now, I'd much appreciate it if you could hold your applause 'till the end of my talk. After all, it's not *me* who deserves applause...it's *God*!" He jutted a fat finger in the air, grinning, living for the applause. "Friends, I know you might've heard about me. Some folks are saying some unkind things about me. Well, let 'em talk...let 'em talk. These same folks who're bad-mouthing me..." He scowled with a constipated look. "...they're *Satan's* tools. They're here to spread *lies. Blasphemy.* Heinous words straight from the *devil's mouth*! Now...I just want you children to make up your own minds. Make your own decision as to who's right and who's wrong. For, I'm preaching straight from the Bible itself. *God's* words. And for these blasphemers who don't believe in God's word...well..." He paced the length of the platform, mopping the sweat from his forehead with a handkerchief. "...I think we all know *where* they're going." The audience applauded. *Hooray for Hell.*

He gripped the edge of the podium, squeezing it tightly. "There's one sin, in particular, that's prevalent in our world today. Does anyone know what that is?"

"Gays," yelled a boy several tables over.

Danvers clapped his hands together hard, as if bringing down a thunderclap from Heaven. He pointed in the direction of the voice, wagging his fat finger about. "That's right, that's right...*homosexuality*. The bane of the evil world we live in. Liberals might tell you differently. Might say it's all right...but it's not." He pinched his lips together, his jowls bookending his mouth. "*Homosexuality* is a curse. The Bible clearly...*clearly*..." He pounded a fist into his palm. "...*clearly*...states homosexuality is a sin. It says 'man shouldn't lie down with another man!' And if I'm the only one brave enough to spread God's word, then so be it. So be it. I just hope you boys and girls will follow me on my path to righteousness. To help pass on the word of God. And to let these *sinners* know it's *not* right in God's eyes."Danvers paused, hitched his pants up by the belt loops."These other so-called 'churches'…they say God loves everyone, that Jesus loves everyone, and that he even *died* for everyone. Lies. All *lies!* Lies made to *justify* the sinful nation we live in. God *despises* homosexuals!" Those hateful, destructive words again. "God is *disgusted* by homosexuals. *God* wants them to rot in *hell*!"

Olivia shot up from her seat, everyone staring at her. "I can't listen to this anymore." She pushed her way through the crowded aisles, stomping her feet and storming to the exit. A handful of students quietly joined her. The rest of my friends sat in stunned silence.

Danvers raised his hand to appease the murmuring crowd. "It's okay. It's okay," he said, jerking his head with each uttered "okay." "Let them go. There'll always be dissenters, helping to perpetuate the fake news the media, the liberals, the false prophets spread. Truth will win out in the afterlife. Now, how many of you are looking for your just rewards in the afterlife?" A few hands raised. Like a wave at a sporting event, more hands went up, the contagion spreading rapidly.

"Good, good. That's a *mighty* fine showin'," continued Danvers. "Now I want you all to let these *homosexuals* know what they're doing is not all right. It's *not* all right! Let them *know* their choice of sinful lifestyles goes against God's wishes. Their kind isn't wanted here on Earth and *especially* not in God's *glorious* kingdom of *Heaven*." Fists pounded the tables, feet tramped the floor, Hell's own cacophonous *Riverdance*. Sister Augustine stepped out of the shadows, a thin smile across her face.

"But don't stop there, boys and girls! Keep spreadin' the good word. Let your parents, your brothers and sisters, your friends, and your teachers know that God's judgment is coming sooner than any of us think. Come join us at the Clarendon Baptist Church next Sunday. With your help, we can build an *army*!" Danvers raised his hands to the rafters, his suit jacket pulling back on his wrists. Every time the crowd's roar began to wane, he reignited the audience by lifting his palms. I caught Allie's attention. She averted her gaze, staring down into her lap.

Once Danvers finally milked the audience for all they were worth, he hit the money mark. "Now. We'll be passing the offering basket amongst you to help us fight this *evil* sickness. And don't forget to spread the word to your parents. *Every* little bit helps. If they could find it in their hearts to make a donation to the Clarendon Baptist Church..." He ran his tongue over his lips. "...we might—just *might*—accomplish our mission." He offered a sweeping wave and shook Sister Augustine's hand before breaking into a slow jog for the back door.

"I can't believe this," I muttered. Most of the kids were on their feet applauding wildly. Earlier in the day, they'd been more or less sleepwalking. Now they're a fired-up collective of town villagers, ready to string up any "Franken-sexuals" they can find.

"Okay, ladies and gentlemen," called out Sister Augustine. "Take some time amongst yourselves to discuss what you've heard. Dinner will be served at five; then campfire discussions will commence afterward." She left the stage, escorted by her colorfully-dressed sidekicks.

Behind me, a hissing sound rose above the murmuring audience. The black cat sat on the windowsill, seemingly calling me out.

Ignoring the cat, I said, "Parker, you *can't* be on board with this…crap."

"It's as he said…are you going to deny God's word?"

I looked around the table. "What do you guys think? Surely, you can't—"

"It's wrong." Elizabeth, of all people, came to my rescue. She forcefully stared at Donovan, defying him to disagree.

Donovan flourished his hands in the air. "Hold on, hold on. Let's not get over-heated about this. We're *all* friends here."

"Elizabeth's right," said Allie, her cheeks flushed red. "We have gay friends."

"They're not *my* friends," said Parker.

Elizabeth aimed her chilly blue eyes in his direction. "A caring, loving God wouldn't condemn someone for the way He created them—"

"*God* didn't create them that way," said Parker. "They *chose* their lifestyle. Now they have to live with it…and die with it."

I pressed my palms into my eyes, hoping to wipe away the stupidity and narrow-mindedness surrounding me, glad Olivia didn't hear this conversation.

Donovan placed his hand on top of Elizabeth's folded hands. "I think…maybe…there is some merit in what Danvers said." Elizabeth's scowl sent him back-pedaling. "But, of course, there's truth to the other side of the argument as well. I just think we could all use some time to soak in the information. That's all I'm saying…" For the first time, he appeared unsure of his golden tongue's power. Elizabeth narrowed her eyes and stuck her lower lip out. There'll be no chaste kisses passed between them tonight.

Dickers had remained uncharacteristically quiet until he broke his silence. "This isn't what the Young American Christians is supposed to be about…" I almost felt sorry for him, his sense of profound disappointment apparent.

"Whatever," said Parker. "It *is* the word of God."

"Enough, already, Parker," I shouted. "Danvers is manipulating and interpreting the Bible—"

"Not *this* argument again, McKenna—"

"It goes against the teachings of Jesus," said Allie. "Jesus loved *everyone*. He died for everyone—"

"Didn't you hear a *word* Pastor Danvers said? Those are *lies*," spat Parker.

Allie's eyes brimmed with tears. She buried her face in her hands, a quiet sobbing bubbling up from between her fingers.

I placed an arm around her heaving shoulders. "Wow, way to go, Parker. I've heard *more* than enough for now." I eased Allie off the bench and guided her toward the exit.

Behind me, Elizabeth said, "I've had enough for now, too, Donovan." She quickly strolled past us, head held high. Looking back, I saw Dickers, Donovan, and Parker, their heads together. Speaking *very* quietly.

\*\*\*\*

Fuming, Olivia paced back and forth outside her cabin. "Tex," she said, "this is by *far* the worst thing you've ever gotten me into."

"Olivia, calm down! Shhh—"

"Don't you dare *shush* me. These damn hypocrites are full of *hate*...and *crap*...and *gah*!" It's probably best she take her anger out on me, rather than jeopardize my thus-far worthless investigation. Allie went inside the cabin while Olivia wound down, slumping to the dirt in defeat. "It's all so...really stupid."

I sat next to her. "I know. Just remember we're here to find out what we can—"

"And what have you found out so far? That YAC's nothing but a front for more of Danvers's sick crap? *Duh*!" Suddenly she dropped her voice. "That creepy Sister Augustine is watching us."

Standing in the doorway of the central building, Sister Augustine glared at us, looking very much like her cat.

"Crap. Try to act casual."

Olivia leaned back and whistled, wagging her head to her melody-free tune. "How's that?" She tossed a devilish smile my way.

"Oh, *real* cas! Look, O', I think we're closer to finding out who the killer is. It's all connected. I'm just asking you to stay cool...just for another night, okay?"

She trumpeted her lips. "Whatever."

\*\*\*\*

At the campfire, Dickers displayed his marshmallow-roasting prowess. He pulled the stick out of the fire, the blackened marshmallow sliding to the ground with a splat.

"Way to go, Dickers," said Olivia.

"Well, the next one will be perfect." Dickers' false bravado sounded weak in the chilly, night air.

While Parker mercifully avoided us, Allie appeared to be in agony. Parker sat at a nearby campfire, gravitating toward a small blonde girl. Every time the girl tittered, Allie shot not-so-obvious glances in his direction.

"Hey, guys," said Dickers, finally giving up on his marshmallow mastery, "I just wanted to, you know, sorta apologize for all of that Danvers's stuff. I had *no* idea he was going to be here—"

"It's not your fault," I said.

"Yeah, but what he said…it was pretty—"

"I know, Dickers. But didn't you sorta tell me YAC was against homosexuality, too?"

Dickers threw his hands up. "Well, they're not *crazy* about it. And YAC *does* believe it's a lifestyle choice, but they don't take such a hard line. I mean, we're all about saving them…rather than, you know, condemning them to Hell or whatever. Anyway, sorry…"

Allie said, "No one blames you, Clark."

"Okay, okay," said Olivia. "*Enough* of the feel-bad hour. When's the fun gonna start?" The fire cracked, snapped, and lightened Olivia's eyes. "So far, fun hasn't been the order of the day—"

Dickers laughed. "Yeah, tomorrow's paintball and—"

"No. I said, 'when's the *fun* start?' And what's the deal with paintball, anyway? Since when does shooting one's peers teach us about God?"

"Olivia, it's a team-building activity, interacting

with one another. Build Christianity between brothers *and* sisters." Dickers seemed pleased with himself he remembered to include "sisterhood" for Olivia's benefit. "And it might be fun—"

"*Fun.*" Olivia snorted.

I grabbed Dickers' abandoned stick and jabbed it into the burning embers. "Speaking of 'fun,' let me ask you guys a question. When we first showed up here, everyone seemed to be acting like they were sorta…medicated, kinda sleepwalking through everything. You know, like Brandon? But once Danvers started talking…they all sorta came alive. Crazily so."

Allie nodded. "It's been getting worse."

"What do you mean?"

"When we first started going to YAC meetings, it *was* fun. I learned things, felt my life being filled by God. But as time went on, there seemed to be a lot more seriousness. There was less…laughter."

Dickers sat up, staring at Allie. "Oh, my God. I thought it was just my imagination."

"I didn't want to say anything. I thought people would think I'm nuts."

I blinked rapidly, partially from the smoke but mostly trying to digest this information. "You guys, *what's* going on here?"

Three sudden sneezes racked my body forward. Then sharp needles dug into my back. *"Whoa!* What the *hell?"* I shot up, something heavy attached to my back like a leach. I whipped back and forth, clawing my hands behind me, and let out a high-pitched squeal.

"Tex," shouted Olivia. "It's the cat!"

I finally made an impact with a bulk of fur, and the

cat dropped. It turned on me, arching its back, hissing. Illuminated by the firelight, its eyes glowed green, a color I now associate with black magic. I tossed the stick in the cat's direction. It scampered off into the woods, growling louder than any cat I've ever heard.

"Hey, you okay?" said Dickers, barely covering his amusement. "You got attacked by Bigfoot."

I swiped at my back and pulled away bloodied fingertips. "Yeah, funny."

"That was weird," said Olivia. "What's the deal? I thought you had a…special thing with cats." Allie and Dickers looked puzzled by her statement.

"Yeah, me, too. Guess just not this cat."

"What? So, you like talk to animals or something?" asked Dickers.

"Yeah, that's right, Dickers." I sat back down to the warmth of the fire, occasionally rubbing the claw marks on my back. "Damn weird."

Weird's right. Numerous campfires burned brightly across the grounds, sparks flying into the dark of night while kids gathered. I wondered if this is what a town under siege looks like.

\*\*\*\*

"What are you planning, Tex?"

"What do you mean?"

Olivia stomped her foot into the dirt. "Don't give me that crap! What, you think I don't know you by now?"

I grabbed her hand and pulled her away from the girls parading into the cabin. "What makes you think I'm planning something?"

"Okay, first of all, whenever you're about to do something stupid, you get quiet. You didn't say a word on our way back from the campfire." From within the woods, an owl hooted as if in agreement.

"Um, maybe I was just quiet 'cause I'm enjoying nature?"

"Bullcrap! You just flinched when you heard an owl. You don't like nature, and you look worried."

"Okay, okay. I didn't let you know because there's no sense in us both getting into trouble if we got caught. Besides, it might be a worthless, um, endeavor."

"How many times have I got to tell you I can take care of myself?" She glowered like an angry schoolteacher. "Now, what are *we* going to do?"

"I give, already! I want to take a look inside the main building—"

"Why?"

"Dunno. But it's where Sister Augustine and her color-coded people do their business. Maybe, I can find something on paper or see something—"

"Sounds really, *really* dumb. I'm in."

"Olivia, come on." But she stood resolute on this. "Okay, but I don't think you should enter the building. You stand guard outside. Let me know if you see anything or if anyone comes. Text me—"

"Fine!" She huffed. "But I don't think you're gonna find anything."

"Why?"

"I don't think these people are stupid. If they're tied up in this murder somehow, do you *really* think they'll leave anything incriminating lying around?"

She had a point. "No, I guess not. But I don't know what else I can do. And Elspeth said I should come to this retreat and—"

"Agh!" She swung her fists in the air at an

imaginary opponent. "Elspeth, again. Do you believe *everything* she tells you?"

"Everything she's told me before has panned out." I splayed my hands in a "have mercy" motion.

"Whatever!" She folded her arms, erecting her defense shield. "What's the plan?"

"I'll meet you in front of your cabin at, say, midnight. Oh, wait, what's that in military time?"

"*Tex!*"

\*\*\*\*

Snoring ran rampant throughout the cabin. A day full of worshipping takes its toll on even the most stalwart of God's soldiers. I crawled off the bed, the thin mattress providing inadequate muffling of the springs. Having "slept" in my jeans, I slipped on my YAC shirt and tennis shoes, foregoing socks. While tiptoeing past the slumbering YACCERS I wished I had picked a bunk closer to the door. The moon, bright and full, forced streaks of white light through the flimsy curtains. A monstrous-sounding *snork* arose from one of the kids, sending my heart racing into my throat.

I pulled the cabin door open a hair, testing for squeaky hinges. Halfway open, the hinges decided to give a good groan.

A sudden shuffling of blankets froze me in my tracks. "Where you goin', McKenna?" whispered Parker.

"Go back to sleep," I whispered. "I'm just takin' a walk. Can't sleep."

Without waiting for his response, I stepped out onto the stoop and pulled the door shut behind me.

Sprinting across the field, I tripped on an untied shoelace. I fell, rolling onto my shoulder, my cheek landing in the dirt. Sitting up, I surveyed the buildings, ensuring my tumble hadn't awakened anyone. All the cabins remained dark. But light burned from the second floor of the stone building. I jumped to my feet and ran toward Olivia's cabin.

Pressed up against the cabin's wall, Olivia rubbed her shoulders against the night wind. "Ready?"

"Yeah. Let's go."

"Did anyone hear you leave?" The wind picked up, sending a shrill whistle between the buildings. I held my finger to my lips. For no real reason other than we'd seen it in movies, I guess, we crouched the rest of the way to our destination. Coming up on the far edge of the main building, I peered into the window at the lunch hall. Dark, and no sign of any night owls.

With our backs sliding across the stone, we edged our way toward the door. I grasped the brass door handle. I whispered into Olivia's ear, "Be sure and text me if you hear anyone." She bobbed her head up and down. Taking a deep breath, I opened the door and stepped into the hallway. On the left, a slight arc of light flowed down the hall. I looked at Olivia once more, her face pale in the moonlight, and nodded reassuringly to her before closing the door behind me.

I entered the dimly lit corridor. Light trickled out from beneath the closed door of the registration office. A tinny male voice, nothing more than a murmur, came from the room. I leaned in to listen. It sounded like a one-way conversation, full of "yeahs" and "uh-huh's." No doubt Mr. Green was on the phone with his wife, explaining his crazy, late hours.

Thinking it a dead end, I retraced my steps back to the stairwell, Mr. Green's voice diminishing behind me.

With only the first few steps illuminated by the moonlight, I carefully mounted the first stair. The carpet runner absorbed most unwanted creaks and tics. Feeling the area out with my foot before placing my full weight on each stair, I slowly ascended the flight. I opened and squeezed my eyes several times, hoping to adjust them to the darkness. My hand ran out of railing, my right foot taking one more instinctual step up to clump solidly on the carpet. Something felt close, to the right; a lack of open air in front of me...a wall. On my left, two ancient-looking sconces attached to the wall faintly lit the hallway. Slowly, I crept down the hall. I passed several doors on either side, no light streaming from beneath them. Voices, speaking in hushed tones, drifted out from the last closed door on the left. I placed my ear against the door but the solid, wooden architecture stymied my ability to hear.

I kneeled at an old-fashioned keyhole, large enough to peek through. Shutting one eye, I looked through the opening.

Two plush chairs positioned with their high backs toward me occupied the center of the room. Between the chairs rested an antique coffee table, a small lit lamp upon it. On the armrest of the left chair lay an older woman's hand, holding a wine glass. The hand's owner had to be Sister Augustine. Two voices sounded restrained, but their tones spoke of urgency, deep in a heated discussion. I pressed my ear over the hole.

"What about the McKenna boy?" Definitely Sister Augustine. She kept her voice controlled in that scary, authoritative manner of hers.

"What about him?" the other voice whispered. It could've been male or female. "I said I'd take care of him."

"I've heard that before."

"Don't worry about it." The voice rose enough to be discernible as a male's voice. "I'll take care of him!"

"You better had." Sister Augustine raised her wine glass and extended her index finger toward the unknown male. "For your sake *and* mine."

A heart-stopping *thump* came from the end of the hallway. I swiveled, squinting into the darkness. Two, very small green circles danced by the stairwell. *Crap.* Guinevere, Sister Augustine's demonic cat. She silently strolled down the hallway, announcing her intentions with an extremely small, yet somehow self-satisfied, *meow.* I felt like a mouse, trapped and ready to be toyed with. I waited. The only thing I could do.

Finally, she entered one of the sconce's soft spotlights. Slowly strutting toward me, her mouth open, almost s*miling.* Still on my knees, the cat boldly rubbed up against my thighs. I shook my head, repeatedly mouthing the word *no,* hoping my pathetic pantomime would instill some pity into the sadistic feline. I swallowed hard, the resultant gulp sounding thunderous to my ears. The back of my throat tickled, and my eyes itched and watered. As I nudged the cat back gently, she retaliated with a claw to my hand. I shot up, ready to run back down the hallway.

"*Ahh-choo!*" I sneezed three times, loudly and rapidly. The cat let rip a hellish *rowr* and dashed off down the hallway. The voices within the room abruptly stopped. Footsteps approached. Below, at the bottom of the steps, I heard Olivia talking animatedly to an irate Mr. Green. *No way out.*

Behind me, another door flew open. A hand

grabbed my shoulder and yanked. Falling back into the darkened room, I twisted to see my attacker.

Elspeth held a fingertip to her black lips. She sidestepped me swiftly, entered the hallway, and closed the door behind her. I heard the door across the hallway yank open. Brighter light poured in underneath the door.

And then a deafeningly long silence.

"*What* are you doing here, young lady?" asked Sister Augustine angrily. I heard her pull her door shut.

"Um, sorry, ma'am," said Elspeth. "I was...lost and...just wanted something to eat—"

"You are *not* a member of YAC. I certainly would remember someone...who looks and dresses like *you* do!"

"No, ma'am."

"I *thought* I heard a male sneeze. Are you alone?"

Elspeth lowered her voice a notch. "That was me. I have a cold...being out in the woods—"

Heavy plodding footfalls hammered down the hallway. "Sister Augustine," cried out Mr. Green. "Is everything all right up here?"

"Mr. Green, it would appear you've let a trespasser enter our quarters."

"Sorry, Sister, I...don't know how it happened. I was busy with another 'wanderer' downstairs—"

"Oh, for *God's* sake! You're *all* incompetents. Who's this so-called 'wanderer?'"

Mr. Green's pause sounded ripe with fear for his job security. "Uh, nobody. I mean, it's one of the YACCERS. She said she couldn't sleep...and wanted a cup of hot chocolate. I caught her coming in the front door."

"And what have I said about locking the doors?"

"Sorry, Sister, it won't happen again—"

"See that it doesn't."

"Should I call the police?"

This time Sister Augustine paused, weighing her options. "No. For Heaven's sake, *no*! The last thing we need is to have the police sniffing about our affairs."

"What do I do with the girls?"

"Give this one a warm meal and kick her out," she said with a sigh. "We don't need to be taking in any runaways. They'll just invite unwanted attention. Tell the other one we have no cocoa and send her back to bed."

"Thank you, ma'am," said Elspeth.

"*Don't* call me 'ma'am'!" Sister Augustine slammed her door closed as Mr. Green led a chatty Elspeth down the steps toward the kitchen.

Leaning up against the wall, I slid down to the floor, finally allowing myself to breathe. If Mr. Green's going to lock the front door, my only chance of escaping unnoticed is if I spend the night in here. I'll sneak down during breakfast, and blend in with the rest of the kids. Olivia's probably going to spend the entire night awake, worried about me, but I had no other recourse.

I silenced my phone and texted Olivia. —*R U okay? I'm fine, but will have 2 spend the night here. C u @ breakfast.*—

She instantly texted me back. —*I'm OK. Be careful.*—

And Elspeth! Once again, she saved my ass. And it sounds like she's fine, even getting a free meal out of the deal. It'll probably appeal to her impish sense of humor.

But *who* was in the room with Sister Augustine?

I waited by the door, looking through the keyhole. I fell asleep at some time around two in the morning, before Augustine's mysterious visitor left.

Chapter Thirteen

The sound of YACCERS tromping in through the front door woke me up. Reacquainting my foggy brain with my impromptu sleeping quarters, I crawled to my feet. With a full bladder, undoubtedly ghastly breath, and my hair all over the place, I needed to rejoin my fellow campers. I opened the door, saw the hallway empty, and sprinted toward the stairwell.

I descended the stairwell, trying to adopt a casual stride, avoiding eye contact with the kids who glanced my way. I dove into the mob, acknowledging those closest to me with nods and smiles. Scanning the lunch hall, I found Olivia standing just inside the doorway.

"Morning, O'." I leaned in and gave her a quick kiss.

"*Gah!*" She waved her hands in front of her face. "Gross!"

"Yeah, um, sorry." I lowered my voice. "I haven't had time to brush my teeth."

"Man! So…you're okay?" She placed her hand on my shoulder, probably to keep my morning breath at bay more than anything.

"Yeah. What happened to you last night?" The crowd seemed more animated this morning, buzzing about the day's impending events, so I thought it safe to talk freely.

"I had the front door open a crack and heard

someone coming down the hallway. I popped inside before Mr. Green went up the stairs. I told him I couldn't sleep and wanted some cocoa." She grimaced at the thought of again having to play the helpless little girl. "Then I heard voices upstairs, and Mr. Green told me to wait while he ran up there."

"Yeah, that would've been me…and Elspeth."

Olivia sighed. "Yeah, I *saw* her. She got a meal, while I got sent back to sleep." She shook her head at the unfairness of it all.

"Did Mr. Green find out your name? Who you were?"

She shook her head. "No, never came up. What did you learn?"

"Sister Augustine knows who I am and is working with someone to get rid of me."

Olivia jerked her head back, her eyes huge. "*What? What do you mean 'get rid of?'*"

"I'm not sure. Maybe she just doesn't want me joining YAC, or maybe it's something worse. I didn't see who it was. Just know it was a guy—"

"Ladies and gentlemen, may I have your attention, please?" Sister Augustine assumed her position at the podium, looking much more irritated than before. "While you gather your breakfast, several fellow YACCERS will explain today's activities and rules."

I followed Olivia to the food window, grabbing a paper plate full of powdered eggs and cold toast, lumps of butter refusing to melt on top. "Eww," said Olivia. Looking at the unappealing food, I nodded in agreement.

Leaving the window, I bumped into Elizabeth, Donovan close behind her. "*Good* morning," said

Donovan, full of too much cheer this early in the morning.

"Morning." I looked around for a place to stash my plate to free up my hands in anticipation of one of his welcoming greetings.

Olivia sidled up. "Morning, guys." She gave Elizabeth a mock appearance of concern, rapidly fluttering her eyelids. "Why, Elizabeth, you look tired this morning." I suppose Olivia couldn't help herself, but...*uh-oh*.

Elizabeth looked past Olivia, freezing me with her ice cube eyes. "Yes, I *suppose* I didn't sleep very well last night." A blonde eyebrow arched up her forehead's mast, and she frowned.

"Um, sorry to hear that," I said, staring at the ceiling.

Donovan intervened like a marvelous *deus ex machina*. "Well, Elizabeth *always* looks wonderful to me." He bent down, his entire face drawn taut in a painful-looking smile. She returned the scrunched-up face. I suppose it's their "thing." Olivia seemed mortified at the cuteness overdose.

"I guess you guys patched up your little falling out yesterday," said Olivia. I pinched her elbow. Now really isn't the time to antagonize anyone.

Elizabeth held her chin up imperially. "*Not* that it's any concern of yours, Olivia, but Donovan and I are doing just fine. Although we still have some things to discuss." Donovan dropped his smile. Poor guy. I've been on the receiving end of Elizabeth's ire. Can't imagine what it's like to receive it in daily portions.

"Okay, guys, take your seats." Sister Augustine had vanished, to be replaced by two burly, short-cropped-haired boys in tight YAC shirts and cargo pants. Indistinguishable in appearance, they looked as if they were on their way to the local marine recruiting center. Tweedleduh and Tweedledunce.

We spotted Allie, Dickers, and Parker already wolfing down their breakfast.

"Mornin'," said Dickers, his mouth stuffed full of toast. He aggressively tore into his meal as if the "testosterone fairy" had visited him overnight.

"What's up?" said Parker. A corner of his mouth pulled up, suspicious eyes glaring at me. "Hey, McKenna, did you even come back last night? After your walk?"

"Um, yeah, Parker, you were zonked."

"That's weird…" He tapped his lips with two fingertips. "…you weren't in your bunk when I got up this morning."

"Oh, well…early riser." Hoping to ward off more questions, I turned to Dickers. "Damn, Dickers, way to devour." He scraped the rest of his eggs off the plate and dropped them into his mouth as if he hadn't eaten in days.

"Gotta keep my strength up," he said around his mouthful. "For paintball."

Olivia grimaced, probably more at the thought of paintball than Dickers' display of poor table manners.

"Okay, now for the rules of paintball," yelled one of the boys, adopting a hoarse, drill-sergeant manner. The YACCERS went wild. Fists pummeled the tabletops, feet stomped in unison. Several of the more boisterous boys grunted and howled like a zoo's monkey house residents.

"Okay, listen up, *especially* you newbies." Some

derisive laughter arose at the expense of us poor newbies. "We'll be divided into four teams, each designated by a different colored tape wrapped around your arms and your guns. The four teams are made up of the four cabins." That'd put me on "Team Blue." Poor Olivia was stuck on "Team Pink"—pink, of course, being what she calls the "most sexist color in the universe."

"We'll be playing in the woods, a two-mile perimeter around the campsite marked off by tape. Playing outside the tape is strictly *forbidden*." The audience cheered, although I couldn't understand why. "You'll each be given a designated starting base at four separate locations, each out of view of the other. The object of the game...*elimination*." Fists pumped assertively in the air. Allison looked frightened, paler than usual. "To eliminate an opponent, you need to shoot them, leaving at least a nickel-sized paint splotch on their body." While Tweedleduh delivered the rules, it was Tweedledunce's job to rile the audience by raising his hands in the air. "Splatter *will* be accepted as long as a nickel-sized spot is left on your opponent."

Dickers leaned in to whisper. "'Splatter' is when a paintball hits a rock or tree and the paint bounces off onto your opponent." He closed his eyes and nodded authoritatively.

Tweedleduh bellowed on. "Once a player is eliminated, he's to go to the Dead Zone...a safe haven for eliminated players. The Dead Zone is the cabins and the immediate area in front of them. If you're *unsure* you're hit, call for a *'paint check'* and the closest player—no matter what team—is to stop and check your body."

"There's a couple bodies *I'd* like to check," yelled out a boy. A hush fell over the crowd. I sorta felt bad for him as it obviously wasn't the proper venue for lecherous good times.

Tweedleduh continued unfazed, while Tweedledunce cupped his hand over his eyes, making a show out of scouting the audience for the wrong-headed offender. "Once a player is eliminated, he's to raise his rifle over his head and yell, '*I'm hit,*' to any player he sees, until he safely enters the Dead Zone. It is *strictly* against the rules to shoot a player who's already hit. We're setting a time limit of three hours. The team with the most survivors will be declared the *winner.*" A rowdy roar filled the lunch hall.

"*Now*, the safety rules." Groans went up throughout the building. Apparently, safety isn't nearly as fun as elimination. "You are *always* to wear your masks until you reach the Dead Zone or the game is finished." Tweedleduh held up a stubby finger. "There is *no* blind firing."

Once again, Dickers shared his vast knowledge of all things paintball. "'Blind firing's' when you don't see an opponent and you just start shooting like crazy." He leaned back, entwined his fingers across his chest, and pursed his lips like a smug teacher.

"You are to *always* allow surrender, if said opponent should want to surrender." Tweedledunce appeared appalled at the notion someone would be so weak as to even contemplate surrender. He balled up his fists, rubbed his eyes, and opened his mouth wide to pantomime a crying baby. "And *finally*, you are *not* to shoot your guns over two hundred fifty FPS! You're allowed to use your own gun if you have one and have it calibrated at two hundred fifty FPS!"

Dickers rocked back and forth on the bench, nearly panting, a soldier looking forward to a tour of duty. "That means 'feet per second.' There's an indicator on your gun. They can shoot a *lot* higher than that."

"*Okay*, I think that covers the basics. You have *one* hour until game time. Gather your gear, get comfortable with it, and *let's play paintball*!" Tweedleduh and Tweedledunce lifted their cannon-like arms in the air, urging the crowd to mass hysteria. Eyes lit up with the promise of ensuing violence. Kids slapped backs and punched shoulders.

Sister Augustine took the stage, silencing everyone with a few no-nonsense hand waves. "Ladies and gentlemen..." The crowd behaved like anything but. "Before you are released to the game, let's keep in mind what our goals as YACCERS are. That goal is brotherhood." And, here I thought the goal was elimination. "This is a team-building exercise. You need to trust your fellow team members. You're united in fighting a common enemy." Her lips spread slowly into a cryptic smile. "Just like everyone in YAC is united against a common enemy in our fight to spread God's word."

*Ah, there we go!*

\*\*\*\*

"So stupid," groused Olivia. "So, so stupid!" Sitting on a log in front of her cabin, we were trying to make sense of our paintball equipment.

"I know, right? I never thought we'd be doing something like this."

The skies were no longer the beautiful deep blue they'd been for a two-week streak, having taken on a depressingly dark life. Earlier the wind whipped at the heads of trees, bending them down, forcing them to bow to nature's majesty. But the wind had stopped, packed its bags, and migrated elsewhere. Likewise, yesterday the woods were filled with noise. Leaves crackled underneath animals' paws. Yips from coyotes and hoots from owls were the norm. Today, an unsettling quiet, a disturbing calm, permeated the air. The later the morning grew, the darker the skies became. Yet there hadn't been a hint of rain, a whisper of thunder.

"You think they'll call off this stupid game if it rains?" asked Olivia.

"I doubt it. Everyone seems pretty hell-bent on going through with this."

Olivia looked up toward the ominously-colored skies. "Huh." She picked up a plastic container that resembled a bicycle helmet. "What the hell is *this*?"

"I think that's the container for the paintballs. Dickers called it a 'hopper.'" I took it from her and found a slot where it attached to her gun.

"These rifles look like tricked-out water guns." She tried out different stances, aiming into the now vacated woods.

"I think they look like mini-machine guns…from space."

Olivia rolled her eyes at my geek sensibilities. The guns were obviously used, probably not the newest in models. Yet, they did have a sleek, futuristic design about them, all plastic and smooth contours.

"At least it doesn't weigh much." Olivia yelled, "*Hah,*" and shot at another imaginary predator. She picked up a cylindrically-shaped device from her pile of gear. "Wait, now, what's this? Do we *really* need all of this crap? I'm maybe gonna take a cue from your dodge-ball rules and run right out into the line of fire just to get it over with."

"That's gotta be the air tank. You can't shoot your gun without it." I connected mine to the back end of the gun.

She eyed me suspiciously. "And just how do *you* know so much about paintball? You're not a closet paintballer, are you?"

I laughed. "No. Didn't you hear Dickers tell me everything? While we were in line to pick up all this junk?"

"Yeah. Well, no. I heard him going on about *something,* but I tuned him out since he was boring the hell outta' me." She hooked an air tank onto the back end of her gun. "So, this gizmo...just sorta rests on your arm?" She held the gun out, looking through the sights, the tank nestled comfortably in the crook of her arm.

"I think so." My gun proved way too short for my long arms, making it tough to balance it.

Olivia rolled some paintballs between her fingers. "These are kinda cute."

"Olivia, *don't* let the rest of these guys hear you refer to a paintball as 'cute.'"

"They do seem...damn gung-ho, don't they?" She dropped the gun to her side, an unusual seriousness darkening her features.

"Something's wrong. It just doesn't *feel* right—"

"What do you mean?"

"It's just...when we got here, everyone was a zombie. Then they got fired up over Danvers. And, today, it's like they're actually, I dunno, as you said 'gung-ho' but way too much. I mean you saw the way Dickers scarfed through his breakfast. And how he's *way* excited about this game. It's almost as if…"

"What?"

"I'm not sure. But it's not…*natural*. Maybe Augustine's spiking their sports drink or…something else entirely."

"What? You mean witchcraft stuff?" I motioned for Olivia to quiet her voice.

"Maybe."

"Gah." She plopped down onto the log next to me.

"Yeah. Which, I guess, is another reason we have to go through with this dumb game. I just *feel* like something's gonna happen."

Olivia rested her head on my shoulder as I stroked her hair. "I don't like the sound of this."

"Neither do I, O', neither do I."

We watched the rest of the crowd, running to and fro in a panic, excited about the forthcoming game. Fists were bumped, teasing insults traded, voices raised to maximum effect. It's like the entire world had gone insane. Is this how people would react if they found out Armageddon loomed? Would they live out their violent war fantasies, any last semblance of civilization abandoned?

Olivia and I sat alone on our small remote log, the last bastion of humanity, an island unto our own. Our lips formed a bridge of unity in a lasting kiss. We held each other for a long time, practically floating on our raft of love while the ocean of madness splashed around us. In that single moment, the fears of my future, YACCERS, hate crimes, evil pastors, deranged

Spencers, hooded murderers…none of it mattered right now. None of it. In that solitary moment frozen in time, all of my confusion and problems simply vanished. Being in love is enough to carry us through anything. I kissed her again, lingering on her soft lips basking in her sweet fragrance, appreciating who she is…feeling like the luckiest guy in the world.

When we broke away, Olivia said, "Well, I'm damn glad you finally brushed your teeth."

I stood, pulling Olivia up beside me. "Anything for you."

"*Don't* be going all Donovan on me, Tex."

We held hands, laughing, until we noticed our audience twenty-five feet away. In the middle of the field, Sister Augustine stood, arms folded, glowering at us. She looked out of place, an imperial older woman, standing amidst all the chaos surrounding her. Kids came close to knocking her over in their exuberance, yet she seemed to have no fear and a natural force-field around her.

"You two better get to your designated starting bases." She walked off without waiting for an answer.

Olivia shot me a wide-eyed stare before we broke into laughter. Our way of coping.

Reaching one final time into her gear pile, Olivia pulled out her mask. She put it on, planted her feet wide, and pretended to cock her paint gun. "How do I look? Bad-*ass*?" She kicked one leg high into the air. "Hoo-*rah*!"

The bulbous plastic goggles hid her eyes, the green mask looking like some sort of insect shell. I *wanted* to stop myself but couldn't. "You look like a giant bug."

She whipped off her mask. "All right, we'll see

how long it is before I kiss you like *that* again."

****

"*Game on*," a voice called out through the woods. My teammates scattered, seemingly with no thought given to strategy. With total bedlam the name of the game, everyone ran in random directions, the chuffing of the rifles filling the air. Players rolled, ducked into the woods, and shimmied up tree trunks. A chorus of voices screamed in the distance, echoing throughout the woods. Welcome to the YACCERS version of *The Hunger Games*.

Parker polished the shaft of his gun with a lover's touch. "Go on, McKenna," he gestured with his rifle. "What are you waiting for?" His voice sounded hollow within the mask, impossible to gauge his mindset.

"I don't really know where to go—"

"Just start shooting the other players." He shook his head mockingly and scurried into the woods.

Dickers clambered up to me, dropping into a crouch. "Come on, McKenna, let's go take 'em out!" He sprang up with a giddy leap, roaring an unintelligible battle cry, and flattened himself against a large oak tree. Peering around it, he dove into the woods.

I pulled off my mask and wiped the visor with my T-shirt. A roadmap of scratches across the eye sockets made it next to impossible to see. Realizing I couldn't improve my vision, I put the mask back on. Behind me, I saw red tape strung between trees cordoning off the playing area. How easy it'd be to just duck under the tape, hide in the non-playing field and wait out this ridiculous game. But Elspeth told me I needed to be here. For *whatever* reason.

Following Dicker's lead, I ran toward the line of trees and sought shelter behind the largest trunk. Voices raged from every direction, urgency and panic supplanting merriment. "*I'm hit*," were the only words I could make out, a repetitious shout-out spreading like social media.

Peeking around the tree, I saw a girl with pink tape around her arms. I swung the gun up, nearly dropping it. Steadying the rifle, I caught the girl in my sights and squeezed the trigger. *Whiff.* The paintball fell far short of my intended target. The girl pulled a double-take and brought her gun up. I repeatedly shot higher, eventually landing a paintball on her leg. Standing paralyzed, a stunned deer in the forest, she stared at her artificial wound before turning her attention to me. I couldn't see her eyes, but her stance told me she was pissed. "*I'm hit*," she said.

"Um, sorry," I said as I ran by her.

The skies deepened into an angry purple, darkening the woods into formless shadows. Entering the most heavily wooded area, the trees folded in upon themselves, forming a bridge of branches and leaves overhead. I moved quickly, clumsily, craning my head back and forth for player sightings. Twigs snapped loudly with every footfall, making stealth not a viable option. A stifling, abnormally humid. Sweat poured down my face, condensation forming on the goggles.

I came up to a ravine, a creek resting dormant within it, merely a trickle of water still alive. I hopped into it, squatted, and looked over the edge. It proved an advantageous position as I could spot anyone approaching from all four sides. If I could just remain "alive" in my bunker, I should be able to pick off anybody who approaches. I heard someone running toward me around a bend in the creek. Squelches popped and belched from the mud underneath their feet. I pointed my gun toward the bend as the footsteps grew louder. The player rounded the corner, his gun hefted in my direction. Seeing the blue tape around his arms, I waved my hands frantically. Even though I couldn't distinguish anyone in their mask, I recognized Dickers' goofy gait and his unfortunate high waters.

"Dickers, it's *me*, Tex. "

"Whoa, I about took you out, dude." He knelt beside me. "How many kills have you got?" Out of breath, he panted like a dog.

"Just one."

"Lame! I've got three! They never saw me coming." He placed one knee underneath him and planted the other foot solidly in the mud. "Here's a tip, McKenna. When you're squatting and shooting, always keep one foot on the ground. That way, in case you need to run quickly, you can get right up. If you have both knees on the ground like you do now, you're a sitting duck. Also, if you're gonna be on your knees, put your feet underneath your butt. Not out to the side. Otherwise, someone can nail your foot."

"Oh, yeah. I can see that. Thanks, I—" Before I could finish, he raced down the creek, growling.

I traveled down the creek, this time slowly and keeping my head below the ravine's edge. Stopping every few feet, I listened carefully. Nothing but far-off, ghostly voices claiming their death tolls. But the ruckus appeared to be dwindling at a rapid pace.

I heard male voices and stopped. Carefully edging my head up, I saw two figures emerging from the woods, green tape wrapped around their arms. Soon they'd be right on top of me. I jumped to my feet, spraying my gun in an arc. One of the guys brought his gun up and dropped to his feet before he realized he'd taken a hit. I missed the standing kid with my first sweep, so I fired again, nailing him with a *splat* on the chest.

"*Damn it*," said the upright boy. He threw his gun down and folded his arms over his chest. The other one stood and raised his gun above his head. "*I'm hit*." As they slumped away to the Dead Zone, one of them placed a supportive arm across the other's shoulder. These YACCERS are taking their battles *way* too seriously.

"Sorry, sorry, sorry…" I repeated while running past them. I hated to leave the creek because it seemed to be a pretty good strategic position, but I couldn't just hide there, waiting for the game to come to me. I needed to be proactive.

Running from tree to tree, I now entered the center of the woods. Hearing no interlopers, I took a moment to catch my breath. I sorely needed to take my mask off, the sweat making me as uncomfortable as being in a personal hellish sauna. No sooner did I sit down on a pile of large rocks and yank off my mask, when I heard someone tiptoeing through the leaves less than six feet from me. I raised my gun as my heart thumped against my ribcage. I couldn't *believe* how I started to enjoy this.

"Tex?" whispered Olivia. "Is that you?" She approached me cautiously, her gun leveled at my chest.

"Yeah. It's me." I lowered my gun as she did the same.

She plopped down next to me, laughing. "How many kills do you have?" She took her mask off, her hair matted to her head.

"Three. How about you?"

"Six, maybe seven, hard to say." She flexed her muscle. "Hoo-*yeah*! I *obliterated* Dickers."

"Yeah, I'm sure that went over well." The thought of Dickers being taken out by Olivia brought a smile to my lips.

"He never saw me coming. He looked like a chunk of modern art before I was done with him, all splotched up. I also think I got Donovan. But I can't tell who anybody is in these damn masks."

"Yeah, I know, right?" I stretched my legs out, letting them dangle over the rock pile. "What about Allie and Elizabeth? Are they still in the game?"

She hitched her shoulders up. "I don't know. I haven't seen 'em since I tore out of the starting zone. Tell you what, though…I don't think there're too many kids left out here. Most of 'em got shot at the start."

"That'd explain why there's not much yelling going on now. Has there been anything weird going on? That you've noticed?"

She tilted her head. "Really, Tex? *Really*? We're playing paintball at a YACCER retreat, and you want to know if there's anything '*weird*' going on?"

"Well, besides the obvious, I guess. I mean, I'm trying to figure out why it's so damned important for me to be here."

"I dunno. It's kinda weird. These guys are all super-pumped and psyched about playing paintball to the point of psycho…but when they get taken out, it's like they lose the will to live or something."

"Yeah, I've seen that. It's like Jekyll and Hyde, two different people, almost. Huh."

"And then there's the sky. I don't know if you'd categorize *that* as weird, but it almost looks like night. And everything's so…still."

I looked up, trying to glimpse the sky through the wooded coverage. Olivia's right. The skies were such a dark blue they were nearly black.

I jumped to my feet. "Okay, time for me to re-enter the game." I grabbed Olivia's hand and pulled her up. "Olivia…sorry for this." I shot repeatedly at the rock closest to Olivia until paint splattered the back of her jeans.

She twisted her head, trying to inspect her backside. She threw her gun down with a crash and put her hands on her hips. "You dick! I can't *believe* you just *did* that."

"Sorry," I said, chuckling. Which is *not* the way I should've responded. "I'm just putting you out of your misery. I knew you didn't want to play—"

She pummeled her fists against my chest, knocking me back. "I was just getting into it, too!" Maybe a little *too* into it.

"Sorry! Ow! Sorry!" I tried to pull her into a hug, not only to pacify her but for self-protection. "Come on, O', it's kill or be killed."

She held her hands out and shook them angrily. "*Gah!*"She picked her gun up and held it over her head. "I still can't believe you did that." Shaking her head, she stormed away. "*I'm hit.* Enemy from team blue over here. Come and get him. Blue *jackass* right here. Get him while you can…"

I took that as my cue to leave. I called out another

apology to Olivia, but she didn't want it. As I wound my way through a maze of trees, I could still hear her calling out my location.

Footsteps approached. The trees being too thin to provide shelter, I dove to the ground, gun raised for action. Five feet in front of me stood two figures, green tape on their arms. I fired at their legs, covering their pants with multi-colored splotches.

"Man," said one boy. The two sulked off to their destination, yelling, their voices void of emotion.

I sat, my back butted up against a tree trunk. I wrestled my mask free again. The clammy air supplied little relief. The voices had practically vanished, a few stragglers mournfully calling out their fates. The quiet felt nerve-wracking. It didn't seem like a tranquil calm, but rather, a foreboding omen of things to come.

To my right, I heard a soft whistle. I leaped to my feet, my mask uselessly residing on the ground. A figure materialized from behind a cluster of thin tree trunks, carefully stepping through the leaves. I rocked my rifle up and scrabbled to hitch it onto my forearm. When I saw the blue tape around his arms, I lowered my gun. He swaggered toward me, full of cocky confidence.

"Parker," I sighed and felt my muscles unwind. "How you doin'?"

He stopped four feet in front of me. "Hey, McKenna." He yanked his rifle up, the barrel sticking in my face.

I stumbled back a step. "What are you doing? We're teammates!"

He chuckled, the sound of his laughter strangled by his mask. "Let's call this 'friendly fire.'" I turned at the last moment, the paintball exploding onto my ear. The impact knocked me onto the ground. My ear felt raw and burning like I'd stumbled onto a wasp's nest. The paint entered my ear, obstructing my hearing, my heart somehow throbbing within my head.

Parker stood over me, a dark silhouette, his rifle pointed into my face. "Parker! What the hell are you doing?" I tried to scuttle backward, my feet slipping against the leaves.

"This is *really* gonna hurt." His finger enclosed around the trigger.

A sudden wisp of wind sliced through the air followed by a thump. "*Ow!*" cried Parker. The sounds repeated while Parker screamed in pain. He dropped his rifle and danced like a clumsy marionette, jerking and bending, his hands flailing at his back. When he swiveled around, numerous paintball marks covered his back. His body continued to convulse from shots to his front side.

A dark figure dropped out of a nearby tree, landing with a *thump*. Elspeth stepped out of the shadows, her paintball gun continually spraying Parker as she advanced. "How's *that* feel?" she asked.

"*Who...ah!* Who the hell are you? *Oww!*"

Elspeth's mouth twisted into a wry grin. "I'm the one who took you out...*bitch*." Walking casually toward Parker, she never let up shooting. Stopping three feet shy of him, she pirouetted and landed a drop kick onto his chest, knocking him into the dirt next to me. Parker groaned, clearly disoriented, and shook his head.

Elspeth extended her hand and aided me to my feet. She looked down at Parker and clicked her lips. "What a jackass."

I tried to shake out some of the paint from my ear. "Yeah, no kidding."

"How ya' doin'?" Elspeth had one hand cupped under her elbow, the other holding the rifle up over her shoulder. In her black leather garb, she looked like a deadly assassin.

"Um, okay…I think." My hearing returned bit by bit. "Thanks for the save again."

She nodded, no big thing, before her expression turned dark. "Hey, something *bad's* about to happen. You need to get back to the cabin."

"What do you mean?"

She shrugged, the creaking of her leather jacket sounding unnatural in the woods. "Dunno. Just get going." She slapped a hand on my shoulder and shoved me.

"What about you? Are you coming?"

"No. I've got to go back and get Elizabeth's clothing," she said in a hushed tone. "Left 'em back by the creek. Now *go.*" With that, she turned, running and leaping like a leather-clad fawn, her faux-hawk waving back and forth.

I nearly tripped over Parker. On his knees, he struggled to get up. "*Damn*! That wasn't…fair. Help me up, McKenna."

I fought the urge to give him a good, swift kick. "Oh, whatever, Parker. You could've blinded me."

Parker pulled off his mask and looked up at me, his eyes glassy and sharp at the same time. "It was…just a joke."

I almost launched into a tirade, but Elspeth's warning held more importance. I set off through the woods, remembering to yell, *"I'm hit,"* during my mad dash. But it hardly seemed necessary as I didn't see or hear anyone. Game over, I guess.

Several tree limbs seemingly jumped into my path, thwacking at my face. I absorbed the pain, not letting it stall my progress. Looking above me gave me no sense of my locale, but the woods thinned out in front of me. I broke through bushes, scraped up against trees, and gathered a small collection of prickers, but the pain seemed like nothing compared to what I imagined could be happening back at the cabin.

I found a well-trodden path and followed it. Finally, an opening lay ahead. Across the vast field stood the main building, the paintball-eliminated milling about like disgruntled ants. The skies above hung even deeper, darker, and still as death. And that's when I heard her ear-piercing scream carry out across the meadow.

*Olivia.*

Chapter Fourteen

My fists jacking, I raced across the grounds, my feet thudding onto the turf and jarring my teeth. *Please let her be all right, please*! I burst through the last of the woods and into the field in time to see Olivia run out of her cabin, her arms thrashing about. Behind her, Allie and a few other girls tumbled out of the cabin, baffled looks on their faces.

"Oh, my *God*," shouted Olivia. "He's in there!" She rushed toward the gathered onlookers, her thumb hitched back toward the cabin.

I bulldozed through the crowd, barely slowing down. Allie held an arm around Olivia's shoulders. "Shhh, Olivia," she said, "it's okay."

"Olivia!"

Upon hearing me, she broke away from Allie and dashed toward me. Flinging her arms around my neck, she nearly took us both down. "Are you okay?"

"Oh my *God*, Tex. He came after me!"

"Who? What happened?" The gatherers formed a circle of nosiness around us.

Olivia shuddered within my embrace. "The *Reaper*. I was washing my face in the bathroom…when a gloved hand clamped down on my mouth and the other went around my waist. In the mirror, I saw a guy wearing a Reaper's costume!"

"Oh, my God—"

"I knocked my head back hard as I could…and I nailed his chin I think. He fell back into the bathroom stall…and then I ran like *hell* out of there." She gripped me again, burying her head into my chest.

"What did he say?"

She looked at me, her eyes wide and round. "Nothing."

"Did anybody see anything? *Anybody*?" A few onlookers shook their heads, most of them ignoring me. "Stay here, O'!" I rushed into her cabin. It appeared to be empty. And quiet. Cautiously entering the bathroom area, I ludicrously thought…so *they* get bathroom stalls. I pushed the stall door open directly behind the sinks. Empty. I bent down and looked underneath the stalls of the other two, seeing no feet or signs of occupancy. I kicked the next two doors open wide, stepping back quickly in case a toilet squatter might lunge at me. Nothing. Just well-cleaned bathroom stalls, very much unlike ours.

When I walked back outside, Sister Augustine, flanked by two of her sidekicks, had encircled Olivia. Parker stood directly behind Olivia, attempting to console her with his hollow charm.

As I approached, Sister Augustine glared at me, angry eyes glowing. "What seems to be the problem here?"

"One of your YACCERS attacked Olivia." Ready to match Sister Augustine's righteous indignation, I stood my ground. "Maybe you should search everyone's belongings."

"I *hardly* believe that to be the issue here, Mr. McKenna." She raised her sharp chin, the better to slice me in half with.

"Then what *is*? Olivia was attacked! During *your* retreat. By *someone* here. You're not going to investigate this?"

Sister Augustine looked at her henchman and inclined her head toward the cabin. "Go check it out." They left in a blur of burly green and brown. "Young lady, *what* exactly happened?"

Olivia explained while Sister Augustine shook her head. "I find it *very* hard to believe a YAC member would be involved in such nonsense. Did you antagonize anyone? Do something perhaps unforthcoming?"

"You have *got* to be kidding me," said Olivia. "I was attacked. And you're acting like *I* did something wrong. Or '*unforthcoming*'!" When Olivia punched the last word, she adopted a snooty manner.

Sister Augustine's eyebrows raised, a scary sight. But not as scary as the sudden, blaring siren in the distance.

When Mr. Green and Mr. Brown came out of the cabin, Sister Augustine waved them over and whispered into Mr. Green's ear, sending him galumphing away. Seconds later, the unconfident voice of Mr. Green crackled over the loudspeaker. "Attention, boys and girls! There's been, ah, a tornado sighting close by. Let's all head toward the center hall and file into the cellar in, um, an orderly fashion."

The YACCERS stopped their mindless wandering about, some of them breaking into a sprint toward the building. Sister Augustine stared up at the still, dark skies, and shot us one last look before setting off for the central hall.

"Tex," said Olivia. "I *knew* it felt like tornado

weather." Allie nervously scanned the sky while Parker ran toward the hall, overtaking many in front of him.

"Come on, O'. We'll figure out the Reaper later, but right now..." I pointed toward the sky. As we made our way across the field, drops of rain fell upon us.

Inside the building, we joined the line snaking toward the back of the building. A new nervousness filled the eyes of the YACCERS, their lively energy dissipated. Donovan walked in the opposite direction of the line, checking out everyone he passed. He stopped in front of us, concern screwing up his handsome features. "Hey, have you guys seen Elizabeth?"

Olivia shook her head. "No. I'm sure she's here somewhere. She's—" Donovan bolted before she could finish.

*Crap.* Elspeth's still out there. "Olivia, I've got to go back to the woods."

"What? *Why?*"

"Elspeth's out there. She helped me. I'll explain later...but, I think she's still out there."

"Tex, what can you do that she can't do?"

She made sense, but I had to try. Elspeth has helped me out *way* too many times. "I've just got to."

Olivia looked into my eyes, hers flitting back and forth. "Okay, then... Do what you gotta do."

I looked down the line and gestured toward Dickers, Parker, and Allie. "Maybe you should join them, O'. Safety in numbers."

She yanked my arm and pulled me back, planting a quick kiss on my lips. "You be careful."

"Always." I exited the line and pushed my way out of the building.

Outside, I scanned the horizon, hoping to see

Elspeth—or Elizabeth—running toward the shelter. The sirens augmented in volume, a mournful and frightening sound. With the skies nearly pitch black, it could have been midnight. In the distance, I saw a cloud in the shape of an umbrella threatening to open up. Living in Kansas all my life, I knew what that foretold. I didn't have much time.

I tore across the field. The rain dwindled as if it, too, feared what loomed in the distance. I entered the woods and called out Elspeth's name—even trying *Elizabeth* several times for good measure. Recognizing the dirt path from before, I followed it to the middle of the woods where Elspeth said she stashed Elizabeth's clothes.

"*Elspeth!*" I saw her cutting through a swath of trees, carrying a bundle. "We've got to go. *Now!*" When she ran toward me, I grasped her hand. Her eyes filled with fright, her black lower lip trembling. When Elspeth gets scared, I get *petrified.*

With no time for words, I pulled her along behind me, recklessly dashing through the dark woods. A blast of cold wind blew down the path, stirring up leaves and spinning them. Tree branches bent down. Limbs snapped and dropped about us, exploding like fireworks. My arm up, I warded off one falling branch with a lucky blow.

We exited the woods to a ferocious howling. The wind lifted Elspeth's wig and sailed it back into the woods. Off to the north, a funnel cloud cut through the woods, a boiling wall of black steam. Cracks emanated from the forest as trees lifted and flung back down, toppling others. The howling wind grew in intensity, an insane banshee. The funnel cloud quickly traveled toward the complex. And we were still half a mile away from the shelter.

"Elspeth! We're not going to make it to the center in time!" Yet the woods would be even more dangerous than staying out in the open field. 500 feet away, the parked cars sat to the left of us. Parked in the front row, Elizabeth's bright yellow sports car stood out, beaming like a golden steed. "Do you have the keys?"

She had them in her hand before I finished screaming the question. We took off running into the wind, the devil chasing us.

"I can't drive," she shouted.

"Throw me the keys!" She did, and I nearly dropped them to the hellish winds. With fumbling fingers, I unlocked the car and reached across to open her door. She crawled in fast.

"Go! *Go, Tex!*" Elspeth leaned forward, fingers digging into the dashboard.

The dirt access road's entrance sat no more than ten feet away, and I gunned the car in that direction. The funnel broke through the woods, the farthest cabin on the lot forestalling it. My cabin. Racing onto the narrow road, I risked a glance back. In mere seconds, the tornado chopped through the cabin. Logs and other debris swirled about the bottom of the cloud before being discarded as deadly projectiles. The roof vanished, and the cabin caved in.

I stomped the pedal down as far as I could without ramming the car into the trees. The wind whipped a large branch onto our windshield with a loud *smack*. A giant vein spread across the glass. I screamed, clamped down on my bladder. Elspeth looked behind us. "Go, go, *go!* I think it's turning back this way!"

*Can a car even outrun a tornado*? I maneuvered through the twisting road. In the rear-view mirror, I saw a large tree trunk plummet to the ground we just passed over. The car's tires skidded at one hairpin turn. I yanked the wheel in that direction as if driving on snow. The car righted itself, and we pulled out onto the highway. I plunged the gas pedal down, reaching 95 MPH.

"*Tex!* It's coming this way!"

The cloud, almost as if following us, carved its deadly path through the woods.

"A pen and a piece of paper, Elspeth!" Without questioning me, she grabbed a notebook and pen from the floor of the car, poised to follow my next instruction. "Write down these words!" I recited the Latin spell to fend off a snowstorm Mickey had taught me two years before. Didn't know if it'd work on tornadoes, but we were out of options.

Behind us, the tornado exited the woods, knocking trees across the highway. It followed us down the highway, quickly narrowing our lead. "We're not going to be able to outrun it!"

Elspeth nodded grimly, clutching the spell in her hand.

"We're going for the ditch! Hold onto that spell no matter what!" I wrenched the car to the side of the highway, slamming on the brakes, skidding across the pavement. The car swerved, pulling an involuntary u-turn and came to a jerking halt, sending us into the ditch. Our heads crashed into the padded dashboard. Wet warmth trickled down my forehead.

We jumped out of the car and ran behind it. The funnel came at us like a runaway fourteen-wheeler from

Hell. I pulled Elspeth into the ditch and jumped on top of her, attempting to burrow our way deeper into the mud. I dug, scrabbling, throwing mud aside. Elspeth joined me, back-paddling with one hand. In her other hand, she held onto the spell, the paper rattling in the wind, threatening to take off like a kite. I clamped my eyes shut.

The wind increased, threatening to lift us out of the ditch. The back of my shirt snapped out, flapping like a storm-tossed sail. The roaring of the funnel cloud grew, five freight trains on top of us, my eardrums close to bursting. A loud swooping sound followed by an enormous grinding metal crunch shook the ground beneath us. I took a look back. The tornado closed on us, the tip of it darting in and out of the ditch as if actively searching for us. Elspeth clasped the paper tight against my back, her fingernails digging in like thumbtacks.

"*Hold on, Elspeth!*"

As the cloud drew closer, my legs lifted into the air. I thought of my loved ones, seeking comfort in their faces. Olivia…Dad…my friends. Tears fell from my eyes and were swept away by the callous, uncaring wind.

My feet suddenly dropped as though a protective bubble formed over us. An unexpected silence. A profoundly deep silence, quieter than death.

*Are we dead?*

I opened my eyes and looked up. We lay in the eye of the tornado. A strong gas smell permeated my nostrils, rendering it hard to breathe. Directly above us loomed a circular opening, around 75 feet in diameter, possibly a quarter-mile away. Flashes of internal lightning illuminated the cloud walls, rotating at a stomach-churning speed. The lightning appeared alive, bouncing furiously from side to side, looking for a means of escape. Small, offspring tornadoes birthed with a loud hissing sound before being released to wreak havoc of their own. A cow briefly popped its head in before being sucked back out to oblivion. Paralyzing terror and awe swept through me. And then…the tornado moved on.

Once the tornado passed, the brutal loudness fired back up, then quickly subsided, the tornado taking its menace elsewhere. The wind died down. The air felt still, but not in a sinister fashion. Release came in the form of cool raindrops sprinkling my back. I looked down at Elspeth, whose icy blue eyes seemed oddly at peace. She offered a weak glimmer of a smile. Sitting up, I pulled Elspeth next to me. Off in the horizon light blue skies glowed, promising the end of destruction. Mud caked, we sat, arms draped around one another, survivors, marveling at the beauty of the beckoning blue skies. We laughed, slowly at first, before hysteria overtook us both. I stood and stretched my arms above me, welcoming the cleansing rainfall.

"Uh-oh," said Elspeth, the first words either of us uttered in some time.

"What's wrong now?" I asked, feeling terror re-enter my numb brain. Elspeth pointed silently toward the cornfield next to us. Elizabeth's car had been overturned, smashed flat to the height of two feet.

"She's *not* going to be happy," said Elspeth.

I cleared my throat. "Um, no." Elspeth rested her elbow on my shoulder as we gave Elizabeth's valiant, dead car an appropriate silent memoriam.

\*\*\*\*

Quietly, we walked hand in hand down the highway, side-stepping the rubble. I felt a new unspoken bond between us. Comrades-in-arms, we shared an experience born of the relentless fury of nature and lived through it. Literally, we stared into the eye of a tornado, beholding unspeakable horrors and incredible, dangerous beauty. The blue skies ahead signified a coda—a happy ending to a waking nightmare.

The ripped landscape surrounding us magnified the surreal nature of our survivor's walk. Large tree trunks lay strewn across the highway like fallen soldiers. Cars were flipped, smashed like accordions, littering the highway like so much abandoned trash of the gods. In adjacent fields, bodies of animals lay like a plague had obliterated a farm's livestock. Approaching the dirt road leading back to the retreat area, I saw part of a cabin's roof nestled tightly between two thick trees, a giant's toothpick.

"I hope only the one cabin was destroyed," I said. "We'd better hurry back. I want to make sure Olivia and my friends are okay. And I'm sure Donovan's totally freaked out about Elizabeth."

She nodded as we stepped onto the dirt road. "Tex, I've seen some wild things…in both realms…but that! *That* totally blew me away. I've never even seen a tornado before, let alone rode one."

"Yeah." It was all I could say.

The woods lay in devastation, trees down everywhere. The ones that survived the apocalypse stood sadly alone, watching over their fallen brethren. We came across a large tree trunk blocking the road, probably the one that nearly clobbered us. We attempted to push the tree out of the dirt road, but it wouldn't budge.

Crawling over the trunk, Elspeth stopped and sat on the dead tree. "Tex?"

"Yeah?"

"She doesn't mind you telling, you know."

"Who? What are you talking about?" I leaned against the trunk.

"Brittany Gerlach. I know you've been struggling to keep her sexual identity—her confusion—a secret out of respect for her, but..." Elspeth smiled, holding my attention with her steely eyes. "She sorta let me know it's okay for it to come out. That way maybe her death won't have been for nothing." She hopped off the trunk, brushing her hands against her leather pants.

"Oh."

"You *need* to do it, Tex."

I turned to face her and gripped both her hands in mine. "Okay, you've been talking to Brittany. Do *you* know who the killer is? Who drove Brittany to her death? Who attacked Olivia?"

"Nope. I just know you'll find out soon. You're closer than you think." Voices rang out from the field at the top of the road. The YACCERS had come out from cover. "Okay, I gotta bounce."

"What? Wait...*what?*"

"Good luck telling Elizabeth about her car. Don't worry." She patted my cheek. "She's got good insurance coverage."

"No, wait. *Don't* you do this to me, Elspeth! Don't *you* make me tell her—"

Elspeth's eyelids fluttered like a hummingbird's

wings. She pitched forward, and I caught her, still holding one of her hands. Her eyes refocused, blinking, as she gazed around at her surroundings. Finally, her eyes settled on our grasped hands.

"*What* do you *think* you're doing?" She yanked her hand away from me. *Welcome back, Elizabeth. And thanks a lot, Elspeth.*

"Um, we need to talk, Elizabeth." The YACCERS were fast approaching us. "Quickly."

"What are we *doing* out here?" Her eyes traveled downward, inspecting herself, a tragic mess. Elspeth's muddied leather clothing hung in strips, her makeup running down her face like a dark, polluted river. "*Why* am I wearing Elspeth's clothes? *What* did you get me into *this* time, Tex?"

"There was a tornado. I, um, came after you—Elspeth, I mean. I saved you…" I so didn't want to tell her. But I doubt Elizabeth would want to be caught in Elspeth's clothes, so I took in a deep breath and braved myself. "But I didn't save your car." Lame, Tex, so, so, sooooo very lame.

The look on her face scared me more than a tornado attack. It looked as if she'd been possessed again, but this time not by Elspeth. Her eyes narrowed into terrifying slits, her mouth drew down, her jaw clenched. "What do you mean?" she growled, low and menacing like a dog.

"The only way we could escape from the tornado was in your car." I glanced around, mentally orchestrating my escape route. "Your car's on the side of the highway. Totaled." I ran the words together as if it might help dilute their meaning. It didn't.

Elizabeth raised her fists, shook them at me, and

babbled in some unintelligible language. Finally, she screamed. *That* I understood. I waved my hands, attempting to calm her, only to be met by flailing fists. "You...*you*..."

"*Hey!*" shouted a voice from the top of the road. "Is someone down there? Are you okay?" The voice echoed eerily throughout the destroyed woods.

I lowered my voice to a whisper. "Listen to me, we don't have much time. I'm really, *really* sorry about your car. It wasn't my fault. Um, not really. I'll explain later." I managed to grab one of her wrists and gently wrestled it down to her side. "We need to get our stories straight. I went looking for you in the woods because I last saw you there before I went back to the retreat. You and I escaped the tornado, but...your car wasn't as fortunate." She bunched her face up in a rare loss of composure. "Needless to say, we shouldn't mention anything about witchcraft. But, right now, unless you want to get caught in Elspeth's clothes..." She wrinkled her nose and nodded. I suppose keeping her appearance pristine trumped the slaughter of her car. "...you'd better run up through the woods to your cabin and get changed. And Donovan's worried about you."

For a moment, her angry demeanor vanished. She placed her hand to her mouth. "Oh, my *God*! Donovan!" She turned on her heels, running efficiently through and over the trees.

"Ah, Elizabeth?"

She turned. "What *now*?"

"Um, you're gonna have to get Elspeth a new wig."

She shot back one final, "*Ooooooooh!*"

****

"He was really going to shoot you again in the

face?" asked Olivia.

"Yeah. I think so. Until Elspeth took him out."

"Why?" Olivia wouldn't take her eyes off me, apparently on concussion watch. I held on tight to the "Oh Hell" handle, hoping she wouldn't crash. I've had enough excitement for one day.

"Beats me. At the time, I kinda thought he was the killer, and he was trying to keep me from finding out."

"I guess that makes sense. I mean, sorta. Parker's a dick and everything…but a *killer*, Tex? *Really*?"

"That's just it. He *can't* be the killer! When the Reaper attacked you at the cabin, Parker was behind me in the woods, still recovering. Every time I think it's him, I get proof it's not him. He has an alibi for Calvin's murder. And it *couldn't* have been him talking to Sister Augustine because he was back in the cabin…and now…"

"What?"

"Well, Jasper told me Parker was spending a lot of time with Brittany before she died. But now, I'm not even sure Jasper's telling me the truth."

"Why would Jasper lie?"

"Because I saw him talking with Hastings—"

"So? Hastings hassles everybody!"

"Not football players. And when they saw me watching them, they broke it off…like they had something to hide."

Olivia sighed loudly. "Do you really think Jasper's Hastings's spy?" She smiled and shook her head. "Too many conspiracy movies for you."

"I don't know. But I've gotta consider the possibility. I'm finding myself trusting fewer and fewer people these days. I don't want to be that guy. But after

Red…and then Danny—"

"I know, I know." She placed her hand on mine. "But you can't let it shape your world view. Not *everyone* sucks…or is a killer or spy."

She's right. For every wrong turn, every hidden killer posing as my friend, there are loyal people in my life, people who love me and would never turn on me. And Olivia topped that list.

"So, tell me again what happened with you and Elspeth and the tornado?"

For the third time, I told her the story. After her initial freak-out over my tornado experience, I detected more than a little jealousy. Because she didn't experience it with me and Elspeth did. But she did relish the fact Elizabeth's car got totaled.

"That's just psycho-nuts."

"Yeah, understatement."

"Do you think Mickey's spell protected you guys?"

I hadn't had time to think about it until now. "I don't know, O'. It was either the spell or.. something else. But *something* definitely saved us."

"Huh." After I closed my eyes, Olivia gave a slap to my cheek. "*Don't* go to sleep, Tex."

"Gah! Olivia, I *don't* have a concussion."

"What? Are you a doctor or something? Just keep talking, Dr. McKenna."

"Well, that was a *wonderful* Young American Christians' retreat, right?"

"Oh, yeah. I *totally* got my four hundred fifty dollars worth of fun. At least Sister Augustine didn't get to pass the offering tray around again."

"Yeah, she did seem kinda pissed about the whole tornado thing. I think we're all damned lucky to have survived the tornado. I mean other than the one cabin, there weren't any casualties. Okay, now about your attack…"

Olivia switched her lips back and forth but said nothing.

"What can you tell me about him?"

She shrugged. "I didn't really see him. The cowl hid his face. And it was dark in those damned cabins."

"Yeah, tell me about it. But more importantly, you guys had actual bathroom stalls."

"Stay focused, Tex."

"We just had open toilet stalls—"

"Tex! *Enough* about the damn stalls. As I said, he was tall…and *oh!* One thing I remember is when he grabbed me, I saw dark stains on the sleeves, darker than the Reaper suit. They looked, I dunno…*oh!*"

Neither one of us said it, but we knew it had to have been Calvin's bloodstains. "Maybe we shoulda called the cops."

"Yeah, fat lotta good that woulda done. He wore gloves. What would the cops have done to help? He was long gone, nothing left behind."

"You're right." And the thought of calling Cowlings seemed less than appealing. "I'm going to get him, O'. Elspeth said I would. That I'm closer than I realize."

"What does that even mean?"

"I'm not sure. Either we'll find out who he is soon, or…it's someone physically close to us."

Olivia sighed. "What's our next step?"

"Well, now that it's personal—since the killer went after you—I'm going to do a spell tonight. I'm going to Mickey's and ask her to help me with the mirror scrying spell. The same one I used a couple of years ago."

"Cool. I'm going with you."

"Sorry, but I have no idea when I'll even get to Mickey's. I have something else I have to do tonight, remember?"

"Crap! Lance. He wants you to be there when he comes out to his father."

The absolute last thing on my mind. I had a killer to catch. Yet I made Lance a promise, one I intended to keep. Besides, if this damned killer strikes again, his next victim could be Lance.

"Yeah."

"Do you want me to go with you to Lance's?"

"I wish you could. But it'd be up to Lance. And I don't really want to ask if I can bring a date to his coming out."

Olivia laughed. "All right. Whatever. But you call me when you find out something at Mickey's. Hell, call me about how Lance's deal goes. But whatever you do, *don't* confront the killer by yourself." I nodded while absentmindedly staring out the window. "Tex! You hear me?"

"Yeah, yeah, I hear you, already. And I *don't* have a concussion." I slumped in my seat. "I'm just going to Mickey's, that's it. Whatever I find out, I'll let you know. And I won't go after the killer, been there, done that."

But I just can't help myself, sometimes.

## Chapter Fifteen

Dad totally lost it when I got home, the tornado's destruction all over the news.

"My God, Tex, are you okay?" He rolled toward me faster than I've seen him move in some time. "Your head! Do you need to go to the hospital?"

I sat down so he could examine my wound. "It's okay, Dad. It's just a minor cut."

"Doesn't look okay to me. Stay there." He left for the bathroom, returning with the first aid kit. "This is going to sting." He grinned when I yelped as he applied the iodine. I suppose payback for the worry I caused him. "Well, you're lucky. Doesn't look like you'll need stitches." He finished with a large white bandage on my forehead. "Tell me again what happened."

After I told him about the attack on Olivia and our harrowing encounter with the tornado, he fell back, exhausted, into his chair. "Tex...you worry me." He rubbed his eyes wearily. "All of this witchcraft business. I just...don't know what to do."

"You don't need to do anything. It's just...stuff I need to take care of." Sometimes I wonder if it'd be a relief to him if I did go away to college. Maybe he wouldn't worry so much. I clapped a hand on his shoulder, which seemed so small and fragile, unlike the broad, sturdy back on which he used to carry me. "I'm sorry I freak you out. I don't mean to."

He covered his face and sighed. "I know. You're your mother's son, all right. I know you have to forge your own path. I just wish it wasn't so...*damned* dangerous."

We hugged, his embrace weak, another sign of his deteriorating health. "Dad, just promise you'll take care of yourself. And I promise I'll do my best to take care of me. Okay?"

"Fine. Guess that's about the best we can do."

"Um, I know you're not going to be happy about this, but I have to go out tonight. After a shower and a change of clothes."

"Don't tell me. More witchcraft stuff?"

"No. Well, some, maybe. But, first I have to help a friend with a problem. And then I need to see Mickey."

"Nothing dangerous, right?"

"Lance and Mickey aren't exactly what I'd call dangerous." I offered him a pacifying smile, for all the good it did. "I'll be fine."

After more typical resistance from Dad, I took a quick shower, tossed away my mud-caked torn clothes, and dressed hastily. I thought I'd better check in with Lance before heading over to his house.

"Tex?" He sounded distant, full of uncertainty, as if we had a weak connection.

"Yeah, hey. Ready to do this? Is your dad home?"

A long hesitation dragged on. "I'm not ready, no, but I *need* to do this. And yeah, he's home."

"As I said before, you're probably never going to be ready, Lance."

"Let's do this."

"Be there in about twenty minutes."

Halfway to Lance's house, I realized I hadn't

driven my car since Spencer put a spell on the brakes. My fear vanished. At least, my fear of driving. After today's earlier tornado encounter, faulty brakes hardly compared.

This time I found Lance's front door with a minimum of confusion. Lance's mother met me at the door, fretting, rubbing her hands.

"Hello, Tex," she said. "How are you?" She brushed her fingertips across my bandage. "I heard you were caught in a tornado. Are you well?"

"I'm fine, Mrs. Nguyen. Ah, is Lance home?"

"Yes." She stepped outside and closed the door. "Are you sure this is a wise thing to do?"

"Oh, Lance told you."

"There's not much Lance doesn't tell me. I'm just concerned about his father. This news will...upset him."

The door cracked open, startling me. In a weird way, I dreaded this more than confronting a killer. "Hey, Tex. Thanks for coming." His hair appeared oddly unstylish, lank, and void of gel. "Dude! Your head! I heard about the tornado. You okay?"

I suppose I'm going to have to get used to explaining the oh-so-very-obvious bandage on my forehead, worse than an unwelcome, ginormous zit. "Yeah, I'm all right. How're you doing?"

His Adam's apple bobbed, a yo-yo in his throat. "Well...you know."

Mrs. Nguyen latched onto Lance's arm. "Lance, would you like me to go with you?"

"Thanks, Mom, but I have to do this without you."

"I understand. It's a very honorable decision. Good luck." She kissed his cheek.

Lance made a playful swipe at rubbing away her love. "Mom!"

I followed Lance down the hallway, stopping in front of two oak doors. After Lance knocked, Mr. Nguyen's controlled voice called out, "Come."

We entered the study. Mr. Nguyen had his face buried in a ledger, refusing to acknowledge our presence. He looked small, engulfed by his large desk, yet still managed an air of quiet authority. Lance and I exchanged glances, waiting for his attention. I'm used to this treatment by Hastings at school. The power of intimidation through ignoring, I guess. Damned effective and nerve-wracking.

Lance cleared his throat. Very deliberately, Mr. Nguyen capped his pen and set it aside. He lifted his eyebrows to gaze at Lance, totally snubbing me. "Yes?" He had such quiet command over his voice that I felt deeply envious. My vocal talents are mainly a collection of squeaks, grunts, ums, ahs and gahs.

"Dad, I need to talk to you."

Mr. Nguyen gestured for Lance to sit, leaving me hanging. What am I even doing here? I'd rather be outrunning tornados.

"Speak," he said, tenting his fingertips underneath his chin.

"Um, Dad…oh, man." Lance looked at me, a visual plea for support in his eyes. "I don't know how to do this…so, I'm just going to say it. Dad…I'm gay." Mr. Nguyen stared unblinking, giving a whole new meaning to the term "poker-face." Or maybe he had just died from a heart attack. "Dad? Did you hear me?" Lance's voice rose, on the edge of hysteria. "Say something, Dad! Anything!"

Mr. Nguyen's lips curled up into a smile. "I know, son. I've known for some time."

"You've *known*? Dad, I said I'm gay!"

"I heard you the first time. And I know."

Lance snorted, prompting Mr. Nguyen to glare at him for his social impropriety. "Well...why haven't you ever said anything?"

Mr. Nguyen raised his hand for Lance to lower his voice. "It wasn't up to me to say anything, Lance. It's your responsibility. I've been waiting for you to come forward...to speak to me."

"Dad, it's not like you're the most accessible guy in the world. I mean physically or mentally..." Lance's voice crawled to a whisper.

"I understand that. It's who I am, and it's how I've come to be in my position today. I also understand that sometimes...perhaps I have a hard time separating business from family. But I have been patiently waiting for you to speak with me, to have a man-to-man talk. To do the honorable thing."

"So...how long have you known?"

"I may be old, but I'm not blind." Mr. Nguyen flashed a reserved smile before reassuming his stolid demeanor. "The clothing, the hairstyle...the interest in dance, musicals, the...ahem...posters on your bedroom wall." Lance's bedroom walls are plastered with posters of Hugh Jackman, Lady Gaga, and shirtless men from cologne ads. I'm surprised it took Mr. Nguyen this long to figure out his son's sexual nature.

"I'm sorry if I'm a disappointment..."

Mr. Nguyen jolted his head upright as if he'd been slapped. "No, son. Never. You'll never be a disappointment to me. I accept you for who you are.

And for what you've done today—the courage you're showing—you're a man of whom I'm extremely proud."

Lance brushed tears away with his hand. "I thought...I thought our culture frowned upon...homosexuality. I thought they considered it—"

"Those were the old ways. But I'd be extremely ignorant...intolerant not to adjust with the times. It's a changing world around us." He reached across his desk, extending his hand. Lance grabbed it and held on tightly. "To be perfectly honest, I did struggle with...the idea at first. But you're my son. A son of whom I'm extremely proud. I love you. Nothing will ever change that." He shook Lance's hand for emphasis, hard to leave the corporate raider at the office I guess. "And I know I would be doing you a great dishonor by forcing change upon you..." He shrugged his shoulders. "A change that wouldn't be possible, from what I understand. I like who you are. I love who you are. I have never been prouder of you than I am now." He walked around his desk and held his arms out. Lance fell into his embrace.

"I love you, too."

As if realizing his emotion showed, Mr. Nguyen broke away from his son. He hitched a thumb toward me, still not gracing me with a look. "Ah, is this...is this your—"

"Um, no. No!" I objected much too loudly when I realized what he inferred.

Lance chuckled. "God, no, it's just Tex, my friend. You remember him from dinner?"

I almost objected, being "just Tex" and all, but whatever.

Appearing embarrassed, Mr. Nguyen returned to his chair. "Yes, I see. So…" He coughed into his cupped fist. "Do you have a…'male friend'?" His color darkened into a deep red.

"No, I'm still—"

Mr. Nguyen halted him with an upraised palm. "Okay, Lance. No need to go any further. I just hope that…one day, when you find someone, you won't be afraid to introduce him to me."

Lance's eyes lit up, whether from happiness or surprise, I couldn't tell. "Sure, Dad, of course."

Mr. Nguyen stacked papers, his rare emotional moment completed. "Might I ask…is there any significance to now being the time you came forward?"

I spoke up, my voice breaking. "Lance is being…harassed, Mr. Nguyen. Someone's sending him notes—"

Mr. Nguyen dropped his papers and folded his hands. "I see."

"And…one gay boy was murdered at our school." Mr. Nguyen lifted an eyebrow. *Barely.* "He received the same letters Lance is getting."

"And what has been done about this?"

"Dad, the police are looking into it."

"Do they know you've been receiving notes?"

"Not yet. I wanted to talk to you first."

"Is your life at risk?"

Lance's mouth fluttered as if at a loss for words. "Maybe…yeah, maybe."

"Perhaps you shouldn't go to school until this killer is caught."

Lance leaned back, placing his hands behind his neck. "I thought about it. But I'm not going to run…or

292

hide. That'd be giving in to him."

"I'd expect no different from you, son. You're a Nguyen." The conversation I just had with my dad flashed through my mind. Apparently, loving father and son relationships are similar, no matter the different cultures, colors, and sexual orientations. "Just be extremely cautious, and please, contact the police this evening. I will be there when you speak with them."

"Okay."

"Well…" Mr. Nguyen slapped his hands on his desk, signifying the end of the "coming out" session. "Oh, one other thing, boys…"

"Yeah?"

"Please don't mention this to your mother. She doesn't know a thing about…your being gay. I'm not sure how she'll respond."

"Um, Dad?"

Mr. Nguyen's mouth tightened in a grim, thin line as we broke into laughter.

****

Well, that went smoother than I thought it would. Even though Lance's dad is a bit of a stiff, it's obvious he loves his son and would do anything for him. On the other hand, he took the news about his wife's secret knowledge pretty poorly. Or at least I think he took it poorly. It's hard to read a robot.

Already late, I headed over to Mickey's, knowing she's a night owl. Too many "stories" to catch up on with her trusty VCR. I should have brought chicken, but it was past dinnertime, and I was way past broke.

The tree limbs in Mickey's front yard rattled in the breeze, the moonlight splashing their bony shadows across the porch. I zipped my jacket tight, shuddering at more than just the wind. Dread pumped through my veins at what I might discover.

I rang the doorbell and waited for Mickey to unlock the mysteries of her numerous chains and locks. Once she cracked the door open, she greeted me with, "What the hell?"

"Ah, hey, Mickey. Sorry I didn't call—"

She yanked the door open and pulled me inside. "Well, don't just stand there like an idiot lettin' the air conditioning out. Come on in." She wore another floral-patterned dress, vibrantly exploding with unnatural-looking petals of pink, purple, and blue. Mickey must be single-handedly keeping the floral-patterned dress people in business. Her closet's probably brighter than her magnificent garden. She stared at the bandage on my head. "What in the world happened to your head, kid?"

After my umpteenth retelling of the story, Mickey gasped and said, "Have you gone to the hospital? I'll go with you. There's a real good-lookin' doctor at the E.R."

"Mickey, why did *you* go to the E.R?"

She stared at me incredulously. "To get my check-up."

"You don't go to the E.R. for your check-ups, do you?"

"Why, yes! As I said, there's a good-lookin' doctor there. He's much better lookin' than the old fart of a doctor I used to go to."

"Um, okay." I'm sure Mickey's quest for hot doctors made her an employee favorite at the Clearwell Hospital emergency room.

"Anyway, you're sure you don't need to see a

doctor?" Mickey sat down on her well-worn sofa, dangling her short legs just off the floor.

I sat next to her. "I'm sure."

"And you actually survived a tornado? With that spell I gave you?"

"Yeah, I guess so."

"Land's sakes. I had no idea that spell was so potent." She chuckled. "Maybe it's the wielder. You're turning out to be quite a powerful witch. Or maybe…"

"Maybe 'what'?"

"Maybe something else saved you." She placed a thin finger to her lips, the sides of her mouth pulling down like saddlebags.

"Like what?"

"I don't know, kid. I'm just tossin' ideas around here, but you and I both know there're strange things going on in all the realms. Anyway…" She trailed off, lost in thought. "A tornado attack! I swear." She cackled and slapped me on the back.

"Um, yeah, that's pretty funny…I guess." Sometimes I think I supply her with more regular entertainment than her "stories."

"So. What are you doing here? It's late."

"Yeah, sorry. But I need to find out who attacked Olivia."

She slumped back into the cushions and harrumphed. "Well, is she okay? Your 'Olivia'?" Mickey's tolerance level for all things Olivia leveled notoriously low, but she sounded genuinely concerned. With a sprinkling of sarcasm.

"She's a little shook up, but there's no damage done. Remember the mirror scrying spell we did two years ago? You think we can try that again?"

She scratched her chin and with some effort, jumped to her feet. "Well, I suppose you are emotionally connected to this now. I'll go get my mirror." With surprising speed, she fled the living room.

Mickey reappeared carrying her large oval mirror. Looking a little worse than I remembered it, the mirror's face remained a solid, painted black with tin foil blanketing the back. With the grape vines and flowers carved into the gold-tinted frame, it could be a refugee from Mickey's floral closet. She carefully placed it on her coffee table, face up. "Go get a chair from the kitchen," she ordered.

When I brought the chair back, Mickey had already drawn a chalk circle on the floor in front of the table. She clapped the chalk from her hands and surveyed her circle like a proud artist. "Put the chair in the middle of the circle. Don't smudge it."

Placing the chair within the circle, I carefully stepped over the chalk line and sat down. "Now, I don't have to remind you to *not* look directly into the mirror, right?"

I nodded my head in compliance, daring a brief glance at the tempting mirror. Mickey caught me, hand raised for a swat. "I'm not looking! Be careful of the chalk line."She grudgingly dropped her hand. My head would remain smack-free as long as I remained within the circle. Maybe I should carry chalk with me when I visit Mickey.

"Okay, now, Tex, relax. Open your mind to find your inner eye." Mickey referred to the "inner eye" in one's mind that helps fill someone with knowledgeable white light. Whatever that means. But it worked several years ago when I found myself in a waking dream, guided by my mother's spirit. Who knows what will happen this time? "Breathe in and out, slowly. Find your rhythm." I closed my eyes, inhaling and exhaling long rushes of air. My mind bubbled, a tingling sensation wrapping my entire body in warmth. My hands fell slack in my lap, my feet asleep. Darkness swam into my brain, stealing away my waking consciousness. Then the darkness edged gently away like a soft blanket pulling off my face. Slowly, a white light materialized, starting as a pinprick and growing into an orb of brilliant luminescence. Swirling lights within lights danced and circled, taunting one another playfully before meeting to form the shape of a body.

"Hey, Tex," said Brittany Gerlach, resplendent in her cheerleader outfit.

I attempted to answer, but my vocal cords didn't cooperate. I sputtered helplessly, finally giving in to my muteness on the spiritual plane.

"What Elspeth told you is right," she said. "I want you to tell the truth about me, about my sexual confusion. I want others to learn from me. And thank you, Tex. Thank you." She smiled, her teeth so blindingly white I had to look away. "Be careful. You still have a long way to go, and it's a dangerous path. Be careful…" Her form imploded soundlessly, turning into a thousand blurry, small white lights, a dazzling Christmas tree.

"Tex? Kiddo? You found your inner eye?" called Mickey from somewhere far away.

Trying to keep a metaphorical foot in both realms, I struggled to bring myself to semi-consciousness. But it would be so easy to surrender completely to the warm feeling of the spiritual world. I wanted nothing but to relax and bask in the comfort, the serenity, of my inner eye. I imagine it's what a day on an exotic beach must feel like, my eyes shut, the sun roasting me with its inviting rays. But my "inner voice" kept nagging at me, telling me I have a job to do. The tingling sensation rippled away like the fading rings from a pond-tossed pebble. "Yes," I mumbled.

"Slowly open your eyes, maintaining touch with your inner eye." I'm not sure, but I think I giggled at Mickey's echoing voice. "Tex! Stay with me." I nodded through my sludge-filled, dream-like state. Forcing my heavy lids open, it disheartened me to find myself back in Mickey's living room.

"Now, call upon the Great Mother of Earth for her divine assistance," said Mickey.

"Great Mother of Earth, please fill me with knowledge and help me to find the answers I seek." Totally groggy, I stumbled over my words. A succession of white lights popped into my head, the spiritual paparazzi stalking me with cameras. My vision reshaped, the after-glow of the flashes leaving flickers behind.

"Envision an object, Tex, and look into the mirror—thinking of that object. But do *not* look directly into it! Don't look at your own reflection."

For whatever reason, Mr. Cavanaugh's cat, Benny, popped into mind. Finding this silly, I smiled while sneaking an askance glance into the mirror. The solid mirror surface transformed into a murky, swimming black liquid. Particles of light broke through the darkness. The mirror blazed intensely, leaving behind a negative image of Benny. To my pseudo-drunken amusement, Benny's tail switched back and forth.

"Do you see an image, Tex?" I nodded. "Good. Now, slowly, carefully…ask your question to the Great Mother."

Slowly, full awareness resurfaced. I hesitated, not really knowing if I wanted to learn the answer. Last time I did this spell, it felt like waking from a wonderful dream into a nightmarish reality. I'd rather not repeat that performance. But a killer needs to be stopped. I gritted my teeth and asked, "Oh, Great Mother, who attacked Olivia Furman in the cabin?"

I gripped the edges of my chair and waited for the unveiling. Dark clouds of swirling smoke streamed into the languid mirror surface, oddly reminiscent of the tornado Elspeth and I had suffered through earlier. The cloud roiled about angrily, concocting its killer stew. A nose poked through the smoke, only to vanish in a frustrating game of peek-a-boo. Two pale eyes materialized, a face chiseled around them. With one last flash, the identity of Olivia's attacker became clear.

Like a dozen slaps to the face, my full consciousness returned with a rude awakening. *Not again, God, please, not again.* I jumped to my feet and stumbled over the coffee table, rolling across the floor. I clamped my hand over my mouth, fighting the tide of rising bile. My stomach churned, my abdominal muscles weak and unsteady. As I crawled toward the kitchen, Mickey plopped a white, plastic bowl in front of me.

"Go for it, kid," she said, rubbing the back of my head. "Let it out."

When I finished, I rolled over on my back, staring at the cobwebs gathering on Mickey's ceiling. Her face came into view, hovering over me like a god from on high. "You sure throw up a lot, Tex."

I said nothing. I felt many conflicting emotions, none of them good. I felt confused, angry, sad, and worst, betrayed.

"Did you see the killer?" asked Mickey.

I coughed several times before I sat up. "Yeah." Taking several deep breaths, I climbed to my feet. "I've gotta go."

When I reached the front door, her hand slapped my back. "Now, *don't* go after the killer by yourself!"

"Fine, I won't. But I gotta go."

As I ran off her porch, she called out, "You better call me when this killer is caught. I mean it, Tex. Don't be a damn fool!"

I stared straight ahead, staggering through her yard, my eyes set on the Bucket but not focusing on anything. "Okay." My voice sounded remote, cold, a stranger in my body. "I won't be a damn fool. Not *ever* again." And I meant it, so sick and tired of being played as a fool. I found myself paraphrasing a song Dad likes, over and over in my head...*Killers to the left of me, murderers on the right, stuck in the middle with you.*

I drove straight to her house.

Chapter Sixteen

I pounded on the door until the outside light snapped on.

"Tex?" Her eyes registered surprise. And fear. "What are you doing here? It's late—"

"*Why?* Why'd you do it?" She fell back against the doorjamb. "*Why'd* you attack Olivia?" She threw her knuckles toward her mouth to muffle a sob. "*Why'd* you kill Calvin? And *Brittany*? *Tell* me, *Allison*!"

"What? No, Tex...*no*."

"You're actually going to stand there and tell me you *didn't* attack Olivia at the retreat?" Inches from her face, I glowered, daring her to continue her lies.

"Oh, God! No..." She crumpled in a heap on her front stoop. Hiding her face between her knees, she held herself, rocking back and forth. "I didn't mean to hurt anyone. I'm so, *so* sorry! It was...just supposed to be a joke."

Realizing my fists were raised in anger, I lowered them to my side. I took several deep breaths and asked, "What are you *talking* about?"

She peered at me between her fingers. "I didn't *want* to do it, Tex. He...he said it was just a harmless joke."

A scratching sound came from the door. Allison's brother leered through the window, the curtain pulled back in his hand, his tongue out. Mocking me. I smacked my hand on the windowpane, forcing him to jump back, then sat down beside Allison. Stewing in silence, I waited for her hysterics to pass. And to make sense of the insanity.

"Okay, Allison. *Explain*. Explain *everything*."

She shuddered, her shoulders heaving up and down. "He said it was a joke. I didn't want to do it, but he said…he said if I put on the Reaper costume and gave Olivia a scare…pretend to grab her…he'd…" She howled like a dog baying at the moon.

I didn't know how to feel. Five minutes ago, rage consumed me, guiding my course, the drive over here blanked out. It terrified me. But now? Now, I felt sorrow, pity. This is Allie, my *friend*. The friend I thought I knew. "Who is 'he,' Allie?" I knew the answer, but I needed her to say it. "And what did 'he' say he'd do for you?"

She stared at me, the flesh around her eyes swollen, her cheeks blotched red. "I'm so sorry!"

"Shhh, Allie, it'll be okay. Just *tell* me—"

"Parker! It was Parker. He said…he'd take me to the dance if I did it."

*Bastard*. I knew it all along. Parker. "But…why, Allie? *Why* did he want you to do it?"

She shrugged. "He didn't really say. He said it was just a joke on Olivia. I told him I didn't think it was a good idea…but he insisted. He…*insisted*. That's when he said…he said he'd take me to the dance—"

"How did he pull it off?"

"He told me to wait. I hid in the cabin's toilet stall during the whole paintball game. Every time someone came in, I peeked through the door to see if it was Olivia. I thought she'd never come in. Parker said he'd text me when Olivia got eliminated. When she came back to the cabin..." Parker must have kept tabs on Olivia during the entire game. When he saw me eliminate Olivia, he texted Allie. I imagine his shooting me in the face just provided him with a bonus kick. Plus it gave him an alibi for Olivia's attack. He set Allison up. An easy target since she had a crush on him. And because she's tall, with broad shoulders, she could easily have been mistaken for a guy underneath the Reaper outfit.

"But...why? I mean, I know Parker said he'd take you to the dance, but...you know it wasn't right."

With the porch light gleaming off her glasses, I couldn't see her eyes. "Tex, some time ago you asked me what happened to my parents." She took a deep breath to ward off another crying jag. "When my brother and I were younger, we lived on a farm in Godwin, Kansas. You ever heard of it?" I shook my head, which gave her a lifeless chuckle. "That figures. Anyway, for years, we lived as a...I guess...a happy family, but we weren't. Not really. There were the four of us: Dad, Mom, Andrew, and myself. Dad had Andrew and me both working in the fields every day before and after school. It was hard. Really tough. And I was never very popular at school. I had no friends. And boys sure didn't like me. I was always too big, too awkward, too...ugly—"

"You're not any of those things, Allie—"

"Let me finish," she shot back. "That's just the way things were at school. I guess I...resigned myself to being lonely and working hard for my dad. I didn't know any better. I thought it was just the way it is. I had nothing to compare it to. I was...I guess, *happy*.

You understand that?"

"Yeah, I think I do."

"Soon, though, things started getting worse. The economy went all to…" Allie stopped to peer behind her. She then cupped her hands and whispered, "…*hell*." I fought the urge to smile, the first time I've ever heard her curse. "So, Dad started losing his equipment to the bank, the crops began dying. He became meaner—more distant. Started drinking every day and night. My brother and I…he was only a little kid at the time. I don't think he remembers much. We tried our best to keep up with the crops…but it was no use. No matter how much work we put in, we couldn't keep up with the bank's demands or the dying crops." Allie brushed at her eyes even though her reservoir had run dry. "Dad turned scary, angry, drunk all the time. Mom—well, she became…nothing, really. Just going through the motions. It was like she lost the will to live. And I saw my brother slipping away. He had…issues. And they got worse while our parents ignored him. They weren't raising him anymore. Or giving him the special…consideration he needed. I didn't know what to do. I didn't know what to *do*!" She leaned into me, pressing her face into my shoulder. "That's why I did it…" she said in a hollow tone.

"I don't get it. What did you do?"

"I *had* to do it, Tex. There was *nothing* else I could do. It was too late for me. Nobody loved me…no one at school…and especially, not my parents. But it wasn't too late for Andrew. I love Andrew…and it was up to me to take care of him." Allison stared up at the full moon. "I called social services. I know… It's terrible to call social services on your own parents, isn't it?"

I hemmed and hawed, having no idea what to say. "Huh."

"You're judging me!"

"No, *no!* I'm really not, Allie. I wouldn't—"

"Oh, just shut up and let me finish. This is hard! So social services came, and saw what a mess my family had become. They contacted my grandmother, and she gladly took us in." She pushed out a long, quivering breath, ending in a sigh. "My parents…didn't seem to care. They let us go without even a hug. The last time I saw my parents they were sitting on the sofa. Like they always did those days. Didn't say a word."

"Wow…I'm soooo sorry…"

"It's okay. Once we got here, things got better for Andrew and me. We no longer had to work in the fields…and thanks to you, I had friends—"

"You did that yourself, you—"

"That's nice of you to say, but it's not true. Not really. You brought me into your circle of friends…and then, boys started actually paying attention to me. First, Ian…and then, Parker…"

Telling Allison her current crush is most certainly a murderer is probably not the thing to say right now. But it sorely tempted me. "You can do so much better than Parker."

She smiled half-heartedly and twisted her hair around a finger. "I don't know… But, anyway, I guess…in a roundabout way of answering your question about why I did what Parker asked me to? That's it. It's lame, I know. But…having boys notice you is something I've never had before. I guess I didn't see the harm…" She started crying again. And here I thought of myself as the only one capable of an endless river of tears. "Oh, *God,* Tex. I'm so, *so* sorry! Will you ever forgive me? And what about *Olivia*?"

The next words out of my mouth weren't exactly what I imagined saying twenty minutes ago. "Of course, I forgive you. And I understand. It's okay—"

"After everything you guys have done for me? *Especially* Olivia?" Her voice rose, setting off several neighborhood dogs.

"Olivia will forgive you, too." *I hope.*

The door squeaked open, and Allison's grandmother poked her head out. "Are you kids okay out here? I thought I heard loud voices."

Allie dabbed at her eyes. "No, Grams, we're okay. We're just…having fun."

Her grandmother smiled angelically. "Well. You kids have a good time playing. And Allison, if you're going to be out here much longer, you'd better get a sweater. There's a cool breeze in the night air." She wrapped her hands around her shoulders and shivered.

"Okay, Grams, 'night." Once she shut the door behind her, we broke into cathartic laughter.

"You really did do the right thing, you know…"

"What?"

"Calling social services on your parents. Look how much better off you are now. And Andrew will have a better shot at…a normal life." *Maybe in a zoo.*

"You think so?" Allie's eyes brightened.

"Yeah, yeah, I do. And you know what? Maybe instead of focusing your attention on Parker…" I fairly spit his name out. "…maybe, you should see about rekindling your thing with Ian."

"No, that ship has sailed." Okay, whatever happened between them, it seemed hopeful to see Allie

306

make her own decisions and take a stance.

"Well, what about Dickers? He's nice enough even though his hair sucks." Allie laughed. "And you guys do share similar interests. I mean, religion-wise and stuff."

"You think so?"

"Yep."

"You know, I never really thought about him that way before…but…" She wiggled her feet absentmindedly, contemplating Dickersness. "…who knows?"

"You should so ask him to the dance instead of Parker—"

My suggestion pulled the emergency brake on her feet. "You don't like Parker, do you?" She eyed me suspiciously.

I sighed. "No, I don't. I have my reasons and—"

"*And,* by the way, *what* was all that other stuff you accused me of?" She leaned forward in full-on interrogation mode. "You asked why I killed Calvin?"

"Oh, um, yeah. That." Think, Tex, think. What can I tell her? If I "unmask" Parker—so to speak—she'd have to be sworn to silence. I can't risk Parker finding out I'm onto him. Not until I have solid proof. But time and again, truth seems like the best option. As dicey as it is. "Okay, Allie. What I'm about to tell you…you might not like hearing, but you have to swear to keep it to yourself, okay?"

Her eyes widened expectantly. "Um…sure."

Why do I always have to rain on parades? "Um, the police have kept this pretty hush-hush, but, Alf, our security guard…you know, the guy who apparently shot himself in his own foot…twice?" Lately, I had to

307

preamble Alf's introduction this way to everyone. "Okay. Alf saw someone dressed as a Reaper go into the bathroom where Calvin was murdered."

Allie gasped when she realized the ramifications of what I said. "Oh my...*God.* You don't think Parker—"

I nodded. "I'm sorry, Allie...but it's looking more and more likely."

"But...why would Parker *do* that?"

"I think...I'm pretty sure he was sending Calvin 'hate notes.'"

"What kind of 'hate notes'?"

"'God Despises Fags,' and 'Homosexuals Go To Hell.' Things like that." I winced but had to ask her, "Does that sound familiar?"

"The YACCERS. The Clarendon Baptist Church."

"And he sent similar notes to Brittany Gerlach—"

"The cheerleader? Why? She wasn't..." Allie covered her mouth as if about to be sick. "Oh, my..."

"What?"

She snagged my arm and squeezed hard. "Parker. He was spending a lot of time with Brittany before she...you know. But, Brittany wasn't gay."

"I don't think Brittany even knew what she was. But she was definitely confused. She had feelings for another girl."

"Oh."

"So, Allie...*Allie!*" I grabbed her shoulders to make sure I had her full attention. She stared at me, a new cool resolve in her eyes. "You see why I need you to keep quiet about this? I have to catch Parker before he does it again."

"What can I do to help?" Out of the many mood swings of Allison Brubaker tonight, this felt the scariest. All emotion had fluttered away, her voice low and somber.

"Just pretend things are normal as usual between you and Parker. Can you do that?"

A low, growl sounded from deep within her chest. "That...*bastard*!" She raised her hands and shook them. "I can't believe he did this. He *used* me. A *killer*."

"Allie, quiet. Can you pretend everything's cool between you and Parker?"

She exhaled slowly and lowered her hands. "I can try." Uh-oh, I've unleashed the beast. "That's all I can say right now. I'll try."

"This is important. Parker needs to be stopped." I could tell she no longer heard me. Hell hath no fury like a woman scorned and all that stuff, I guess. "Please, Allie—"

She shot up suddenly. "I *said* I'll try, all right? I've got to go to bed now. *Big* day at school tomorrow." The way she said "big" troubled me. Just how "big" a day are we talking here?

I scrambled to my feet. I threw my arms open wide, hoping to appease her with a calming hug. Ignoring my offer, she looked at me with cold eyes. Then she slammed the door shut in my face.

Way to go, Tex. Not only did I jeopardize my investigation into Parker, but I might have sullied Allison's faith in God and religion. Not to mention her own newfound happiness.

This is *not* how I saw this encounter playing out.

\*\*\*\*

Sitting in front of Allison's house in the Bucket, I dreaded the call, thought about putting it off. But I couldn't. "Um, hey."

"Hey," said Olivia. "You're *killing* me here. What took you so long? What'd you find out?" If she thinks I'm "killing her" now, just wait.

"You need to promise me you'll keep calm—"

"*Tell* me, Tex."

"Are you sitting down?" A ludicrous question. First of all, I suspected she'd be on her bed. But procrastination is my friend.

"Tell me…*now*!"

"The person who attacked you isn't the same person as the killer…"

"I'm listening…"

"*Allisonattackedyou!*" I purposefully jumbled it into one word, hoping I could subconsciously deliver the message to her without her full comprehension. "And…the killer is Parker."

A soul-shaking silence on her end. "Run that first part by me again…"

"Allison attacked you." This time I whispered it in a tone only dogs could hear.

"'Allison,'" she repeated. "*Allison?* Allison *Brubaker*? Our *'friend,'* Allison? You have *got* to be kidding me!" And so it begins.

"Yeah, I know, but chill. Let me explain—"

"I can't *believe* that…bitch did that to *me*. And you're asking me to *chill*?" I'm glad I had the foresight not to deliver the news in person. I'd had enough beat-downs from irate women for a while. But, of course, I'll pay for it later. "She was our friend, Tex! Our *friend*!"

"Parker used her. He manipulated her." She ranted so loudly, I had to yell to be heard. "He lied to her. He told her it was a joke! She had *no* idea what she was doing. He told her he'd take her to the dance if she did it."

Apparently, the last grenade of info-drop lodged inside Olivia's head as radio-silence ruled. "So…Parker's the killer?"

"Yes! I've been *trying* to tell you that. He gave Allie the Reaper outfit to, um, pull this 'joke' on you."

Her voice lifted off low, slowly scaled high peaks, and crashed like an airplane. "I can't *believe* she did it. Wait until I get my hands on her. What is this *crap*?" I let her scream it out for a while, no other option.

Once Olivia's tirade ran its course, I told her Allison's story. "*Ohhh*," she said. "I *still* can't believe she did that to me."

"But, you can sorta see why, right? *Right*?"

"I *guess*. But, *don't* expect me to BFF her right away." Lunchtime would be fun tomorrow.

"You have to be cool with her. We need to get Parker. That's the most important thing right now."

"Oh, whatever, Tex. I'll bet if you were attacked, you wouldn't be so *damn* calm."

"Um, I was attacked. Several times, in fact." It had to be Parker who pushed me down the stairs that day. Nothing else made sense.

After a loud, exasperated snort, Olivia said, "So, how are we going to get him?"

"I don't know. I guess I'm just playing it as it goes. As usual."

"Oh, good plan, McKenna." She laughed, a much more pleasant response than what I just endured.

"Well, yeah. But I've been thinking. We know Parker has a Reaper costume, possibly with Calvin's bloodstains on it. If we can find it, we're golden."

"Mighty big 'if.' Maybe he got rid of it after my

attack."

"Maybe. But as long as we keep him in the dark, we're onto him. I think his 'work' isn't over yet. He still may go after Lance."

"You're *not* thinking of using Lance as bait, right?"

I truly hadn't thought about it, but now it didn't sound like a terrible idea. "No, no, of course not."

"No one else can get hurt. Especially our friends."

As always, she's right. I'm just sick of the entire situation. *Gah*! I need to wrap it up and move on with my life…such as it is. It seems unfair we know who the killer is, but can't prove it. I can't call Cowlings on a suspicion—pretty damn good one though it is. "I'm stuck. I don't know what to do—"

"You'll think of something. You always do. By the way, if Parker's the killer, what about his alibi? For Calvin's death?"

"His parents must've lied. I mean, we all know what love can make people do—"

"You mean like Allie?"

"I mean like…being human."

"*Whatever.*"

"I guess we just need to keep our eyes on Lance and especially Parker. And you and Allie need to be cool tomorrow with one another. And toward Parker—"

"It's gonna be tough, Tex." Yes, it will. I'm going to have a hard time facing Parker. But I'm particularly worried about the girls. "But I'll try." Just like what Allie promised. "By the way, you said you wouldn't confront the killer by *yourself.*"

With all the bombshells I dropped at Olivia's feet, I hoped we could by-step this minor explosion. "Um, technically, I didn't confront the killer."

"Bullcrap! You *thought* Allie was the killer."
*Nailed.*

"Okay, okay, sorry. I just knew Allison wouldn't,
um, pose a threat, and I..." I let my lame reasoning
drop into the nether. "It won't happen again."

"Better not!"

"It won't. We're a team."

"You're damn *right* we're a team." And we are,
too. Now more than ever. Which makes my imminent
decision regarding college so much tougher.

"Okay. I'll pick you up tomorrow, 'kay?"

"All right."

"And, O'?" I shouted, trying to catch her before
she dropped the call.

"Yeah?"

"I love you." Quickly, I snapped shut the phone.
It's odd. We spent the last three years off and on as a
couple, mostly on. The first time I told Olivia I loved
her had been when she broke up with me. Poor timing,
but whatever, truth wins out. Yet neither one of us has
had the courage to say those three important words
since we got back together. I guess I take it for granted
our mutual love is an unspoken truth between us. At
least I hope it's a mutual feeling. Maybe in some weird
way, we're afraid to jinx our relationship. Or maybe
I'm scared. I hung up before she could respond or *not*
respond. Either response felt terrifying to contemplate
as I knew those damn three words could shape my
future.

My phone buzzed. —*I luv u, too. Duh*!—the text
read.

It gave me all the encouragement I need for
tomorrow.

Time to catch a killer.

I took one last look at Allie's house. Allie's brother danced in front of the window, opening and closing the shades with each turn. Watching me. I now understand Allie and her brother better. But, he *still* freaks me out.

## Chapter Seventeen

*Lunch time!* The part of the day I'm dreading most, and not because of the usual "lunch-tastic" treats served up by the cafeteria ogres.

Earlier, Olivia spoke to Allison and sorta forgave her, at least as much as she could. Given time, I'm sure Olivia will come around. *Maybe.*

Olivia confirmed what I suspected about Allison's behavior. She said Allie seemed different, colder. Her abundant hugs had gone the way of the dinosaurs. A new ice age rocked her world, and I, the cosmic orchestrator, hurled my meteor of painful words down upon her.

So far, we'd successfully avoided Parker except for a quick "drive-by" he pulled on us this morning. While gathered in front of my locker, he passed by us, dropping a few snide comments. I overcompensated by being unusually friendly, while Olivia ignored him, gnashing her teeth in powerless rage. Allison, on the other hand, glowered at him, her eyes two daggers of glistening steel. Parker gave her a double-take, his suspicion obvious. I would have to watch Allie. Parker obviously thought her behavior odd.

A lot of dark secrets lurked around the lunch table today.

Lance arrived first at the table.

"Hey." I sat down across from him.

Stuart R. West

Olivia slid in next to Lance. "I heard about last night. Cool! You did awesome."

Lance smiled, looking more at peace than he had in a while. "Oh, whatever. I should have taken care of it a long time ago."

"And it went okay, right?" I asked. "I mean, after I left? Did you call Cowlings?"

Lance tilted his head toward Olivia. "Um…"

"Lance," said Olivia. "Don't worry. I know about it all."

"Of course you do," said Lance. "Tex, that Detective was *really* curious about your dealings with this Reaper and everything else." *Great.* "And when I told him about Olivia's attack, well, he seemed pretty pissed you didn't call him." Even greater. "Did I screw up? I mean, everyone knows about Olivia's attack. It's all over the sites, and Dickers was texting and calling everyone—"

"Gah! Now I'm a social media 'thing,'" said Olivia.

"It's cool, Lance. I'm going to tell Cowlings about everything soon, anyway. I doubt he's much of an online guy." But, man, did I dread *that* encounter.

"So, has he got a raging 'mad-on' against you or something?" said Lance. "He turned sorta…purplish whenever I brought your name up." I imagined Cowling's bald pate ringed with the color of anger, the opposite of an angel's halo.

"We have history," I mumbled.

Ian and Brandon joined us. "What the hell, Tex? You survive a tornado, Olivia gets attacked, and *you* don't call me?" Ian slapped the back of my head, apparently a favorite pastime of just about everyone I

316

know.

"Ow, dammit, Ian! Look, sorry I didn't let you know. I was going to. But I was, you know, dragging from everything that happened. I went to bed early."

"Did they catch your attacker?" Brandon's gazed at Olivia with an anime character's wide-eyed worry. I couldn't help but wonder if he still cares about her romantically. He didn't seem all that shaken by my tornado encounter.

Olivia smiled. "No, they didn't catch her, um, him. Whatever." Olivia saved her flub through instant diversion. "I'm okay, though. Thanks for asking. You gonna eat that?" She pointed at his green gelatinous mystery goo.

"No." Brandon scooted it across the table. "Have at it."

"Thanks." Olivia plunged a plastic spork into the gelatin, attempting several jabs before successfully slicing its rubber sheath.

"I missed all the action this year," said Ian.

*Lucky you.* "Man, did you *really* want to go to the Young American Christians' retreat? God must have been so happy with what he saw, he sicced a tornado on us." Olivia shot me a dirty look. "Sorry, sorry…"

Dickers bounded up, white socks exposed in all their glory. "Dudes! Did Tex and Olivia tell you what happened yesterday?"

Ian sighed. "Always too late, Dickers."

Defeated, Dickers flopped down on a chair. "And I was there, too. Shoulda been my story to tell…"

"Don't worry," said Lance. "One of these days you'll give us late-breaking news."

Guffawing, Olivia ran around the table and draped

her arms around Dickers. "Thanks for the laugh, Dickers. You get a one-time freebie hug, but *no* hug-backs."

Ian grumbled, ever the young curmudgeon, while the rest of us joined in the merriment. But it didn't last. Allison walked up, an aura of despair following her like a dust storm. "Hi," she said quietly. Allison and Olivia exchanged a cold glare that spoke volumes before Olivia refocused quiet contemplation on her gelatin. While Allie gobbled up her lunch in silence, everyone else looked mystified over her sullen mood.

"What's up, Allie," said Ian, obviously out of his comfort zone, "are you, ah, okay?"

Allison stared down at her salad as if inspecting for stow-away bugs. When she finally looked up, she said, "I'm fine. Thanks for asking."

Looks were dared, spared, and covertly shared around the table.

"Hey, Allie," said Dickers. "I think there's another YAC meeting next Sunday. After the disastrous retreat, I think we've earned something, right?" When none of us laughed, he nervously glanced around feeling like the odd man out.

"I'm *done* with YAC, Dickers." Crap. Allie never calls him Dickers.

Dickers looked like a hurt child on the playground. "Why…why are you done?"

"I'm…just done." Those three words unsettled me. There's no way this can be good.

"But, Allie…" I understood Dickers' confusion, but I wish he'd just shut up.

"Hey." While I was relieved for Jasper's good timing, I still have issues with him. He pulled out a chair, his tray carefully balanced in his other hand.

"Jasper," I said, "you think that's such a good idea?" Ian stared at me as if I'd gone crazy.

Jasper hesitated, his tray hovering above us. He looked around the table. "What's up?" Nothing ever riles Jasper. I bet he can go through major surgery without an anesthetic.

"Why don't you go ask your friend, Mr. Hastings?" I said.

Jasper's lethargic gaze swam around the table, looking for a sympathetic compatriot.

"Jeezus, Tex," said Ian. "What's *wrong* with you?"

Jasper held up a commanding hand to halt Ian's defense. So overflowing with confidence, I guess he doesn't feel the need to accept charity. "It's cool. Look, Tex, I don't know what your problem is but..." He shrugged his broad shoulders and cocked his chin. "...guess I'm outta' here." He walked off, head held high, and sat by himself at a nearby table.

I felt like crap. He didn't appear to be hiding anything. And I turned him away because of unfounded suspicion.

"What the hell, man?" asked Lance. "Jasper seems pretty cool." The rest of the table agreed, including Olivia. I felt a small pang of jealousy because I know she thinks Jasper's cute. Maybe that has something to do with my dickish behavior. I dunno.

"Gah! Sorry, guys. I'm just...worried about school and stuff." But my excuse sounded rather pathetic.

Brandon, of all people, said, "Maybe you should go talk to him."

Olivia leaned over and spoke quietly. "Brandon's right. Go. I think Jasper's okay."

When you're wrong, you're wrong. I trudged toward Jasper, head hung low. He's the only guy I know who makes eating by himself look cool. Casually leaning back as if in a recliner, he surveyed the cafeteria activity around him. In his situation, I would've buried myself in my food, hoping to blend in with the tabletop.

Jasper bit into a sandwich when he saw me. He raised his free hand, palm up, silently asking "yeah?"

"Ah, hey, can I sit?" Without disrupting his meal, he kicked the chair out opposite him. "Um, thanks." I cleared my throat as I struggled with what to say. "Look, hey, I want to apologize. I know I was…well, a jackass." He nodded at my self-assessment. Must be a hell of a sandwich for him not to edge a word in around it. Or maybe he just wants to see me sweat. Mission accomplished. "It's just, well, I saw you talking to Hastings the other day…" His eyelids flipped up like twin window shades. "…and it looked like you didn't want me to see you."

Jasper continued mulching his food, holding me in his stony expression. I had no idea what was going through his mind. Finally, he swallowed. "And?" Not much pay-off for the suspenseful sandwich chewing build-up.

"And I guess I thought Hastings might have told you to, um, 'infiltrate'…" I used the dreaded finger quotes. "…um, to spy on us."

Jasper nearly choked on his sandwich and wiped his mouth with a napkin. "Really, Tex? A 'spy'?" He laughed. "What the hell, dude? Why would I 'spy' on you? What's there to 'spy' about?" He volleyed back my air quotes each time he said "spy."

"Yeah, I guess it does seem kinda stupid now that I think about it. It's just, we're not exactly the coolest, or most popular kids in school, and you're way beyond our status. You could hang with anyone. When I saw you with Hastings, I guess my paranoia kicked in. I'm an idiot..."

"Hastings told me to stay away from you guys. He hassled me, said you guys were the biggest problems here, and was disappointed in me. I told him I'd hang with who I wanted to."

"Oh." I scrunched down in my seat, hoping I could slide into oblivion.

"Wow. Just...whatever. You know, I wanted to hang with you guys because...well—especially, you, Tex—seem to have your shit together."

"*What*? That's the first time anyone's ever accused me of having my shit together. My life's messier than diarrhea. It's sloppy and gross and runny and...and..." Jasper tossed his sandwich down due to my bathroom metaphors. "But, really, I don't know what I'm ever doing. Or what I'm going to do. Ever!"

"Maybe that's how you feel. But a lot of us see it differently."

"Like...how?"

"Dude, you *always* get results. You've done a lot of good here. I mean, you've put away two killers. What's up with that, anyway?" He contemplated the uneaten portion of his sandwich, quickly abandoned it. "I don't know how you do it or even why you do it, but you seem to have, I dunno, a reason to be here. I wish I could say the same about my life. I have no idea what I'm doing once I graduate—"

"Neither do I."

He splayed his hands. "As I said…you get results."

"Huh." It's nice to hear good things for a change. Even if I don't necessarily believe them.

Jasper straightened up in his chair and leaned forward. "By the way, what have you found out about Brittany? Or Calvin's death?"

"Um, what do you mean?" I rubbed the tabletop in a circular, nonchalant fashion. When I realized I was massaging the table, I stopped.

"Come on, Tex. Really? I mean, you've been asking me questions about Brittany. And I know you were there when they found Calvin. So, it doesn't take much to figure out you're looking into it."

No sense in lying to him. He's *way* too smart for a football player. "Okay, yeah, I'm 'working' on it, I guess you'd say." I really needed to quit using geeky air quotes.

"How are they connected?"

I couldn't tell him everything. Not yet. But he'd proven to be a valuable asset with information. My "football man on the inside," I guess. I lowered my voice. "Well, you're right. I think they are connected. But what I'm going to tell you stays between us, cool?"

"Cool."

"Both Brittany and Calvin received notes—"

He furrowed his brow and leaned in. "What kind of notes?"

"Well, you know Calvin was gay…" He shrugged. "…and Brittany thought she might've been gay." I waited for the bombshell to blast his stoic expression away only to be met with more impassive detachment, my desire for drama defeated. "Brittany thought she was gay, Jasper."

"Yeah? So? Go on."

"Did you know that? I mean about Brittany?"

"I had my suspicions. What about the notes?"

I suppose it's not surprising Jasper knows practically everything. He has friends in many popular cliques and is pretty observant and shrewd. The truth behind Brittany's turmoil certainly stunned me. Guess I should quit "profiling" football players. "Okay, well, they're 'hate crime' notes." I stopped myself midway from using more finger quotes. "They say things like 'God Despises Homosexuals' and—"

"What do the notes look like?"

"What? They're notes. Handwritten…blocky letters—"

"Are they on yellow paper?"

I fluttered my eyelids as if it would help me comprehend his question. "What?"

"I said 'are they on yellow paper'?"

"Yeah, yeah, actually, they are. How do you know that?"

"Okay, dude, I liked Brittany. And even though she played the dumb cheerleader, she wasn't. Not really." Note to self: quit profiling cheerleaders and pretty much everybody. I suck at it. "So, when I found out your boy, Parker…"

"Um, not 'my boy.'"

"Whatever." Jasper wiped the air clean with his hand. "Anyway, when I told you Parker was hanging with Brittany and saw your response, I put two and two together. I started watching Parker."

"Okay."

"He's in my study hall, not too far from where I sit." He nodded his head toward a cafeteria table in the back. A lot of study halls take place in our fine eatery, the kids spread out amongst the tables to deter chatting or any semblance of fun. "Last Friday, Parker was scribbling something down…on a yellow piece of paper. At the time, I thought it was weird, kinda girly. When he saw me watching him, he crammed the paper into a notebook and threw it in his backpack. He kept looking back at me, freakin' out."

*Got you.* Jasper just handed me a way to catch Parker, evidence and all. Now, I just need to get my hands on his notebook. But how?

"Jasper, I think you just saved the day." I stood and held my hand out to him. "You're welcome to join us anytime you want to."

He looked somewhat puzzled but accepted my handshake, nearly crushing my hand within his. "What's going on, Tex? Is Parker—"

"Please don't say anything yet to anyone. But, yeah, I think so. I'm gonna get him."

"Good. Let me know if I can help."

"You've already done tons. Why don't you come back to our table?"

He shook his head. "Maybe tomorrow. I'm done eating, anyway."

"Um, yeah…the diarrhea. Sorry."

"Yeah. Just don't bring it up tomorrow."

"Cool. But I mean it, come hang with us anytime. And again, sorry for what I thought earlier."

Jasper gathered his tray and nodded. "It's cool."

I swiveled to return to our table, a huge smile plastered across my face. It slid away when I saw Parker lingering by my friends. My heart leaped into my throat as I dashed through the crowd.

"Parker!" I clapped him on the back. "How ya' doin'?" My excitement felt way over the top, one more reason why you'll never see me pursue acting.

Parker's lips pulled into a thin, tight line. "What's your deal, McKenna?"

"Oh, nothing, just good to see ya."

Allison scowled while Olivia studied the suddenly fascinating tabletop.

"Whatever. Hey, Allie, how's it goin'?" He grinned at her, pouring on his translucent charm.

Allison shot to her feet and brushed by Parker, intentionally bumping into him.

Parker called after her. "Allie? *Allison*?" He smirked, his pointed teeth ready to devour. "Her time of the month?"

Olivia slammed her hand down onto the table. "Oh, yeah! That's it. It's her 'time of the month!'" She couldn't bring herself to look him in the eyes.

"Um, everyone's still a little upset, I guess, about the tornado." I attempted to smile but felt my mouth wavering.

Parker shook his head, an insulting wag I had grown more than sick of. "Yeah, right." He slowly walked away, craning his head back several times, uncertainty in his eyes.

I sat down at the table. "So, what's up guys?"

"You tell us," said Ian. "You're the one acting weird. First Jasper, then Parker. What the *hell's* going on?"

Olivia said, "We're still upset about the tornado." From the look she shot me, she didn't seem happy about keeping the façade up.

Lance stood up. "Well, I've got to get to class.

Maybe things will be more normal there."

"Look, guys, we only have a couple weeks left. Can't we all just be friends?"

"Sure, Dickers." Olivia attempted a half-smile. "I've gotta go, too." She pushed her chair back and made a beeline toward the tray window.

Ian, Brandon, and Dickers remained at the table looking like the last members aboard a sinking ship, not comprehending how or why they found themselves in this predicament.

"You know, everyone's just tense now because of the tornado and the end of school…and…" I turned and saw Olivia headed for the hallway. "I gotta go." I chased after her.

"O'! Olivia," I called. "Wait up." I caught up to her at her locker.

"*What*? Do you know how *hard* that was?"

I placed my hands on her shoulders, feeling her tension. "I know. I know. But I've found a way to get Parker. Just stay with it a little longer. It's almost over."

"Oh, my God! What? Tell me. *What?*"

"Jasper said he saw Parker writing on yellow paper. It's in his notebook. This was last Friday, and Lance didn't say anything about getting any more notes. So…I bet Parker still has the stationery and maybe more notes."

"Day-um!"

"I just need to get hold of his notebook."

"How?"

No clue. But I'm all in. I need a desperate ploy, something crazy. Before he kills again. "I'm gonna go 'Kamikaze' on his ass, that's how," I said triumphantly. But it felt like nothing but false confidence.

\*\*\*\*

Philosophy class. The philosophy of catching a killer. Gah!

I tried several deep breathing exercises to settle my nerves, much to the bemused curiosity of the students sitting beside me. Sweat dripped from my brow, my armpits turning into swamps. I had no plan, no idea what came next. All I knew is it had to happen. *Now*.

Parker swayed in, lugging his backpack. He acknowledged me with an arrogant chin thrust and sat down. I dragged my sweaty palms across the desktop, resulting in a squeaking mouse sound. I wiped my hands on my jeans, my knees nervously bounding up and down.

Parker pulled out a blue notebook when he noticed me watching him. "*What?*"

"Um, nothin'. Just spacing out."

Parker thumped his fingers over his notebook before replacing it in his backpack. He placed the backpack underneath him, sneaking glances at me. Clearly, he smelled something off.

Mr. Jensen strolled in and clapped his hands. "Okay, class, let's get started." Everyone took their time settling down, the laughter and conversations slowly dwindling.

It's now or never. I stood up and stretched, knocking my philosophy book onto the floor. Mr. Jensen sighed impatiently.

"Sorry, sorry," I mumbled. Parker acted antsy, his attention focused on me. Bending over to pick my book up, I seized the moment. I snatched Parker's backpack from underneath his seat.

Parker jumped to his feet. "Hey! What are you

*doing,* McKenna?"

Hefting the backpack, I ran to the back of the class. Parker stared at me dumbfounded.

"Tex! Give Parker his backpack," said Mr. Jensen.

I ripped at the backpack's zipper, snagging it once on the material before it opened. I pulled out several books, tossing them aside with dull *clumps*, before I found the notebook. I flipped through it, my fingers trembling over the pages. My heart roller-coastered, rising and then sinking when I didn't find what I sought. Parker stormed toward me. I backed to the opposite side of the classroom, putting as much distance between us as possible.

A loud clatter shattered my nerves. Parker had fallen to his knees next to Paul Jacobsen, whose foot extended into the aisle.

Paul, leaning back lackadaisically, shrugged. "I'm sure you got your reasons, dude." He'd awakened long enough from his weed-induced stupor to trip Parker.

Parker scrambled to his feet and stalked toward me. I slung the backpack at Parker, keeping the notebook. "Damn it, McKenna! Give it to me!"

Several students tittered. Mr. Jensen, recovering from his initial shock, made his way up the aisle, quickly closing in on me.

"Just give me a minute, Mr. Jensen. Just a second!" My legs shuffled me around the classroom as if they had a mind of their own. I plowed through the notebook again. Dashing through the middle of the room toward the windows, I quickly tore through more pages.

*Where's the damned yellow stationery? Did Jasper make a mistake? What if Parker destroyed the evidence?*

"Just another *second*, I swear!" Parker stampeded after me. I kept moving. Ring Around the Rosie gone wild. Mr. Jensen flanked me on the opposite side. I took refuge behind Mr. Jensen's colossal desk, a formidable barrier.

In the back of the notebook, I discovered a side flap. I wedged my fingers inside, feeling a folded piece of paper. My digits trembling, I pulled it out. Yellow stationery. *"Here!"* I struggled to open it up.

A sudden blow knocked the wind out of me. Parker swung again as I fell against the chalkboard. Desperately holding onto the piece of paper in one hand, I tried to fend Parker off with the other.

*"Give* that to me! *Damn it!"* He lunged at me again, slamming me to the floor. I scrambled back. He clung to my legs, pulling himself up along my torso, clawing me, fingernails digging in, reaching for the yellow note. "God *damn* you, McKenna!"

Out of breath, Mr. Jensen loomed over us. Grabbing Parker underneath his arms, Mr. Jensen yanked him to his feet with ease. "Damn it, Tex! You better have a good reason for this! Parker, settle down!" He gripped Parker around the chest, his burly arms holding him tight, and lifted him off the floor. Parker kicked and struggled but couldn't escape Jensen's bear hug. Parker screamed toward the ceilings, his words incomprehensible.

I sat up and unfolded the paper. *GOD DESPISES FAGS.*

Somehow, I climbed to my feet, my entire body shaking from the encounter. I waved my vindication through the air like a baton. "Mr. Jensen…this is one of the 'hate notes' Parker was sending to gay students.

And I'm pretty sure—either in his locker or his bedroom—you'll find a Reaper outfit…with Calvin Sturgess' blood on it."

The uneasy giggling of the students stopped. Mr. Jensen's jaw dropped. Parker slumped within his grasp, deflating like a burst balloon. He stared at his feet, his head bobbing, his blond hair whipping up and down.

"Just what're you saying?" asked Mr. Jensen.

"Parker killed Calvin. He also drove Brittany Gerlach to do what she did…by sending her these letters."

Slow realization whitened Mr. Jensen's face. He pointed at the student closest to the door. "Go get Alf! *Now!*" The student disappeared into the hallway. "Tex, why do you think Parker sent letters to Brittany?"

My dry lips clicked like a cricket. "Brittany thought she might be…gay." Gasps spread throughout the room. "She was confused. And Parker found out and used it to harass her."

Mr. Jensen gently nudged Parker toward his chair and sat him down. "Is this true, Parker?"

Parker looked up, his eyes glassy and red. He said nothing. Mr. Jensen straightened, fists on his hips. He glanced at me, then Parker, before finally resting his eyes on the grassy fields outside the windows. He sighed a deep, heavy breath, his usual warm-up for a speech. "Helluva thing…it's a helluva thing." He remained still for several seconds as my classmates looked to him for guidance. Finally, when he saw the blank stares across the room, he regained control.

"You know…I don't know what's true or not true. I'm not sure *what's* going on here." Students murmured agreement. "But…" He crossed in front of his desk, effectively blocking the class's view of Parker. I continued stupidly waving the yellow paper before finally dropping it to my side. "I know many of you are puzzled...shocked, even, from what Tex said. I know I am. But that's okay. It's human nature." A slight wave of calm washed over the students. "It's also human nature to be different. If you question who you are...or your own sexuality, it's normal, people. It's *okay* to be gay if that's who you are. *Never* be ashamed of who— or what—you are, people. *Never!*" He shot an angry glance at Parker, who seemed oblivious to today's philosophy lesson. "If Brittany was gay, or questioning herself...I can't even imagine what pain she must have been going through...for things to have ended..." He fell silent. "Do *not* go through life despising yourself. Talk to someone. Talk to me. Anybody. Just don't...keep your sadness and pain inside until it eats away at you. It's okay who you are... It's okay..." Mr. Jensen continued repeating the phrase, making sure the students comprehended his message. Or maybe, he did it for his own benefit. I know he'd valued Brittany as a student.

Alf burst in, eyes wide as plates, his hand on his holstered gun. "What's going on here, Mr. Jensen?"

Mr. Hastings followed, his roving, buffalo eyes landing on me at the front of the classroom. He wiggled his finger at me. Seeing this, Mr. Jensen intervened and called for a hushed three-way conference with Alf and Hastings. I stood at the front of the room, silent, feeling as useless as one of "Hastings's Hallway Heroes" monitors. Parker appeared nearly comatose, unmoving.

Mr. Jensen broke away from the impromptu huddle and flourished his hand toward the classroom. "Read chapter sixteen, people." The classroom, still in a state of mass shock, stared at him flabbergasted. "*Now,* people!" Pages rattled and chairs scraped across the floor. Parker and I were escorted out of the classroom as if being led to the gallows, not my first rodeo.

\*\*\*\*

The long walk down the hallway seemed like a pitiful, silent parade, onlookers gathering in classroom doorways to gawk at the dead men walking. Hastings, the self-important ringleader, determinedly strode past the students, ignoring them as if embarrassed that yet another killer could possibly be in his school. Alf and Mr. Jensen brought up the rear, both silent. Whispered words sailed our way as we passed "gay" and "murderer" amongst them. Parker fixed his gaze on the floor, all of his swagger and bluster gone.

I turned to Alf and asked, "Would you please call Detective Cowlings?" I think I might need a "get out of jail" card.

"Already done, Richard." He tucked his salt and pepper mustache into his lower lip. "Called him while I ran to the classroom."

We entered Hastings's torture dungeon of an office. Alf and Mr. Jensen stood guard behind us while we sat down. Hastings took his time getting situated, getting comfy before the inquisition. "So, you boys killed Calvin Sturgess?"

"Wait. What? *No!* I didn't do it." Not so subtly, I inclined my head toward Parker.

Hastings looked at Mr. Jensen, eyes narrowed skeptically. Mr. Jensen cleared his throat. "Arville, I don't think Tex had anything to do with this. Show him the note, Tex."

I nearly forgot the crumpled-up evidence I desperately clutched. I tossed it onto Hastings's desk. Parker glimpsed at it before returning his attention to the floor.

Mr. Hastings looked at it stoically and threw it back on his desk. "What am I to make of this?"

I waited for Parker to reply, but he seemed out of it. "Um, Parker was sending notes like these to gay students—Calvin, Lance Nguyen…Brittany Gerlach."

Hastings thick eyebrows shot up. "Brittany Gerlach was *not* gay."

"Ah…" I glanced at Mr. Jensen for backup, but got nothing but a grim nod. "I think she might have been, Mr. Hastings. Her diary pretty much said so—"

"Her *diary*? Why—and *how*—did you read her diary?" Hastings lips formed a sadistic smile as if he'd finally nailed me for evildoing.

"That doesn't matter. Parker killed Calvin, and he drove Brittany to kill herself."

"I did it," Parker said quietly, following it with a loud snuffle. "I did it."

Against my better judgment, I felt a surge of sympathy for Parker. "Um, Parker, maybe you want to get a lawyer…or something." Hastings pierced me with a hateful stare.

"No. No, it's okay, McKenna." He shut his eyes and straightened his shoulders. "I want to talk about it. It's been bothering me…" His hands flew to his face. "Oh *God*! What have I *done*?" His anguished bellow filled with pain, agonizing to hear. "*What* have I *done*?"

"Go on, son." Mr. Jensen placed a supportive hand on Parker's shoulder.

"I didn't mean to…kill Calvin. I just meant to scare

him. Shake him up a little bit. But he fought back. He fell and hit his head on the sink. It was an accident!"

"And you sent Brittany the letters?" I asked.

"Yes!" he shouted. "But I *never*...I never thought...she would..."

If not exactly liking Parker, I saw honor in his confession. He showed more character than he had the entire school year. I felt empathetic, yet torn. Anger and a sickening sadness twisted my stomach. Sometimes, it seems like we're all treading upon a very frightening, fragile layer of humanity. Some of us are just luckier than others in navigating a path of sanity. "Why did you attack me, Parker? Why'd you push me down the stairs?"

"To send you a warning. You were butting into places you shouldn't have." He lowered his hands. "I am sorry, Tex. For all of it...I'm so sorry."

I pushed back the urge to shed tears for Parker. Maybe later. "Why'd you do it? I mean...all of it? I understand your religious beliefs...but, why?"

He faced me, panic widening his eyes. "That's just it. I don't *know*! It's like something...took me over. I felt...out of control." He looked lost, bewildered, wondering how his life had come to this. At the expense of the lives of others.

Yet I also saw a strong sense of clarity burning in his blue eyes. Like he'd awakened from a living nightmare, fully conscious for the first time in months.

And that's when it clicked. The signs have been there all along. It explains why the YACCERS became so pumped up during the rally led by the loathsome Pastor Don Danvers; why the YACCERS unwaveringly lent their support—and their parent's cash—to the cause; how a purportedly fun game of paintball turned into a chest-thumping display of testosterone. There's more going on here than just religious beliefs. My flood of anger rushed away from Parker and soaked into a new target. Parker had been brainwashed—drugged?— by the Clarendon Baptist Church.

I leaned over and gave Parker a quick bro-hug. He clung to me, digging his face into my shirt, weeping like a baby. I uttered embarrassing inanities such as, "It'll be okay." I rocked him back and forth while Hastings frowned disapprovingly at our show of male weakness.

A knock hammered at the door before Cowlings poked his head inside. Surveying the emotional carnage, he strolled in and said, "Well. I see there's an interesting story here."

\*\*\*\*

Feeling nauseous, I quickly dashed out of Hastings's office once my involvement seemed no longer necessary.

Behind me, the door opened, and Cowlings called out, "A moment of your time, Tex."

I stopped, one hand on the hallway door to freedom. "Okay."

Students piled up outside the office's glass walls, hoping to catch a glimpse of drama. I felt like a hapless fish in a bowl, on display for their amusement. Cowlings pulled me down into a chair, our backs facing the crowd. He looked up at Mrs. Carbody, fake busy shuffling papers, one ear cocked to listen. I guess age shows no boundaries when it comes to a person's desire to partake in human suffering. As long as it's not their own.

"Excuse me, Mrs. Carbody, is it?" Cowlings asked. "Yes?"

"Would you please give us a few moments here? Alone? Official police business."

Mrs. Carbody stamped the ream of paper down onto the desktop. "I suppose so." She huffed off to the back of the office, angry she'd been dethroned.

"Okay," said Cowlings. "I've heard your story. I've heard Parker's story. It looks like I have the murderer. He told us where to find the Reaper costume. But why don't *you* tell me how you found out about him?"

I sighed. "Detective, I knew about the notes. My friend, Lance Nguyen started getting them. Then, another friend…" Cowlings cocked a loaded eyebrow. "…told me he saw Parker writing on yellow stationery in study hall." I shrugged. "Not too many kids in school use yellow stationery paper. I took a chance—"

"A helluva chance, Tex. What would you've done if you were wrong?"

"Well…I wasn't. It paid off. I guess."

"Yes, well…speaking of which, why didn't you report Lance Nguyen's letters to me?"

"I've a good reason. Lance…um, he thought his father didn't know he was gay. He didn't want his dad hearing it from a policeman. He needed a little time. He wanted to be the one to tell his father before the news came out—"

"I suppose I can understand that. But, as always, you seem to revel in playing at risky business. And withholding *important* information from my investigations." I flustered around for a response before he cut me off with a raised finger. "*And* Olivia was attacked. Why in hell didn't you call me?"

I hid my face in my hands, mostly so I wouldn't have to meet Cowling's accusatory scrutiny. "I *just* survived a tornado attack, literally in the damn center of the thing—"

Cowlings leaned back and crossed his legs. "Oh, really? You were literally in the center of the tornado, Tex? You know…" He shut one eye and tapped his pen to his lips. "…I don't know too many people—*ordinary* people, that is—who can say they've survived being in the literal center of a tornado. Don't know a single one, as a matter of fact. Just how'd you do that, exactly?" He tilted his head, grinning. "I *really* would like to know."

"Oh! Did I say 'literally?'" I laughed uneasily. "That's not what I meant. I mean…it *felt* like we were in the center of the tornado. It was pretty scary, Detective." I faked a shudder with way too much drama.

"Uh-huh. Anyway…you didn't report Olivia's attack because you were shaken up by the tornado? Is that what I'm to understand here?" I nodded, hoping wide eyes of innocence are my ally. "Because you've survived much worse before. Let's see…" He started ticking off his fingers one by one. "…a serial killer, gangsta killers, a religiously fanatical killer—"

"Yeah, it does seem like a lot. Look, I apologize for not calling you. I was just freaked out."

Cowlings pushed his glasses up with his pen and sighed. "Tex, Tex, Tex. So, why did Parker have this other student attack Olivia?"

"I think…to make me believe he wasn't the killer."

"Mm-hm. And does Olivia want to press charges against her attacker?"

"No! Detective…Olivia's attacker didn't know the truth. Parker told her it was a joke. Since he's confessing to everything else, I'm sure he'll man up to that, as well."

"So, Parker knew you were, ah, investigating him, is that right?"

"Hey, I leave the police work to you."

"Yeah, like you've ever done that before." A slight growl arose in his tone.

I quickly changed the topic. "Detective, I'm not so certain Parker is completely at fault here."

Cowlings rolled his eyes and threw his hands up. "What are you talking about now?"

"I think he might have been brainwashed or something—maybe, even drugs—by the Clarendon Baptist Church." I paused, waiting for Cowlings to scoff. He just blinked at me as though an annoying fly had splattered on the windshield of his glasses. "I think they're taking advantage of kids—the YACCERS—and using them—"

"Tex, I know the Clarendon Baptist Church are not good people…but come on!" He glanced out the window at the crowd. "I'm loath to ask this…but do you have any proof to back you up?" I told him everything I could, obviously leaving out pertinent bits regarding witchcraft.

"I'll look into it. But I doubt there's much I can do. What you're accusing them of sounds pretty preposterous, and it'll be hell to prove. *Even*—and I'm not saying I do—*even* if I do believe you." He shook his head grudgingly. "But…I've learned to trust your—let's call it 'intuition.' Even if I'm not sure how you come by it. Or if I *want* to know."

"Do you think this might make it easier on Parker? I mean…I'll testify and everything, if I have to—"

"That's something for the lawyers to work out. But, if you really believe in your friend—"

"Um, I don't know that I'd call him my—"

Cowlings sliced his hand through the air. "*If* you believe in Parker, get with his lawyer." Cowlings stood, the master of the last word. "I'll be in touch, Tex. But right now, I've got a murderer to book."

"Um, bye, Detective."

He turned around before re-entering Hastings's chambers. "Oh, this *isn't* goodbye. We'll be talking again very soon."

"Ah, okay."

"As I said before, I find you very interesting," he said with a knowing wink. "I make it my business to know *every*thing I can about people I find interesting." His accusation reminded me of a Chinese curse, "May you live in interesting times."

"I'm not interesting. I'm really boring. In fact—"

"We'll see, Tex. We'll see." He chuckled as he vanished behind Hastings's door, definitely *not* amused.

As I edged my way through the students, they tried to stop me, hungry for gossip. Many of them I didn't even know. I ignored them. It's not my place to air any more dirty laundry. Particularly laundry soiled with suffering, tragedy and death….and blood.

"Tex," shouted Olivia. She shoved her way through the crowd and fell into my arms. "What happened?"

Grabbing her hand, I pulled her out onto the front steps. Several police cars were parked in front, their ominous cherries announcing, "*Drama! Come one, come all, and see the drama! Hurry, hurry, hurry!*"

Students blatantly pointed at me, making it no secret of my buzz-worthy status. They cupped their hands over one another's ears, whispering who knew what.

"Olivia, I'm leaving. I can't take any more of this place today." Although the sun shone with brilliance on another magnificent spring day, my mood had turned dark.

"Well, I'm going with you. You're not leaving without telling me what happened." She blocked my path.

"You'll probably get in trouble tomorrow—"

"Hoo-yah!" She kicked her leg into the air. "I can handle another damn detention."

"Okay. Well, you probably heard Parker confessed."

"Is it true? Did he?"

I nodded, but felt no satisfaction. Not like I thought I would. "He pretty much confessed to everything—"

"How in the hell did you get him to do it?" I recounted my less-than-action-hero chase through Mr. Jensen's classroom. "Damn!" She subdued a guffaw with the palm of her hand. "Wish I could've seen it." When she realized I didn't feel like jokes, she embraced me. "Tex...it's over now."

"No, Olivia. It's not over yet." *Not by a mile, it isn't.*

Chapter Eighteen

I spent most of the afternoon trying to persuade Olivia she shouldn't go with me. I should have known better.

"Damn it, Tex. What happened to that whole speech about us being partners?"

"O', Sister Augustine has all those goons—"

"Mr. Green? I ain't afraid of Mr. Green. Or Mr. Brown. Or Mr. Polka-Dots or whoever." She stamped her feet defiantly. "You're *not* doing this without me!"

"Okay, fine." I knew when to quit. "You can come. But stay out of sight, all right?" She played around with one of my action figures, pretending not to hear me. "All right?"

"We'll see." A huge grin spread across her face.

I had to confront Sister Augustine, maybe even Don Danvers. Didn't know what good it'd do. But I needed to let them know I'd uncovered their manipulation of the YACCERS, possibly even having turned Parker into a murderer. Parker has to share some form of culpability in his involvement...but where it started or stopped, I could only venture a guess.

Maybe it's possible to put a stop to their future abuse of kids; maybe not. A threat from a teenage boy won't hold much weight in their tower of faux-Godliness. But I *have* to try—for Brittany, for Calvin, even for Parker.

Olivia refused to leave my side, possibly out of fear I'd ditch her. When Dad and Ruth came home, I asked if Olivia could stay for dinner. I knew what the inevitable culinary consequences would be, but if Olivia intends on shadowing my every more, then I think it only fair she suffer through Ruth's meal with me. We're partners, after all.

Before dinner, though, I called Mickey and let her know how the killer's unveiling went.

"Hey, Mickey, it's Tex."

"Kid, I've been waiting to hear from you. How'd it go?"

"As good as can be expected, I guess…" I explained the tale once again.

"I knew you could do it, Tex. I *knew* it."

"Yeah, thanks." With the living encyclopedia of witchcraft at my disposal, a wild question popped into my mind. "Hey, Mickey, if someone's able to persuade people, is that maybe a witchcraft thing?" I gave it a lot of thought over the past several hours and felt fairly convinced something supernatural might be about. And it seemed more and more obvious who Augustine's mysterious retreat visitor had been.

"I don't know nothin' about brainwashin', kid, but, some witches do have a power—a power to 'push' people to do their bidding for them. The good witches who have this power—who abide by the rule of no personal gain—have a hard time dealing with their powers—"

"Why?"

"Because they basically can't use their powers, kid. No one's figured out a way to use this particular power for good. That's why most of these types of witches fall into the black magic side of the spectrum." Mickey's amused tone quickly changed to frantic worry. "Why are you asking me about this?"

"Well, I think Parker—um, the 'killer'—might've been 'pushed' into doing what he did."

"You're gonna have to tell me more than that."

I told her my suspicions regarding the Clarendon Church and the YACCERS. During my telling of the tale, I heard the doorbell ring. By the sound of things, Dad and Ruth were entertaining someone in the living room.

When I finished, an extended silence fell on Mickey's end. "Mickey?"

She cleared her throat with a wet-sounding rasp. "Yeah, kid, I'm here. Describe this 'Sister Augustine' to me."

"Well, she's old…er, um, middle-aged. She's tall, with what looks like prematurely silver hair. Let's see, she dresses nicely, and I guess you might say she's attractive." Olivia scrunched up her nose in disgust. "She carries herself well, speaks well. That's about all I've got. So, um, what do you think, Mickey? You think this might be witchcraft-related?"

"I think I'm gonna go with you, kid, that's what I think."

This is *so* not a good idea. I didn't want to worry about protecting Mickey as well as Olivia. "Mickey, it could be dangerous—"

"You damn *better* believe it's gonna be dangerous," she snapped. "*That's* why I'm goin' with you. *Numbskull*. You need to be prepared. You've never dealt with witches like this before."

I didn't understand her anger but reluctantly

343

agreed. "Okay. But maybe you should wait in the car—"

"Kid, you need me, and I'm not sittin' this out. And respect your *goddamned* elders."

"Um, okay. Respect, got it, you got it." My head issued a merciful thank you for avoiding one of her head slaps. "I'll come pick you up in an hour or so."

"Let me go get my face on." She clicked off to go don her "battle armor" makeup.

"Crap. I guess Mickey's coming, as well."

Olivia rolled her eyes and bounced off the bed. "*Why?*"

"I'm not sure, but she was insistent…" I lowered my voice and quietly added, "Like someone else I know."

"Oh, shut up! Come on, I'm starving. Is it dinner yet?"

*Oh, yes, Olivia. Yes it is.* I damn near wrung my hands and issued a villainous chortle.

We bounded down the stairwell to be met by Ruth, her eyes round and worried, her face flushed. "Tex!" she said. "Your…*friend* is here." She swept her arm across the living room. Dad sat with his back toward us talking to someone on the sofa. Rounding the corner, we saw Elspeth, lounging on the sofa, dressed in her punkesque finest.

"Hey, Tex," she said, her unfathomable smile always a mystery. "Olivia."

"Elspeth! *What*…um, how are you?" My voice once again reclaimed the squeaky nature of adolescence.

Dad looked as if his world had been shaken by a leather-clad hurricane. "Tex, ah, we've just been getting

344

to know your, um, friend, Elspeth here."

"I can see that." So stunned by her unexpected appearance, I barely made it to the sofa before falling upon it.

Olivia snapped, "Elspeth," before sitting next to us. Dad faced us like a judge to our jury. Hope he's not wearing his hanging judge robes.

"Elspeth was just telling us a little bit about herself." His forehead rippled with waves of concern. Ruth hurried back in, wringing her hands, appearing on the verge of a stroke. She stood behind Dad, using him as her protective barrier from the wild couch creature.

"Oh, I can't *wait* to hear this," said Olivia.

I shot her a look to rein in the sarcasm. "Elspeth is, ah, a new student at Clearwell this year. I met her in art class. Um, she wants to be an artist." Maybe I should've claimed her as French, since Dad, for some reason, never understands the French.

Dad relaxed slightly, accepting Elspeth's outré appearance as a natural by-product of her artistic sensibilities. "Is that right, Elspeth?" he asked. "What kind of artist are you aspiring to be?"

She fixed her cold-blue gaze on Ruth and added, "I like drawing nudes."

"Oh, *my*," said Ruth. "I...need to tend to supper." She ran toward the safe confines of the kitchen.

*Crap.* Time for a change of direction. "Um, yeah, anyway, what can we do for you, Elspeth?"

"I'm going with you, Tex."

Dad's ears perked up. "Where are you going, son? I thought you were in for the evening." Suspicion darkened his eyes.

"Yeah, something came up. But, please don't

worry. Everything's fine."

"Is this related to…ah—"

I nodded. "But it's okay. I promise. I'll explain everything when I get home." It did nothing to soothe his fears. "Dad, I *swear* this will be the last thing I need to do."

He closed his eyes in deep-Dad concentration mode. Now I'm thankful Elspeth and Olivia are here. Dad won't cause a scene with company in the house. He inhaled deeply and let it out. "Okay, son. I trust you." He turned toward Olivia. "Are you going on this…excursion too?"

"Yes, Mr. McKenna," she replied. "Hey, I'll take good care of your son." Elspeth smirked, which didn't escape Olivia's attention. "I've done it *many* times before," she said to Elspeth, ignoring Dad.

"Oh, I'm *sure* you have, Olivia." Elspeth dangled her head, caressing her cheekbone with a black-covered fingernail. "I'm sure you have."

Seething with fury, Olivia struggled with battling her one-upmanship inner demon. An intervention felt needed. "Dad, if it's okay, we might just eat leftovers when we get home." I jumped to my feet. "We probably should get going." I jerked my head at the fighting girls on the sofa. "Come on."

"I'll let Ruth know, son," he said, rolling into the kitchen. He stopped, hands frozen on his wheel rims, and called back, "Tex?"

"Yeah?"

"Be careful, okay? I love you…"

"I will. And I love you, too."

Elspeth grinned as I pushed her and Olivia out the front door. "Elspeth, *what's* going on here?" Elspeth and Olivia were too busy shooting daggers at one another to pay me much heed. "*Elspeth*!"

She lifted her shoulders, still staring at Olivia. Taunting her. "*What?* You asked me why I never rang your doorbell." She appeared totally incredulous at my line of inquiry. "So I rang."

"I mean, *what's* going on?"

Elspeth rubbed her elbow, making the leather sing. "If you're going to pull a…siege on the Clarendon Baptist Church, I'm going. I'm told I'll be needed."

Much to Olivia's dismay, I readily agreed. When Elspeth says she's needed, you can count on it as fact.

"But I was really looking forward to dinner," said Olivia in a hushed mumble.

"Trust me, no you weren't." I lowered my voice. "Ruth's a terrible cook—"

Olivia wrinkled her brow. "*What?* You were going to feed *me* crappy food and not Elspeth?" She folded her arms, indignantly tapping her foot on the driveway.

I pulled off an exaggerated, earth-shattering eye-roll. "Gah! Let's go do this, already."

Elspeth yanked open the driver's side door and crawled across the front seat. "Oh, hellz no! You don't get shotgun," shouted Olivia.

"Olivia, please! Just get in. We can *all* sit in front."

"Fine, but she is *not* sitting in the middle."

Olivia scooted in, staring straight ahead of her, her mad face on. She let out a brief roar while Elspeth, the top of her faux-hawk brushing up against the Bucket's ceiling, uttered a small chuckle.

Horrible silence filled the first part of our journey. "Where are we going, Tex?" Elspeth finally asked. "I thought the Clarendon Church was in Overland Park."

"It is. I looked it up on the 'Net earlier." And what a heinous website it is, too. Full of hatred and disparaging comments about homosexuals. Hard to believe it's legal. Yet, in between the vile epithets and ugly cybernetic behavior, the site's filled with ridiculous, contradictory slogans such as *The Clarendon Baptist Church welcomes all!* And, *We're here to save your soul!* "But we've got to pick up Mickey first."

"Okay," said Elspeth, matter-of-factly.

"Elspeth…What do you know about tonight anyway?"

"Not much. All I know is it was strongly…indicated I come along." Seeing my disappointment, she quickly added, "I can tell you *something's* going to happen tonight."

Olivia piped in. "What do you mean 'indicated?'"

"I can't tell you that," Elspeth fired back, taking obvious delight in befuddling Olivia.

Olivia's lips turned pale as she pinched them tight.

"Your dad seems nice, Tex," said Elspeth. "And, Ruth, well…" Olivia glowered at her, daring her to make an insulting remark. "…she seems sweet." Elspeth looked out the window, drawing a circle with her fingertip on the glass. "They sorta remind me of…my parents." Her audacity had vanished, replaced by a despondent voice belonging to a different girl.

"Are your parents still alive?" asked Olivia.

Elspeth struggled to dredge up a smile. "Yes. Maybe, I'll see them again someday." She fell into a quiet huddle of leather.

"Elspeth, um, you know this might be dangerous, right?" I asked.

"I know," she said, brimming with confidence once again. "Danger's fun."

"Bring it," shouted Olivia, flexing her muscle. A brief glimpse of mutual respect passed between the combatants, a shared bond of strong womanhood making them temporarily forget how they hated one another. It didn't last long.

Elspeth patted Olivia condescendingly on her arm. "I'll be interested to see how you do, Olivia."

"You know what, Elspeth? I was fighting bullies and serial killers with Tex *long* before *you* came along!"

Elspeth chuckled and flicked a finger at Olivia's button-bedecked jacket. "I saw them, you know."

"*What?*"

Elspeth pointed at one of Olivia's buttons. "The Clash. I saw them back in '79…maybe '80."

Olivia's eyes expanded. "Get out!"

"It's true. I saw them in New York at the CBGB."

"No *way!* What were they like?"

"Hot!"

I became a non-entity as the girls continued talking about punk bands from the '70s and '80s. No matter. At least they had finally found a topic other than their mutual antagonism and disdain.

We were a half hour early, yet Mickey stood on the porch waiting for us. Even though a nice spring evening—the temperature in the upper '70s—she wore a tan, bulky overcoat buttoned to her neck. Clutching a large, purple purse to her chest, she cradled it like a valued heirloom. Her makeup had been elaborately applied, with large swatches of purple and pink splashed about. She looked ready for a church social, rather than a church siege.

When I walked toward her, though, I saw anxiety in her eyes, something I usually don't associate with her.

"Hi, Mickey."

"You're early."

"But…you're ready. "

She craned her head to peer behind me. "Who's the slutty rooster?"

Elspeth walked up behind me. "Who's the bag of prunes?" *Uh-oh.*

Mickey sucked in her lips like she'd been punched in the gut. To my shock, she let out a long, braying laugh. "Oh, kid, is this the channeler you told me about?"

Elspeth nodded once sharply, her faux-hawk snapping like a whip. "Yeah, I'm Elspeth."

"Well, I've been wantin' to meet you." Mickey bent down from her stoop and inspected Elspeth like she would a trick-or-treating child on Halloween. "I'm Mickey."

"I know who you are."

"Can't say I approve of your wardrobe."

"Who dressed you? 'Potato Bags 'R' Us?'"

"This one's got a smart mouth on her. Speaking of which, where's Olivia?"

Olivia sidled up and sighed. "Right here." She stood patiently, waiting for Mickey's inevitable verbal abuse. "I see you're as charming as usual."

Mickey clapped her hands once before loudly proclaiming, "Well, the gang's all here. Let's get going."

Olivia and Elspeth raced to the Bucket, squabbling

over "shotgun" rights. Savoring the moment, Mickey bypassed them and slowly worked her way onto the front seat. Sullen and grumbling, the girls crawled into the back.

So. *Tex's Angels*. And *none* of them can get along. How in the world am I supposed to shape them into a cohesive fighting team?

I broke the cold silence and asked, "So, um, Mickey, why do you need to go with us, again?"

Mickey thumped her heavy purse onto her lap. "Kid, you need help. If you're gonna face down a 'pusher'—and who knows *what* else—I've gotta prepare you. As a general rule, 'pushers' usually can't affect other witches. But, if what I suspect is true, Augustine won't be alone. Usually, 'pusher witches' have people under their sway helpin' them do their dirty work. Even other witches. So—what is it you kids say? We're gonna have a 'cram session.'" I saw Olivia roll her eyes in the rearview mirror. "You've got to pay attention and memorize all these spells you can."

"Mickey…do you *know* Sister Augustine?"

She rocked her purse back and forth in her lap. "I dunno, kid. Maybe. But we're wasting time. Now, pay attention. This is gonna be hard." Over the next twenty-five minutes, Mickey pulled parchment paper, napkins, and assorted vials out of her purse, plying my brain with spells in Latin and English. She continued harking on me, pushing me to repeat the wording until I got it right. With her incessant slave-driving, I felt as if preparing for the toughest test of my life.

I hate being right.

\*\*\*\*

The sun vanished under the dark cover of night. I

crawled the Bucket down the street. Parking the car several house lengths away, I studied the church.

Nestled right in the middle of downtown Overland Park, Kansas, between unsuspecting suburban neighbors, sat the domicile of evil. Positioned on a corner lot, the church sat far back from the street, the vast lawn at a slight incline. The makeshift church appeared to have been a home at one time, refurbished for Danvers's nefarious needs. The front of the building housed no windows, all white paneling, except for the entryway. Five steps led up to double red doors under an arch. A dimly lit lantern next to the doors seemed to be beckoning wayward stragglers to…*something*. A small red cross, the color of blood, hung over the doors. The green-shingled roof vaulted high in the sky, pointing to Heaven, no doubt. Running across the back of the building, a long rectangular add-on resembled a trailer home. A small sign sat in the front yard displaying the words *Welcome to the Clarendon Baptist Church. Let us take you to Heaven.* It read more like a threat than a promise of eternal salvation.

I braved myself. "Let's go," I said, quickly hopping out of the car. Olivia and Elspeth followed my lead, while Mickey struggled to get her car door open.

"Tex," she called from within the car. "Damn it, *let* me out of *here*."

I looked back and said, "Sorry, Mickey." I hoped by the time she scooted out the driver's side, we'd be finished with our impromptu confrontation. I knew she'd make me pay for it later, but I'd gladly suffer a head smack if it meant her safety.

"*Don't* you go in there without me, Tex!"

Elspeth grinned back at her and asked, "Okay,

what now?"

"I don't know. I guess we'll see if anyone's in there." I crouched down and ran through the neighbor's yards, the girls following me. A narrow strip of cement, serving as a small parking lot, took up most of the east side of the church. Four parked cars. Something's going on. On the west side of the church were several high-set windows—each comprised of fifteen smaller panels—that stretched nearly to the roof. Standing on tiptoes, I was barely able to peek inside.

I looked into the chapel. A dozen wooden pews spread across the hardwood floor, an aisle dividing them. Phony-looking white pillars stood off to the sides, appearing like decorations more than physical support. Low-lit sconces lined the walls, flickering, bouncing shadows over the pews. I pressed my face against the window, angling to get a look at the back of the chapel. A small stage lay underneath a white arched ceiling. On it sat several plants and a podium, and a large cross hung on the white brick wall above it.

A sliver of light crossed the stage floor, an expanding quadrilateral of yellow as an unseen door opened. Sister Augustine and Don Danvers stepped toward the podium, appearing to be in a heated argument. I glued my ear to the windowpane, unable to make out their words, but they were definitely squabbling. Hoping to block out the glare from a streetlamp, I placed both hands to the side of my head, resting them on the window. My palm slipped and slid across the glass. *Screeeeech*!

"Crap!" I fell back from shock. On my way down, my hand swung around and smacked the wood paneling. *Thrump*!

"Tex!" Olivia pointed toward the window. Mr. Green's face, contorted into an ugly scowl, stared out at us. Behind him, the lights grew brighter. By the time I got to my feet, Mr. Green had vanished from the window.

Angry as a gun-shot, I heard the front door crack open. Footsteps trampled through the grass. Mr. Green rounded the corner, holding onto the side of the house to slow his trajectory. "*You*," he shouted. "*What* are you *doing*?" He brandished a candlestick like a knife. Raising his weapon, he ran full tilt toward us.

Elspeth stepped in front of him, forcing him to a sudden stop.

"What do you think *you're* gonna do?" Mr. Green spat. "'*Goth*' me to death?"

She swung her foot up into his crotch. "Yeah, something like that."

Holding his groin, Mr. Green fell to his knees as another man approached from behind him. Green crawled to his feet with the aid of his crony. "You little...*bitch*." For each step Green took forward, Elspeth hopped back, a dangerous tango.

My full attention on Elspeth, I didn't even see him coming. "*Oooof!*" The other man blind-sided me, taking us both down into the grass.

"Get *off* him," screamed Olivia. Wielding one of her favorite weapons—her Ramones pin—she jabbed him in the shoulder with the jutting needle. Shrieking, he landed his elbow into Olivia's chest, bashing her to the ground. The man launched onto me, pinning my body with his own. I kicked and punched. The momentum propelled us down a sharp slope in the yard, our bodies ludicrously tumbling over one another.

When we stopped rolling, I laid helpless underneath his weight.

I saw Elspeth backed up against a tree with Mr. Green closing in. Olivia clambered to her feet, her face bone-white in the moonlight.

"Run! *Run*! Get help," I yelled. The man backhanded me hard in the face. Stunned, maybe even out for a second, I wrenched open my eyes. Elspeth had disappeared. Olivia crouched in a runner's starting position. Noticing my disorientation, the man released me and started after Olivia.

"*Run*, Olivia!" This time she bolted quickly, disappearing around the back of the house. I pounced on the back of the man's legs, driving him down. He fell with a thud, kicking back at me, landing a shoe on my cheekbone. I released his legs. At least I had given Olivia time to escape.

"The girls got away," said Mr. Green, huffing. "Bitch!" He massaged his crotch from the kick Elspeth had given him.

"Well, we got this one." The other man pulled me roughly to my feet. "Help me get him inside. I think Sister Augustine's been expecting him."

The two thugs dragged me toward the front of the church. Mickey stood on the stoop, preparing to enter, just a little old lady walking into the house of God. Except not. Mr. Green dropped his hold on me and squatted beside her, hands pawing at the air.

Mickey stared disbelievingly at him. "Oh for *God's* sake," she said. "Are you going to *hit* me?"

The two men stared at each other, contemplating the idea. Mickey pushed by them and opened the red doors. The men shoved me in behind her. After entering the small, dark entryway, we were immediately faced with a second set of red doors. Mickey threw them open as the blinding light of the chapel flooded over us.

Sister Augustine, standing by Don Danvers at the podium, glared at us. Her cheekbones pulled up a cadaverous smile, her teeth white as bone. She snatched off her glasses, letting them dangle on a chain around her neck, and focused on Mickey.

"Hello, Mother," she said.

Chapter Nineteen

"Augustine," said Mickey.

Stunned, I fell out of Mr. Green's grasp onto a wooden pew. Why does no one bother to *tell* me these things?

"What are you up to now?" Mickey took a step forward, determination in her stride.

"Your *mother*?"asked Danvers. Leaning on the podium for support, he appeared as baffled as I felt.

"Be quiet, Don," snapped Augustine. "Mr. Green, Mr. Shaffer, you may leave the church now. I have things under control."

The two men exchanged puzzled glances, remaining frozen. "But…do you want us to call the police, Sister?" asked Mr. Green.

Augustine fixed him with an intimidating stare. "I said *leave!*"

The two men backed up and fled the building.

"Mother, I'd like you to meet my husband, Pastor Don Danvers." Augustine displayed her hand toward Danvers.

Danvers stepped away from the podium. "Hello, ma'am. Ah, it's…a pleasure to meet you." He removed his cowboy hat and mopped the sweat from his forehead.

Mickey disregarded him, her full attention on Augustine. "You married this…*weasel*?"

Danvers sputtered, and stretched his jowls to speak. Augustine cut him off with a glower. "I can assure you, Mother, it's not out of love." She purred like a cat.

"So, what are you up to, Augustine?" said Mickey. "You been 'pushing' these kids to get money?"

Augustine let rip a one-note laugh. "Well, yes, the money's nice...but that's not what this is about. I've progressed beyond that, Mother. I now have political aspirations." She pointed a crooked finger at Danvers. "He's nothing but a figurehead."

"Augustine," shouted Danvers.

"I found this foolin Texas. He created a church...nothing more than his ridiculous family as the congregation. But with his talents for raising awareness and controversy and my ability to...*m*anipulate people, I saw a future. A future where I'd become prominent in politics. With the money I've accumulated through his church, I've been raising capital for my march to power."

"You always were a greedy little bitch."

"Language, Mother, language."

I stood up. "Is *that* why you 'pushed' Parker? Is *that* why you made him into a killer?"

Augustine fixed her eyes on me. "The prodigal young witch boy, Mr. McKenna. You've become quite a pest. I was rather hoping that nasty tornado might've taken care of you, but ah well. One of these days, I'll find a witch who can actually harness nature." She tapped a long finger across her cheek. "Be that as it may, I've been expecting a visit from you once I heard Parker'd been stopped—"

"*Stopped*? Is *that* what you call preventing a kid from murdering someone? You're ultimately responsible for the deaths of two other kids."

"Yes, well…" Augustine showed a flicker of emotion for a second. One of disappointment. "I suppose there are expected casualties along the road."

"You don't have any remorse, do you?" said Mickey.

Augustine shook her head. "I can't be held responsible for young Mr. Pennett's actions. I didn't exactly *push* him to kill anyone—"

"Augustine," said Danvers. "What are they talking about?"

"Oh, shut up, you moron." Danvers obediently fell silent, swaying his hat in front of his belly. "Parker's a special boy. It didn't take much of a 'push' to make him a…shall we say, a believer. He was looking for something. All I did is give him something to believe in—"

"Like *hatred*? And homophobia…and *murder*?" I couldn't believe how she tried to justify her actions.

"No, Mr. McKenna. As I said, I never told Parker to kill anyone. He took that upon himself. Personally, I don't even believe in the absurd teachings of the Clarendon Baptist Church. It's just business."

"Augustine," said Danvers. "How can you *say* that? After everything we've talked about and *learned* together…" His voice shriveled up, his shoulders caved in, a raisin of a man.

Augustine roared with laughter. "Have you not been listening to a word I've said, Don? If you want to keep your beloved church and your growing following, you're going to shut your mouth and listen to my every instruction."

Like a cornered criminal, Danvers hung his head

and struggled to sit down on the stage. He mumbled quietly—a prayer, maybe—attempting to come to terms with how his world had suddenly upended.

"You ruined Parker's life because of *'business'?"* Seething anger raged through me. "And you don't *accept* any blame."

"Oh, poor, naïve Mr. McKenna. What is 'blame' anyway? Perhaps you're as much to blame for Parker's descent as anyone." Her eyes widened accusatorily. "Without your incessant meddling, perhaps none of this would have happened."

I tried to wrap what she said around my brain. Does she have a point? If I hadn't intervened, would Calvin still be alive? *No.* Brittany would still be dead. This is *not* going to be laid at my feet. "That's total bullshit!"

"Well, I see you've picked up foul language from my mother."

"And, you 'pushed' all those kids, the YACCERS, into bringing you money…into believing your hateful rants against humanity. You even pushed them into bloodthirsty behavior during the paintball game, didn't you? And yet you still *stand* there and say you're not to blame for the two deaths? *Unbelievable!"*

Augustine made a clucking sound. "You have so much to learn yet. So much about your aforementioned humanity. And about witchcraft." A slow grin stretched across her lips. "Why, you don't even know the truth about your mother, do you?"

"What…what are you talking about?"

"Oh, shut your pie-hole, Augustine," belted out Mickey. "She's just trying to mess with you, kid." She extended a clenched fist toward Augustine. "You may as well have pulled the trigger on those two kids as much as your puppet did. Just like you killed your own father."

Augustine's self-assuredness vanished. "He had a heart attack."

"Yes, he did." Mickey wiped a tear away with the back of her palm. "But it was because he heard what you were up to. About how you were using your powers for personal gain...pushing people for money. Then when he confronted you about it...you laughed at him. Defied him! Told him you weren't gonna stop. You left him in a crumpled ball on the floor...clutching his chest. You didn't even call for help..." Mickey reached for a pew to steady herself, her small frame visibly trembling. I ran to her side and enveloped her with my arms, pulling her close to me.

Augustine shrugged. "What was I supposed to do, Mother? I knew you'd blame me. So I left."

"You could have called for an ambulance!"Mickey fought through her sadness, letting fury stoke her words.

"You have a lot of blood on your hands, Sister," I said quietly. "We're going to stop you from hurting anyone else—"

"Oh, *really*, Mr. McKenna? And just how do you propose to do that?" Something felt off. Mickey said witches aren't able to 'push' one another. Yet, her confident arrogance suggested she had the upper hand.

"Any way I can...I guess."

Augustine crossed the stage to where she and Danvers had entered earlier. "Do you truly think I'm unprepared for you?" She pulled the door open. "Come out. It's time."

Spencer strolled onto the stage with slow, deliberate timing, still wrapped in his too-small, purple Nehru jacket. Stopping at the edge of the stage next to the spent Danvers, he broke out an aggressive grin.

"I believe you know Spencer Pritchett," said Augustine.

"Oh, yeah, we're old friends."

"Spencer," spat Mickey. "So, you're *still* using kids to do your dirty work."

"Oh, Spencer's no ordinary kid, Mother. He's *very* special...and powerful." Augustine smiled coolly at Spencer. "Mr. McKenna, you've already experienced some of Spencer's special gifts?"

"Yeah. There was the spell to take my breath away. And you tried to make my car crash. Didn't work though, did it, Spencer?"

Spencer straightened his shoulders, making the fabric of his jacket groan. "This time I have a ring of protection myself." He patted a large ring on his stubby finger with flair. "We'll see what works today." Dropping into a crouching position, he splayed one hand toward me like an inexperienced karate practitioner and rattled off an unfamiliar spell in Latin.

As if being hit by a baseball bat, I felt a painful thrust to my chest. My legs yanked out from underneath me, I flew back into a pew. "*Mickey,*" I cried out. "Take cover!" Gripping the back of the pew, I pulled myself up. Mickey rushed past me to the back of the church. Spencer repeated the spell, this time screaming the words. The blow to my chest hit me twice as hard as I sailed through the air. Landing in the center aisle, I dove for cover between the nearest pews.

"Kid," shouted Mickey. "Remember what I taught

you!"

My brain searched for the precise spell Mickey lambasted me with earlier. Various phrases swam to the forefront, but they cluttered together in a confusing jumble. Right now I just wanted to survive.

I jumped up, holding a palm out like Spencer did, hoping it'd bolster my powers. With jackhammer speed, Spencer countered. An invisible bullet blew through my chest. The impact knocked me back into the pew, bringing it crashing down upon me.

"Kid," said Mickey. "Reverse the damn hex, already!"

The spell flooded my brain like an ocean wave. I stood, muscles aching, and chanted, "Spell, spell, spell be gone! Back to which ye belong. Back to the caster, take your disaster!" I jolted my hand out toward Spencer and added one of Olivia's "Hoo-yah's!"It couldn't hurt.

Spencer's eyes grew into round orbs, his mouth forming a similar circle. He grunted as he fell to the floor beside Danvers.

Danvers covered his face with his meaty hands, whimpering like a whipped dog. He crawled off the stage and tumbled to the floor. Screaming, he ran past me down the aisle and burst through the doors, no doubt seeking the sanity of non-witch-like activities. Hate crimes are considered sane in his world. Just not witchcraft.

Winded, Spencer clambered his way up to the podium. "God *damn* you, Tex!" He raised his arms above him, fingers spread wide. I climbed out from the fallen pew into the aisle, attempting to rush him, hoping to take him in a physical challenge. *Maybe.*

He bellowed out another Latin spell, his voice shrill. My head split open, painful jags swinging back and forth like lightning strikes. Pressing my palms against my temples, I tried to alleviate the pain. I dropped to my knees and screamed. The anguish increased, my vision diminishing.

"*Tex*! The third eye rite! The third eye *rite*!" Mickey's voice aggravated the pain. I struggled to recall the spell, attempting to cut through the barbwire around my brain.

"I invoke thee, Oh Great Mother…" Somehow, the words bled through. "…and call upon the ruler of clairvoyant powers, I ask thee now to open my third eye, to protect my mind, to see the past and the future, and to show me the hidden light. Let me perceive the divine kingdoms of the unknown! So mote it be!" The pain lifted like tendrils of smoke from a dampened fire. A sudden clarity—a warm glow within—told me everything will be all right. My sight returned as I heard Spencer repeating the spell. I got to my feet and grinned. Panic crossed his face.

"*Okay*," Spencer cried out. "You *asked* for this!" Again he raised his hands toward the roof. But his dramatic flair had dissipated, replaced by a fearful uncertainty. When he finished reciting his spell, a low, rumbling sound emanated from beneath the wooden floors. The noise crawled up, as if alive, claiming the walls and shaking the pillars. The rafters creaked, the lamps swayed back and forth. Spencer appeared terrified as he looked around the pulsating church.

"*Spencer,* what have you *done?*" The moaning sound erupted into a large roar as if Satan himself clawed his way up to claim us. The back doors blasted open, and a powerful gust of wind blew down the aisle, pushing me aside. The small windowpanes exploded; then burst into smithereens with the sound of firecrackers snapping.

Augustine stepped out from her hiding place. "Spencer, make it *stop*! *Now*!"

"*I can't!*"

Suddenly enlightened, I remembered another spell Mickey taught me several years ago. She nicknamed it the "Hail Mary" of spells, only to be used in case of emergency. I'd call this circumstance eligible.

"*Thrice around the circle bound, evil sink into the ground*," I screamed, trying to raise my voice above the groaning church so the spirits—or whatever—could hear me. A sudden intake of air at my back felt as if the wind reversed direction. Abruptly, the building stopped shaking. The horrendous moaning and groaning slowed to a mild gurgle, a demon's upset stomach. A lantern fell to the ground, splintering glass, a crescendo to the black magic melody.

My gaze locked onto Spencer's, hoping his foolish spell snapped some sense into him. His eyebrows raised. "Now you've *really* had it!" He thrust his shaking hands in front of him.

"Oh, shut up!" Elspeth stepped out of the doorway behind Spencer and swung a gold object at the back of his head. Spencer collapsed. Elspeth dropped the weapon to the floor with a clang, the light catching the gold collection plate as it rolled around her feet. Spencer groaned and sat up. Elspeth picked up the plate and whacked him again. "Just stay down," she ordered.

Augustine backed a few steps away from Elspeth and took up position behind the podium. Still unflappable. She squinted, looking out into the damaged chapel. "You can come out now, Mother."

Mickey stepped underneath one of the still-swinging lanterns, shadows creeping up and receding across her face. "Augustine…we *won*."

"Maybe, maybe not. But…what now?" Augustine grinned her Cheshire cat smile. "You can't exactly go to the police and tell them I'm a witch, now, can you?" She sighed resolutely. "I suggest you pack up your little…entourage, go home and forget about us. In exchange, we'll do the same about you. I won't send Spencer after you again. His performance has been less than satisfying anyway." Spencer sniveled, cowering on the floor. "What say you, Mother? Do we have a deal?"

Mickey strolled self-assuredly down the aisle toward me, her arms swaying animatedly back and forth. "You know we can't let you do that, Augustine." She stopped beside me. "We'll continue to fight you until you quit what you're doing."

"With *what*?" She tittered and placed her fingertips over her lips. "You have *nothing*."

"Oh, I wouldn't say that, *beeyotch*!" Olivia stood at the back of the church, flaunting her phone in the air, waving it back and forth. "I've been hiding in the back of your *stupid* church since this whole freak show-and-tell began. I recorded *everything*." Olivia joined us. I reached for her hand.

"Well, Augustine," I said, refusing to call her "Sister" any longer. "Looks like we have more than a stalemate here. Unless you and your crew pack up and vanish, we're going to put this video all over the web. How do you think your political aspirations will go if everyone knows Danvers married a witch?"

Augustine's tongue darted in and out of her mouth like a dried-up lizard. "You wouldn't dare! *All* of you are on that recording as well!" She smiled, but *man,* it looked forced. "Besides, no one will believe it. They'll think it's phony—"

I shrugged. "Could be. But I doubt it. Are you willing to take that chance? We are. Besides, we can easily edit our part out. Either way, it's gonna cast enough suspicions on you and your 'organization' to hurt you."

Augustine gathered a few papers on the podium, obviously playing for time. "Fine, then," she finally said. "We'll leave."

"Don't *even* think of starting your hate *crap* up anywhere else," said Olivia. "Or *else!*" Once again, she flashed her phone like a weapon. She seemed to enjoy this *way* too much. But so did I.

"We'll see." Augustine walked past Spencer, carefully side-stepping Elspeth, toward the door. She stopped and turned toward Mickey. "Goodbye, Mother."

Mickey stared at her and snorted. "No, Augustine. Good riddance!" Augustine walked regally off the stage and through the door. Mickey lowered her head. I saw tears sliding down her cheek, her makeup running. She took in a deep breath and walked toward Spencer. "Spencer, we're *not* going to have any more trouble out of you, are we?"

Spencer shot a frightened look toward Elspeth. Elspeth grinned and pulled the collection plate back. Spencer raised a hand in defense and cried out, "No. I promise! No more trouble." Elspeth lowered the plate.

"Okay, then," said Mickey. "But you can bet I'm

taking this up with the Witches' Council!"

"Mickey, what *is* the 'Witches' Council'?" I asked. It's just the second time I've heard the name in my three-year tenure as a witch, and I wonder why it's only becoming a "thing" now.

"Later, Tex, later." She brushed her hand back and forth like a distracted parent. "Did you *hear* me, Spencer?"Mickey leaned against the stage, and the moment of her sadness passed.

Spencer nodded rapidly. "Okay, *okay*. Fine! Just...don't let her hit me again."

Elspeth chuckled and tossed the plate down to the stage. It wiggled to a halt next to Spencer's head. "Poser," she said.

"Let's get out of here." Mickey led our troop of conquering warriors down the aisle of our battleground.

Once we all quietly climbed into the car, I turned to Mickey. "About your daughter—"

She held a hand up to ward me off. "Not now, Tex. I don't want to talk about it."

"Okay. But...unless you have a problem with it...I lied. I'm gonna go viral with Olivia's recording." I watched her carefully, hoping she understands what I have to do, and the possible implications for her.

She closed her eyes. "I don't know what 'going viral' means. But if you're talking about exposing Augustine and this mockery of a church...then you do what you gotta do. I wouldn't expect anything else from you."

\*\*\*\*

When we reached Mickey's house, I opened the Bucket's door for her. "Thanks, kid," she said as she inched out of the car. "Hey, girls." Olivia and Elspeth tumbled out, preparing to race for the front seat. "You both did really good tonight." To my surprise, she reached up and hugged Olivia.

"Thanks," said Olivia. "You weren't so bad yourself, you know."

"Yeah, well, that's me. I've still got a few miles in the old wagon."

"You're one of us," said Olivia.

"And you, Elspeth…" Mickey tossed her arms around her as well. Elspeth looked so uncomfortable with the unexpected warmth it took her a moment to respond. She patted Mickey, resting her chin on her shoulder. "…if you ever want to talk about your channeling, or maybe I could help you hone your gift or something, you know where I live."

"Thanks." Elspeth winked at her after breaking their embrace. "I just might do that."

Taking Mickey by the elbow, I escorted her up the sidewalk. "Try not to kill each other," I called back. "Mickey, are you going to be okay? I mean, that couldn't have been easy for you…with your daughter."

As soon as we reached the shadows of Mickey's porch, she stopped on her steps. "Oh…" That was all she said before she fell against me. She buried her face in my chest, her blue head dipping up and down, stifling her sobs. In many ways, it seemed more unsettling than seeing my dad cry when Mom died. Mickey'd been my rock for three years. For the first time, I saw her as a little old lady, mourning the loss of her daughter. If I could use my witchcraft to take her pain away, I would and damn the consequences.

With my arm around her shoulders, I guided her down to the step and sat next to her. Her other hand reached out and I held it. "Oh, Tex…oh, my…" We sat in the dark for minutes, just holding hands.

When she regained herself, I said, "Mickey, do you want to talk about your daughter now?"

"Tex! *Dammit*! I don't want to talk about it ever. I *told* you that already." With blinding speed, she brought her open palm up onto the back of my head. *Thwack*!

"Gah! What was *that* for?" So much for the kinder, softer Mickey model. Oddly enough, it relieved me to have her back.

"First of all, you need to listen to me, kid," she said. "If I say I don't want to talk about something, what do you think that means? It means I *don't* want to *talk* about it." Mickey looked over-heated in her heavy coat, yet a sudden breeze brought on a shiver. "And you weren't paying enough attention to me in the car earlier about the spells."

"But…we won, Mickey." I followed Mickey's lead and stood up.

"Don't get cocky. We *barely* won. You need more refinement."

"It's kinda tough remembering spells when you're under assault."

"And I'm telling you, kid, you need more training." She shuffled her feet and stared down at the sidewalk. "Have you decided what you're going to do after school yet?" That's what this is about. Mickey still wants me in her life, her roundabout way of telling me not to be a stranger. Outside of her monthly witch meetings, I might be the only person in her life.

"Hey, I know I need more training. And you're my one and only teacher." I bowed. "Even if I do go away, I'll be back every weekend. And I hope we can schedule a weekly training session." Even though I never want to use my witchcraft powers again. "If that's okay with you, that is."

Mickey's smile stretched across her face, her eyes reduced to slivers of happiness. "I think that can be arranged." She grasped my arm, an iron grip for a small, elderly woman. "You *did* do good tonight, Tex. I'm proud of you." My turn for a hug.

"I'm proud of you too, Mickey. You're a force to be reckoned with."

"Okay, kid. You can let go now. I don't want the neighbors thinking I'm robbin' the cradle." Laughing, she lit a cigarette.

I waved the smoke away from my face. "One of these days, you should really consider quitting."

"Look, kid, what fun do I get these days?"

I waved my hands in surrender. "Um, Mickey?"

"Yeah?"

"What did your...um, Augustine mean tonight when she said 'I don't know the truth about my mother'?" At the time, those words had made the hair on the back of my neck stand up. But during the ongoing battle, I pushed them out of mind. Possibly, intentionally so.

Mickey took a long drag from her cigarette and exhaled, watching the smoke wisps curl into the night. "I don't know kid. I think she was just tryin' to mess with your head—"

"Did she know my mother?"

Mickey dropped the cigarette and stepped on it. She nodded her head while watching the remaining embers snuff out. "Yeah, kid. Most of the witches in Clearwell knew your mother. It'd be hard not to."

"Huh."

"But I wouldn't put too much stock in what she said." Mickey averted her gaze. "Okay, it's getting chilly out here."

"Not really," I muttered.

"You'd best get your girls home. It's a school night."

"Okay, Mickey, 'night."

"Good night, Tex." I watched her curse at her ring of keys until she found the correct one. She turned one more time and gave me a half-hearted wave before closing the door behind her.

Walking back to the car, I wondered if Mickey had been upset about her daughter. Or if she lied to me about what Augustine said. Something's definitely off with her behavior.

In the car, Olivia and Elspeth busied themselves arguing about who the bigger badass is. They stopped when they saw me sitting still, my fingers lingering over the key. "Are we done?" I asked.

"Whatever," said Olivia. Elspeth shrugged and looked out the window. "Is Mickey okay?"

"I guess so." I pulled the Bucket into the street. "Hey, earlier I was really hoping you guys went to get the cops—"

"What would we've told them?" said Elspeth. "The Clarendon Baptist Church is secretly a coven of homosexual-hating, murderous witches?" She stared at me unflinchingly, her radiant eyes nearly glowing.

"Really," agreed Olivia. "We took a cue from you, Tex. We winged it. Elspeth took the back of the church, and I snuck in the front as soon as the two goons left." The girls shared a fleeting smile, once again united over their fierce warrior status.

"I found an open window and climbed in," said Elspeth.

"Guess I'm glad you didn't go for help. This turned out way better than I thought it would."

"Tex, do you really think we shut them down?" Olivia absentmindedly stroked the lock of purple hair over her eye.

"I don't know. I'd say, definitely, here in Clearwell we did. But I'm willing to bet Augustine will resurface somewhere at some point, probably with a different scheme. I'll tell you one thing, though. After I post your video everywhere, it's gonna make it damn tough for her." It thrilled me that Augustine, Danvers, and crew wouldn't be getting away untarnished. They needed to pay for their sins, for everyone they hurt. My momentary happiness just as quickly faded away. "You know, the news about YAC is gonna devastate Allie and Dickers…and all the other YACCERS."

"Crap. You're right," said Olivia. "I didn't even think about that."

"I wouldn't lose any sleep over Elizabeth," said Elspeth. "I think she just joined YAC because of Donovan. And she's just trying to pad out her resume. I betcha she's way more pissed off about her car than this news." We all nodded wearily in agreement.

"Do you guys think it's the right thing to do?" I asked. "Posting the video? What about everyone who's gonna have their world rocked by the news? We're gonna destroy their beliefs."

"Tex," said Olivia. "An entire culture was once wiped out in the name of Christianity. But people are strong. It's *way* better to deliver a few blows now instead of having them going on believing in a buncha liars."

"As much as it kills me, I have to agree with Olivia. Bring 'em down, Tex. They deserve it. And their clueless followers deserve to know the truth."

"Do it for Calvin, Lance, and everyone who was persecuted by these bastards," said Olivia. "And even Parker."

"And Brittany would want it, too," said Elspeth, smiling knowingly.

"Yeah, you're right. I'm doing it tonight."

"Of course, we're right, Tex," said Olivia. "We're women." The girls roared with laughter.

"Elspeth?" I asked. "Do you want me to drop you at Elizabeth's house?"

Elspeth ran her finger along the window seal, staring up into the stars. "No. It's a nice night. I'm gonna take advantage of it. I might not get another chance for a while."

"Ah…okay." I knew it was Elspeth's cryptic way—and, really, with her, is there any other way?—of telling me she's taking a hiatus from this realm again. "Elspeth…will you be back?"

She remained silent for the rest of our trip.

\*\*\*\*

I let the girls out in my driveway.

"Tex?" called out Elspeth. "Can I talk to you?" While Olivia and I headed toward my front door, Elspeth had started down the driveway. She flashed a mirthless grin at Olivia before readdressing me. "Alone?"

*"Fine,"* huffed Olivia. "I'll wait for you inside."

"Thanks, O." I lowered my voice to a whisper.

"Don't eat anything unless my dad says he cooked it."

Both girls laughed. Elspeth called out. "Olivia?"

"*What*?"

"You're really…kinda all right, you know?"

"Thanks. You can hold your own, too." Olivia raced into the house. No hugging greeting card moments, but it seemed like a start.

"Elspeth, I know you're leaving again. Will you be back?"

"That's not important right now," she said. "I need to tell you something. It's about the tornado."

"What about it?" We stood in the moonlight, looking like two hesitant lovers before a breakup.

"We had help, you know."

"What do you mean?"

"Your witchcraft spell helped, but…" She looked upward and hefted an eyebrow. "…come *on!* We couldn't have survived without *something* helping us."

I guess I halfway suspected as much. "Did somebody tell you that?" I wrapped her hands in mine, a move I must've mastered from watching Donovan Goode at work. "What helped us?"

She shook her head, the mischief in her smile gone. "Tex, you know I can't tell you that." Her stock answer. It's like pulling teeth that don't need extraction. "It was strongly—*strongly*—insinuated we had help from another…area."

"'Area', Elspeth? *Really*? Area is like a place you shave. Is that *all* you can give me?"

"Yep. That's all you're gonna get," she said, batting her eyelashes.

"Okay…can you tell me why we were given help?"

"I think you know the answer to that." She stared at

me, waiting for my synapses to fire up. "It means there's still work ahead for you to do. The 'powers' want you around."

*Here we go again.* I had hoped my days of being an active witch were behind me. No such luck in the craptacular world of Tex McKenna, boy witch. "I don't suppose you know what that's all about, do you?"

"No. But hang in there." I flashed back to the cat on my counselor's poster. *Hang in there, baby.* "I have a feeling everything's gonna work out for you." Her leather-jacketed arm creaked while she grabbed my neck and gave me a quick kiss. "So long, Tex."

"Wait," I said before she could prance off. "Will I see you again?"

"Chances look like you might, Tex. Gotta bounce." Her hands on the small of her back, she strolled down the driveway.

"Goodbye, Elspeth. I'll miss you…"

She shot me a quick glimpse over her shoulder and wiggled her fingers at me. Kicking her boots high and humming "Anarchy In The UK," The Sex Pistols' song, she vanished into the night.

Chapter Twenty

Graduation day! An hour to go before the ceremonies, but Dad and Ruth insisted I get here early. And I *still* don't know what the hell I'm going to do with my life.

The auditorium is awash in a sea of blue gowns, squeals of giddy laughter reminding me I don't have anything to celebrate. They instructed us to sit in our assigned seats, awaiting our triumphant march into the gymnasium, but no one is following protocol. Parents strutted about, snapping photos, full of encouraging pep talks. Like any other school day, students gathered in their cliques, bragging about their future accomplishments. Aren't things supposed to change once you graduate?

"Did you decide about KU yet?" Ian wouldn't let up.

"No idea, man."

"Tex, you gotta make a decision. Time's running out." Ian looked strange in his ceremonial garb, dark-dyed hair, and eyeliner; a goth kid in a blue gown.

"I gotta consider my dad." Ian shook his head in frustration. "He's not doing so well."

"Damn it. You're just making excuses." Maybe I am, but that doesn't stop the fact Dad's health is failing him. And, of course, there's Olivia. A long-distance relationship would suck. I'd miss not seeing her every day.

"Tex!" Olivia's open gown flowed behind her as she raced toward me. "You look…goofy."

"Yeah, well, this damn cap won't stay on." It was just my luck to have a cap too small for my head. I had to hold onto it with every step, a tiny blue ice cap on top of my looming mountain of a head.

Olivia attempted to pull the cap tighter around my skull. "Maybe you should try and get a bigger hat." She tried to quiet her laughter, but she's never been good at doing so.

"I already tried. They said they didn't have any extras left."

"Maybe you should strap it around your head," said Ian. "Get some rope. You *do* have a big head."

"Oh, that's soooo funny."

Brandon and Lance joined us. Lance, looking dapper in a paisley dress shirt, began shimmying in the aisle. "Way to go, guys. You made it. Hope I get there next year."

Olivia jumped next to him, spinning like a top and kicking her legs impossibly high. She could out-perform the entire Clearwell cheerleading squad. "Aw, I'm gonna miss you, Lance."

"I'll be around. You guys know where to find me."

Ian rolled his eyes. "Jeezus, you guys, chill with the dancing." Ian's grumpiness goaded Lance and Olivia to really break out their moves. Brandon joined them, barely moving, but still managing a calm cool. Of course, I sat the number out. The three of them finished, collapsing into a group embrace. "Tell me again why I'm friends with you guys?" said Ian.

"Oh, don't be such a tight-ass," said Olivia.

Brandon said, "This is it. No more of this place." He swiveled his head around, taking one last school inventory.

"Yeah." I took one last look as well. The others fell silent, a quiet wake for our Clearwell trauma. And the good times. "Can't say I'm really gonna miss this place. I mean, I'm gonna miss you guys...but—"

Jasper Stafford strutted up, rolling his football player's shoulders with the rhythm of ocean waves. "Hey."

"Hey, Jasper," I said. "You're coming tonight, right? To my party?" Dad and Ruth were adamant about throwing an evening graduation party for me. I reluctantly agreed after I took Dad aside and insisted it be catered. I didn't want to be held responsible for giving my graduating class food poisoning.

"Yeah, sure, I'll be there."

"Are your parents coming? All parents are welcome, too."

Jasper shrugged. "Nah. I'm bringing a date. I'll be tired of the 'rents by then."

"Cool, cool. Hey, Jasper, I wanted to thank you again—" Elizabeth and Donovan's magisterial appearance derailed my train of thought.

"Hey, guys," said Donovan, displaying his expertly maintained dental hygiene. "Tex." He grasped my hand in both of his, more comfy than sitting in front of a fireplace. "Congratulations!"

"Same back at you." Donovan shook everyone's hand, tossing out personalized comments, leaving behind a rippling effect of beaming faces. I'm *so* going to vote for him some day.

Elizabeth looked resplendent in a blue flowing

dress, her long blonde tresses splayed perfectly across her bare shoulders, a fairy tale princess. "Yes, congratulations are in order to all of you," she said, enunciating each word with precise care. She nodded curtly to all of us.

"Hey, Elizabeth," said Ian, grinning mischievously. "Did you get a new car?" Elizabeth's cold blue-eyed gaze snagged Ian.

I nudged Ian's shoulder and quickly changed the subject. "Um, hey, I didn't get a chance to talk to you about it before, but I'm having a graduation party tonight at my house and want to invite both of you."

Donovan blinked and looked genuinely pleased. "Tex, it'd be my honor to come to your party. That is, if it's okay with Elizabeth." He looked at Elizabeth for approval. Like all powerful First Ladies, Elizabeth will be the one truly running the country someday.

"Yes, we'd very much enjoy that." But the way she said it left a lotta doubt about her level of enjoyment.

Ian groaned. I yelled, "Great," hoping to cover up Ian's anti-social display. "We'll see you there. Starts at seven. My address is—"

"I *know* where you live, Tex," snapped Elizabeth. Donovan's face wrinkled in bafflement. As they strolled off, arm linked in arm, I saw Donovan questioning her how she knows where I live.

"Tex," said Olivia, "did you *really* have to invite her?"

Lance intervened. "Come on, O'. It's time to party. Everyone gets their party on." Ever the social beast, Lance propelled himself into the aisle again, gyrating his hips, punctuating every flawless move with a "yeah" or "uh." Jasper showed a rare exhibit of emotion and erupted with laughter.

Dickers ran up and hopped alongside Lance. Awkwardly swaying his hips, rowing his oars, he looked like an arthritically-challenged old man. Underneath his gown, unfortunate white socks glowed like they were radioactive. Allison stood next to him, obviously amused at the impromptu dance-fest. Not to be outdone, Olivia and Brandon once again joined in, this time swinging one another around the crowded aisle. We gathered quite a crowd of amused—flabbergasted?—spectators, but who cares? We'll probably never see most of them again and graduation day merits some form of liberating release.

Out of breath, Dickers managed, "Hi, guys."

"Hey," said Allie, who proceeded to pass around hugs. It didn't take long for Allie to return to her old self. I don't know when the turning point happened, but it warmed my heart. And reminded me I've been meaning to have a conversation with Allie and Dickers for too long now.

"Hey, guys, can I talk to you?" Allie and Dickers glanced at one another before nodding in unison. "I mean somewhere quieter? We still have about forty-five minutes."

Olivia immediately knew what I had in mind. "I'm going with you," she demanded.

I led them to the cafeteria where several students sat sullenly with their families. They appeared mortified to be spending time with their parents when they should be whooping it up in the auditorium with their friends. It seemed like a holding tank to keep parents hidden away.

We sat down at our usual table. "Okay, I don't

know how—or where—to start—"

Allie said, "Just say it."

"It's about YAC and the Clarendon Baptist Church." I felt inadequate talking about religion with Allie and Dickers. But Olivia insisted on it. She'd promised to be my backup in case I screwed it up. "You guys obviously know about the, um, video that was posted all over the Internet about YAC and Sister Augustine?" Naturally, I didn't tell them I anonymously posted it and discretely edited our participation out of it.

"Yeah. That was…weird," said Dickers. "And, I gotta say disappointing." He flashed a glance toward Allie, who bobbed her head in support.

"I get that. And, you know, there are a lot of naysayers about the video. People said it was doctored…or photo-shopped. But some experts said it was real. Sister Augustine and Don Danvers disappeared after that. It's gotta mean—"

"What are you trying to say, Tex?" snapped Allie, on the defensive.

"Oh, for God's sakes," said Olivia. "Tex, you take *forever* to hit a freakin' point. Look, guys, whether you believe Augustine was a witch or not, she *did* admit she was in it for money and power. None of the 'so-called' online experts ever even disputed that part." While Dickers' gaze fell to the table, Allison glowered.

"Ah, yeah," I continued. "I just want…no, I *need* to hear from you guys that this…disappointment about YAC isn't going to put you off religion…or your beliefs."

Surprise lit up Allie's eyes. Dickers gave me a double-take. "Why would you even think that? And, to tell you the truth, I didn't think you even cared about our beliefs."

I shook my head. "No. *No!* That's not true at all. I mean, I can see you two truly do have strong faith and…anytime anyone has solid beliefs, it's a good thing. Dickers….Clark—" He smiled when I called him by his first name. "Clark, your beliefs are so strong they led you to your future vocation."

"And, Allie," said Olivia, "I think you're the kind person you are today…well, because of your Christianity." Her words shocked me. Just a little while ago Olivia swore off Allie for attacking her. But Olivia never lies. She meant every word.

"Thank you, Olivia." Allie blinked her lashes as if shuttering tears.

"I guess what I'm saying is I'm totally jealous over your beliefs," I said. "You know what you believe in."

"Let me ask you something," Allison had experienced a positive change through the ordeal. She's now braver, more upfront in her interactions. "Do you believe in God?"

I didn't expect this question. I looked to Olivia for reinforcement, but she merely raised her eyebrows, wanting to hear my answer. An answer to the same question she asked me a few weeks back. "Well…" I stuttered and stumbled, contemplating my answer. "Someone recently—okay, it was Olivia…" We exchanged smiles. "…asked me the very same question. I didn't have an answer. At the time, I said 'no.' But now…I don't know. Maybe, things have changed. Maybe *I've* changed." I squinted at the ceiling as if looking for a definitive sign of heavenly activity. "I've seen things. Proof of activity from the dark realm—" Olivia kicked my leg underneath the table.

"What's *that* mean?" said Dickers.

"Oh, well…um, the dark side. Parker, Danvers, Augustine, you know." I attempted a weak laugh. "So, if the 'dark side' exists, then it just goes to figure there's a 'good side' as well. I mean, I've lived through a lot of weird stuff. Some of it dangerous. I survived a tornado attack."

Dickers practically salivated from his tornadic memory. "Yeah, we all did."

"Um, yeah. But maybe…just maybe, we had 'divine intervention.'" I glanced at Olivia, who looked more surprised than the others. "I used to think there wasn't a God. Where are the modern miracles? Why did my mother have to die? There're so many tragedies…they're easy to see. Happens every day. Sucks. Then I started thinking, maybe the Devil's just a show-off. What if God's miracles are still out there? Maybe the miracles…are just in everyday life."

"Exactly." Dickers pointed an authoritative finger toward me.

I shrugged. "Okay, long answer to a short question, Allie. I'm not quite ready to accept there's a long-bearded, white-haired, Santa Claus-looking figure, sitting above us in clouds, doling out rewards to the just and punishment to the bad. But, I think it's awfully narrow-minded of me to definitively say there's not a God. I believe there is a power of good, something we don't understand. So my answer is…maybe yes…with reservations?"

"Wow, Tex, way to commit," said Olivia with a laugh. "It sounds like you're hedging your bets a little." And, yeah, honestly, truth in that. The way I roll.

Several weeks ago, I considered myself a card-carrying atheist. But with what Elspeth told me about the tornado—and my visits from evil and good spirits—how could I dispel the possibility?

"I think that's awesome," said Allie. "And to answer your worries…" Allie tossed Dickers a look. "Clark and I have had some long talks lately about religion."

Dickers took up the slack. "We were…well, as I said, both disappointed about YAC, but it didn't take long to figure out that one snake in the garden wouldn't put a stop to what we believe in." He held his upturned hand across the tabletop. Allison reached out, and held it. "We helped each other through the crisis. Actually…we're, um—"

"Oh, just tell them, Clark," said Allison. "We're dating."

"Wait. What?"

Olivia rocketed around the table, dropped her head between theirs, arms falling across their shoulders. "That totally…kicks *ass,* you guys." She bounced up and down, tugging their heads alongside her. "I'm so happy for you."

"Enough, Olivia! *Please* let go." Dickers scrunched his face up like a pug dog beneath Olivia's stranglehold.

"That's cool," I said, kinda at a loss for anything else to add. Shock shuts me up.

"And I've decided to join Clark at Parkway," said Allison. "I'm going to study art there."

"Way to go, guys." People were filing out of the cafeteria. I checked my phone. "Um, we'd better get back now." Olivia wouldn't stop clapping and hooting on our trek back to the auditorium. Somehow this unexpected news made my world feel like a better place. But that warm, fuzzy feeling didn't last long.

A familiar voice spoke from behind me. "Tex, can I have a minute of your time?" Detective Cowlings stood in the hallway, hands in his pockets. Instant concern fell over Olivia's face. Cowlings said to her, "It's okay, Olivia. I just want to talk to your guy." Olivia reluctantly entered the auditorium.

"Hi, Detective. Um, did you come for the graduation ceremony?" A lump in my throat struggled its way down. Anytime Cowlings shows up, bad news surely follows.

"No." He looked at the crowds filling the hallway. "Let's go outside and get a breath of fresh air." He brushed by me and turned back. "Coming?"

"Ah…sure." Struggling to keep up, I followed Cowlings outside where he sat at a picnic table in the commons. I awkwardly sidled onto the bench across from him, my gown snagging on the wood. *How do women manage in dresses*? "What can I do for you, Detective?"

Cowlings looked up at the sky, shading his eyes with his hand. "Nice day for a graduation."

"Yeah, it is."

"But you and I both know I don't want to talk about the weather."

"Yeah, kinda."

"I went out to the Clarendon Baptist Church after we had our chat. It appeared abandoned. Along with some destruction inside." I framed my face with faux curiosity. "There was no sign of Don Danvers, this Sister Augustine, no one. It was like something wiped them off the face of the earth."

"Wow. Huh. Weird."

"Yeah, I've been running into a *lot* of 'weird' lately, Tex. Then the video came out. Other cops were interested since most of them despised the Clarendon Church and the problems it caused. But Sister Augustine's revelation about witchcraft?" He cocked an eyebrow. "That really had everyone talking."

"Yeah. The kids at school were, um, talking about that, too."

"Tex…did you have anything to do with that video?" He lowered his voice and leaned forward.

"No! I mean…why would I?"

"Why do you think I'd think that?" He pulled out his damned notepad. When that comes out, I want to retract into my clothes like a turtle. "Let's see, you had inside information about the football player killer two years ago. Remember that?"

"Of course I do."

"Then there was the Modern Gangstas from last year. And now, there's Parker Pennett and the Clarendon Church." He shook his police scroll in the air, his sermon from Detective Mountain. "Can you now understand why I think you might have some involvement with the video?"

"I really don't know." I sounded like a slaughter-bound chicken clucking for its life.

"It's past time you stopped lying to me, Tex."

"Lying? I'm not lying! I'm just—"

"You're a witch."

"What?" I hemmed, hawed, squinted, laughed, stared disbelievingly, wrinkled my face up in overly dramatic disbelief, and ran out of things to do. "Wait…*what*?"

"You're a witch." He crossed his arms over his chest with self-satisfaction. "I've suspected something's been up with you for a while. But once I started digging into this 'Sister' Augustine's background, I found out her mother is Mickey Goldfarb. That's your 'friend,' right?"

I scrunched down onto the picnic table bench, ready to pass out. "That's right."

"I've looked into her before. She shops at a new age store...and goes to monthly 'witch meetings.' Your friend is a 'witch.'"

"That's crazy! Surely, *you* don't believe in witches?"

"Tex, I work as a detective in Kansas." He chuckled. "Do you know how many practicing 'black magic cults' I've run into over the course of my years on the job? Most of these people are heavy metal listening, high school idiots...but I still have an open case regarding a homicide—an apparent 'sacrifice' if you will. Some of them obviously take it quite seriously."

"Huh." My first new day of life began to crash and burn.

"Anyway, most of them are relatively harmless, but I'd be a fool to discount the notion of people who at least believe in witchcraft."

Maybe I can get off with a slap on the wrist if Cowlings thinks I'm just a believer and not a full-blown witch. "Okay, so *maybe* there *are* some people who believe in witchcraft, but—"

"You're different, Tex. Last week, a retired cop came into the station. We kicked around old cases. He brought one up from years ago about a missing child.

He said they'd received an anonymous tip as to the child's whereabouts. The tip paid off, and the child was rescued from a sewer he'd fallen into." He waited for me to acknowledge the tale. I shrugged although I knew what he referred to. "What the caller didn't know was she stayed on the phone long enough to be traced. Well, the investigating detective rightfully made it a precedent to find the child. When it was obvious there'd been no wrongdoing to the child—an accident—he ignored following up on the call. Something I wouldn't have done, by the way, but that's neither here nor there. The call came from *your* house. The caller was your mother. She was a witch, too."

My arms went limp. Am I too young to have a heart attack? No way out, no way but down. "Fine. I guess...I am a witch," I said quietly.

Cowlings smiled, but I couldn't tell what lay behind that emotionless grin. "Tex, we're *finally* making progress. Does this mean you're finished lying?" I said nothing; did nothing; maybe nodded once; I have no idea. "You've left me in quite a quandary. You know it was too much of a coincidence for you to just stumble across three murderers, right? Tex?" *How complex the intricate nature of a picnic table is.* "So. What am I to do with you?"

"Nothing?" I peeped.

"As far as I can see, you've broken no laws. Sure, I could be a hard-ass and try and hang you up with obstruction of justice...but I'm not sure what good it would do. Also..." He lifted an eyebrow. "...I'd probably be persecuted at work if I ran around ranting how a teenage witch boy helped me close three murder cases." I looked up, hopeful for a possible silver lining on the horizon. "I thought about it long and hard...and I'm not going to do anything."

"Really?"

"Really. You've done a lot of good over the past three years. You've been stupid at times..." He scowled briefly. "...and endangered yourself when you could have trusted me all along."

"I know..."

"But, you have a bright future ahead of you. I'd be doing the world a wrong if I took you away from that. So, my graduation day gift to you is...nothing." He smiled broadly, an unusual and somewhat unsettling look for him.

I exhaled a calming breath. "Thanks, Detective. I *really* appreciate it! Kinda cheap gift, though." Uh-oh. Too early in our revised relationship to joke?

"Excuse me?" Yep! Way too early.

"Just trying to lighten the mood. Sorry."

"One condition, though. If you insist on, ah, investigating in the future, you'd damn well better consult with me first. Is that understood?"

"Yes, sir."

"And one of these days, you need to explain to me the full extent of your powers. Just so I know what I'm dealing with here. Understood?"

"Yes, sir."

He consulted his watch. "Okay, you have to go graduate." He stood up, brushing his suit. "By the way, what are your post high school plans?"

"I don't know yet."

"Huh. Well, if you ever consider a career in law enforcement... come and see me." He held his hand out. "I really mean it. We could use someone like you on the force. Not only because of your…'powers,' but you're bright and very determined. I'm glad you're on the 'good side.'"

I shook his hand. "Thanks, Detective. I guess that's one option I have."

"Good man. Happy graduation." He strolled down the sidewalk, staring up into the afternoon sky. His step seemed lighter, as if the weight of the world slid an inch from his weary shoulders.

I checked my phone for the time. *Crap!* I ran as fast as I could up the stairs, the robe curtailing my speed, trapping my legs in its net. But I just wriggled out of one seemingly inescapable web; surely I could suffer through wearing a skirt for a day. The last of the students chugged into the auditorium as I played caboose to the blue train. I excused myself through an irritable line of seated students, holding onto my cap.

The proceedings were predictably long and dull, with the valedictorian spouting nonsense about a yellow brick road and "goodbye to you, Scarecrow, Tin Man, and especially you, Cowardly Lion." I have no idea what Frank L. Baum's creations mean in relation to graduating, but I sucked it up, knowing I won't have to endure Clearwell High for very much longer.

Excluding the awful top-40 song, the powers-that-be threw a surprisingly tasteful tribute to the students no longer with us, sadly a long list. A slide show displayed larger-than-life images of Josh, Bob Bellman (I hoped the scant applause he received wouldn't dredge him up from Hell again), James Badger, Calvin, and finally, Brittany, who received thunderous roars of appreciation. Mrs. Bennesh, my counselor, delivered a speech regarding being true to yourself and talking to someone about depression, a thinly veiled salute to Brittany, but not a word of homosexuality was mentioned. No matter. I have a feeling Brittany's hard lesson in life (and death) will ultimately help other struggling students. I know Brittany would approve.

Vice Principal Hastings took the stage, warned us to hold our applause, and cleared his throat. I thought I caught a glimpse of Principal What's-His-Name lurking behind the stage's curtains. Maybe he's the valedictorian's "man behind the curtain", the Wizard of Oz, himself.

With the possibility of detention behind me, I hooted and roared when my friends' names were called. After a mind-numbingly long period, I approached the line forming at the bottom of the steps. When I reached the stage, my cap fell to the floor. Providing the audience with much amusement, I swooped to pick it up and gripped it firmly onto my head.

"Richard Mc…Kenna," called out Hastings, stumbling over my last name, undoubtedly determined to make my last few minutes prickly. When I heard Mickey call out from the back of the auditorium, "*Give 'em Hell, Tex*," I scurried across the stage. Dad and Ruth were probably embarrassed, but it felt good, nonetheless. I grasped Hastings's hand and shook it for the first time ever.

A buzz grew throughout the gym. Light applause sprinkled the auditorium before erupting into a thunderous storm of handclaps. I wondered what I did this time to cause such a commotion, if I didn't zip up or whatever. I looked out into the audience and what I saw stunned me. Over half of the student body stood, applauding and stomping their feet. My name ricocheted throughout the gym like a multi-voiced echo in a canyon. Mr. Jensen, standing as well, utilized the two-fingered, ear-blistering whistle only gym teachers know how to do. I glimpsed at Hastings, still clutching my hand in a vise-like grip, who glowered at the audience. The applause and screaming continued until I took off my cap and waved it at the crowd to quiet down. It only evoked even louder cheering.

I couldn't believe it. I thought I spent my entire four-year tenure in this prison as an unknown shadow, just adhering to the walls, making way for the physical embodiment of people who count. But...perhaps I *did* count. Maybe what I did over the past three years mattered to the student body. Maybe I gave them hope in a weird way. If I—Tex McKenna, a skinny, regular, awkward in his own body kid who possesses no special skills or talents or hopes of ever being popular—can make a difference, anyone can.

*The hell with it.* Like a rock star, I tossed my cap into the crowd.

Hastings finally released my hand. He bent down to whisper into my ear.

"Do good out there, Richard," he said. Hours later, I'm still contemplating his last words to me. Did he mean to encourage me? Inspire me, even? Or did he want to make sure I never forgot him? I guess I'll never know.

****

The party blew into full force with over sixty people chowing down the hors d'oeuvres. Ruth took on commandeering hostess mode, floating around like a fairy, magically filling up punch glasses before they ran dry. Somehow she'd latched onto Lance and promoted him to her first lieutenant. I had no idea whether she knew about his sexuality, but it didn't really matter.

Lance said, "Ruth's a riot."

"Yeah, she's pretty great. Just don't take cooking tips from her."

"What?"

Olivia swatted me. "Oh, shut *up*, Tex. Ruth's fine."

"You haven't eaten her cooking," I mumbled.

Mr. and Mrs. Nguyen joined our group. "Tex, how are you?" asked Mrs. Nguyen. "Have you decided which school you're going to?"

The question on everyone's mind. "Ah, no, not yet."

"Oh! Well, I'm sure you will. Lance is going to Harvard after next year—"

"Mom, this is Tex's day, *not* mine."

"Of course you're right. I'm sorry." She placed a maternal hand on my shoulder.

"It's okay."

Mr. Nguyen pulled me aside. "I just wanted to thank you for supporting Lance. I know you mean a lot to him."

"Mr. Nguyen, you don't need to thank me for being Lance's friend. In fact, I should thank you for having such an awesome son."

His somber face brightened. "Yes. Lance is…awesome, indeed." I had to leave before I burst out laughing at Mr. Nguyen's awkward slang usage.

Allie and Dickers stopped me. "Tex," shouted Dickers. "That was so cool how you got a standing ovation." He held his hand out toward me. "Congratulations!"

I grabbed his hand. "Oh, whatever. It's you guys I

should be congratulating. So…congratulations!"

Allie blew off my extended hand. "You know better than that. Come here." She pulled me into her bone-crunching hug, holding me far too long. Dickers and Allie are truly a match made in Heaven. They can hug the crap out of one another and leave unwary others alone. "I appreciate everything you've done for me," she said, her voice breaking.

"Allie, you did it all yourself. Don't forget that."

I spotted Dad by the food table. Tired of tearful farewells, embarrassing congratulations on my standing ovation, and especially, questions about my future, I swam for safe harbor. "Hey, Dad, how's it going?"

He swallowed a cheese cube before responding. "I'm eating what I can while I can, before you know…" He hitched a thumb toward Ruth and smiled.

I clapped him on the back. "I get it."

"Son, I'm proud of you. I've always known you're special. But to see the audience give you what you deserved today…well, you must be doing something right."

I sighed. "Dad, come on, Let's just forget that." I reached for something fried and popped it into my mouth. Discovering a jalapeno pepper in the middle of it, I scrabbled for a glass of punch, putting the fire out much to Dad's amusement.

"Looks like we still have some food issues going on." His cheeks looked a healthier rose color than I've seen in some time.

"And how're my two favorite McKenna men doing?" said Ruth, wrapping her arms around our shoulders.

"Great," said Dad.

"Really good turnout," I added.

"Tex, I'm really proud of you. I know I'm not your mother, but…I certainly *feel* like it today. And I know your mother is proud of you, too." She looked toward the ceiling. "I just know she's smiling down on you."

Even though I still wrestled with concepts such as Heaven, I appreciated her heartfelt sentiment. I gave into my emotions and embraced her, Allie style. "Thanks, Ruth. And thank you for everything." I kissed her cheek, her blushing apparent through her heavy foundation.

She slowly drew her hand across her cheek as if relishing the afterglow of the kiss. "You're very exceptional, you know."

I cleared my throat and thought it best to leave before I turned into a blubbering mess. "Okay, gotta make my rounds."

I saw Jasper chatting up a pretty girl in the corner of the living room. "Hey, Jasper."

"Hey," he said, his sleepy eyelids flitting open. "This is my date, Katherine. She's a junior."

The blonde girl spread her mouth into a beauty pageant smile. "Hi, Tex. I've seen you around school."

"Yeah, I think I've seen you, too." It'd be hard not to. "Jasper…" I pulled him a foot away. "…I wanted to thank you for your help with Parker. Without your info, he'd still be out there, doing…you know—"

"Hey, no problem." He shrugged. "Brittany deserved it."

"Yeah, I think she really did."

"So, what are you going to do now? I mean…after school."

"I don't know. If I had a buck for every time

someone asked me that, I could retire already."

"I hear ya', I hear ya'." He shook his head, his shaggy, blond hair flopping over his brow. He jerked his head back to reposition his mane. "That's why I'm going to JuCo. Until I decide where I'm going next."

"Oh. Good for you." While happy for him, trepidation shared space with that emotion. Panicked jealousy swept over me as I realized he'd be going to the same school as Olivia. He'd see her every day. And she thinks he's cute. I'm coming closer and closer to a college decision, and it smells a lot like JuCo.

As if reading my thoughts, Ian rapped me on the back. "We gotta talk, dude."

"What about?" Like I didn't know.

"Dude! You gotta cut me some slack. What are you going to do?"

"I don't know!" Party guests stopped what they were doing to stare at my flare-up. I waved a hand through the air. "It's okay, it's okay." I mumbled. "Hey, go try those fried things at the food table. They're *really* good."

"Jeezus," said Ian. "I kinda really need to know if you're gonna be my roommate."

"Sorry, Ian. I'm just freakin' stressed out."

"Okay, it's cool, it's cool." Ian glowered at Allie and Dickers across the room. "What's the deal with them anyway?"

"Um, they're going out now...I think."

Ian slumped his shoulders. "No shit? And you're just now telling me about it?"

"Ian, you *had* your chance. What happened between you and Allie anyway?"

He rocked his head back and forth as if cranking up

for a full truth disclosure. "I don't know. I think I was scared. I never had a girlfriend before. Or sex. So…I guess I kinda put some distance between us."

"Yeah, I think I get that." He looked totally despondent. Knowing he's not the hugging type, I gave him a few manly claps on the back. "You'll get your time. Just think of all the hot chicks waiting for you at KU."

"Oh, yeah." He pumped his fist into the air. "Ian rockin' the chicks." He looked around the crowded room. "Hey, Tex?"

"Yeah?"

"Next time, invite some girls to your party. It's a real sausage-fest in here."

"Got it."

Elizabeth and Donovan strolled in, Donovan greeting those around him, Elizabeth barely nodding acknowledgments. They headed directly for Dad.

"Hello, Mr. McKenna," said Donovan, doing the two-handed tango with Dad. "Tex has told me so much about you." Which is a bald-faced lie. But I guess every politician needs to master that skill.

While Donovan worked his mojo, Dad fell under his sway. "Nice to meet you." He turned toward Elizabeth. "And you are?" A look of confusion crossed his face.

"Elizabeth Blackmer," she replied. "Pleased to meet you, Mr. McKenna. Thank you for inviting us to your party."

Dad scratched his head. "Have we met before, Elizabeth? I could swear we have. Your eyes are very distinctive—"

"Sorry to interrupt, Dad, but I really need to talk to

Elizabeth." There's probably no need to keep Elizabeth's double identity from Dad, but a crowded party's not the best venue for such a revelation. I pulled her aside. "Elizabeth, have you heard from Elspeth?"

She smiled wistfully. "No, she's gone. For now." I knew that. But I guess I hoped for a postcard from beyond. Or something. Anything. I already missed her.

"Yeah. I kinda thought she was leaving. Did she say when she might be back?"

She shook her head. "But I'm sure she'll return at some time. She always does."

"Hey, I wanted to apologize again about your car—"

She narrowed her eyes, pinpointing me with her darts. "The less said about *that*, the better." Suddenly she melted. Scary. "Besides…Daddy bought me a new car."

"Good, um, good."

"*Elizabeth*," said Olivia from behind me. "Glad to see you could make it."

"Olivia…"

"Tex." Olivia grasped my arm and bobbed her head toward Dad. "I think you'd better go rescue your dad." Dad faced the sofa, hands in his lap, looking uncomfortably toward the ceiling. Brandon sat opposite him, munching on something, staring wide-eyed at Dad as if he provided his entertainment for the evening.

I sat down next to Brandon. "Dad, I see you've met Brandon."

"Oh, yes," he replied. "He's…ah…" Dad gave up, dropping his hands to his chair's wheels.

"Hey, Brandon," I said. "What are your plans after school?"

Brandon studied his plate of potato chips. "Well, I'm at your party—"

"No. I mean, what're you going to do with your life?"

Brandon took his time swallowing a mouthful of chips. "My uncle owns a garage. He said I could work for him. Maybe even take it over some day." He shrugged. "I'll be getting sixty thousand to start—"

"Sixty *thousand*? Um, do you need an assistant?"

Dad coughed and gawped at me, attempting to fathom my seriousness.

"I can ask," said Brandon.

"No, no. I'm just kidding. I don't know the first thing about cars." Dad sighed in relief. "But that's really cool, Brandon."

"Yeah, I like working with cars."

"Good for you."

Lance and Ruth glided by, offering punch refills. Dad took the opportunity to make a fast getaway and rolled back toward Donovan and Elizabeth, much more his speed. Brandon appeared to have found a new fascinating person to study in Ruth.

I saw Mickey step out the front door and hurried after her. She faced the front yard, puffing on a cigarette, and clutching another monstrous purse in her other hand.

"Mickey?"

"Hey, kid, congratulations on your graduation."

"Thanks." Risking her ire, I plunged ahead. "Um, hey, I'm still really sorry about your daughter and everything."

She waved her cigarette at me, trailing a smoking Z through the night air. "It's all right, kid. I hadn't seen her in twenty years or so anyway. Probably won't ever see her again. The news said she pulled a vanishing act after your video went out."

"I know, Mickey...but she's still your daughter. I'm just...I'm sorry."

"Don't worry about it."

"Hey, there's something I've been wanting to ask you about for three years now."

"What's that?"

"What *does* 'mote' mean, anyway?"

Mickey let loose a cat-screech of a shriek. "Oh, Tex, you just slay me. One of the most powerful witches I've ever seen, and you're asking me what 'mote' means?"

"Heh, okay." I guess I'll *still* never know what "mote" means.

She reached inside her purse. "Here." She pulled out a gift-wrapped package and handed it to me. "I wanted to give you your graduation gift where no one could see."

"Thanks, but you really didn't need to."

"Just shut up and open the damn gift and be thankful for it. *Honestly.*"

I tore the paper off and held an ancient leather-bound book, the pages yellow and the binding loose. On the cover, several Latin words were inscribed in gold. Flipping through it, I found hand-written entries in Latin and English. "What is it?"

She took a step toward me. "That's the best book of witch spells I've ever owned. It was my mother's before she handed it down to me. And now, I'm giving it to you."

"Wow, thanks. But...shouldn't you keep this in the

family? I know Augustine and you are on the ropes, but maybe, someday you could give her the book—"

*Smack!* Mickey's hand landed on the back of my skull. "Ow!"

"*You're* my family now, Tex. Just accept the gift and be done with it."

"All right." The back of my head throbbed, yet I felt great otherwise. "Thank you, Mickey." I threw my arms around her tiny frame and held her tight. "You're my family, too."

****

The partygoers were gone by ten thirty p.m., Olivia and Ruth the last to leave. After walking Olivia to her car, I made my way back inside.

The house seemed incomplete, quiet, after the endless stream of chatter. Paper cups littered tables, ghosts of parties past. The rooms felt stifling, eerily devoid of life. The hair on the nape of my neck stood up. Something felt *wrong.*

"Pretty good party, huh, Dad?" I called through his bedroom door and only silence greeted me. "Dad?" Light seeped out from the bottom of the door. I knocked. "Dad?" My heartbeat kicked up a few notches. Slowly pushing the door open, I saw his wheelchair on its side, a wheel still spinning. He sat on the floor, propped up against the bed, his chin resting on his chest. So very still. Eyes closed. "*Dad!*" My heart leaped into my throat, adrenaline flooded my body. "Dad! Oh, God, *no,* Dad! Get *up! Please* wake up, Dad!" I shook his shoulder, hoping, praying for a response, yelling non-stop pleas to whomever—whatever—for help. "Dad! *Don't* you leave me, too! Please*, please,* Dad, wake *up!*" Tears rained down my cheeks. My phone fell out of my shaking hands and dropped onto his chest.

He snorted suddenly as if waking from a nap. "Tex?" His voice sounded quiet, fatigued. His hands fell limply to the floor. "What's going on?"

"Dad! God, Dad!" I slumped next to him, my shoulder resting against his. "Are you all right?"

He rubbed his eyes, blinking. "I'm okay. I guess...the party was a little much for me. Tired me out. I must've fallen." He offered me a faint smile of reassurance.

"Dad..." My voice choked.

With effort, he managed to wrestle his arm around my shoulders. "Tex...I'm okay. It's all right. I'll be good as new after some rest."

"No, Dad! You're getting *worse*. You don't think I see that? And you *expect* me to go away to *college*?"

He arched his eyebrows and frowned. I welcomed his anger as a sign of life-force. "I expect you to do what's best for you. And if that means going away to school, yes, that's what I expect."

"I know. It's just...*hard*."

"Life *is* hard, son." As if getting a second wind, he straightened up and withdrew his arm. "There's something else I've been meaning to talk to you about...but I wasn't sure how you'd feel."

"If you're gonna say you want to go to a home, forget it. I'm *not* going to let you do that."

"What? Tex, I'm not ready for a home. Not just yet. You can't get rid of me that easily." He nudged me with his shoulder.

"So...what then?"

"I'm thinking of asking Ruth to marry me." He

rushed out the last few words, exhaling deeply when he finished.

"What?"

"I'm thinking of asking Ruth to marry me. But I was afraid of how you might feel about—"

"Whoa…wait. *What*?"

"If you're not ready for this yet, I understand—"

"No, Dad, *no*. It's not that. It's just…wow…I wouldn't even think to stand in the way of your happiness. Have you talked about it…you know, with Ruth?"

"Yep. We're both ready to take the next step. If you're okay with it." He raised his eyebrows in anticipation, but he knew it'd be a slam-dunk with me.

"Dad…Dad…" I threw my arms around him.

"Okay, easy, son, easy."

"I'm really, really happy for you guys. This is…awesome. Of course I'm okay with it." At that moment, things finally looked clear. If this isn't a ginormous sign of what I should do after high school, it's at least a subtle shout-out. I worried about Dad being alone if I went off to school, but now he wouldn't be living by himself. "When are you guys planning on doing this?"

"Well…we're hoping for a summer wedding."

My giddiness galloped in a surge of energy, a long-shot racehorse crossing the finish line. "Dad, I've got news for you, too!" Always expecting the worst, the look of familiar fear overtook him. "No, no, no. This is *good* news. I've been offered a scholarship to KU….in English!"

"Tex, why didn't you tell me? This is…this is just…" He threw his hands up in the air for loss of words.

"I know, right? I'm gonna go to KU in the fall!" We sat on the floor, laughing, hugging like long-lost relatives. Once we let the unusual tide of good news ebb away, I managed to help Dad back into his wheelchair. "One thing, though, Dad…"

"What's that?"

"You *are* going to get a cell phone…." He pressed his lips into a thin, hard line. "No, you're going to get one. I'm not going to KU unless you do. In case you fall, and Ruth's not available, I can be here in an hour or less. But you need to have a means of communication with you at all times."

Acting like a chided child, he swept his gaze back and forth across the room then begrudgingly said, "Oh, all right, if that's what it's going to take—"

"That's what it's gonna take."

"You drive a hard bargain, son."

"I learned from the best." I leaned down and embraced him once again. "Dad?"

"Yes?"

"Are you going to be all right for a bit? I need to go tell Olivia."

He put up a show of irritability. "Son, you *don't* need to 'baby' or pamper me. Who's the parent here, after all?" He tried to restrain his amusement. "I'll be all right. *Go.* You need to tell Olivia."

"I'm outta here." Already halfway out the front door, I called back, "Love you, Dad."

"Love you too, son."

\*\*\*\*

Eleven o'clock might be considered too late for me to be banging on Olivia's door. But this is something that can't be discussed through a text or phone call.

The front porch light came to life, and through the window, Olivia blinked her eyes at me in shock. I suppose I should get used to this response I have on my loved ones.

"Tex? What's wrong?" She waved me in, but I grabbed her hand and pulled her onto the porch. "You're scaring me!"

I shook my head. "No, there's nothing wrong. I just needed to tell you—"

"What? Dammit! Tell me."

I swallowed the lump in my throat. "Olivia…I've made a decision…about what I'm going to do."

She nodded sadly, slowly, no words needing to be said. She embraced me, pressing her head into my chest. "I know. You're going to KU," she whispered.

I followed the line of her cheekbone with my fingertips. "How did you know?"

"What? You think you'd come running over here to tell me you're staying with me at JuCo?"

"I guess not. O'…Olivia? Are you okay?"

She pushed off me with sudden ferocity. "Of *course,* I'm not okay. *Idiot.* But…I'm happy for you. I think it's the right decision for you. I'm just feeling sorry for myself…"

"I know. I'm feeling kinda…lonely, too. I haven't even left yet…and I already miss you."

"Dammit, Tex. Don't *you* start crying. Or we'll both be out here blubbering all night." She thumped the back of her hand against my chest.

"Okay." I readjusted my shoulders, hoping it would magically man me up. "You know I'm coming back to see you every weekend."

"You better…"

"And I swear to make video calls to you every day!"

She nodded, her eyes closed tight.

"I'll just be an hour away. You call…I'll come runnin'."

"Okay…"

"And you can visit me whenever you want."

"At least…Ian's gonna be thrilled." She smiled a sad smile.

"Yeah, he's got a roommate he can live with now, I guess. I just hope I can live with him."

Olivia chuckled. "Good luck with that."

"Thanks. I'm gonna need it…I think."

"You do realize I'll be up there with you in a year, right?" She poked her finger into my chest. "So, don't you even *think* about looking at other girls."

"You're the only one for me, O'."

"Damn right!"

"You are. I love you, Olivia Furman."

"And I love you Tex…always…"

We stood in the spring breeze, holding one another, quiet for nearly an hour. Even though we had all summer together before I moved, it felt like we were saying goodbye. Yet, at the same time, it felt like an affirmation of our relationship, a new beginning. We knew our bond, our love, can weather a long-distance relationship. We've been through a lot worse and have survived. "I love you, always and forever, Olivia."

## AFTERWORD

Even though the Clarendon Baptist Church is a fictional creation, their so-called "ideology," unfortunately, is not. Their beliefs about homosexuality, other faiths, Heaven, and funeral protests are based upon all too real "churches"—sects, really—springing up across the Midwest. Sometimes truth *is* scarier than fiction.

This is the final *Tex, The Witch Boy* book. At least for a while.

But Elspeth and Elizabeth will return in *Elspeth, The Living Dead Girl.* Coming soon.

### A word about the author…

Stuart R. West is a lifelong resident of Kansas, which he considers both a curse and a blessing. It's a curse because…well, it's Kansas. But it's great because…well, it's Kansas. Lots of cool, strange and creepy things happen in the Midwest, and Stuart takes advantage of them in his books. Call it "Kansas Noir." Stuart writes thrillers, horror and mysteries usually tinged with humor, both for adult and young adult audiences.

Stuart spent 25 years in the corporate sector and had to bail, splitting his time between writing and real estate. He's married to a professor of pharmacy (who greatly appreciates the fact he cooks dinner for her every night) and has a 29 year old daughter who's dabbling in the nefarious world of banking.

If you're still reading this, you may as well head on over to Stuart's blog at: http://stuartrwest.blogspot.com/ It's what all the cool kids are doing.